CAPTIVE HEART

"Do not bite me again, white woman."

Unafraid, Emma shoved the handsome Indian chief away from her. With hands on her hips, she glared at him. "What do you expect when you sneak up on me like that? If I'm not allowed to go for a walk by myself, then just tell me so."

Striking Thunder's eyes narrowed to two furious slits. "Do not push me, Emma. As long as you obey our rules, you are free to move as you please. But not at night. It is not safe."

Emma snorted and sent him a look of derision. "Don't try to frighten me with tales of bears and wolves. I'm not stupid. If there were any wild animals—besides you—the dogs would bark."

Striking Thunder advanced. Emma stood her ground until inches separated them. He reached out and touched her chin, and when she rolled her eyes, he forced her to look at him.

"Did you hear *me* behind you? If I'd been the enemy, you'd have been dead or long gone by now. Our prairie tribes raid each other for prizes and even pleasure. You, Emma, with your flame-hair and white skin, are a prize."

His gaze dipped to her heaving bosom. "A prize any warrior would risk war over." Releasing her chin, he trailed the backs of his fingers along her jaw, down her throat and down the center of one breast. His voice became gentle. "No one will steal you from this warrior. You are mine." He lifted a hand to still her protest. "Like it or not, you are mine."

White Flame

Susan Edwards

LEISURE BOOKS   NEW YORK CITY

A LEISURE BOOK®

October 1999

Published by

Dorchester Publishing Co., Inc.
276 Fifth Avenue
New York, NY 10001

ISBN 0-8439-4613-X

*In loving memory
of
Patrina O'Donnell.*

*Grandmother of my heart if not my flesh,
we shared a love of birds and kids.*

*I pray the song of birds,
and the laughter of children,
are your companions in that better place
to which you've gone.*

*We will always miss you here, Grandma Pat,
but whenever I hear the sweet song of a canary,
I will always think of you.*

White Flame

Prologue

U.S. Major Grady O'Brien stared at a portrait of a young woman with misty-green eyes. His fingers gripped the edge of the mantel, his knuckles white as the cool marble. Grief swept through him. "Margaret Mary, don't hate me for what I must do." Pain laced his whispered words.

Footsteps vibrated across the wooden parlor floor, intruding on his private moment of pain. "You're a fool, Grady."

Grady glanced over his shoulder at his sister. "Ida, please. We've been through this." His eyes burned with remorse.

"Then listen to me. Forget this foolish notion. The army doesn't need you as much as your children do." She moved into the room and stood beside him.

Grady's gaze strayed back to the portrait of his deceased wife. His vision blurred at the thought of never hearing her sweet laughter or being able to gaze into eyes alight with her love. Somewhere overhead, the wooden floorboards creaked. The sound echoed the breaking of his heart. How could he go on without her? A hand touched his shoulder.

"Please, Grady. Give yourself more time. It's only been two weeks since Margaret Mary, bless her sweet soul, passed on. The pain will ease. Don't leave. Your children need you."

11

Grady leaned his head against the back of his hands for a moment, then straightened. "No," he whispered, "they don't need me. They have you."

Ida arched her narrow brows. "Emma barely understands her mother is gone. Do you honestly expect her to understand your disappearance as well?" Folding her arms across her ample bosom, she waited.

Frustrated, wanting only to be left alone, Grady rammed his fingers through thick waves of bright, golden-red hair that fell in waves to his shoulders. "Dammit, I'm not deserting her. I'll be back." He turned his back on Ida. Shame ran through him. She was right. He *was* abandoning his children. But not forever, he promised himself—just until the pain of his loss dulled.

Ida didn't understand, but how could she? Nearly ten years his senior, she'd never married, didn't know the pain of having her heart ripped out from inside of her or the bleak despair of losing part of her very soul.

"When?" The woman's voice was quiet.

He glanced at her over his shoulder. She waited, back straight, hands loosely clasped in front of her and lips pressed into a tight disapproving line, reminding him of an old spinster schoolmarm. Though he knew she loved him in her own way, had been more mother than sister to him, he couldn't stay, not even for her. He answered honestly. "I don't know."

Ida turned away. Silence filled the room. Finally, she shook her head. "You're running again, Grady, using the army as an excuse not to stay and face your grief." She whirled around. "Just as you did when Father and Mother died. You ran then, joined the army the day after the funeral. Mark my words, if you return to duty, you'll never come back. You'll never stop running."

Grady wandered to the window and stared out, not seeing the carriages and citizens bustling about their business. "Maybe it's better this way," he whispered, his voice low, barely audible.

"Better for whom? Emma will be devastated."

He closed his eyes, his throat burning at the very thought of leaving his little princess, the ray of sunshine in his life, but he couldn't bear to look into eyes so like her mother's. "I'll hurt her far worse if I stay." He straightened when he heard a carriage stop out front.

"Grady—"

He swiveled around, once more the stern major his men knew so well. "No more. It's time."

Ida tipped her chin, her eyes bright but determined. "I'll fetch Emma. You won't steal out of her life like a thief in the night." Her skirts rustled as she left the elegantly appointed parlor.

Grady donned a travel coat over his military uniform and left the room his wife had loved. After seeing to the loading of his bags, he went into his den to await Ida. Picking up a neatly folded sheaf of papers, he tucked them into the inside pocket of his coat then poured himself a brandy. He dreaded telling his small daughter goodbye. Before his wife's death, they'd been close, spending every evening together reading or playing games, but the loving and devoted father he'd once been had died the day fever had cruelly snatched his wife from him.

He leaned against the book-filled shelves behind his desk and closed his eyes. He felt cold and empty inside. There was nothing left that he could give Emma or the infant. No, he was doing the right thing. The girls were better off with Ida. They needed a mother figure. A moan slipped past his lips. If only Margaret Mary had lived to rejoice in the birth of another daughter. If only . . .

At the sound of running feet, he downed the remainder of his brandy in one gulp. He turned when a small girl of eight burst into the room, a frilly dressed doll under each arm. She skidded to a stop before his massive oak desk.

"Papa, 'tis teatime. Will you join me?"

Grady clenched his fists at his side and stared into eyes sparkling with misty laughter. Waves of pain swelled and crested within him. He slammed his glass down on the desk.

Emma backed away, her eyes wide and fearful. "I'm sorry for running in the house, Papa. I forgot the rules—again."

Her voice, small, full of hurt and fear, twisted the knife in his soul. His thoughtless reaction to her childish exuberance only proved how unfit a father he was without his loving wife at his side. He forced a smile to his lips and knelt in front of his firstborn. "No, child. I'm not angry."

Grady drew a deep breath. His gaze roamed over her delicate features as he memorized hair the same shade as his, creamy skin, rose-tinted cheeks and eyes the shade of dew-kissed shamrocks on a misty morning. Those bright eyes shone with the same love of life as her mother's had until death dimmed them forever.

Emma clutched her dolls and regarded him solemnly. "Then you'll have tea with me?"

Staring into those earnest depths, filled with uncertainty and hope, he knew they would forever haunt his dreams. His fingers trembled as he cupped her face between his large calloused palms. "No, my precious, Papa cannot stay."

Noting her father's attire for the first time, Emma's brows furrowed. "Are you going out, Papa?"

"Yes, child. Papa must go away."

She pouted, then brightened. "But you'll be back very soon," she announced with certainty. Then she glanced at him coyly. "And you'll bring me a surprise?"

Grady fingered one red curl. His voice cracked. "Papa will be gone for a long time, Emma." He smoothed her wrinkled brow but before he could reassure her of his love, Ida spoke from the hall.

"A mistake, if you ask me." She entered, a tiny blanketed bundle in her arms.

Standing, Grady picked up his hat. He avoided looking at his sister or the infant. "We've said all that's to be said."

"Then it needs saying again. You're a fool." She

14

blocked his escape and thrust the wiggling bundle into his resisting arms. "The babe needs a name."

His hat fell to the floor as he reluctantly cradled his newborn daughter for the first time. He thought his heart had shattered completely the day he'd buried Margaret Mary. But when those intent blues blinked open without warning to stare at him, he knew he was wrong, so very wrong. Grady fingered the crown of peach-soft, golden-red fuzz. Tears slipped from his eyes, blurring his sight.

Margaret Mary had chosen Elizabeth for a girl baby, but before he could speak it aloud, another name came to mind. "Ranait," he whispered. "Her name is Ranait, after our mother." His breathing quickened when the infant turned toward him as if recognizing her name. Her tiny bow-shaped lips puckered as she rooted, searching for nourishment. A tiny balled fist caught him on his chin.

Grady felt his resolve slipping. He had to leave, now. He swallowed past the lump in his throat then knelt to place the baby in Emma's small arms. "You're a big girl now, Emma. Promise Papa you'll be good and always look after your sister."

His throat tightened when she nodded uncertainly, her bright gaze clouded with confusion. Grady caressed one lock of long hair then pulled his knife from his belt. He cut the tight red curl clinging to his finger, put the knife away then ran a finger down her soft cheek. She looked frightened by the strained undercurrents surrounding the adults. Bending forward, he kissed her forehead. "Papa loves you, Emma. Remember that always." With one last caress of the baby's head, he stood. "Call her Renny," he choked before fleeing the room.

"Papa! Don't leave," Emma cried, her voice high, tight.

Grady didn't reply. He hurried out of the front door to the waiting carriage. As he rode away with the silky soft curl wound around his finger, he glanced back then wished he hadn't. The sight of Emma standing on the front steps, the infant cradled in her arms, burned itself indelibly in his memory.

Chapter One

Late Summer, Nebraska Territory, 1856

Emma O'Brien stared at her sketch pad in disgust. The tall cottonwoods she'd drawn lining the banks of the Missouri River loomed dark and sinister. Glancing at the bank for comparison, she noted sunlight filtering through the spread boughs, falling across the bank and river in thin, golden streaks. A perfectly peaceful setting. Nothing like what she'd captured on paper. Her own frustrations had colored her work. Crumbling the paper, she stood.

A cool breeze washed over her as she put away her supplies and drew on her gloves. Too frustrated and restless to sit still any longer, she sent one last disgusted glance over the rail into the shallow murky-brown water of the river then left the rail. The steamboat *Annabella* was grounded—again. Crossing the deck, she addressed the captain. "How long will we be delayed this time, Captain Billaud?" She waved one pristine, white-gloved hand toward the sandbar and tapped the end of her parasol on the spotless wooden deck.

The pilot, a small rotund Frenchman with a thick black beard, frowned briefly, then beamed. "No more zan a few hours," he said, his accent as thick as the muddy bottom of the Missouri. Seeing Emma's dismay, he added, "We will warp over zis sandbar and be on our way—like zat!" He snapped his stubby fingers.

16

Emma allowed herself an unladylike snort. She'd heard that promise more times than she cared to recall since boarding the *Annabella* more than two months ago.

Captain Billaud patted her hand. "You shall see your papa very soon, *ma cherie*. Be patient. The Missouri, she's like a female, no? One day she's right where she should be and ze next? *Voila!* Gone. Picks herself up and moves while we sleep."

Emma stared at the sluggish river with distaste. Never had she seen or heard of a more contrary river.

The riverman wiped beads of sweat from his face, then tipped his hat. "I must see to my duties, Miss Emma. Go below, leave zis heat. It is not good for a beautiful young lady to remain in ze sun so long." He patted her gloved hand in a fatherly fashion then strode away, a white handkerchief sticking out of his back pocket like a flag.

Emma listened quietly as he shouted orders for a rope to be tied to a tree along the bank. She knew from witnessing this procedure many times that the other end would be wrapped around the capstan on the bow, which allowed the steamboat to pull itself off the sandbar. Biting her lower lip, she swallowed her disappointment at yet another delay. The trip from St. Louis to Fort Pierre should have taken fifty-one days, but one problem after another had slowed the boat's progress up the Missouri River. They were now three weeks behind schedule.

Worry churned through her mind like a paddle wheel agitating the water. They had to reach the fort before her father left. In his latest letter, her father had indicated he'd be at the fort until the end of summer, then would head west to Fort Laramie for the winter. By her reckoning, they had a little more than a week, give or take a day or two.

Hooking her parasol over the railing, Emma pulled out the worn letter from the pocket of her navy-blue woollen dress. She scanned her father's boldly penned missive. Like the rest of his correspondence, the page was filled with news of his career—his promotion to colonel had been a frequent topic and he was likely now bucking for a generalship. The letter ended as always, with a bid for Emma to take care of Renny.

Dropping her hand to the wooden rail, Emma stared out across the water at the stand of cottonwoods lining the bank. As the sun dipped low in the sky, the huge trees cast deep angled shadows across the river, encroaching on the remaining light on the water, much like the bitterness welling inside her heart. While she'd accepted a long time ago that she wouldn't have a father figure in her life, it wasn't fair to Renny.

Over the last year, she'd written several times, begging her father to come home and take up parental duties for Renny's sake, but his answer had always been the same: The army needed him. Those words cut deeply. His family needed him, too. Mentally, Emma kicked herself for believing that this time, given the circumstances, the colonel might actually put his daughter's needs above his career. Emma folded the letter carefully and slid it back into her pocket.

She squeezed her eyes shut. At seventeen, the crushing pressure of playing mother and father to her nine-year-old sister weighed her down. Emma had never forgotten the promise she'd made to her father. Nor had she resented the sacrifices she'd been forced to make to keep that promise. But since their aunt's death six months ago, Renny had grown surly and unmanageable. Emma, at her wits' end, had turned to a father who wanted no part of their lives. Fool that she was, she'd admitted to needing him. It was the first time she'd admitted that since he'd walked out the door, leaving her holding her baby sister. And once again, he'd turned his back on her.

Emma's gaze narrowed with contempt. As far as she was concerned, Grady O'Brien could stay away forever. In nine years, he had never come back, and if it hadn't been for Renny who desperately needed and wanted a father's reassurance and love, she would never have left her home to travel through this wild, untamed land to try and force him to return home and resume his parental duties.

Once again, her attention wandered to the men hard at work trying to free the boat before sundown. Now she wished she'd left home sooner, not waited so long; her plan had been to arrive at the fort and catch her father between assignments. If he had to escort them home, it would be too late for him to leave for Fort Laramie. Then, if he stayed the winter with them in St. Louis, perhaps he'd stay for good.

And if he refused? Emma rubbed her eyes. If he refused, then she'd have to find a way to ease Renny's hurt. Discouraged that all her careful planning might have been for nought, Emma straightened, pulled at her gloves and left the railing, clutching the unopened parasol Aunt Ida had insisted a young woman always carry. Lifting her skirts, she went downstairs to see what mischief Renny was getting into.

It came as no surprise to find empty the cabin she and Renny shared. Emma tossed her parasol onto the bed, having a pretty good idea where to find her errant sister— in the stable area. Sure enough, when she went below she found Renny in the steerage, caring for horses that belonged to a contingent of soldiers also traveling to Fort Pierre. Her gaze traveled over the men sitting around a bale of hay, playing cards. Sniffing the air, she caught the scent of alcohol. This was definitely not a place for a young, impressionable child. And one glance at the girl's disheveled appearance confirmed she'd been down here most of the afternoon instead of doing her studies.

Renny, unaware of Emma's presence, continued to chatter away to the captain leaning against the wall. Folding her gloved hands in front of her, Emma spoke in her firmest voice. "Ranait, it's rude to intrude upon the captain and his men. You've taken up enough of their time for one day."

Captain Derek Sanders, a tall blond man in his midthirties, pushed away from the wall and stepped forward

with a warm smile. He removed his hat. "Good afternoon, Miss Emma. I assure you that your delightful
young sister is no trouble. In fact, you are both welcome
to join me anytime."

Emma smiled politely. The captain was a handsome
man, tall and fit, always neatly attired, and groomed with
clean, short nails, and hair most women would kill for.
Blonde and glossy, he kept it short, the ends just brushing
against the collar of his uniform. "That's very kind of
you, Captain, but Renny mustn't neglect her studies."

Derek brushed his fingers over his moustache and
smiled, his voice a low, seductive hum for her ears only.
"You're a breath of fresh air to this weary soldier, Miss
Emma. It will be a pleasure to have two beautiful ladies
visiting at the fort."

Emma lowered her gaze, embarrassed yet thrilled at
his flowery compliment. She pulled at her gloved fingers.
"That's very kind of you, Captain Sanders."

Derek stopped her nervous fidgeting by taking her fingers firmly in his grasp. Lifting one hand to his lips, he
pressed his lips to her gloved palm. "Merely the truth,
Miss Emma."

She glanced warily at him. Was he making fun of her?
He stepped closer. His soft, honey-brown eyes reminded
her of a soulful puppy. Her heart raced at the desire in his
eyes.

"I think I'm falling in love with you, Emma. I hope
you'll allow me to get to know you?"

Flustered by his boldly stated feelings, Emma pulled
her hands from his grasp and turned to watch Renny
brushing down a chestnut mare. "There's much for me to
consider, Captain Sanders."

Derek clasped his hands behind his back, his gaze following hers. "Ah, yes, your young sister. As I said, a
delightful child."

Emma lifted one brow. "My dear, Captain. I fear
you've taken in too much sun." *Delightful* was not a

word she'd choose to describe Renny of late. Head-strong, willful and rebellious came to mind; right now, her sister looked like an abandoned urchin. Bits of straw clung to her soiled pinafore, and her hair hung loose, the neat braids long gone. Searching the straw on the floor, Emma spotted a lone blue ribbon. The other one was nowhere to be seen. She sighed. "Appearances can be deceiving, Captain. You have not seen Renny at her worst. I fear her escapades have sent many a brave man running."

Derek laughed softly and twisted the ends of his mus-tache. "Ah, my dear Miss Emma. I am not most men. Do not worry about me. I can handle a mere child. In fact, I find her high spirits quite entertaining."

Emma smoothed the wrinkles from her skirt then folded her hands demurely to still their nervous trem-bling. "Time will tell, Captain. Since my aunt passed away, I fear Renny has grown even more headstrong." A wistful sigh escaped at the thought of never seeing her beloved Aunt Ida again. How she missed her. Though she'd become fragile with age, giving over the running of the household and the raising of Renny to Emma, she'd retained a calming effect on the young girl.

Renny had been a happy and content child without their father. But as the years had passed, and as she'd observed her friends and their families, Renny had become more aware and concerned with the absence of their father. The sporadic letters and gifts along with the empty promises that he'd return when his duty was over no longer appeased or fooled her. Emma's lips twisted at that bald-faced lie. Colonel Grady O'Brien's tour of duty would never be over.

Putting the bitter thoughts from her mind, she watched her sister, noting how happy the girl seemed as she groomed the horses. A far cry from the sullen and rebel-lious child of late. Remembering her own early child-hood, the horses she'd had and the time she and her father had spent riding, Emma frowned. At Renny's age, she'd had her own horse and had loved to defy convention and ride bareback.

But her father's abandonment and the early responsibility forced upon her had been the end of that. Aunt Ida hadn't seen reason to incur the expense of maintaining a stable when they could just as easily walk or hire a coach. But now that Emma knew how much Renny loved horses, she decided to purchase a pair for them to ride when they returned to St. Louis. If caring for the huge beasts put the sparkle of happiness back in Renny's eyes, she'd provide her with a whole stableful!

"Miss Emma?" Derek's voice drew attention back to him. "I'd be honored if you'd join me for a turn around the deck."

Emma reluctantly shook her head. "Thank you, Captain, but I'm afraid I must take Renny back to our cabin."

He bowed low. "Very well. Perhaps you'll find it in your heart to honor a poor, lonely soldier with your company later this evening?"

Emma made a noncommittal response then hustled a complaining Renny up the stairs, eager to get away from the group of staring soldiers, especially the captain. It wasn't that she objected to his attentions. She didn't. He made her feel attractive and special. But she didn't want to set herself up for hurt and disappointment later on. And until she saw her father, any plans for the future must be put on hold.

Back in the small, barely larger-than-a-closet cabin, Emma sat Renny down and picked up a hairbrush. The girl squirmed and complained as Emma drew the brush through strands of hopelessly snarled hair. "Do sit still, Renny." She pulled out more bits and pieces of straw.

"Aw, Em. I was having so much fun. You ruin everything." Renny folded her arms across her chest and frowned.

Separating the strands into three thick bunches, Emma quickly plaited the girl's deep auburn hair into one long braid down her back, then refastened the pale blue ribbon. "I know you like being around the horses, Renny, but you really mustn't bother the captain. He's a very busy man."

Renny jumped off the edge of the narrow bed, her mouth set in a mutinous line. "Captain Sanders don't mind. He told me so." The last was spoken defiantly.

Emma turned away. "Nevertheless, we shall spend tomorrow on your studies. Your teacher will be most displeased if you return behind the other students." She held up a hand when Renny opened her mouth to protest. "That is final."

Renny pouted, her gray-blue eyes darkening with resentment. "I bet Papa isn't such a bore. When we get to the fort, I'm gonna ask him for a horse of my very own. He won't make me study or do stupid stitches all day. I hate it! I wish Aunt Ida were here. She wasn't such a bore. She let me have fun. Wait until I'm with Papa. Then you can't boss me around." With that, the nine-year-old ran out the door.

Emma started to follow then stopped. She knew her sister didn't mean the hurtful words. Before Aunt Ida had fallen ill, forcing Emma to take over the discipline and day-to-day raising of Renny, Emma had been the fun one, the one who'd sneaked desserts into the nursery, or sneaked her sister out to the park for some girlish fun while their aunt napped. And now, because of her authoritarian role, Renny resented her and believed their father would be more loving and fun.

Fighting pangs of hurt, Emma watched her sister run down the narrow corridor, her long braid whipping from side to side. The ribbon slipped off, leaving Emma to wonder why she bothered: with her sister's hair, with this trip, with her determination to make her father see them.

How would Renny feel when they had to return home alone? Would things get worse? Like the ribbons that refused to stay in her sister's hair, Emma fully expected

Colonel Grady O'Brien to slip out of his parental duties as he always had.

Derek stood on deck, deep in thought. He leaned against the railing and tuned out the shouts and commotion of the men working to get the steamboat over the sandbar. He had other things on his mind—like Colonel O'Brien's daughters. What a stroke of luck to run into them. He planned to personally deliver Emma and her pest of a sister to the colonel, then bask in the old man's gratitude. Frowning, he rubbed his smooth jaw. But would that be enough to get him the promotion he sought? The colonel was a hard man to impress. After all, Derek wouldn't have done anything more than arrive at the fort on the same steamboat as the girls.

He narrowed his eyes and absently fingered his moustache. A slow smile emerged as he thought of his plan to win Emma's love. As the colonel's son-in-law, he'd have the connections he desperately needed. Anticipation lit a warm glow in his belly. And with those coveted connections came wealth and power.

Yes, Emma O'Brien was the answer to his problems. While he had no desire to marry, he was a man of great ambition. And the colonel's daughter, with her clear, pale green eyes that could drown a man, creamy skin and well-proportioned figure, would serve him well. He grimaced. Too bad she had the colonel's god-awful red hair, which meant her breasts' tips would be a pale pink, not a rich chocolate-brown as he preferred. Ah, but their size and youthful firmness would make up for that defect. Besides, in the dark, he could pretend.

He allowed his imagination to go wild. Just thinking about squeezing and suckling that tender flesh made his body swell with the anticipation of bedding her. Damn. The need for patience chafed him. He hated waiting. He was used to taking what he wanted, when he wanted, but she wasn't some Indian squaw who'd cower and do his bidding. He sighed, this time, he'd have to wed her first.

And therein lay his problem: He needed to coax Emma into accepting him as her future husband, and he didn't have much time. In the two weeks since he'd come aboard, she'd kept her distance. Thoughtfully, he studied the working men. By the look of things, they'd be on their way sometime in the next couple of hours. Barring any more problems, they'd arrive at the fort within a week. But if the *Annabella* were further disabled? A glimmer of an idea formed. Reaching into his pocket, he withdrew a small gold nugget, then stared at it regretfully. But there was more where this one had come from. He wandered over to where two workers dressed in old threadbare pants coiled ropes.

Minutes later, the deed accomplished, Derek watched the two men he'd bribed head for the paddle wheel. He was a gold nugget poorer but if all went as planned, he'd receive his promotion to major. And once he was in charge, he'd step up his plans to rid the Black Hills of all savages. He fingered his last gold nugget. Soon he'd be free to get more nuggets and be rich beyond his wildest dreams, free to do what he pleased and go where he wanted. Forget the army.

And the women. Ah, yes. They'd seek him out.

Whistling, Derek ran his fingers over his moustache, then with hat in hand, he headed downstairs to the dining room. Someone needed to be on hand to comfort Miss Emma when she found out that the *Annabella* had a broken paddle wheel and would be laid up for another few days. Who better than the man who planned to marry her?

Chapter Two

The next morning dawned clear and warm. Standing on the deck of the *Annabella*, Emma watched the half-dozen soldiers lead their horses down the plank from the steamboat to solid land then return to unload an old mud coach that belonged to the Frenchman. The horses, free from the confines of the steerage, pranced with eagerness as they were harnessed.

Emma turned to Derek. "I'm grateful you're willing to escort us to Fort Pierre. Are you sure we won't be any trouble?"

Derek clasped his hands behind his back. "A beautiful woman like you is never any trouble, Miss Emma."

Beyond the bank lay a wild and untamed world. Emma frowned and plucked at her gloved fingers. "Is it safe to travel by coach?" Doubts assailed her. Captain Billaud had advised her not to leave the comparable safety of the boat to travel by coach to the fort. But if they waited out this latest delay, she feared her father would be long gone when they arrived. Then what? She had no intention of following him west to Fort Laramie through Indian territory.

"Be assured, Miss Emma, my men and I will see you and your sister safely delivered to the fort." Derek glanced at her. "No point fretting your time away here when you can be reunited with your father before he leaves."

Emma glanced at the bank. Renny had talked one of the soldiers into letting her ride his horse. Though Emma had her doubts about leaving the boat, time *was* of the essence. She had to reach the fort with no more delays and Derek's offer to escort them seemed an ideal solution. Besides, her sister was thrilled with the prospect of sleeping outdoors. Picking up her valise, she nodded. "All right. I believe we're ready." Confident that she was making the right decision, she thanked Captain Billaud for the use of his coach then allowed Derek to lead her off the boat.

Three days later, Emma wasn't so confident that leaving the *Annabella* had been the wisest choice; the interior of the coach was stifling, her emerald-green travel dress clung to her skin, and the dust of travel filled her nostrils. To top it off, the muscles along her shoulders and back ached from nights spent sleeping on the hard, cold ground and long days confined to the coach with nothing to see.

The passing scenery was all the same. Trees and bushes rimmed the river on one side, barren and depressing land stretched forever on the other. Rolling her stiff shoulders, she swallowed a moan then sneezed. Blotting her forehead daintily with a damp embroidered handkerchief, she wondered how much longer it would be before they reached the fort.

Renny turned away from the window. "Are we nearly there, Emma?"

Emma bit back a sigh of impatience and folded her gloved hands primly in her lap. "Good heavens, Renny, you asked that very same question not more than fifteen minutes ago." Never mind that she'd wondered the same thing.

"But Emma, we've been traveling ever so long. Captain Sanders promised we'd reach the fort in just two days." She wiggled on the cushioned bench, her skirts twisting beneath her.

Settling against the seat back, Emma frowned when Renny shoved her mop of tangled hair out of her eyes.

Just an hour ago, the thick, dark strands had been confined to two tidy braids. "Yes, I know he did, my sweet, but that was before the axle broke. As much as I hate to contemplate it, I expect we'll be forced to spend another night on the prairie before we reach the fort."

She ignored her sister's whoop of excitement. Except for being confined in the coach for long periods, Renny was having the time of her life. Emma bit back a moan of despair. If spending another night camping made her sister happy, she'd find the strength to endure it . . . somehow.

Renny stuck her head out of the window and, after a few seconds, plopped back on the seat. "It's so boring just sitting here." She gave Emma a sulky glance. "I bet Captain Sanders would let me ride up with the driver."

Emma begged the heavens for patience then adopted a no-nonsense look similar to the one her aunt had used. "Young ladies ride inside coaches. Besides, the captain's men do not need to listen to your constant prattle."

Renny crossed her arms across her thin chest and tucked her hands beneath her arms. Her jaw jutted out. "Aw, Emma—"

The young girl closed her mouth when Emma lifted one brow in warning. The two sisters sat in silence for several miles before Renny drew her knees up and rested her chin on them. "Emma? Will father be angry with us?"

Emma kept her features carefully schooled in an expression of indifference for her sister's sake. Grady O'Brien would likely be extremely angry, but she vowed to make sure his displeasure was directed toward her and not at Renny. She reached across the coach to pat her sister reassuringly on the knee. "Everything will be fine. Now, no more worrying."

Renny's lower lip trembled. "Father hates me."

"Ranait! What a thing to say. Father does not hate you."

Tears came into the nine-year-old's eyes. "Yes, he does! It's *my* fault Mama died. Jillyanne said so. That's why he went away and never came back. He blames me."

Renny's distress and quavering voice nearly broke Emma's heart. "Oh, Renny, don't say such a thing." Fury engulfed Emma. Jillyanne, several years older than Renny, was never happy unless she was making others miserable. And the girl's mother wasn't any better. A snob and gossip, she had nothing better to do than spread vicious lies. But anger wouldn't help her sister now. Once again, Emma wondered if this trip would make things worse. *Was* she setting her sister up for a worse disappointment? *Did* Grady O'Brien truly blame his younger daughter for their mother's death?

Staring into the eyes across from her, Emma knew Renny favored their mother in most of her features. Though Renny's eyes were a bluish-gray, her mouth, nose and hair-color marked her as their mother's daughter. But the girl's eyes were her father's.

Clicking her fan open, Emma pulled from her memory an image of a tall man who'd been kind, gentle and loving. She recalled the bedtime stories, the kisses good night, twinkling bluish-gray eyes and always, a tickle to the tummy that left her giggling as sleep claimed her. What was he like now? From his letters, she envisioned a stern and forbidding military man who was all business.

Emma sighed. Their aunt had always been able to reassure her nieces that their father wanted to be there but couldn't because of his military commitments. But when Aunt Ida died, Renny's secure little world had shattered. Nothing Emma said could convince her that she, Emma, would always be there for her. Renny wanted her father.

Her sister's hurt and confused voice brought Emma back from her contemplations. "Then why did he leave us? Why hasn't he been back to see us? He didn't even come to Auntie's funeral," she accused.

Emma sighed. They'd been over this more times than she could count. She gentled her voice. "You know very well he didn't learn about it until three months ago. Sometimes our letters take a very long time to reach him. Enough now. We'll see father soon." She deliberately changed the topic of conversation. "I've been thinking. Perhaps we can buy a couple of horses when we return. Would you like that?"

"Truly?" Renny breathed, her eyes bright with longing. Emma nodded.

Renny clapped her hands. "I can't wait to see Papa and tell him I'm to have my very own horse."

Holding on to the side of the coach, Renny balanced on her knees and asked, "Em, are you going to marry Captain Sanders?"

The sudden change of topic and mood so characteristic of the energetic child caught Emma off-guard. "Ranait, mind your manners! I hardly know the man. He simply agreed to take us to the fort." Her voice sounded sharper than she'd intended.

"Well, I like him. He's got horses." Again, Renny shifted positions, this time to sit on her knees and peer out the window. "I see him." She waved.

Emma wasn't sure how she felt about Derek Sanders. Part of her thrilled to his attentions, yet she was afraid to let herself hope for his affection. Many other suitors had balked when they had found out that marriage to her meant taking on Renny.

Hiding her lower face behind her fan, Emma allowed herself a smug grin when she recalled several times that the prospect of raising Renny had sent less-than-desirable prospective suitors running. She sighed. Maybe, maybe this time, it would be different. Hope stirred deep inside her heart. Derek had made his intentions clear, even if he was getting rather pushy about it. Perhaps she'd give him a chance. She did find him attractive. Catching sight of his broad shoulders as he rode past, she waved the fan a bit faster.

Renny continued to bounce around. Emma drew her brows together in her sternest glare and snapped her fan closed. "Renny, do sit still. Young ladies don't squirm and wiggle about." As usual, her reprimand fell on deaf ears. The girl's youthful energy knew no bounds.

"Ranait!"

"Oh, Emma, you sound just like Aunt Ida." Renny flounced back against the leather seat with a pout. But a half hour later, the young girl's eyes grew heavy and drifted shut.

Grateful for the blessed silence, Emma closed her eyes and despite the jarring ride, she too dozed, dreaming about the handsome captain. She woke hours later when the coach came to a standstill.

Glancing out of the window, she saw Derek approaching. When the door opened, she sighed in relief. "Are we stopping for the night?"

He nodded and held out his gloved hand. Emma gratefully accepted his assistance from the torturous confines of the coach. Renny jumped down on her own, wide-awake and chittering like a magpie.

Leaving the men to set up camp, Emma walked down to the river, easing the tightness from her legs and back. After finding some concealing bushes to take care of her needs, she went to the water's edge and knelt down to splash the cool, revitalizing water on her face and neck. She rubbed her aching shoulders, longing for a nice hot soak in a tub. She was sick of traveling. Sick of wearing the same dress.

She brushed at the dirt and wrinkles lining her green dress, but it didn't help. Now she wished she'd kept more than two changes of clothing with her, but she hadn't expected further delays. Sitting back on her heels, she tried to still her impatience. This whole trip had been fraught with delays from the very beginning. What was another day or two?

Enjoying her solitude, she luxuriated in the peace and quiet. Across the river, a flock of birds hidden in the tree-tops took to the air in wild chattering flight. Her tired gaze lowered to the deep shadows across the river. She let out a sharp gasp when Indians on horseback emerged from the shadows. Frightened by their sudden appearance, Emma jumped to her feet, picked up her skirts and ran back to camp.

"Derek!" Her voice squeaked with fright. "Look!" Pointing, she pulled his arm, interrupting his conversation with two of his men.

Derek took one look at the approaching visitors and swore. He pulled her behind him. "What the hell does *he* want?" He signaled his men. Rifles were drawn.

"You know him?" Emma's voice quavered when one of the savages dismounted and approached. The other four remained on horseback a short distance away.

Derek kept his gaze trained on the approaching Indian. "I know him. Wait here." He handed her over to a young private named Edmond who stepped in front of her, his body shielding hers. Another soldier joined them.

Nervous and afraid, Emma glanced around. Renny, where was she? She breathed a sigh of relief when she spotted the child surrounded by three soldiers, all of whom had their rifles trained on the group of intruders. She returned her attention to Derek and the Indian. Fear trailed down her spine. What did these savages want? Seconds ticked into long, agonizing minutes. Emma peeked between her two guards' shoulders at the rag-tag group of natives.

Never had she seen such a frightening sight. Their hair hung down over their shoulders in dull, stringy strands and their bodies bore several days' worth of dirt and grime. Faced with such sinister-looking savages, she dearly regretted leaving the comparative safety of the *Annabella*.

But she didn't have time to bemoan the vulnerable position in which she'd put herself and Renny. Heated shouts filled the air as an argument broke out between Captain Sanders and the warrior. When the fierce-looking savage glanced at her and pointed, she shivered, instinctively sensing that he wanted *her*.

Derek shook his head, his hand going to the pistol he wore around his waist. After a final spat of words, the angry warrior mounted his horse. With a harsh shout, he shook his fist in the air and glared at them through hate-filled eyes. Emma breathed a sigh of relief when he rode off.

After the Indians crossed the river and melded into the lengthening shadows, Derek rejoined her. "It's all right, Miss Emma. They're gone." He reached for her and drew her into his arms.

Instead of feeling comforted by his embrace, a feeling of suffocation assailed her. Derek's bold attentions since leaving the steamboat had grown from flattering to tedious, increasing to the point where she felt uncomfortable and rushed. She didn't understand her conflicting emotions. She pulled free but, not wanting to hurt his feelings, laid a trembling hand on his arm. "What did they want?"

"Not to worry, Miss Emma. Just a bunch of beggars. I sent them away. They won't bother us again."

"Are you sure? Why was he pointing at me?"

Derek patted her hand then carried her fingers to his lips. "My dear, these are savages. They probably haven't seen a white woman before. Now, don't worry none. I won't allow anything to happen to the woman I hope to marry soon. Trust me, Emma. I'll take good care of you."

Emma hid her impatience at his assumptions. She hated feeling helpless and dependent on Derek, but until they reached the fort, both her life and Renny's rested in his hands. Though she felt far from reassured, she forced a smile. "Thank you, Captain. I do appreciate all you've done for us."

She turned to go, but Derek pulled her back to him. His hands cupped her face. His head lowered.

"Captain!" Her voice rose in panic.

"Derek," he breathed. "Say it, *Emma*. Let me hear you say my name."

Emma planted her hands against his chest, fearful of the underlying tension she felt in him. "Derek," she complied.

Satisfied, Derek smiled and touched her lips briefly with his. "You have no idea what you do to me, Emma." His hooded gaze drifted down to the tailored fit of her bodice. "I want you. When we arrive at Fort Pierre, I will ask your father's permission to wed you. Then you'll be mine—forever." Derek took her by the arm and led her away from the rest of the soldiers.

"Now, why don't you rest while my men see to supper?"

Shaken and uneasy by what felt like a threat more than a declaration of intent or love, Emma called Renny to her and gladly made her escape into their tent.

As soon as the tent flap closed behind Emma, Derek posted his men around the temporary camp, then went to the one remaining soldier tending the horses. Gus, a simple boy around nineteen, was one of the soldiers Derek could trust to do whatever he ordered. "Keep your eyes open. I don't trust Yellow Dog. He's getting greedy. I'm putting you in charge of the colonel's daughters. I don't want anything to happen to them." Derek knew the boy would die protecting the girls if he ordered it.

"Wha'd he want?"

"Guns," Derek scoffed. His gaze hardened. *And Emma*, he added mentally. Slightly uneasy, he studied the camp, calculating their weakest positions.

"Guns? You ain't gonna give him any more, are you?" Gus looked horrified.

Only paying slight attention to Gus, Derek scowled. In his distraction, his voice lost the refined quality he strove hard to maintain. Long ago, he'd vowed to leave poverty behind forever and live the life of a gentleman. "Hell, no. I'm no fool."

"Why's he after payment so soon? We jest gave him a bunch of stuff. Even had to give him my pa's old huntin' knife," the young soldier grumbled.

"Yeah, well, seems he decided to kill some chief's squaw instead of just harassing the Sioux like I paid him to do. Now he wants guns to protect himself."

Gus sent a worried glance over his shoulder. "Cap'n, we didn't pay him to do no killin'—especially not some chief's squaw."

Derek stared out toward the distant hills on the far horizon. He twirled one end of his moustache into a sharp point. His plan had been for Yellow Dog to seem that he was under the colonel's orders to drive out the Sioux, which was why he'd given Yellow Dog the colonel's silver belt buckle as payment. He knew the renegade Indian would brag about his prize and importance.

His voice was thoughtful as he smoothed his moustache with his thumb and forefinger. "Maybe Yellow Dog did us a favor. This should rile the Sioux enough to attack the fort. Then that damn Indian-loving colonel will have to take action and get rid of them."

Gus scratched his greasy brown hair and looked confused for a moment, then he grinned, revealing a mouthful of rotting teeth. "If they attacks us, we gets to attack them, and if we does, then we gets their women. Right, Cap'n?"

Derek shook his head at the boy's eagerness. It was a mystery to him how the boy had survived his stint in the army, but that very naivete and eagerness to please made Gus a valuable asset. All it took to keep Gus loyal was an occasional lay with a willing or unwilling squaw.

He lowered his voice. "Right. I'll even give you first choice. Now, not a word. If anyone finds out our plans, they'll take all the young maidens and leave you the old wrinkled ones."

Gus frowned. Derek gave him a none-too-gentle shove. "Get to your post, soldier. We don't want the others to get suspicious, do we?"

"No, sir." Grinning ear to ear, Gus dashed off to stand guard at Emma's tent.

Hands on his hips, Derek watched him. Little did the boy know, there was much more at stake than rutting with a bunch of women. Sliding his hands into the pockets of his pants, he fingered the remaining gold nugget he'd taken from a widowed squaw who'd come begging to the fort.

He'd gone to her tipi to check her out. After she'd

proven her willingness to spread her legs for food—with a little encouragement, he thought—he'd gone through her pitifully few possessions.

His hands closed over the cold rock. He'd been shocked to find a pouch with several gold nuggets of a size and weight he'd never before seen. Those alone would have made him a rich man, but he wanted more. After plying her with drink, she'd told him about the sacred mountains where the shiny rocks turned streams the same color.

Not about to let anyone else learn of gold in the hills, he'd strangled her and buried her far from the fort. No one had questioned the disappearance of another squaw. He narrowed his eyes. If only he could get into those hills and hunt for the gold. But not with all the Sioux there. That's when he'd come up with the idea of starting Indian wars by pitting the Arikara and the Sioux against each other. The two tribes were long-standing enemies. And if tensions between them escalated, the army would be forced to step in and he'd have the perfect excuse to drive the Indians out of the area.

So far, his plan had failed. Damn the colonel for trying to work out peace treaties with the Indians. But the colonel was due to leave soon. Derek fiddled with his moustache then chuckled softly. Pleased with this new turn of events, he headed back toward camp.

When Emma and her bothersome sister emerged from their tent to eat, he sat beside them, his rifle loaded and at his side. Emma, still on edge from Yellow Dog's earlier appearance, kept glancing over her shoulder. Derek decided to shamelessly play on her fear, hoping she'd exaggerate the scene to her father. He would get what he wanted: gold.

Long before the sun rose the next morning, Derek gave orders to break camp. Emma sensed his tension and hustled a sleepy Renny into the coach. As the coach rumbled along the uneven terrain toward the fort, she cast worried glances out the window. Her loving gaze fell to her sister, asleep in the seat across from her. If anything happened to Renny, she'd never forgive herself. After several uneventful hours of travel, she relaxed.

Dozing, she woke when the wheels hit a rock, slamming her shoulder into the side of the coach. Emma moaned and rubbed the bruised flesh. The jarring bump had woken Renny, too. She sat up and rubbed her eyes then opened her mouth. Emma held up one hand. "Don't ask. We'll get there when—"

The coach unexpectedly surged to the left. The driver sitting above their heads cracked his whip and yelled at the top of his lungs, sending the coach careening forward at such speed that Emma and Renny were tossed to the floor.

"Emma?"

Renny's frightened voice penetrated the haze of pain surrounding Emma. She struggled to her knees, her head aching where she'd hit it against the door but the wild rocking of the coach made keeping her balance nearly impossible. "Stay down." Her own heart pounded in unison with the throbbing of her head. Hearing the sound of an approaching rider, she glanced out the window to see Gus riding hell-bent-for-leather toward them. When he drew close to the window, Emma grabbed hold of the door and stuck her head out. "What's going on—"

Suddenly, the air exploded with bone-chilling screams followed by shouts and gunfire. Gus stared at her, white-faced, his eyes wide with fright. "Git down, Miss," he shouted. "We're under attack—"

His body jerked, his warning ending in a strangled cry. Emma watched in horror as he slumped forward, the feathered shaft of an arrow protruding from his back.

Chapter Three

Emma screamed when Gus fell from his horse. Glancing behind the coach, her heart stopped when she saw the Indians who were chasing them. An arrow whizzed past, close enough for her to feel the soft scrape of feathers brushing her cheek. Jerking back, she crashed to the floor. An arrow flew in, the sharp head plunging into the back of the seat inches from where Renny had sat only moments before. Oh, Lord, this couldn't be happening. Fighting an onrush of pure terror, Emma covered her sister's small body with her own. "Stay down!"

She cringed when another arrow pinged off the side of the coach. Cold fingers of fear slithered through her; the loud whoops of the attacking Indians grew louder. "Oh, dear Lord."

"Emma, I'm scared," Renny whimpered.

"Me, too, sweetheart." Overhead, the crack of the driver's whip alternated with the loud report of his rifle and his frantic yells at the team of horses. Swaying to her knees, Emma buried her sister's head in her lap and braved another peek through the open window. Where was Captain Sanders?

After a few frantic seconds, she spotted him riding off to the right, fleeing into a stand of thick cottonwoods near a bend in the river, with an Indian on horseback in hot pursuit. Turning in his saddle, he fired. The Indian fell from his horse but instead of returning to fight, Derek kept riding as though the devil himself were after him.

Disbelief left Emma speechless. She loosened her hold on Renny and gripped the coach through the open window to keep her precarious balance. Surely he wasn't leaving her and Renny to the Indians, was he?

"Derek!" The name came out a hoarse gasp. She screamed again.

Renny lifted her head. "Emma?" Her voice wobbled with fear.

The sound of an approaching rider prevented Emma from answering. Peering behind the careening coach, her heart nearly stopped at the sight of a garishly painted Indian closing in on them. Gunfire from the driver sounded overhead and the hideous savage toppled from his horse. Emma sagged with relief, but her relief was short-lived when an ominous thud sounded above her. Seconds later, the driver's arrow-pierced body pitched off the roof.

With no driver, the horses bolted wildly. Both girls screamed as the coach swayed precariously from side to side. Emma grabbed Renny and held her tightly, bracing herself on the floor between the seats. She tried to reassure her hysterically crying sister, but couldn't force the words past her own fear-clogged throat.

The coach continued to careen through the rocky landscape until Emma feared they'd end in a pile of splintered wood. Still, dying in the coach seemed better than facing the pursuing savages whose horrible war cries surrounded them. Stories of atrocities done to captive white women and children numbed her mind and filled her soul with terror.

After what seemed like hours, the coach slowed and came to a halt. Emma lay still for a moment, her heart thumping and her mouth dry. With Renny clutched to her bosom, she listened. Outside, she heard the restless sound of horses, the jangle of a harness but nothing else. No voices. No screams. No loud whoops.

The comparable silence after the thunderous noise of the runaway coach seemed stark and oppressive. Who was out there? Her eyes skittered from one set of doors to the other. At the same time, she tried to find something she could use as a weapon. *Please, God,* she prayed, *let it be Derek out there.* The door wrenched open and Emma found herself staring her worst nightmare in the face: a savage with a hideously yellow-painted face.

The Indian stuck his head inside. A deep jagged scar ran down one cheek from just beneath his eye, ending at the corner of his mouth. When he grinned, the yellow-caked crevice deepened grotesquely. Emma gasped, recognizing him as the same Indian who'd come to the camp last night, the one who'd stared at her and had made it obvious he'd wanted her. Horror as she'd never known gripped her when she realized he'd cold-bloodedly killed the soldiers to get *her.*

Laughing, he reached inside and grabbed Renny by the foot. Her sister screamed, kicked and clutched Emma around the neck. Emma yanked Renny free from the savage and shoved the girl onto the seat behind her, then threw herself backwards, using her own body as a shield.

"No! Go away, leave us alone." Her voice shook, her throat so clogged with fright that she could barely speak. She kicked out, but the Indian, amused by her futile efforts to avoid capture, reached out and grabbed her by the ankle. With one strong yank, he pulled her down off the seat.

Emma landed hard on her backside on the floor of the coach. The savage used her moment of dazed pain to pluck Renny from the coach. Her sister's frantic screams brought Emma to her knees. She hurtled herself at the warrior, slammed her body into him, and sent them both flying to the ground.

The Indian tossed her off of him. She landed in a sprawled heap in the prairie grass several feet away, the wind knocked from her. Lifting her head, she struggled for breath and glanced around, searching for help. There were no soldiers to be found. Her blood pulsed loudly in her ears. She and Renny were on their own. Crouched in the grass, she stared at the five hostile Indians surrounding her. Their faces were painted, their chests scarred and slashed with color, and their bodies naked but for a strip of cloth dangling between their legs. One of the savages held Renny.

Emma scrambled to her feet but her skirts were twisted and tangled around her ankles. She tripped and fell flat on her belly. When she finally gained her footing, one savage behind her yanked on her hair while another reached out to grab one breast. Prepared to fight them all, Emma whirled around. The savages crowded close, their hands snaking out to touch and taunt. Then the savage with the yellow-painted face stepped forward and yanked her to his chest. He grinned down at Emma and thrust his fist victoriously in the air, yelling and whooping. Victory shouts from the other warriors joined his.

Emma used her forearms to put distance between her and her captor but he tightened his hold until her breasts were flattened against his chest and her face within inches of his sweat-drenched body. She gagged and turned her head. He smelled of filth, sweat and death. Fighting the rising wave of nausea, she closed her eyes and prayed. *Please, God, don't let them rape me.*

Then he spoke, his voice harsh and guttural in a language she couldn't understand. He grabbed her by the back of the head and addressed her in broken English. "Yellow Dog kill enemy, take woman from soldier with cheating heart and lying tongue. You belong to Yellow Dog."

Emma could barely understand his thick, coarsely spoken words, but their meaning was clear when he dragged her toward his horse with his arm hooked around her neck. Desperate, she swung her fists and kicked with all her might, all the while screaming for Derek to come and rescue her and Renny.

Her screams echoed over the treetops, lost in the vastness of the open prairie. Using her nails, she scratched and clawed. One foot caught the savage in the shin and a wildly swinging fist connected with his nose. The warrior grunted and backhanded her, knocking her to the ground. Dazed, she shook her head and glanced around.

Renny followed her lead and tried to bite the hand of the warrior holding her, but the savage only laughed. When he tossed the girl over his shoulder and strode over to one of the horses, Emma shoved her hair out of her eyes and charged the warrior who'd mounted his horse, Renny held tightly in front of him.

Her sister screamed, trying to struggle free.

"Renny!" Emma ran forward, but Yellow Dog grabbed a fistful of her hair and threw her down onto the ground then straddled her. Though she continued to fight, he had no trouble binding her feet and hands with thongs of leather. Done, he leered at the flesh revealed by the ripped neckline of her dress from the rough handling, but to her relief, he didn't touch her. Instead, he flung her over his horse and mounted.

Emma tried to push up, but the savage held her firmly in place. He lifted a hand and gave an ear-shattering whoop. The small band of Indians surged forward.

The sinking sun cast gray-violet shadows over a band of warriors following their enemies trail. The trampled prairie grass was a narrow swath through the golden plains that ended at the river. Crossing the river, the band of a dozen warriors dismounted. Several trails, made by animals, both human and four-legged, snaked out in several directions.

Chief Striking Thunder crouched and parted the short prairie grass to study the soft, moist soil close to the riverbank. There were many tracks to be studied. Buffalo, deer, elk, horse and man. With several different tribes roaming the land, it made finding the set of tracks he followed difficult but finally, he spotted the faint print of a scarred hoof. Shouting, he gathered his warriors.

Pointing at the tracks and the day-old horse droppings, he spoke, using his Lakota tongue. "Yellow Dog was here. We gain on our enemy." His voice nearly cracked with the onslaught of emotion, but he forced his voice to remain neutral. "We will have justice for the killing of our people."

The others nodded in response. For three days, he and his band of warriors had followed Yellow Dog's flight across the plains. He noted the solemn faces around him and knew each was remembering the Arikara's brutal attack on a small group of their people during the buffalo hunt. They'd lost several loved ones that day. He drew in deep controlled breaths and concentrated on the furious pounding of his heart.

Long Arrow, an older brave with a bandaged thigh limped forward. "I will avenge my grandmother and grandfather!" On that day, he'd been left with two other warriors to guard those too weak or sick to go on the hunt. Normally, all who could endure the grueling work followed the herd and took care of the meat after the warriors killed what was needed.

Meadowlark and several other women had left to return to the village with the first load of meat and furs. Before the rest arrived, at a time when they were vulnerable, the tribe had been attacked. Long Arrow had fought well, but he'd been no match for the renegade warriors who thought nothing about cutting down those weaker than they in order to reach their objective—Striking Thunder's wife. Six of their tribe had died that day and Long Arrow had been wounded.

Afterward, though he was in pain from his injuries, Long Arrow had insisted on joining the war party. Striking Thunder noted with pride the brave's impassive features—a good warrior didn't allow emotion to blind him. The boy would be strong. Still, looking closely, he saw the lurking anger deep in the boy's earth-brown eyes. He knew only too well the effort it took to keep one's emotions tightly reined. Striking Thunder's own anger over losing his wife coiled tighter within him, fighting for a release he dared not give into.

"Long Arrow becomes a warrior this night," he announced. "He will avenge the spirits of his grandmother and grandfather." The boy stood taller with each of Striking Thunder's carefully chosen words, spoken to remind him of his warrior's training.

Long Arrow spat on the ground. "The Arikara are no match for our mighty chief. They are cowards. They attack old men, women and children. They will pay for their crimes against the Sioux and against our people." He punched a fist into the air.

Everyone nodded at the boy's words and while each was equally set on seeking justice, sadness filled the air when they looked upon Striking Thunder. He closed his eyes against a fresh wave of pain. It would be a very long time before he forgot the sight of his young wife—dead from a self-inflicted knife wound. Rather than allow her enemy to defile her body, Meadowlark had taken her own life. Their marriage had been much too short, only two months.

Breathing deeply, flaring his nostrils, Striking Thunder pulled from memory a vision of a young, petite girl of sixteen winters with knee-length shiny black hair, smooth skin the color of the nutmeg spice his mother loved and eyes the shade of a newborn fawn. A cry of rage rose from deep in his soul and clawed at the back of his throat. Though not a love match, he'd cared for his wife.

He tried to block the searing pain and guilt of his thoughts. If he hadn't married her, she'd still be alive. The council had ordered him to marry, and he'd chosen Meadowlark. Forcing the anguish from his mind, he focused on the task of catching the enemy. Though he longed to continue on and close the distance between them, the horses needed rest and food. "We stop here to thank the spirits. With the help of *Wambli*, the spirit of the mighty eagle, we gain on our enemy."

Each warrior wandered off a short distance. Striking Thunder knelt where he stood. The *wanagi* of the slain were restless. They demanded justice before their journey to the spirit world to live in spirit tipis. He turned so the fading light of *Wi* fell on his face. Emptying his mind of all anger and thought, he prayed. First to *Mahpiya,* the spirits of the heavens, asking for continued good weather. One storm could wash away all traces of Yellow Dog. A gentle breeze caressed his cheek. He'd been heard.

Then he prayed to the spirits of the west. He asked *Wiyohipeyata* to preside over the evening and coming darkness. He opened his eyes and scanned the sky. When he spotted the wide soaring wings of a hawk searching for its evening meal, he added a prayer to the spirit of *Cetan,* asking for swiftness and endurance.

When he was done, he led his brown-and-white-spotted mare, Rides-to-War, to the water. His gaze slid over her, checking for signs of exhaustion. She lifted her nose and shook her head as if to tell him she could go on. For the first time, his lips softened. "Drink, my friend, then eat and rest." His gaze shifted to the mare's back where a black raven perched.

He'd found the bird injured two months ago and nursed her back to health. In return, she shared her wisdom. Flying across the sky, she shared her vision with him by her actions.

"You too, my friend," he said to the bird. With a loud caw and spreading of wings, the raven, Black Cloud, flapped her wings and lifted high into the sky. Striking Thunder watched the bird circle several times then return to the stream to drink.

His hand closed around the leather medallion he wore tied around his neck. It depicted a raven sitting on a perch, wings outstretched. The bird was his personal helper, and knowing by the bird's actions that there were no enemies close by, Striking Thunder took his own pouch of dried meat and berries and sat in the grass to eat, anxious to resume the pursuit.

Long before *Wi* rose the next morning to show her face in the east, the warriors resumed traveling with speed over the flat prairie land. By mid-morning, they reached the Big Muddy River. A short distance away, they found an overturned coach and the strewn bodies of dead soldiers. Striking Thunder examined an arrow shaft protruding from the back of one soldier. "Yellow Dog!"

The other warriors glanced around, uneasy in the presence of the dead left to rot under the heat of *Wi*. Striking Thunder, about to remount, spotted articles of clothing strewn on the ground near the overturned coach. Picking up a bonnet, he stared at it for a long time then crushed it in his hands. The situation had grown worse. Not only had Yellow Dog and his renegade warriors killed white soldiers, but they'd taken a white woman captive. Stepping over an empty valise, he snatched up a smaller dress and closed his eyes, battling his fury.

Ever since the soldiers had arrived at Fort Pierre, once an old trading stop on the Missouri that was now a military outpost, tensions between the whites and Indians had been shaky. This atrocity would bring down the wrath of the white army upon all Indian tribes. Arikara, Cheyenne or Sioux, it would not matter to the soldiers when they found their slain comrades and learned of the missing woman and child.

Two-Ree, his closest friend and brother-in-law joined him. "We must leave. If soldiers come upon us, we will be blamed for Yellow Dog's crimes. The soldiers already wait for an excuse to kill our people."

Striking Thunder tossed the clothing to the ground, his lips compressed. With the arrival of the soldiers had come raids on Indian villages. Women were raped, tipis were shredded and furs were stolen by the greedy whites who believed they owned the land and everything on it.

But this land belonged to The People. They would fight for it. "You are right, my friend. There is nothing we can do here. We must stop Yellow Dog before he brings the wrath of the white soldiers upon our people." With one last look at the clothing fluttering in the breeze, he mounted and left the scene of death.

Sitting next to a small, nearly dry creek, Emma held Renny who slept fitfully. Around her, the late-afternoon air burst with the song of a meadowlark and the hum of bees in frantic search for a last find of sweet nectar. Above her, the sun beat down on her and a cool breeze caressed her reddened neck, bringing a measure of relief to her overheated body even as it intensified the sting of pain in her burned skin. She stifled her own moans so that she didn't wake Renny. Emma hurt all over from three days of constant travel. Her eyes, swollen from the sun and wind, and gritty with lack of sleep, fluttered closed. A buzz went through her body but she jerked her eyes open. She longed to sleep but didn't dare let her guard down.

So far, Yellow Dog hadn't raped her. Putting distance between them and the murdered soldiers left no time for him to do much other than terrorize her, but it was just a matter of time. Emma pushed the fearsome thoughts from her mind and did what she could to block the burning rays of the sun from Renny's blistered face. Her own wasn't much better. The burned skin felt tight and her lips were bruised and swollen from Yellow Dog's slaps. Her shoulders sagged. She no longer fought him. Instead, she hoarded her energy, watching and waiting for the chance to escape.

Renny stirred. "Em, I'm so hungry," she moaned, opening her glazed eyes.

"I know, sweets." Emma's stomach rumbled. She'd given her sister most of her ration of food when they'd stopped at noon, eating only enough to keep from passing out. Tenderly, she patted Renny's damaged skin with the edge of her dress, which she'd soaked in the creek. Ripping off another strip of her petticoat, she tied it around her sister's lower face to keep the sun off the burned skin. It wasn't much, but it was the best she could do. She gathered Renny back into her arms and they sat in silence while the warriors conferred in a huddle a short distance away.

"Emma?" Renny whimpered.

"Hmm?"

"Do you think Papa will come after us?"

"Of course he will."

"Is that why Cap'n Sanders ran away? Did he go to fetch Papa?"

Emma closed her eyes. To give Renny hope, she'd told her sister of Derek's flight into the trees. "Yes, when he saw he couldn't stop the Indians, he went for help." Secretly though, she doubted her own words. He'd run long before the Indians had overtaken the coach. While part of her couldn't blame him, she hated him for it. He'd sworn to protect and deliver her safely to her father. And now, he was her only hope. She prayed he made it to the fort to alert her father of their capture. A sharp command startled her. Wearily, she rose.

Just before dusk, they came upon three warriors camped on the prairie. Yellow Dog shoved her off the horse. She fell to the ground, rolling as best as she could to ease the pain of impact. Struggling to sit, she ignored her throbbing shoulder and watched her captor greet the warrior who came forward. The two warriors communicated with hand gestures and grunts while the other warriors from both sides remained in the background, poised in case of trouble.

Renny ran to her. Emma dropped her bound wrists over her sister's head to hold her close. "It's okay, Renny," she whispered, wishing she could give her sister more than empty assurances. Would things ever be right again?

Seconds turned into minutes. Emma kept her gaze trained on the two groups of warriors. After what seemed like heated haggling, Yellow Dog motioned for her to come to him. Emma held Renny tightly as she stood and went to him. She noted that the other Indian seemed better dressed and neater in appearance. His hair hung braided over his shoulders, and he was clean and young-looking. His eyes brightened with interest when she stopped several feet away. He pointed a long finger at her.

Yellow Dog shook his head. His hand slashed the air in a downward movement. He pointed at Renny. The other warrior frowned. Emma's eyes grew wide. Cold fingers of fear slithered up her spine. She took a step back, pulling Renny with her when Yellow Dog reached out. Two other warriors held her while Yellow Dog yanked Renny from her arms.

Renny held her arms out to her and whimpered. "Emma!"

To Emma's horror, Yellow Dog thrust her sister into the hands of the other warrior who carried her away, screaming and kicking. Emma, frozen with horror, watched the two groups of warriors exchange horses. Understanding dawned. Bile burned the back of her throat. Yellow Dog had just traded her sister for fresh horses. She lunged, broke free and ran. "No! Renny! Don't take her."

Her sister's screams tore her heart to shreds. Rage filled her. When Yellow Dog grabbed her, she lashed out, her nails scraping down his cheeks. This time, his punishing blows didn't stop her. She fought until a final blow of fist ramming into her jaw sent her skidding across the golden grass. She lay there, defeated, her heart shattered, her head pounding from the blows and ears ringing with her sister's cries, which grew fainter and fainter. Tears ran down her cheeks, and screams of despair tore from her throat. She'd failed her father. She'd promised to care for her sister, but her impatience to reach the fort had cost Renny her sweet, young life. Emma sank into a dark world where there was no pain or fear.

Chapter Four

A large fire lit up the night sky. Yellow Dog's renegade warriors danced and celebrated around the flames, sending grotesque shadows weaving across the prairie. As the night deepened and thick, slate-gray clouds drifted across the sky, concealing the moon, they passed around a flask of whiskey taken from a slain soldier. The flask emptied and one by one, the band collapsed near the fire or stumbled to tipis where their women waited. Eventually, only two remained huddled by the dying fire.

Nearby, cloaked by the darkness, Striking Thunder's band of Sioux warriors watched and waited. With no revealing light from Old Woman Moon, the crouched figures blended with their surroundings, their hushed voices harmonized with the cadence of insects chirping into the night. At the sound of a slightly louder series of chirps and clicks, Striking Thunder crept forward, a long knife gripped in his right hand. He paused, waited for the second signal. When it came, he replied softly. Seconds later, Two-Ree joined him.

"What have you found?" Striking Thunder asked, sliding his knife back into the sheath strapped to his thigh.

Two-Ree stuck his knife into the hard prairie earth. "Our enemy celebrates the killing of the white soldiers. They dance and drink the white-man's firewater." His features twisted into lines of contempt. "They are drunk and do not know we are here. I say we attack and take our revenge. The warriors of Striking Thunder will return to our people victorious."

Adrenaline surged through Striking Thunder. "What of the woman?"

Two-Ree spat on the ground. "The woman is in the tipi of Yellow Dog. There is no sign of the girl-child."

Striking Thunder frowned. He knew from the tracks they'd followed that Yellow Dog had traded his weary horses for fresh ones. He suspected the child had been used as barter. "We will kill our enemy tonight."

He led the way back to where the rest of the band waited silently. Using hand signals, he positioned his men around his enemy, then settled down to wait for the night to lengthen. Staring into the darkness, he thought of the captured white woman he'd glimpsed earlier before the sun had fully disappeared over the horizon.

He'd known from Black Cloud's reactions when she'd circled the sky earlier that the enemy was close. His people had a special affinity with the animals who roamed the earth and sky. By watching and learning from them, special powers and knowledge were obtained.

In order to keep from being spotted by his enemy, he'd crawled slowly on his belly to survey Yellow Dog's camp and there, had witnessed the warrior's treatment of the woman. She'd kicked and fought Yellow Dog as he'd dragged her to his tipi. She had courage, wasn't afraid of her enemy; for that, she'd earned his respect. And if the spirits were willing, he'd free her before Yellow Dog did her harm.

Striking Thunder had never desired to take a white woman to his tipi as his father had done with his mother; the illustrious White Wind had once been known as Sarah Cartier. But today, after looking upon this woman's flame-red hair and pale skin, he'd briefly considered taking her from Yellow Dog to keep for himself. The beauty he saw beneath her blistered and bruised flesh

51

made her a tempting prize worthy of a great warrior, and the spirit he'd witnessed in her was doubly precious. Still, there were other considerations. If he took her for himself, he risked the lives of his people at the hands of the soldiers. No matter how much he wanted her, Striking Thunder could not risk his people. He had his duty to them.

Yet he couldn't stop thinking of her, which disturbed him. He'd just lost his wife and shouldn't feel such emotions. Meadowlark had been a good mate, deserving of his loyalty and affection.

Sliding a glance up at the cloud-blanketed sky, he made a decision. After he killed Yellow Dog, he'd see that the woman reached the fort safely. He would ask her to inform the soldier in charge that the Sioux were honorable, that the killing had been done by the Arikara. Yes, that was what he would do. Then he would put her from his mind. With that settled, he narrowed his gaze on the scattered circle of tipis in the distance. He tensed when Yellow Dog stood and left the fire. Filled with the whiteman's firewater, he staggered to his tipi. The other warrior had fallen over in a drunken sleep. Striking Thunder forced all thoughts of the woman from his mind and palmed his knife. Revenge for his people would be his.

In a tipi on the outer edge of the village, Emma struggled against the leather binding her hands behind her back. Though her arms ached with effort and bruises covered them, she pressed on. She didn't know how much time she had before Yellow Dog returned. The camp had grown quiet except for the squeals of women followed by low grunts of their warriors.

Her breathing quickened and a sob rose in her throat. There was no doubt in her mind that Yellow Dog planned to have her tonight. She'd seen it in his eyes when he'd brought her to his tipi earlier. She shuddered and tried to blot out the feel of his hands fondling her before he'd left. Even the memory made her feel sick and once again, all the stories of what happened to captive women rushed forward and sent stark fear darting through her mind.

Tears ran down her swollen cheeks, stinging in her open cuts and abrasions; her raw and bleeding wrists burned as she struggled against the leather thongs. Sticky warmth continued to slide down her palms but she didn't stop. With a smothered moan of pain, she finally felt the leather loosen. Filled with a small ray of hope and alert to every sound, she worked frantically to free her hands. When the leather thong fell from her throbbing wrists, she swallowed her cry of relief and set her numb fingers to working on the knots binding her feet. Panic welled when they refused to yield, and she bit her lip to keep from crying out.

Hurry. Hurry. The beat of her heart grew louder. *Hurry.* Finally, the knot gave way enough for her to tear it apart. Free, she jumped to her feet, ignoring the prickling sensation as the blood rushed through her veins. She stumbled toward the tipi opening and freedom. Cautiously, she pushed against the flap and peered around its edge. Suddenly, a large dark shape loomed before her. Emma cried out and stumbled back, her eyes wide with fright when Yellow Dog entered. The drunken warrior swayed from side to side. With a lustful leer, he reached for her. Having nowhere to run and nothing to lose, Emma shoved past his weaving body.

Thrown off balance by her direct attack, Yellow Dog's harsh laughter filled the air as he nabbed her long hair. With a hard yank, he trapped her against his sticky, unwashed chest. "White woman belong to Yellow Dog." He lowered his head.

Emma's stomach roiled at the smell of his fetid breath and sour body. Turning her head, she shoved against him, willing herself to remain strong. *Don't give in to hysterics. He's drunk. This is your chance to escape.* When his arm slid around her back, forcing her closer, she reached out with her fingers and twisted the tender skin on the underside of his upper arm.

With a roar of rage, he released her. Emma backed away, stepping into the cold ashes of the fire pit. He lunged. She jumped back, but the slanted sides of the tipi stopped her. When he came at her again, she ducked and managed to avoid his arms but fell. He towered over her, trapping her against the hide wall.

When she crawled away, Yellow Dog stalked her for sport. Every time she neared the flap, he shifted until she was scooting back the other way. Desperate, she searched the ground for a weapon. When her fingers closed around a large, palm-sized flat stone, she gripped it and came up swinging. It caught him on the side of his head. Harsh words poured from his mouth. Though stunned and drunk, he pulled his knife from the sheath hanging at his waist. The look in his eyes promised painful retribution.

Emma's stomach lurched and her mouth went dry. Fighting for her life, she swung again. But this time, Yellow Dog was ready. He kicked her feet out from under her, knocked the rock from her hand and straddled her hips with his knife clenched between his teeth. She screamed and struggled, but though his movements were slower and jerky, she was no match for his strength. In short order, her arms were pinned above her head. His eyes—glazed with drink, lust and revenge—narrowed and, with one hand holding her captive, he palmed the knife and held it above her face.

Emma closed her eyes and held her breath. This was it. She was going to die. Some distant part of her prayed for a swift end while another part desperately prayed for a miracle. Renny was out there somewhere, alone and frightened. She blanched when she felt the blade of the knife skim her throat then move down her breastbone. Suddenly, the sound of blade slashing through her bodice rent the stillness of the night.

She felt him withdraw the blade and unable to help herself, Emma opened her eyes, then wished with all her might she hadn't when he lifted his hand in a sudden upward movement. The muscles in his arms bunched when his hand slashed downward. She screamed again and closed her eyes tightly against the expected sharp thrust of cold steel.

It never came. Hearing his laughter, she opened her eyes to see the knife poised a heartbeat from her chest. Her gaze shifted to his face and she realized he was playing with her. Sobbing, she tried to jerk away, which amused her captor even more.

The horror of what this savage planned left Emma reeling with fear. Each time Yellow Dog lifted his hand, she cringed, her eyes on his hands, the tightening and relaxing of his fingers. He laughed and continued the game until Emma thought she'd go mad. *Oh please, Lord,* she prayed, *help me.*

Her prayers were answered. An arrow tore through the back of the tipi and flew over Yellow Dog's head. Startled, Yellow Dog reared back, freeing Emma's hands as he twisted his torso to stare at the shaft embedded in one of the poles. Taking advantage of his distraction, Emma grabbed the stone she'd dropped and sprang up with her arm swinging.

A look of disbelief came over him when she smashed him on the side of his head with all her might. He fell forward, unconscious. Sobbing hysterically, Emma pulled her legs out from under him and ran through the hide doorway. She smacked into a hard body. Strong fingers reached out and held her immobile. Emma gasped. "No, oh no," she moaned, staring into the glittering black eyes of another Indian.

Tears blurred her vision. Freedom had been so close. Snatches of moonlight fell to the earth as clouds drifted across the night sky. The pale beams of light revealed a warrior much taller than Yellow Dog. He held her effortlessly, his sheer size alone reducing her to a trembling mass of flesh. Long black hair flowed around his shoulders, shrouding him in stormy darkness. Somehow Emma knew he was dangerous, much more so than the Indian she'd just knocked unconscious.

Ready to fight once again for her freedom, her heart stopped when she heard a bellow of rage behind her. Yellow Dog had regained his senses. Terror gripped her in its numbing hold. Oh, God, she didn't want to die.

A shake of her shoulders snapped her from her numb stupor. "Go."

The sound of clear, fluent English rolling off this dark warrior's tongue startled her, but she didn't take the time to question it. When the warrior shoved her toward the shrubbery, she didn't need further urging. She ran.

Before she reached the shielding bushes, a burst of activity exploded around her. Battle yells, much like those of Yellow Dog's band when they'd attacked her coach, sounded, sending shivers of renewed fear down her spine. The high-pitched cries of women and children followed along with the sound of arrows zinging overhead. Glancing around wildly, Emma realized her captors' tribe was under attack. The screams splitting the air propelled her forward. Looking over her shoulder to see if Yellow Dog was coming after her, she breathed a sigh of relief to see him and the tall warrior circling each other with knives drawn. With the village in turmoil, this was her chance to escape.

Forcing her mind to remain calm, she ducked between tipis to get out of the battle. Breathing hard, she stared out into the dark prairie. How far would she get before someone came after her? Not far. She needed a horse. After a brief hesitation, she ran around the outer circle of tipis and stopped when she came to a horse tethered to a stake in the ground beside its owner's tipi. No one stopped her as she grabbed the lead rope and pulled the nervously snorting animal away.

Tangling her fingers in the horse's coarse mane, she bunched her skirts and jumped as if she were once again that carefree child who loved racing bareback across the park. With the sound of battle raging behind her, she galloped off into the night.

* * *

Minutes after the attack began, it was over. Drunk on the soldiers' spirits, Yellow Dog had been no match for the consuming fury that drove Striking Thunder's blade. Striking Thunder stared down at the body of his enemy. The joy of victory should have been his, but rather than feeling avenged, frustration and disbelief churned in his gut along with anger.

Though he'd killed his enemy, the spirits of the dead weren't appeased. Yellow Dog had cheated him of happiness by telling him that he'd been paid by soldiers to raid and cause trouble with the Sioux. Wiping Yellow Dog's blood from his knife, Striking Thunder shoved the blade back into the sheath strapped to his upper thigh and considered Yellow Dog's confession. The villain had known death was upon him, known nothing he said or did could avert it. Had he lied just to make trouble?

Not willing to relinquish his hard-earned victory so easily, Striking Thunder searched the tipi of his slain enemy for proof that Yellow Dog told the truth. There wasn't much to go through. In a matter of minutes, Striking Thunder had found several flasks of liquor, an old rifle and the silver belt buckle Yellow Dog claimed had been given to him as payment. He turned it over. As Yellow Dog had claimed, it had the colonel's initials etched into the metal.

Yellow Dog had spoken the truth. Clutching the incriminating buckle, Striking Thunder threw back his head. Pain and the fury of defeat erupted from his throat. His loud cry tore through the sudden silence of the night. "Hear me, spirits of our slain. I will set you free. I will avenge your deaths. Hear me. I speak true. Those who speak of peace but act in war will pay."

With that vow, he stormed from the tipi.

When the soldiers had first come, the colonel in charge had met with him and the other chiefs. He'd assured them that they only wanted peace. Yet now, whenever they tried to meet with the colonel, talk with him, his captain always refused them entrance to the fort. With each passing day, each act of harassment, it had become clear the soldiers wanted the Indians gone at any cost. And now he had proof. The white man with the red hair lied.

Banking his rage with difficulty, Striking Thunder knew nothing further could be gained here. Yellow Dog and his band of warriors were dead and their women and children scattered into the prairie. Taking up his bow from the ground where he'd tossed it in order to fight Yellow Dog, he shot a single flaming arrow into Yellow Dog's tipi, then whistled loudly, giving the command to go. He glanced over his shoulder one last time. Flames lit up the night sky.

A shout from Brave Arrow, half-leading, half-dragging Two-Ree caught his attention. Striking Thunder hurried forward and gently lowered his injured brother-in-law to the ground. He scanned Two-Ree's body. Blood streamed from a knife wound in the warrior's gut. His own gut wrenched and sorrow filled him. "We will get you home quickly, my friend."

"It is too late, my chief," the dying Indian gasped, taking Striking Thunder's arm in his weak grasp. "Star Dreamer—she'll know—hates gift—important to people."

"Save your breath, my friend." Striking Thunder said, though he knew there was nothing to be done to save him. His wife, Striking Thunder's sister, would be crushed, but she had likely already forseen his death in her visions. She had been blessed—or cursed, as she saw it—with the sight.

"No." Two-Ree's pained voice cut through Striking Thunder's sorrow. "Must—listen. Flame-haired woman— go after her."

Striking Thunder glanced around him. He'd forgotten about the white woman. "No. I need to take you back to our people."

Two-Ree shook his head and coughed. Blood trickled from the corner of his mouth. "Star—vision—woman—

destiny—" Two-Ree's grip tightened, his breath came in short, weak gasps. "Promise. *Promise* . . . "

Covering Two-Ree's hand with his own, Striking Thunder whispered, "I will go after the woman, my friend."

Two-Ree lifted his head. "*Kola*," he whispered with his last breath. His head fell back, his eyes glazed with death.

Striking Thunder bowed his head, tears streaming unashamedly down his cheeks. "*Mitakola, mitanhan.*" *My friend, my brother.* Striking Thunder knelt there in the darkness, fresh waves of grief tearing through him. He'd just lost a man who was closer to him than his own brother. Never again would he hear his dearest friend's name mentioned aloud. But there wasn't time to grieve now. After several minutes, he composed himself and stood. With a heavy heart, he whistled for his horse. Another death to be avenged. "Let us leave this place."

Brave Arrow stepped forward. "What of the woman?"

Taking a deep breath, Striking Thunder surveyed the black void of endless prairie. Heartsick, he wanted to go home, work through the layers of grief clouding his mind and heart. Unbidden, came the memory of the woman as she'd stood outside Yellow Dog's tipi, her face white with fear, her hands clutching her torn bodice over her creamy flesh. His fascination with the white woman bothered him. Instinct warned him to keep his distance, but he'd promised. To Brave Arrow, he said, "I will go after the white woman." He ordered his warriors to carry Two-Ree home for burial.

Brave Arrow pointed south. "She went in that direction."

Chapter Five

Emma sat on her horse in the middle of nowhere. Miles of dark, frightening prairie surrounded her. She glanced upward, cursing the thick cloud cover blocking out the stars and moon. Which way should she go? She had no idea and was tempted to remain where she was until daylight allowed her to search for the river Yellow Dog had followed.

But fear urged her to put distance between herself and the Indians. Twisting herself around, she listened for the rush of water. Nothing. A cool breeze drifted across the bare flesh of her breasts. Glancing down, she attempted to retie the ragged ends of her bodice while she considered her options.

Stifling a yawn, Emma closed her eyes and lowered her forehead to the horse's neck. It seemed forever since she'd slept. The animal nickered softly and stood still, as if sensing her exhaustion. The sound of crickets soothed her raw nerves. She would just rest her eyes for a moment. Clouds scudded overhead, leaving patches of stars and moonlight to peep through.

Sometime later, she was startled awake when her horse snorted and pranced, nearly dislodging her from its back. Disoriented, Emma peered into the darkness, searching for the source of the horse's excitement. She didn't see anything, but knew someone or something was out there. The horse didn't seem afraid, which meant it wasn't some wild animal. That left only one thing—Indians. "Dear God, they're coming after me," she breathed.

Her heart slammed against her ribs. Fear of becoming a prisoner again chilled her. Kicking the horse in the ribs, she twined her fingers in the animal's long, silky mane, urged him forward, then held on for dear life as she fled her unseen pursuers. Too late. Already, she heard the sound of an approaching rider. Glancing over her shoulder, she saw a dark shadowy shape gaining on her. Panic welled in her throat. Terrified, she hunched over the horse's neck and urged the animal faster.

When the rider drew abreast, she yanked on the rope halter. The horse turned sharper than she'd anticipated and she felt herself slipping off. Strong arms whipped out and swept her from the horse. Her feet dangled just above the ground before she was pulled up against a wall of solid muscle. Realizing that she was once again a captive, she struggled against the one strong arm holding her as securely as two. "Let me go," she screamed. Her struggles nearly unseated the both of them.

"Be still. You will not be harmed."

The shock of hearing English stilled her. This wasn't Yellow Dog. It was the same warrior she'd run into outside Yellow Dog's tipi. Instantly, she also became aware of several differences other than his fluent command of English. He lacked the sour, foul body odor and from the feel of his chest pressed against her back, she knew he was much bigger and stronger than her previous captor.

And though he didn't act in a violent or threatening manner, he was still an Indian. And his actions were suspect. He hadn't stopped her before. Why had he come after her? What had happened to Yellow Dog? Had this man killed him so that he could take her for himself? Not wanting to wait around and find out, she jabbed him in the ribs with first one elbow, then the other, catching him off guard. His hold loosened and she slid off the horse, fell, then jumped to her feet and ran for all she was worth.

He passed her on horseback, whirled his mount around and blocked her escape. The Indian, a dark, imposing figure, sat tall on his horse. "You go the wrong way." He pointed. "Big River is to the east." He held one large hand out to her. "Striking Thunder will return you to the fort. I swear. Yellow Dog will not harm you again."

Emma backed away, watching his every move. The tall grass and uneven ground hindered her retreat, causing her to stumble and nearly fall several times. When she spotted her horse grazing a short distance away, she turned and headed for the animal. To her dismay, Striking Thunder kept pace on his horse. She moved faster. "Go away. I can find my own way. Just leave me alone." Terror rose when he shook his head and dismounted.

"I cannot leave a woman alone to wander the *maka*."

Emma swallowed the rising hysteria sweeping through her. Those bulging arms had effortlessly swept her off her horse and could easily capture her once again. She knew he was playing with her, that he could stop her anytime he chose, but she ignored him and kept going. The tension within her grew as he followed.

She broke into a run, but Striking Thunder dismounted and sprinted in front of her, clearly letting her know she could not escape. The warrior stopped when she did, moved when she moved. No matter where she turned, he was there, blocking her escape. She clenched her hands, her ragged nails digging painfully into her palms. What was she going to do?

More clouds drifted apart, allowing rays of moonlight to fall and hit the prairie. They bathed the man before her in silver splendor. He stood tall, strong and proud. His stance emphasized the strength of his thighs and the slimness of his hips and the powerful set to his broad shoulders. She took a small step back, awed and fearful of this magnificent warrior whose very presence spoke of power and ageless strength. Here was a man in his prime.

The sight of all that raw masculinity took her breath away. Her legs went weak and her heart pounded. Where

Yellow Dog's body had repulsed her, something about this Indian captivated her, reached out and touched her deeply. Some primal instinct warned that this warrior was much more a danger to her than Yellow Dog.

"Please leave me alone," she begged, her voice low and husky.

A slight breeze sprang up and tugged at his long flowing hair, revealing the shadowed valleys of his face. His lips firmed. "No. Enough. We go."

Emma shook her head, her throat gritty and sore. Uncertainty assailed her. He spoke English, said he would help her. Was he telling the truth? Would he take her to the fort? Maybe he was one of the scouts the soldiers used? Remembering Yellow Dog and the dead soldiers, she didn't dare trust him.

Tears brought on by the hopelessness of her situation blurred her vision. There wasn't one part of her that didn't ache. But she couldn't give in now, not when she'd nearly made it. When he moved toward her, she jumped, held out one hand to ward him off. "Stay away. Don't touch me," she croaked.

"I give you my word of honor. You will not be harmed. I will return you to the fort. You will tell them that the Sioux people are honorable." His voice was soft, enticing, as if he were calming a spooked mare. "Come." He held out one hand, palm up, his fingers beckoned hers.

Confusion and fear warred within her as his deep voice lulled her, tempted her to put her trust in him. *Trust.* Her father had *trusted* her to keep her sister safe, but Renny had been traded away as if she'd been nothing more than horseflesh and it was all Emma's fault. "No," she shouted, breaking his spell. "Stay back. Don't touch me. My father is an important man. I'm warning you, leave." She tossed her head and eyed him with bold defiance.

The warrior stopped and cocked his head to one side. He appeared to consider her words. "Your father? And who is this father of yours?" he asked, sounding amused.

Emma tilted her chin and drew upon all the strength she could muster. "My father is Colonel Grady O'Brien. He's in charge of Fort Pierre." She said the words confidently, pleased when he took a step back.

"Colonel Grady O'Brien is your father?"

Emma nodded, finally feeling as though she had the upper hand. "I'm his daughter Emma." She waited a beat then sought to strengthen her position by adding, "Captain Sanders is my fiancé. He was escorting me to the fort where we shall be wed when Yellow Dog attacked. He escaped."

Something in the warrior's stance caught her attention. All trace of amusement had faded and his eyes had narrowed into glittering slits. Staring at his clenched fists, she continued, her voice uncertain. "At this minute, my father is probably out looking for me. So you see, I'll be fine on my own—"

"Sanders!"

The single word exploded between them. Emma backed away when the warrior closed his eyes as if in pain. His menacing glare frightened Emma. Her stomach tightened painfully. *Something's wrong.* Why had the mention of her father and Derek produced a reaction of hatred instead of fear? Emma hugged her arms to her chest, looking for answers in the warrior's face but his eyes were shadowed by the night. Yet there was no doubt he was furious. And she didn't understand why. "The captain is very kind," she whispered, trying to soothe the Indian.

Striking Thunder's shoulders stiffened and his hands curled into fists. He took a step forward. "Sanders and your father are responsible for the murder of many of my people, including my wife."

The world tilted. Suddenly, Emma was very afraid of the dark storm of fury raging in this warrior who stood before her with hatred glittering in eyes black as the night. This time, when he advanced, she picked up her skirts and ran for her life.

* * *

Striking Thunder didn't need the soft guiding light from Grandmother Moon to follow the white woman. His upper lip curled into a sneer of contempt. "She thinks to outrun this warrior?" He tensed, staring off across the darkened prairie in the direction she'd fled. His thigh muscles bunched, his body quivered with anticipation of the hunt. "Let her run," he spoke, forcing himself to relax. There was no hurry. The spirits were with him this night. The colonel's daughter would escape only if he allowed her to do so.

"*Emma.*" The name rolled off his tongue, smooth and silky, as beautiful as the woman with her wide, frightened doe eyes the color of spring grass, flame-red hair and skin as pale as freshly fallen snow. Seeing up-close the bruises marring that flesh brought forth fresh waves of fury. Realizing where his thoughts were taking him, Striking Thunder looked to the moon to clear his thoughts of the white woman. To his dismay, Emma's features were imprinted on the disk's glowing face.

He closed his eyes. Why did this woman draw him so? She was a white woman *and* the daughter of his enemy. He summoned the image of Meadowlark's lifeless body to drive all desire for the white woman from him. His wife's life-giving blood had flowed across the *maka,* seeping into the dirt. Wasted. Gone forever.

A shaft of pain pierced him, sharp as the blade Meadowlark had used to end her life. Anger, fierce and as hot as a fire whipping across the dry prairie raged within him. He'd failed to protect her life. He would not fail to appease her spirit.

Colonel O'Brien and Captain Sanders would pay for their evil crimes and how better than with the life of the colonel's own flesh and blood: the daughter and wife-to-be. Both would pay, not with their lives, but their suffering would be far worse than death.

A pang of regret for what he must do tore through him. That hesitation, that small show of weakness, displeased him. Warriors showed no mercy to the enemy. The colonel must suffer the loss of his family as Striking Thunder's people had suffered the loss of their loved ones. His resolve firmly in place, Striking Thunder took off after Emma on foot. After a few minutes, he bore to the left. He didn't need to see his prey. He felt her, sensed the direction of her flight. The spirits guided him, just as they had led him to Emma once before.

As he gained on her, her ragged sobs led him to her. Then he saw her running ahead of him, a dark wraithlike shadow that grew clearer the closer he got. When only a few feet separated them, she glanced over her shoulder, the trail of tears luminescent on her pale skin. A tug of something pulled at his heart, but he ignored it. Not watching where she was going, she stumbled and fell. He stood over her. "You cannot escape Striking Thunder. You are mine."

"No. Never!" Emma's hoarse gasps signaled her exhaustion, yet still she tried to get to her feet and run.

Tired of the game, Striking Thunder reached down and grabbed her by the arm. Like a she-bear, she came up kicking and clawing, until he knocked her feet out from under her. He followed her down, his length falling atop hers. His size and weight easily pinned her to the grassy mat beneath them. With ease, he captured both her wrists in one hand and held them high above her head. Despite his anger and the driving need for revenge, he admired her courage. She fought well though she was no match for his strength.

"Let me go," she begged, her voice raw and gritty, her face inches from his.

"No."

Her eyes, their color eclipsed by his shadow, glittered with tears. Her body trembled beneath his and with a shock of awareness, he realized they were flesh to flesh. Her breasts, bared by her torn clothing were pressed against his chest.

Lifting his upper body without releasing her wrists, Striking Thunder stared down at the generous swells revealed by the torn bodice of her dress. His blood surged with the urge to palm that supple flesh, to bask in the feel of her. Desire, hot and thick as honey, flooded his veins and he felt his organ stir and harden in response to her womanly softness.

Her beauty, her spirit, summoned something deep inside him, releasing a hunger he'd never known existed, not even with Meadowlark. His lips parted, tempted to bend down and capture one of those beckoning pale buds and suckle until she cried out with pleasure and her body writhed beneath his with the same hot need that raced through his veins.

He fought for control, for command of his emotions. From boyhood, his every action and thought had been carefully planned. The quest to become the great warrior his grandmother had foreseen ruled his every waking moment. Even marriage, when he'd been told to take a wife, had been dealt with in the same methodical manner. He allowed nothing to interfere with his duty—not even his own needs and desires. But this woman threatened that and he didn't like it. Not one bit. Too much was at stake.

"You pr-promised to take me to the fort."

Her fear-laced words jarred him. It took a long moment for him to absorb the full meaning of her words. *"Tuwakaksa!" Impossible!* He released her hands. Immediately, she covered her nakedness but his desire had already fled as his plan for revenge crashed down upon his shoulders for the second time that night.

Unfortunately, she spoke the truth. He *had* given his word to return her to the fort. And though it had been before he'd learned that the colonel was her father, he was honor-bound to keep his promise. Biting back an oath, Striking Thunder stared up into patches of star-studded sky, seeking answers, for he could not release her. Without revenge, the sweet innocent spirit of his young wife would roam forever, caught between the two worlds. Yet by his own words, killing Emma to set Meadowlark's spirit free was not possible.

He'd have to kill the colonel and captain. To do so would take much planning and thought. A sharp breeze swept across his bare back, signaling summer's retreat and winter's approach. Time was short, for once the snows fell, he'd be forced to wait until spring for his revenge.

Time, the spirit of the winds whispered in his ear. *Time*. Striking Thunder held himself still and listened. Could time be his ally? The colonel would soon discover Yellow Dog's ambush of his soldiers and daughters' capture. At first, the soldiers would concentrate their search among the Arikara tribes. That afforded him and the council plenty of time to formulate their plans. When spring arrived, his people would be ready. That settled, his only problem lay with the woman. What to do with her? Honor demanded that he keep his word. He studied her, pretending to himself that he felt no relief at not having to kill her.

The distant howling of a wolf pack drifted on the night breeze. The wolf was smart, shrewd and wily. Closing his eyes, Striking Thunder asked for the spirit of the wolf to advise him. Seconds later, the corner of his mouth twitched.

He'd never said *when* he would return her to the fort, nor had he promised to return her to her *father*, which left him free to keep her captive for the winter, use her as bait to lure her father and captain into his trap. Only then would he release her to the soldiers at the fort. In the meantime, he was honor-bound to keep her safe and unharmed. Pleased with his cunning, he stood and pulled her up. "I've changed my mind. I choose to keep you for now."

His words sent her into a panic. Her cries tore through the night. "Please, I need to go to my father. My sis—"

"Enough!" He lifted his head and pursed his lips. A shrill whistle echoed across the prairie. From a distance, his horse answered. Moments later, the animal halted before them, snorting and pawing the ground. Gripping

Emma's wrists behind her back, Striking Thunder ignored her cry of pain and shoved her forward.

Emma half-turned to stare at him with teary, reproachful eyes. Her hair spilled to her waist in a tangled mass of silky strands. The shimmering color seemed to have a life of its own in the pale moonlight as it fell across his arm, the soft, satiny strands caressing him with feathery kisses. Fascinated, he watched one wispy curl fall across her throat and unfurl, luring his gaze downward.

Once again, his gaze latched on to the flesh exposed to the white light from above. Silvery moonbeams rippled over her young, pert breasts, each capped with a blooming rosebud. Her sharp intake of air lifted those generous swells high, thrusting them forward. His manhood throbbed with the need to have her, now. Never had he felt this wild urge to bury his face between a woman's breasts.

Sharing Meadowlark's mat had been pleasurable, they'd found mutual release but she'd never roused him to this feverish pitch, which had been fine. Passion clouded one's vision; it led to loss of control. He swallowed his groan of lust and thrust her aside. "Cover yourself."

Emma moaned in shame, turned her back and tore off a long piece of her skirt. She wrapped it around her chest to hold the tattered bodice in place. By the time she'd restored her modesty, Striking Thunder had a short length of rope ready. He grabbed one of her wrists. Once more, she cried out in pain. Frowning, he held one thin wrist up for his inspection, then the other. Raw wounds gleamed in the moonlight.

He released her hands and held the rope up. She cringed. "I will not bind you unless you run. The choice is yours." Though he harbored hatred toward her father and the captain, he saw no reason to make her suffer needlessly.

Emma cradled her wrists close to her body. "I won't run," she whispered, her voice filled with defeat.

He mounted his horse, then stared down at the woman.

The thought of having her soft breasts pressed against his back sent arrows of desire darting through him once again. Furious that she affected him so, he thrust out his hand. When she complied with his silent command, he pulled her up behind him and rode off, his mind at war with his body.

Derek Sanders lay on his belly near the river, his body wracked with pain and fever from the self-inflicted knife wounds he'd been forced to give himself. Moving carefully to avoid additional pain from a deep cut in his upper left arm and one in his side, he drank greedily then splashed the soothing liquid over his burning face. Soaking a strip of his torn uniform, he gritted his teeth and forced himself to his feet. The throbbing in his thigh kept beat with his heart. He'd gotten drunk off a flask of liquor tied to his saddle before he'd inflicted the wounds. His knife had slipped, slashing into him deeper than he'd intended.

He breathed deeply and slowly to ease the pain. Damn, he hurt. At the time, his fear of hurting himself had outweighed his fear of the colonel's reaction to his arrival at the fort unharmed and without his daughters.

Glancing around, he figured he still had a good two days' walk before he reached safety. He'd planned to arrive at the fort before infection set in, but his horse had bolted, ruining his dramatic return and forcing him to walk. Following the river, he cursed with each painful step. "Damn double-crossin' Indians," he raged. If not for Yellow Dog, he'd have been at the fort already, basking in the colonel's praise.

Blinking his eyes, he eyed the setting sun and calculated the passing time. By now, the *Annabella* would have arrived at the fort and the colonel would know that something had happened to Emma. Derek's only consolation was the certainty that a search party was likely already underway.

Derek grimaced. He dreaded facing the colonel. He'd failed to protect Emma. As sure as the sun rose each morning, he knew that Yellow Dog had taken her and her bratty sister captive. The thought of that savage touching Emma made his blood boil.

Exhaustion overwhelmed him. Derek made his way to the shade of a cottonwood and eased himself down. Leaning against the rough bark, he closed his eyes and considered his options. He winced as he tended his wounds with an alcohol-soaked rag. Old Doc Gil would patch him up; he wasn't worried about dying. No, he'd live. But all his carefully laid plans were in ruins. What was he going to do now? He had to secure command of the fort before the colonel left for his next assignment.

He opened his eyes and took stock of the sun's position. It would be dark soon and he just didn't have the energy to go another foot. Maybe he'd remain where he was and let the search party come to him. He lifted his brows. That was not a bad idea—let the colonel find him and believe he'd collapsed from fever and loss of blood. If he appeared sicker than he was, his recuperation time would give him a chance to form a new plan, discover what happened to Emma and judge the colonel's reaction. After all, Doc Gil wouldn't allow anyone, not even the colonel, to browbeat a sick and injured soldier. Yes, he had to appear worse off than he was.

Gritting his teeth against the forthcoming pain, Derek deliberately reopened some of the already healing surface cuts on his chest and arm, then took his knife and made a few shallow cuts on his chest, knowing they'd bleed and scab quicker but make him look worse than he was. Then he did the same to his thigh, ripping the pants even more. But when he used his fingers to pull apart the jagged edges of the gash on his thigh, white-hot shards of agony shot through him, leaving him gasping and shaken. Warm fresh blood trickled over his fingers.

"Damn," he moaned. Breathing heavily against the

throbbing pain, he welcomed the graying of his vision. He leaned down to lie in the mat of leaves and grass near the river. As he allowed sleep to claim him, he reminded himself that a little pain was nothing compared to what was at stake.

Chapter Six

Streaks of light elbowed through the darkness, chasing away the shadows and warming the air but Emma appreciated none of it. It was all she could do to concentrate on the horse beneath her and keep from falling off. The steed, plodding along, rocked her, luring the edges of consciousness to close around her. But to close her eyes and sleep meant leaning against the savage in front of her, something she refused to do.

Striking Thunder had pressed onward throughout the night, allowing only brief rest stops for his horse. Emma, unable to remain awake seated on the hard, cold ground had dozed reluctantly, until Striking Thunder had woken her with orders to remount. The short snatches of sleep left her feeling sick and nauseous.

It had been days since her last decent meal. And to add to her discomfort, she ached all over from the beatings she'd endured and the long hours on horseback. Her muscles screamed for rest but she stayed tense, fighting against the movement of the horse in order to hold her body away from Striking Thunder as far as she could. With Yellow Dog, she'd had her hands tied around her waist, leaving no choice but to lean against his filthy, sweaty and smelly body.

But Striking Thunder was different. He was clean and his skin was smooth, not sticky. He had bathed in the river at their first rest stop. And his scent didn't repulse her. In fact, he smelled rather pleasant, it all added to the temptation to lean her head against him and close her eyes.

But she forced herself to stay awake and try to concentrate on her surroundings. Though she'd promised not to run, she planned to escape the first chance she got. As they traveled farther west, she noted landmarks: to her right, a lone tree, gnarled and long dead, and to the left, prairie grass blackened by fire.

There were also the many rivers. Some branched off the main one they'd crossed earlier. The water flowed from west to east. If she found the river, she'd be able to follow it to the Missouri, then from there to the fort. Another landmark for her was the towering black hills in the distance.

Rubbing her eyes, Emma gave up trying to focus them on objects in the distance. Instead, her attention wandered back to her captor. During the dark of night, she'd only had to deal with the closeness of his hard-muscled back mere inches from her, the feel of his long hair whipping across her cheeks and the outdoor scent of wood and smoke that surrounded him. But in the cool light of day, his proud features and nearly naked body took turns assaulting her senses.

Emma tried not to stare at his bare flesh, but it was difficult with his broad back so near to her face. How could she not notice shoulders wide enough to shelter a woman from danger and skin richly bronzed and warm to the touch? Her gaze slid downward. Embarrassed warmth seeped through her. He wore only a thin flap of animal hide around his waist, which did little to hide what no civilized man would dare bare. And with each forward movement of the horse, those naked rock-hard buttocks nestled between her thighs rolled forward, revealing taut golden skin before slamming back down to once again press into the cradle of her pelvis.

With each jostling bump, each contact of his flesh grinding against her, a strange ache filled her lower body. She squirmed self-consciously. As if sensing her thoughts, he glanced over his shoulder, his dark eyes flashing with amusement. Her face flamed and she scooted away from him. In her haste to put some measure of distance between them, she slid too far back and felt herself slip.

The horse, disliking her weight on his hip, crow-hopped, throwing her forward. The movement slammed her into Striking Thunder's back.

He reached around and pulled her tight against his back. "Put your arms around me."

Emma did as told, but at the feel of his hardened muscles and smooth flesh, she let go, holding herself as far from him as she could without falling.

"Do not be foolish, woman. Hold on to me or I will bind your hands around me." Striking Thunder's voice brooked no argument.

Emma gingerly grasped his hips with her fingertips, careful only to touch the thin thong of rawhide circling his lean, narrow waist.

Striking Thunder growled and yanked her arms fully around his waist, which pulled her entire front to rest against his back. "Leave them," he ordered.

Emma gave in and leaned against her captor. Though he'd so far kept his promise not to harm or mistreat her, she didn't trust him.

He'd been friendly only until he'd learned the identity of her father. His accusation replayed in her mind. Striking Thunder's wife had died and he blamed her father and Captain Sanders. The idea was preposterous. Colonel Grady O'Brien might be many things, but he was no murderer. Of that she was certain, even though she hadn't seen him in nine years.

His military career revolved around his communication and negotiating skills with hostile Indians. Fighting against the thick haze of exhaustion, Emma wished she had the packet of letters her father had sent over the years. Each was full of compassion for the Indian people and would prove to Striking Thunder he was wrong. But

her letters, her most treasured possessions, were in her
trunk aboard the *Annabella*—all but the one she'd tucked
into a pocket in her valise, which was more than likely
scattered across the prairie by now.

If she could convince him to take her to the fort, she
could show him those letters, prove to him he was wrong.
She would promise not to allow her father to cause him
harm, let her father know he'd rescued her. Maybe he'd
even give him a reward. She lifted her head from the
warmth of his shoulder and took a deep breath. "My
father is no murderer." Striking Thunder nudged the
horse into a canter. Emma tightened her grip around his
waist, her frustration mounting. Desperation lent her
courage. "I can prove you wrong."

His head swiveled around and his gaze confronted her.
"We will not talk of this." Striking Thunder clicked his
tongue and the horse leaped into a fast gallop.

Emma grasped him tightly to keep her seat. Her breath
came out in jagged gasps, but she refused to back down.
"Tell me what happened. You've kidnapped me because
of some crime my father is said to have committed. *I
have the right to know!*" she shouted in his ear.

Striking Thunder drew on the leather reins, bringing
his mount to a sudden halt. He twisted his torso around
with such speed that it nearly unseated her. "The man
you claim as your future husband paid Yellow Dog to kill
my people—under your father's orders!"

The blood drained from Emma's face. "It isn't so," she
whispered, more to herself than to the furious warrior.
Her heart pounded. For the first time, doubt crept in. She
recalled the kind captain, his gentle nature and gentle-
manly behavior aboard the *Annabella*. Even after they'd
left the boat, he'd remained solicitous, even if he was
more demonstrative than she was comfortable with.

But a murderer? And so underhanded? No. She
refused to believe it. Derek might be a coward, but he
was not a murderer. "Derek would never do such a vile
thing." But as soon as the words left her mouth, she

recalled the heated exchange between Yellow Dog and Derek the night before they were attacked. Derek *had* known Yellow Dog. Could the captain have had underhanded dealings with the savages? Had that been the cause of their argument?

Striking Thunder narrowed his stormy gaze. "I see in your eyes that it is so."

Emma cringed inwardly then raised her chin, feeling guilty for allowing herself to believe Striking Thunder, even for one moment. For if he spoke the truth, that meant, she, in her innocence, had endangered her sister by trusting the captain with their lives. She couldn't face that, refused to believe it. Yellow Dog had attacked for one reason: to obtain her. The fault lay with her and her eagerness to leave the *Annabella*. Had they remained and chanced another delay, none of this would have happened.

"I believe Yellow Dog killed your wife and if not for you, I would have been next. But do not ask me to believe my father or Derek had anything to do with his vile actions. You have no proof to back up your claims."

"Proof! You want proof?" Anger spiked his words. Striking Thunder dismounted and yanked her down as well, uncaring when she stumbled and fell at his feet. Emma swallowed her cry of pain at his rough handling. He towered over her, his eyes snapping with restrained fury. Removing a long, narrow leather pouch from around his waist, he threw it down at her.

"Open it," he commanded. "There you will find your *proof*." Folding his arms across his bare chest, he waited.

Fear, icy cold, traveled up her spine. Slowly, she got to her feet, feeling less vulnerable standing. Pulling open the mouth of the pouch, she reached in and withdrew a cold metal object. When the sunlight struck it, she gasped. "Where did you get this?"

"Yellow Dog. It was his payment."

The world tilted beneath Emma. In the early-morning sunlight, the silver belt buckle winked at her. She recognized it. How could she not? She and Renny had sent it to the colonel last winter for his birthday. Her mouth went dry. How had this Indian come by it? She shook her head in vehement denial. "No, there's a mistake. My father wouldn't—"

Striking Thunder snatched the belt buckle with a spate of angry-sounding words. Turning on his heel, he led his horse down to a stream a short distance away. Emma followed slowly, more worried and confused than before. What was going on? How had Yellow Dog come to possess her father's buckle? Her heart stopped. A horrible thought came to her. Was her father alive? Had Yellow Dog killed him? She refused to believe Grady O'Brien had paid Yellow Dog to kill the Sioux.

Running up to Striking Thunder, she stepped in front of him, her hands clasped tightly in front of her as she pleaded, "Take me to the fort. I can prove my father had nothing to do with the killing of your people. I'm sure there's a simple explanation of how Yellow Dog came to have my father's belt buckle. Please. Let me prove his innocence."

Striking Thunder shoved her out of his way, his glare full of contempt. "You think to fool this warrior, white woman? The minute your father lays eyes on you at my side, he will shoot first and ask questions later. No. You are mine until after *siyo istaheapi wi* has passed."

Emma stared at him. "What does that mean?"

"It means, *moon when the frost covers the prairie chickens' eyes.* It is our name for your month of March."

"March! I can't stay with you that long. You must return me. *Now.*"

Striking Thunder knelt at the water's edge and drank, ignoring her.

"Why can't you let me go now?" Emma cried out in frustration.

Standing, Striking Thunder pulled back his shoulders and lifted his head proudly. "After I have dealt with your father and the captain, I will release you." Eyes black as a moonless night held hers. His lips curled in disdain. "You will learn from your father's mouth that I speak the truth before he dies."

Frustration turned to horror when Emma realized, for the first time, that this warrior planned to lure her father into a trap—using *her* as bait. "You can't do this," she whispered, shocked and horrified.

"Please—"

Striking Thunder slashed the air with his hand. "No. Do not ask for release again or I will remove your tongue."

Emma hugged herself. Tears of hopelessness and fear gathered in her eyes and spilled down her cheeks. "What of my sister? She's only nine. Yellow Dog traded her for horses. She's out there somewhere, alone and scared. Please—"

"No more! Your sister is no concern of mine."

The true extent of her situation slammed into her, leaving her breathless. Without her father's help, she'd never find Renny. Emma clamped her trembling lips together. She doubted Striking Thunder would carry out his threat to remove her tongue but refrained from pushing him too far.

Wiping the tears from her face with the hem of her dress, she tried to gather her shattered courage. She'd need all her wits about her if she were to find a way to stop him from carrying out his plan to kill her father. Striking Thunder went back to his horse and returned with a square of rolled-up leather. From inside, he pulled out a flat, square piece of dried meat. Biting it, he tore off a hunk with strong white teeth. He held the other piece out to her.

The thought of eating anything after learning what he planned turned her stomach. She shook her head and backed away, swaying from the wave of nausea sweeping over her.

Striking Thunder followed her retreat. "You will eat. You are of no use to me dead." He thrust out the jerked meat.

Emma slapped away the offending piece of food. It flew from his hand and landed in the short grass. "I don't want any of your food. I'd rather starve."

Striking Thunder took one menacing step forward. He pointed. "Pick it up."

Emma ignored the fury darkening his features. "No." She had nothing to lose at this point. She stood mute and defiant, even dwarfed by his commanding height. They stared at each other, one resolute, the other rebellious.

He narrowed his eyes. "You will do as you are told."

Tired of being threatened, Emma tossed her head. "What will you do if I refuse? Kill me?" She waved her arms. "Do it, I say! Then you won't get my father."

When he lifted his hand, Emma closed her eyes and cringed, bracing herself for his blow. Heartbeats later, when there was no physical form of retaliation, she opened her eyes and found him watching her, his arms folded across his naked chest and an unreadable expression lurking deep in those nearly black eyes of his.

His gaze hardened. "This warrior does not strike women. Now, do as I asked. Much hard work goes into preparing food. We do not foolishly waste it. Pick it up or there will be no food until we reach my village."

Emma scowled. Unlike Yellow Dog, who'd meted out his punishments with physical blows, Striking Thunder's methods were more subtle. The choice was hers. Already, her body felt weak: her head spun from lack of food and her throat felt dry. She could refuse. If she perished, he'd have no bait to lure her father into a trap. But then she thought of Renny. If she died, who then would rescue her sister?

The memory of Renny being carried off screaming was all it took for her to make her decision to survive, no matter what it took. She'd do anything for her sibling, even swallow her pride.

Snatching the leathery strip of meat from the ground, she slapped it into his outstretched hand, wishing she hadn't been so quick to refuse food. Her stomach clenched and her mouth watered at the thought of eating, but she ignored her discomfort, unwilling to give him total victory.

Without another word, Emma stalked past Striking Thunder, her mutinous glare letting him know that he may have won the physical round but he couldn't control her thoughts or emotions. Nor could he force her to eat.

Heading upstream, Emma dropped to her knees and drank deeply from the flowing, cool water. Sitting with her knees drawn up to her chest, she dropped her head into the cradle of her arms. She closed her eyes, longing to drop off into a deep sleep where she could escape the turmoil tearing at her mind and heart. A warm buzz traveled through her as her body relaxed with the sweet breeze. Just as she drifted off, his voice intruded, harsh and commanding, startling her awake.

"Leci u wo!"

Emma lifted her head, blinked to clear her blurred vision. Striking Thunder stood downstream. She didn't move.

Striking Thunder stood, his face dark with displeasure. "Come here. You are captive and will obey."

Sighing, Emma got to her feet and stumbled toward him. "What do you want?"

He pointed to a spot near a clump of brush. "Sit."

Lowering herself to the mat of summer-dried grass, Emma blinked, fighting sleep.

Striking Thunder knelt in front of her with a small round tin. With his knife, he ripped away another strip of her skirt. She stared dispassionately at what had once been one of her favorite day dresses. The material was dusty, torn and wrinkled. It was also a foot shorter from having supplied the material to cover what her torn bodice could not.

Returning his knife to a leather sheath strapped to his thigh, the Indian soaked the material in the river then grabbed her hand. Fearing he planned to bind her, she braced herself for the pain. Instead, he gently cleansed her raw wrists with gentle strokes of the wet cloth. His fingers curled around hers, his palm warm, his thumb caressing the back of her fingers in an unconscious soothing motion. She gasped at the tenderness of his touch. He mistook her gasp for one of pain and frowned. "These must be cleaned."

She steeled herself to accept his ministrations. But after he opened the tin, she wrinkled her nose when he applied the foul-smelling ointment to each wrist. Taking another strip from her skirt, he wrapped her wrists then checked her ankles, which weren't quite so bad. When he was done, he stood and dropped several pieces of dried meat into her lap.

"Do not foolishly refuse."

Grateful for a second chance to ease her hunger pangs, Emma picked up one piece and stared at the reddish-brown strip. It looked like leather. Cautiously, she sniffed it. "What is it?"

"*Wakapapi wasna*—pemmican. It is made of dried meat, animal fat and berries."

Hesitantly, Emma bit off a tiny corner and chewed. She took a second bite at the tough substance, finding it not too objectionable. As she nibbled, she turned to watch Striking Thunder care for his horse. What a strange man he was. So harsh and full of anger one minute, firm but fair the next, then kind, caring and thoughtful. Not at all what she expected from a savage. She held out her bandaged wrists. Already, the searing pain had faded and the tightness of her flesh had eased.

Too tired to think anymore, Emma crawled over to a small bush near the water, seeking shade for her sunburned face. She stretched out beside the water. Sleep claimed her quickly, but even in her exhausted and confused state, images of the virile and vibrant warrior filled her dreams.

Chapter Seven

Striking Thunder stood over Emma. It was time to continue their journey. He had duties to see to back in his village—sad duties—the burial rites of his friend; his family to comfort. Two-Ree had been one of his bravest and wisest warriors, and a devoted husband and father as well. Thinking about his sister, Star Dreamer, and her two small children who'd lost now their father, sorrow filled him.

He knew she'd already be grieving, that she'd have seen her husband's death in her visions. Two-Ree's words came back to haunt him. He'd known of the flame-haired woman, known of her value to his tribe, which meant Star had told him of her before they'd left camp.

Frowning, something niggled at the back of his mind. It was something to do with the woman. An uneasiness took hold of him. Two-Ree had known of the woman, had said she was his destiny. The man had known, yet said nothing to him until he lay dying. Nor had Star. She hadn't confided in him either. Not as her brother or as her chief.

Why? Her visions were never wrong. Why had she not told him of Emma? Scowling, he questioned himself about Emma's presence and what it meant to him and his people. Without hesitation, he rejected the idea that she was to mean more to him than a method of achieving revenge. So why did she affect him so? He was a warrior, a great chief whose destiny lay with his people. This woman meant nothing to him. Would not mean more. He wouldn't allow it. Suddenly, he wished he hadn't gone after her, had left her to fend for herself, but no matter what he told himself, part of him feared Star's vision and the implication that Emma might be tied to his future.

After all, Star had seen Jessie, their brother's wife in her visions. When his brother Wolf had left to lead a group of emigrants to Oregon, Star had seen the danger that threatened his and Jessie's future. By acting quickly, Striking Thunder and his warriors had arrived at Fort Laramie in time to find Wolf and go after the malevolent woman who'd kidnapped Jessie and a small child. All had ended well that time. Jessie was now his sister-in-law and next summer, Wolf and Jessie would return to their people.

Both pleased and envious of his brother's happiness, and confused by his sister's recent silence, Striking Thunder watched Emma sleep. His gaze fell on the rhythmic rise and fall of her breasts and the pale, soft-looking flesh peeping out between the torn edges of her dress. Desire stirred, unfurling from his loins to bloom throughout his body, causing him to yearn for the kind of love his brother and father had found.

Stalking away, he tried to put Star's visions from his mind. He refused to read anything into Emma's presence. She was his bait. Nothing more. Nothing less. With his sister's gift of sight, she'd seen the attack in which he'd lost Meadowlark, though they had been helpless to stop it. It made sense that she would also see Emma, the daughter of his enemy.

Though a great sadness filled his heart, a weight lifted from his shoulders. This white woman was nothing to him but a tool to be used to avenge the crimes committed against his people. He would not think of her; nor would her name touch his lips. The spirits had given her to him to use. He wouldn't allow her beauty's strong magic to cloud his vision. When he was done with her, he'd set her free then forget about the flame-haired woman who fought with much spirit and courage.

A raucous cry from the sky drew his attention upward. Above, Black Cloud circled, then flew down to his shoulder. "You've been gone long, my friend," he said. The bird cocked its shiny black head and hopped down to the ground. The raven, curious, circled the woman and pecked at the unraveling hem of her dress. While most warriors sought the predators of the sky as their talismans, seeking their courage for success in war, he never questioned that he, as a chief should have a raven. He touched the leather charm around his neck and turned away.

When he turned back, he was surprised, for Black Cloud had hopped onto the swaying limb of a bush and spread her wings, as if offering Emma protection from the sun. Displeased and filled with dismay, he stalked away.

Colonel Grady O'Brien ignored the soft knock on his door. The steel pen he held moved across the sheet of paper lying on the blotter of his rough-hewn desk. After signing his name, he pulled the next letter from the stack and repeated his signature after scanning the missive. Setting the completed pile aside for his aide to deal with, he started reading one of several reports sitting in a neat pile to his left.

There was much to be done before the fort was abandoned. Previously under command of General William S. Harney and twelve hundred men, the general had left, taking half of the troops with him to Fort Randall. Pierre had been a poor purchase. With a poor river landing; no timber, fuel or forage within close range; and most buildings in decay and beyond repair, the soldiers hated their stint here, which was why none of his men knew that soon, they'd all be reassigned. If they knew now, they'd grow lax in their duties.

Another knock, this time louder, more demanding,

broke his concentration. Tossing the report down, he called, "Enter." A young, fresh-faced soldier stepped hesitantly into the sparse room, his gaze fixed firmly on the scarred wooden floorboards. Grady furrowed his brows in displeasure. "Snap to, soldier." For the life of him, he couldn't figure out why Perkins, a shy, overly timid boy, had joined the army. "I believe I left orders not to be disturbed."

"Y-yes, sir. B-but the pilot of the *Annabella* insists on talking to you. Says it's urgent."

Before Grady could reply, a small man rushed into the room, clutching an immaculate cap between his stubby fingers. "Please, *monsieur* colonel, I must speak with you."

Perkins whirled around. "Hey! I told you to wait outside. The colonel's a busy man."

Grady held up one hand. "You may go, Perkins. I'll deal with this."

As soon as his aide closed the door behind him, Grady turned to the Frenchman. "What can I do for you, Mr.—?"

"Billaud, Colonel. Jon Billaud, captain of ze *Annabella*."

Leaning carefully back against the broken slats of his chair, Grady steepled his fingers. "Ah, Captain Billaud. I've heard of you. You have the reputation for being one of the best pilots on the Missouri."

The Frenchman's weathered features broadened into a pleased smile. "*Oui*. I love zis river." He sighed dramatically, kissed his fingers, then winked. "Like a beautiful woman, she is a worthy challenge. One must only learn her moods. With patience, she is easily tamed."

Grady hid an amused smile by clearing his throat. "Yes, well, what can I do for you this day, Captain?"

Jon Billaud straightened, his features grave as he recalled his purpose. "I have ze mademoiselles' trunk to unload, but no one seems to know of zeir arrival. Zis worries me greatly. I did not like ze idea of zose two young ladies leaving ze *Annabella*, but ze elder was quite insistent."

Grady held up one hand to stop the tumble of words. "What young ladies?"

"Why, your two lovely daughters, of course, Colonel. Zey should have arrived by now. I was to drop off zeir belongings and pick up ze coach zey borrowed. Please, tell me zey are here, safe and sound with zeir papa."

Confused, Grady shoved his chair back from his desk. Surely the man was mistaken. His daughters were safely ensconced in his town house in St. Louis. "Perhaps you should start at the beginning, Captain."

Captain Billaud worried his cap between his fingers and shifted from one foot to the other as he told Grady of his two passengers and Emma's subsequent decision to leave the steamboat and travel the rest of the way to the fort by coach with Captain Sanders and his men. "She seemed anxious to reach you."

Grady drew his brows together and gave the captain a stern look. "There must be a mistake."

The captain of the steamboat's gaze strayed to Grady's head. He shook his head. "*Non.* Zat hair, it is of ze same shade as your elder daughter." Captain Billaud sighed. "And if I may be so bold, Colonel, you have two very lovely daughters. Ze young one is a spirited filly and ze eldest, a true lady—even if she is a bit impatient."

Grady unconsciously ran his hands through his thick, wavy hair, the same bright shade and thickness at thirty-six as it had been when he was twenty. Troubled, he regarded the captain. If the man knew of Emma, that her hair was the same shade as his, then it meant the captain was telling the truth. Emma and Renny were coming here? Leaning back in his seat, he sat, stunned. It was unthinkable. Emma would never disobey his orders to remain in St. Louis. Would she? He frowned. In her last correspondence, she'd pleaded for him to come home.

He shifted uncomfortably in his seat, recalling his curt

response chastising her for being melodramatic. Had he been wrong? The first feelings of unease trickled through him. Emma had never disobeyed him before. For her to take such drastic measures to reach him must mean things were as bad as she'd indicated.

Grady swiped a hand over his jaw, the man before him forgotten as unexpected emotions broke free of the strongbox in which he'd locked them nine years before. His darling little Emma. As clearly as if it were yesterday, he saw her standing on the porch, crying with the infant Renny cradled in her small, thin arms.

He closed his eyes against the pain. Only by driving himself hard during each and every day could he hold at bay the guilt that continued to plague him. He was a colonel, a man well-used to being in command, a man who controlled his every thought and action—but over the years, that memory and the knowledge of what he'd given up had surfaced to haunt his dreams in the darkest hours of the night when control of one's mind and thoughts fell prey to emotions of the heart.

Jumping to his feet, he paced. Where then were his daughters? Staring out the grimy window, his mind raced. The land beyond was wild, untamed. Beasts, both two- and four-legged roamed unchecked. Shoving aside his fear, he strode to the door, his boots pounding the floor. "Perkins!" His shout halted all movement outside his office.

Perkins came running, his glasses falling from his nose, a sheaf of paper tucked beneath one arm and several thick folders in his arms. "Y-yes, sir?"

"Captain Sanders and his men, where are they?"

"I don't know, sir." The soldier shoved his glasses up his nose with one forearm and nearly lost his armload of papers. "They haven't returned from their last survey, sir."

Grady smacked one fisted hand repeatedly into his palm. "Are they late reporting in?"

Perkins drew a deep breath. "O-only a few days, sir, nothing unusual—"

Grady gripped his hands tightly behind his back. "Has a search been conducted?"

The young soldier swallowed. "N-no sir."

"Why the hell not?"

One of the files fell to the dusty floor. "Colonel, sir. The men are often delayed. We've never sent—policy—"

Grady cut him off with a fist slamming hard against the open door. "Policy be damned. Something's wrong."

Perkins backed away from his fury. Grady ignored him, his mind focusing on possible reasons for Sanders's and his men's late arrival. Had their coach broken down? Or had they run into trouble of another sort? His blood chilled. The natives in the area were up in arms, protesting the presence of soldiers at the fort. Cold beads of sweat broke out along Grady's forehead. If anything happened to Emma or Renny . . .

"Hell's bells!" His roar echoed over the compound outside his open window. "Perkins, fetch Zeb. He's the best damn tracker around. Then assemble a search party."

"Y-yes, sir." Perkins gulped and bent down to pick up the papers.

"Now, soldier! Move!" Grady commanded. "We leave within the hour. My daughters are out there somewhere."

Perkins bolted. Grady followed, his boots tromping the strewn papers.

Behind him, Jon Billaud wiped the sweat from his forehead and then hurried out to unload the trunk belonging to the missing girls.

A pair of golden eagles soared lazily across a cobalt-blue sky. Below them, land touched by shimmering hues of gold stretched beyond forever. The petal-framed faces of sunflowers gazed at the sun, ripening oceans of soft, tawny-colored prairie grass rippled as far as the eye could see, and meadowlarks swayed from their perches atop the ripe seed heads as their sweet song filled the air.

From her seat on a rock at the edge of one of many streams crisscrossing the land, Emma wrapped her arms around her updrawn knees and watched the birds fade into the distance. Her gaze dipped and roamed over the rippling prairie. Strangely, she felt at peace among the trill of birds and the buzz of insects. For reasons she didn't understand, the beauty of the land struck a chord deep within her. She'd always longed to travel, had wanted to see the world, but between raising Renny and caring for her elderly aunt, she'd been firmly tied to her boring and uneventful life in St. Louis.

Emma let out a snort of derisive laughter at the absurdity of her thoughts. In the eight days since leaving the steamboat, she'd seen and experienced much more than she'd ever bargained or wished for. Suddenly, St. Louis and all its dullness didn't seem so bad. Glancing up into the sky, Emma wished she could fly away on the breeze, be free to drift at will, like the eagles and meadowlarks.

Freedom. She'd never given it much thought, never fully appreciated it until she'd lost it. How fortunate she'd been and not realized it. Tears welled up in her eyes. Not only had she lost her freedom, she'd lost the one person in the world who mattered most to her—her sister—and in doing so, she'd cost Renny not only her freedom but her life.

The peace of the afternoon fled. One error in judgment had torn her life into shreds. How she wished to wake up and find her situation was nothing more than a horrible nightmare. Resting her head on her knees, Emma prayed for a miracle. She prayed for her father to come and save her and make her world right once again. It didn't matter that she hadn't seen him in more than nine years. She needed him. Though she'd used her sister as an excuse to go to him, the honest truth was that she herself desperately longed to see him.

For years she'd convinced herself she didn't need

Grady O'Brien, didn't care about him, but deep down, she desperately needed his love and approval—as much now as when she'd been eight. But after this, even if he rescued her and Renny, she'd destroyed all hope of ever receiving those precious things. She'd failed him.

Emma stood, grabbed a handful of stones and threw them into the water with enough force to create loud splashes. "Fool," she berated herself, ignoring the sting of her tears. Whatever had possessed her even to dream that things between her and her father could change? If he truly loved them, he wouldn't have left, let alone stayed away. Grady O'Brien loved only himself and his career. She'd spent a lifetime craving something she'd never have, no matter what the circumstances, and for that, she could only blame herself.

She steeled herself. Who needed Colonel Grady O'Brien?

Gingerly, Emma wiped the tears from her sunburned cheeks then sat back down on the rock, her head bowed. "I do," she whispered. "I need you, Papa, I need you to find Renny." Thoughts of her sister brought forth a fresh wave of anguish. Where was she? Was she alive? Warm? Cared for?

Striking Thunder's voice intruded on her thoughts. "Our meal will be ready soon."

Startled, Emma nearly fell from the rock into the water. How could anyone move as he did, without making a sound? She glared at him over her shoulder, then wished she hadn't done so. He stood directly behind her, his golden-brown thighs mere inches from her nose. Lifting her gaze a smidgen, she stared at the bottom edge of the leather flap. Swallowing, she didn't dare lift her eyes further. Heat infused her cheeks. Looking back out toward the fast-moving river, she tried to ignore the man standing so close behind her, whose heat she felt through her dress.

The scent of a roasting prairie chicken reached her and made her stomach rumble loudly in anticipation. Though her mind rejected all thought of eating, her body craved a hot meal. Turning sideways so she could keep her wary gaze on him, she wrapped her arms around her knees. "I'm not hungry," she lied.

Striking Thunder folded his arms across his chest. "You will eat." A frown deepened the creases between his eyes and along either side of his mouth as he stared at her.

Emma felt self-conscious. She was filthy, her dress in tatters and her hair matted and tangled beyond help.

As if he read her mind, he indicated the shallow stream. "You have time to bathe before we eat."

The idea appealed. The water, while cold, looked inviting. How she longed for a bath, but she refused to take off her clothes to go into the water. And with the autumnal prairie winds, it was just too cold to spend the night in wet clothes. Glancing back at the water to dismiss him, she shrugged her shoulders. "I don't wish to bathe."

Striking Thunder went to the water's edge. "If that's your wish. Go tend our meal. I have no desire to eat until I am clean." With no warning, he pulled the leather band from around his waist and let the strip of leather he wore between his legs fall.

Emma squealed in shock at the sight of his naked buttocks and drew in a ragged breath. Common courtesy dictated she turn her back on him but she couldn't. She watched, eyes glued to his backside until the water rose and concealed flesh as golden brown as the rest of him. *For shame*, she berated herself. *You're a lady, not some common strumpet!*

Emma turned to the side and forced herself to look elsewhere—at the smoking fire, his horse, anywhere. Suddenly, her attention zeroed in on the unattended horse with the black raven still perched on its back. Emma grew still. A quick glance to the left confirmed Striking Thunder was still in the stream, his back to her. She held her breath. Did she dare? Her eyes narrowed with determination. Yes, she dared. This might be her only chance.

As soon as he submerged his head beneath the flowing water, she was up and running. Grabbing the rope bridle, she shooed the bird off and mounted. A shout from the stream warned her that he'd seen her. From on top of the horse, she glanced toward the water.

Striking Thunder waded out. "Get down," he ordered softly.

The sight of him naked held her for long moments. His backside had been impressive enough but oh Lordy, his front . . . His body was a masterpiece of raw, wild splendor. She'd never imagined that a man would look so—so breathtaking. Waves of embarrassment washed over her followed by shame. Why was she was wasting precious seconds ogling the man! Defiantly, she lifted her gaze and gave him a glare of triumph before digging her heels into the horse's sides. The animal took off. The joy of success sang through her veins. She'd done it. She'd escaped!

Chapter Eight

A shrill whistle pierced the air. The horse Emma sat on responded by tossing its head. With ears pricked forward and nostrils flared, the mare obediently made a hard turn to the left. Too late, Emma recalled how Striking Thunder had called the horse to him by whistling. "*No*," she cried, struggling to regain control of the animal.

But the horse didn't stop until it had reached Striking Thunder. No emotion disturbed the hard planes of the Indian's face but in his eyes, the storm of his fury reached out to engulf her. Her shoulders slumped in defeat. Without speaking, he reached up and yanked her down. She toppled into his arms, her feet slamming onto the ground between his wide stance. She struggled against the bands of hardened steel that crushed her against his wet chest, then stilled.

In silence, they glared at each other, lips tightly compressed; his to control his fury, hers to stop the trembling. Emma's green eyes grew lighter in coloring, his browns dark and intense. Her softly rounded jaw tilted upward in defiance, his clenched tighter. Neither gave. Defiance challenged contempt. Chests rose in unison and fell rapidly with suppressed emotion.

With each passing second, the tension between them thickened. Water dripped from Striking Thunder's long hair, soaking into the makeshift bodice of her dress. Moist heat rose between them. Against her palms, his skin felt hot, smooth as warm butter. Pressed against that hard, moist flesh, her breasts swelled. Emma held her breath at the subtle shift of tension in his body. His grip relaxed and the anger in his eyes dissolved. His gaze released hers, his lids lowering as he glanced down at her ragged clothing. Though he couldn't see them, her nipples tightened in response to his seeking gaze.

She gasped, mortified by her body's traitorous response. This abrupt shift of mood from anger to desire frightened her. "I'm sorry. Please let me go," she whispered. Nervous, she moistened her lower lip with her tongue, but when she noticed his heavy-lidded gaze lingering on her mouth, she clamped her lips shut.

His arms shifted. One hand moved to her jaw, the other to the back of her head. His head lowered, slowly. Unable to move, her protests died beneath the warm hardness of his mouth closing over hers. He held her lips captive as easily as he held her body. Emma turned her head but he brought her mouth back to his.

To her surprise, his mouth softened and his kiss turned gentle. His lips played over hers, coaxed her into accepting what he offered. Though she feared this warrior, feared the warmth of him that was stealing away her will, she held herself immobile. When his tongue snaked out and teased her mouth into opening to allow him a quick foray inside, she moaned, mortified to discover that she liked being kissed, liked the heady sensation of his mouth mating with hers.

Breaking off the kiss, he gazed into her eyes, then groaned and bent his head once more. She leaned into him, gave herself over to his expertise. Her blood pounded, and her heart raced wildly against his chest. She pressed closer, seeking the easing of an unnamed aching need. He moved against her. She felt his throbbing hardness against her belly. Fear broke through the languid haze cocooning her. From her married friends, she'd heard about a man's tool and the pain it caused. Fresh panic rose in her. She twisted and pushed but he ignored her protests. Desperately, she bit him on the lower lip. His head jerked up and a startled curse left his full, moist lips. Emma, her breathing ragged, tilted her chin. "You're no better than Yellow Dog. I won't let you rape me."

Faced with Emma's incredible spirit, Striking Thunder's senses sharpened. To subdue her would be a challenge, one eagerly accepted and anticipated. He drew his throbbing lip into his mouth, tasted no blood then chuckled. "Ah, my spirited prize, this warrior does not need to force a woman." Pulling her closer into the cradle of his hips, his hand applied just enough pressure to the small of her back to keep her where she was. Tangling the fingers of his other hand in her hair, he pulled her head back.

"There are other ways to subdue a stubborn filly than violence." Ignoring her squeak of a protest, Striking Thunder slanted his mouth over hers, and teased her lips with his tongue once again before claiming them in a masterful kiss. Her lips softened on a sigh. The blood in his veins sang in anticipation but when he felt her jaw tighten, he eased back, keeping his hand firmly at the back of her head to stay her from inflicting further damage. Frustrated when she found she couldn't bite him again, she opened her mouth. "I won't give in," she panted.

"No?" Capturing her lower lip between his, he suckled, nipped. With his tongue, he teased the crinkled corners of her mouth, traced the full, swollen flesh.

"No." She said again, but this time, her voice lacked conviction.

Leaving her mouth, he trailed his lips along her jaw and down her throat, lingering on the wild pulsing in the soft hollow. Breathy sounds of pleasure vibrated against his lips, her fingers fluttered against his chest. Feeling her acquiescence, he slid one hand up and down her spine then over the curve of her narrow waist. Emma's head fell back, her lips parting. Striking Thunder needed no further invitation. Consumed by his own need, he reclaimed her mouth with a savage intensity.

To his intense pleasure, she kissed him back, her mouth moving with his, accepting all he gave, giving in return. A low moan filled the air. He was startled to find that it came from him but he couldn't stop. An aching need consumed him, made him forget why he'd kissed her to begin with. His tongue found entrance. He stroked and wooed her until she accepted him and allowed him to explore her mouth's inner sweetness. Her arms lifted, her hands moving shyly around his neck and her lower body leaned hard into him, sucking him deeper into the swirling need obliterating all but that of satisfying the thrumming hunger clawing within him.

His hands slid downward to cup and caress her nicely rounded bottom. Lifting her so his turgid manhood lay throbbing against the center of her heat, he nearly cried out with the need to lift her skirts and slide inside the warmth of her moist sheath. So lost was he in this woman's magic, nothing else mattered. Desire. Lust. Neither had ever been this all-consuming before. Mating with Meadowlark had never resulted in this wild abandon. Theirs had been a tender act, prompted by duty and the expectations of producing a child.

Duty. He stilled. Lifting his head, shame filled him. He'd lost his wife at the hands of Yellow Dog who had claimed that this woman's father had paid him to murder her. All thoughts of duty, of his people and their needs had fled with just one taste of this woman's sweet lips. His people suffered, grieved, yet here he stood consumed by the desire to make love to the enemy.

Emma pressed her fingers to her kiss-swollen lips. He stared into her eyes. They'd darkened to forest-green pools of innocence. His nostrils flared. He shoved her from him in disgust, wanting nothing more than to jump on his horse and ride away, leaving her forever. But he couldn't. Not only was she to bait his trap, he had a duty to her as well, one she'd forced out of him before cleverly letting him know who her father was.

He glared at her through narrowed eyes, just now realizing how shrewd and cunning she was. She was wily, like the coyote, tricking him into lowering his defenses. But now he was on to her. From now on, he'd keep his distance. But his body still yearned for release, which further darkened his mood. Standing over her, unable to hide the evidence of his desire, he glared down at her. "Do not challenge me again, foolish white woman. Next time, I may not stop with a kiss." Turning his back on her, he strode back into the cold water.

Emma pressed the back of her hands to her hot cheeks. Shame made her want to curl up and die. How could she have allowed him to kiss and touch her as he had? He was an Indian, a savage, *her captor.* She groaned and squirmed from the remembered feel of him pressed hard against the part of her that ached the most. How could she ever face him again? Sinking onto the dried grass with the horse grazing a few feet from her, it pained Emma to admit she'd enjoyed the kiss and had wanted more. Much, *much* more.

A shrill cry from above caught her attention. Glancing up, she watched the return of one golden eagle. The raven left the water's edge and flew to the mare's back with a shrill cry. But the eagle ignored the blackbird as it circled across the blue heavens. Then, without warning, it dove toward the earth, wings folded back, claws out. Lightning-quick, the bird snatched up a squealing field mouse. Watching the majestic bird of prey fly away, Emma felt as though she herself were caught in the grip of some powerful force and was every bit as helpless as the eagle's doomed prey.

Hundreds of miles away, another pair of eyes scanned the sky, frowning at a flock of circling birds. Buzzards. Dozens of the ugly, revolting things. Grady grabbed his rifle and shot it into the air until every last one of them scattered from sight. "They'll take nothing more," he roared, furious yet sickened.

Behind him, death permeated the air and soaked into the earth. Though Captain Sanders had told him of the massacre and the cloud of dark birds had warned they were near, nothing could prepare him for the grisly sight, nor the overwhelming smell. No matter how many times he faced the ravages of death, it always left him feeling helpless. Many of the soldiers who fell in the line of duty were young men cheated out of long, full lives.

Grady shifted the rifle in his hands, keeping it ready in case of trouble. Scanning the area, he watched his men, with handkerchiefs tied around their noses and mouths, dig shallow graves while three of his best scouts scoured the scene. Grady glanced down. In his hands, he held what was left of his Emma's valise. Reaching inside, he pulled out a single letter. It was the last letter he'd sent to her. Carefully, he tucked it into his pocket, then withdrew a small silver snuff box, the last gift Margaret Mary had given him. He stared at it for a long time. No longer was he that gentleman and nothing could ease the stench of death or the feeling of failure weighing him down. Weary and worried, he fought against the unexpected feeling of helplessness. He was a colonel in the U.S. Army, a man of action. So why was he frozen, unable to move or help his men with the unpleasant job of burial?

His hand formed a fist around the pewter box. Never had his job taken on so personal an aspect. This time, it was *his* daughters in danger. When he'd first arrived at the scene where his men had been slaughtered, the thought of finding them among the dead had nearly driven him wild. Gone was the cold and controlled colonel who'd driven his men hard to reach this spot. Long-buried emotions resurfaced with a vengeance as he'd searched among the bodies.

Though relieved they weren't among the dead, it brought on a new, agonizing worry. Where were they? The thought of Emma and Renny captured by Indians left him trembling anew. Fresh waves of guilt plagued him. If only he'd given in to Emma's plea to come home. But he'd been afraid to face her after all these years. And his cowardice, his failure as a father may very well have cost them their lives.

A shout drew his attention. The demeanor of a cold, forbidding military man replaced that of the fearful father. Putting away the snuff box, he joined Zac. "What have you found? Was it Yellow Dog as Captain Sanders said?"

Zac, born to zealous missionary parents who'd baptized him Zacarias Cristobal Chavez, looked old as the hills in his well-worn deerskin breeches and shirt. His unkempt gray beard hung in tatters down to his chest and nearly obscured the four-inch silver cross hanging around his neck. But his movements were agile and sure-footed, his gaze clear and intelligent. He held up a fistful of arrows and pointed to the nocked ends. "These belong to them Arikara savages, Kern'l."

Grady pinched the bridge of his nose with his thumb and forefinger. His ears rang with the rhythmic clunks and clangs of shovels striking the hard-packed earth. "Are you sure?"

"Yep." He pointed to the bodies of three Indians. "They's Arikaras."

Grady thought of Captain Sanders, the only survivor of the massacre. The search party had come upon him near the river, unconscious and injured. After reviving him, he'd told his story of how Yellow Dog had ambushed him and his men. With pain weakening his voice, he'd begged the colonel to forgive him for failing to save Emma. Out scouting the way, he'd returned but been outnumbered, so he'd ridden for the fort to get help. According to the captain, one of the savages had spotted him and had followed, resulting in the loss of Derek's horse and his injuries.

Sanders had nearly passed out during his recounting of the attack until Doc Gil had stepped forward, insisting on taking the injured man back to the fort. Reluctantly, Grady had no choice but to halt his questions.

Zac, who had gone back to his study of the arrows, cleared his throat. "Kern'l? Sanders was right. See here?" Zac pointed to several crude marks along the shaft of three arrows, near the feathered end. Anger hardened his gruff voice. "These are Yella Dog's marks. Them others, I don't recognize."

Yellow Dog had given Grady and his men at the fort nothing but trouble for the past few months. When they'd first taken over the fort, the Indian had offered his services as a hunter and scout in return for goods, but he'd been banished after they'd caught him stealing guns and liquor. Now he harassed the soldiers.

Staring into Zac's worried eyes, Grady knew true fear. The outlook for his daughters was grim—even *if* he found them alive. Fury mingled with apprehension and guilt. He strode away, filled with determination. No matter how long it took or where his search led, he *would* find his daughters.

Emma received her first glimpse of Striking Thunder's village two days after her attempted escape. Cone-shaped tipis sprouted from the golden prairie, stretching upward to lend the flat, rolling land a bit of color and depth. From the tips of the tipis, plumes of smoke drifted toward the sky to merge with the dark roiling storm clouds gathering overhead. The scene was so dramatic, it had her fingers itching for a paintbrush and canvas, or even a piece of charcoal so she could capture the wild beauty on paper.

But though the Indian village appeared peaceful, not at all frightening, it brought home just how precarious her existence truly was. This was not a civilized settlement where basic laws of society governed. Life as she knew it existed no more. Raw fear crept up her spine and invaded the calm acceptance she'd adopted over the last few days. It all seemed so unreal. She, the daughter of a respected colonel, now faced captivity. Her mouth went dry and her stomach twisted into tight knots as she fought the bleak despair threatening to break like the storm brewing overhead.

Her feet dragged, resisted each step that brought her closer to the unknown. She faltered and came to a stop. Hugging herself tightly, she panned her gaze around, desperately looking for any means of escape. Overhead, the raven circled, following their progress. Around her, open prairie with an occasional deep river valley or flat-topped mesa with steep slopes, stretched into forever. Ahead, behind the grouped-together tipis, towering rocks and forests rose high. There she might find places to hide, but they were still too far away to be of use. Even the river they had followed didn't offer much in the way of concealment.

"*Inanhni yo!*" Striking Thunder ordered, motioning for her to catch up.

A sudden gust of wind whipped her shortened skirts around her legs and several drops of rain hit her face. The impending storm echoed the emotions churning deep within. Emma tried to quell the rising panic, but with each plodding, exhausted step toward the unknown, a sense of doom grew. Beside her, Striking Thunder led his exhausted horse and as much as she longed to ask him what would happen to her, she remained silent, unwilling to risk angering him. Suddenly and shockingly, came the awareness that the warrior who'd saved her from Yellow Dog now represented some small measure of security.

Unbelievably, she felt safe with Striking Thunder. He had kept his promise not to harm her, even if he had taken advantage of her to kiss her. Touching her lips, she recalled that brief, shared moment, welcomed that brief distraction from her fear of what she would soon encounter. But the sound of strange, high-pitched wails threw her back into the harsh, cold reality of her situation. Pinpoints of goose flesh rose on her arms and chills that had nothing to do with the icy wind raced down her back. The beat of drums joined the wailing, lending a frightening undertone to the atmosphere of gloom. The sound cloaked the land, thick and suffocating in its intensity.

Even Striking Thunder seemed affected by the sound. Emma felt the tension radiating from the tightly coiled muscles of his upper, arms, the bunched sinews of his thighs, and the rigid line of his shoulders. Stopping, Emma pressed her hands to her belly. "What is it"

Striking Thunder glanced at her over his shoulder. Eyes of black ice bore into hers. "My people mourn."

Emma tried swallowing past the tight lump in her throat. "Y-your wife?"

Striking Thunder stopped abruptly. "My people mourn the loss of many." His eyes went bleak with pain as he listened to the drums. "A great warrior died while avenging the deaths of our people. He died avenging the wrongs of your father."

Fury filled those dark eyes, causing Emma to stumble back a step. She pressed her fingers to her mouth to still the trembling. He'd again accused her father of murder. She shook her head, denying what he said.

Striking Thunder closed the distance between them. His voice simmered with repressed violence. "For your own good, I give this warning. Be silent. Speak when spoken to and do as told." He stalked away but Emma's feet refused to budge. She trembled with the force of her denial. She had to convince him he was wrong about her father. With a spurt of courage, she ran after him and grabbed his arm.

"Wait!" A ripple of warmth traveled up her arm and lodged in her cheeks at the feel of those hardened muscles beneath her icy fingers. At his contemptuous glare, she clasped her shaking hands tightly behind her back. "My father wouldn't—"

Faster than a striking snake, Striking Thunder's hand shot out to grip her chin. The hard bite of his fingers silenced her protest. "Many will hold *you* responsible for the actions of your father. Do you wish to be stoned or tortured?"

A wave of terror, stark and vivid, chilled Emma. The trembling she'd fought spread to her legs and threatened to bring her to her knees.

Striking Thunder eased his grip and stepped back a pace. "I promised no harm would befall you and I will keep my word. But hear me well, white woman. These are my people, I, their chief. They will do as I ask, but how you are treated during your stay will be determined by your own actions. Do you understand this?"

Emma nodded then followed after him, slowly, fearing even more so the reception of those who would blame her for crimes her father had supposedly committed. She pressed a fist into her stomach to fight the churning nausea.

"Oh, Papa, what is going on?" she whispered, and for the first time, she admitted to herself that she didn't really know the man she called "Papa" or of *what* he was capable.

Chapter Nine

Refreshed by a bath in the cold stream and dressed in his finest loincloth, leggings and moccasins, Striking Thunder strode through the circles of tipis. On his head, he wore a short headdress made from the feathers of a golden eagle. The wind ruffled those feathers and fanned his long, black hair out behind him.

Tonight, around the fire, his warriors would gather to count coup and extol the virtues of the deceased and celebrate the death of Yellow Dog. But in his heart, Striking Thunder didn't feel victorious. He couldn't celebrate until he had killed the colonel and captain for their parts in the death of his people. And he would. It was only a matter of time, patience and careful planning. He'd have his vengeance.

Thinking about the forthcoming meeting and his news brought the white woman to mind. Upon his return, he'd taken her to his tipi and left her. He wasn't worried she'd try to escape—at least not yet—for there was no way she'd get more than a few steps with his people closely observing her.

When he came to the council lodge erected near the center of the inner circle of tipis, he ducked inside where the men of his village, ranging from the youngest brave to the eldest warrior, gathered to await word from their chief. Solemn-faced, they sat cross-legged on either side of the fire, forming two half-circles, with another row of warriors squatting behind.

Silence reigned, all eyes focused on him as he took up his position at the back of the lodge. Sitting, he rested the back of his hands on his crossed thighs, palms open and face up. Once he'd cleared his mind of all thought and emotion, he lit a long wooden pipe.

His voice filled the room as with great ceremony, he lifted the lighted pipe first toward the heavens, then pointed it toward the earth. He then offered it to each of the four winds: South, West, North, East.

Done, he closed his eyes and drew in the smoke from the sacred mixture of herbs. He released it slowly, reverently. Silently, he passed the pipe to his left—with the passing sun. No one spoke, though each was curious to hear what their chief had to say. News of the white woman's presence had spread from one tipi to the next until all had heard.

Sadness filled Striking Thunder's heart. The women outside continued to wail and weep over the death of a brave warrior, echoing his own wail of grief. It would be a long time before he'd be free to deal with the pain of his loss. Deliberately, he shoved the sorrow aside. Across from him, his father, Golden Eagle, who'd once been their chief, sent him a questioning look.

Striking Thunder saw the shadows in his father's eyes and knew he worried over the presence of a white captive in their village. There had been none since Golden Eagle had brought a young girl known as Sarah Cartier into their midst, determined to marry her, even against his father's wishes.

Unease slithered through him at the realization like his father, the son had returned from a war party with a captive woman in tow. But unlike his father, Striking Thunder wasn't trying to protect Emma from a villainous relative. These circumstances were different. The white woman's presence was necessary to secure revenge. So why was he suddenly trying to justify his actions? He knew the answer. He dreaded his mother's displeasure.

Before he could contemplate the difficult scene that

would follow this meeting, the pipe returned to him. Setting it down before him, he stood and, in a voice vibrating with emotion, told in great detail of his days hunting down Yellow Dog and of his victory over their enemy. Cheers filled the tipi.

The mood shifted, quieted, when he spoke of Two-Ree's bravery. Shoulders rounded as grief settled over the gathered warriors. He made sure that all learned it had been Two-Ree who'd known—through his wife's visions—of Emma and the role she would play in their pursuit of revenge. He held out the belt buckle. "This belongs to the soldier in charge of the fort and is proof he lies when he speaks of peace." He allowed each warrior time to absorb his news.

Voices broke out as each man made comment to his neighbor. One loud voice drowned out all others. "Are we to let the white soldiers kill our women and elders? We must prove the Sioux are mighty. I say we call together all our great chiefs, band together and drive the white soldiers from land that doesn't belong to them."

Murmurs of agreement rose. Striking Thunder held up his hand. All fell silent. "There are too many soldiers and the risk to our people great." He waited a beat. "My brothers, I have a plan. This woman's father will search for her, first among our enemy, the Arikara, but he will not find her there. We will use the white woman to lure him to us when the time is right." He raised a fist high. "Revenge will be ours." Loud whoops greeted his announcement.

An aging warrior named Singing Crow stood. In a soft, singsong voice, he trilled, "What is to become of the woman with hair the color of fire and eyes as green as new grass?"

All eyes returned to Striking Thunder. He glanced around at the men sitting before him. "Before I knew of her identity, I gave my word not to harm her and to return her to the fort—to show the soldiers that the Sioux want only peace, unlike our enemy, the Arikara." A rumble of protest arose. Again, he held up one palm.

"It is the will of *Wakan Tanka*. The spirits revealed the truth only after I made my promise. We must release the woman, but not until we have our revenge on her father and the captain."

Though some voices had quieted, others still rose in protest. One, louder than the others, belonged to a young warrior named Waho. He stood, his face flushed with anger. "*Hun, hun, hay!* Yellow Dog killed my sister. Never again will her sweet young voice fill the air. I say this woman should be given to me." His dark eyes shone with lust.

Striking Thunder narrowed his eyes. Waho was a troublemaker. His name, which meant howler, fit well; he was always protesting and stirring up trouble.

Standing, Golden Eagle defended his son's decision. "You question our chief? Have you forgotten that your sister was his wife, murdered by Yellow Dog? It is his choice what is to become of this woman." Murmurs of agreement rose.

Waho flushed a dull, angry red but didn't back down. His glare challenged Striking Thunder's decision. "Have you forgotten my sister so soon that you wish to take a white woman to your mat?"

Furious, Striking Thunder let his silence speak more loudly than any harsh words. Only when Waho finally sat back down, did he address his people. "I have told you of my promise to this woman. It is the will of the spirits or they would have revealed her connection with the white soldier first. The Sioux are honorable. Would you have me break my word, bring dishonor to our tribe of Miniconjou Sioux?" He waited a heartbeat.

"I will return her when we no longer have use for her. Until then, she will lodge with my sister, Star Dreamer."

Waho once more protested. "I say the council should decide where the white woman stays." He glanced around, seeking support. Low murmurs wound their way from one end of the lodge to the other.

Golden Eagle speared Waho with a forbidding glare.

"Was not my daughter's husband the one responsible for convincing our chief to go after this woman? Did she not see this woman in a vision and share this with her husband? Did my daughter not see her own husband's death and start mourning long before his body returned to us? Star Dreamer has no husband. With two young children to care for, my son is thoughtful to consider her needs."

Grateful for his father's support, Striking Thunder's voice rang out strong with conviction as he summed up their course of action. "The spirits led us to the daughter of our enemy. They demand she remain unharmed and be released when we have no further use for her. If we do not honor their wishes, we risk angering them." The last was spoken quietly. No one protested, not even Waho.

Inside Striking Thunder's tipi, Emma turned in a slow circle surprised to find the inside of the cone-shaped dwelling was roomy, bright and airy. Though the top was open, it was pleasantly warm inside. Hides sewn together then stretched over tall poles sheltered her from the gusting wind outside.

From the poles, both beautifully decorated and plain-leather pouches hung. Carefully, she lifted one down. It was covered with exquisite beadwork in yellows, blacks and reds on both sides. Inside, she found sewing supplies: long, colored needlelike sticks, beads, and what she assumed was some sort of thread, though it was quite thick. There was also a smaller pouch with downy-soft feathers inside. She chewed on the inside of her cheek. These had obviously belonged to Striking Thunder's deceased wife.

Setting it back where she found it, she glanced inside the other ones. Each held various food supplies and strange implements. As she handled the strange items, she wished circumstances were different. How many times in the past had she bemoaned her dreary life, wanting nothing more than to leave it behind to explore the world, learn about other people and places. But always, her number one priority had been the duty thrust upon her first by her father, then later, her aunt.

Reminded of her failure to protect her sister, the urge to explore left her. Harsh reality set in. This wasn't some pleasure trip or exploration. She was here against her will and Heaven only knew what had become of Renny—if she was even still alive.

Sinking onto one of the fur-piled pallets, Emma dropped her head into her hands, unable to blot out the sound of her sister's screams echoing in her head. She'd never forget the sight of Renny's face, stark-white with terror as she was torn from her.

"Oh, God." She rocked back and forth. How could she live with the consequences of her error in judgment? "Don't fall apart, not now," she whispered. With effort, she forced the nightmarish vision from her and shoved her tangled hair from her eyes. Exhaustion, fear and worry swept through her. She longed to close her eyes and lose herself in a deep, dreamless sleep. The softness of the thick fur beneath her lured her tired, aching body. She fought it and jumped to her feet.

She had to stay alert. Shoving aside the flap covering the round entrance to the tipi, Emma peered outside. A short distance away, she spotted the river, wide and fast-flowing. The wind from the approaching storm whipped the surface into a white froth. Once again, her gaze shifted beyond the tipis to the dark mountain to the west. It towered like some black, shadowy wall. She bit her lip in anticipation.

If only she could steal a horse, she'd be able to escape under the cover of darkness into the thickly wooded forests. Her nerves fluttered at the thought. While she knew escaping Striking Thunder would not be easy, she had to find a way to do so. Noticing the approach of several women, she ducked back inside.

Unable to sit still, Emma continued to pace. What was Striking Thunder doing? When would he return and what happened next? Questions piled one atop another until a dark head poking through the flap startled her. Emma backed away from the black-haired woman eyeing her with hate-filled eyes. The woman shouted something that sounded awful then disappeared, only to be replaced by another who repeated the process. One after another, the Indian women of the village stuck their heads into the tipi to shout angry words at her.

Unnerved by the outward hostility directed at her, Emma backed away and crouched down against the hide wall, seeking to make herself as small as possible. As the women continued to file past the tipi, she felt like an animal in a cage. Oh, when would Striking Thunder return? Scared that they might swarm in and attack her, Emma grabbed an iron skillet and clutched it to her chest.

Suddenly, something hard hit the outside of the tipi, smacking her in the lower back. She yelped in pain and threw herself forward, away from the sides just as another object struck. At the sound of stones and angry words being thrown at the dwelling, Striking Thunder's earlier warning about being stoned came back to haunt her. She stifled the urge to scream his name.

After a few minutes, things outside appeared to settle. The sudden silence left her free to worry anew about her fate. What would happen to her? Had Striking Thunder lied to her about keeping her safe? Would he rape her as Yellow Dog had tried to do?

The memory of that one brief but oh so heart-stopping kiss burned in her cheeks. Never had she imagined a kiss from a man could make her feel such wondrous things— but to have experienced it from him, a savage, and in these circumstances, she moaned with mortification. To make it worse, she'd enjoyed it, had wanted him to continue. Would he? Staring at the doorway, she both feared and longed for his return. Embarrassed by such thoughts at a time when she needed to keep her wits clear, Emma shook her head.

Suddenly, in a flurry of fury, another woman stormed inside the tipi. This one was younger, somewhere around her own age. Emma went on guard against the hatred spewing from glittering brown eyes. None of the other women had actually stepped inside the tipi. Though her stomach clenched with fear, and sweat rolled down between her breasts, Emma couldn't help but notice the girl was the most strikingly beautiful female she'd ever seen.

Blue-black hair hung past her waist, her eyes, with their slight slant, were dark, nearly black, and added an exotic beauty to a delicate face boasting high cheekbones, a straight nose and full lips. Again, the urge to capture what she saw on paper assailed her—until the woman thinned her lips and bared her white teeth.

"You murderer. You killed my sister."

Emma jumped to her feet, clutching the skillet with both hands, and narrowed her eyes. Wary of the malice directed at her and fearing the burning hatred in the stranger's eyes, Emma decided enough was enough. If these women were intent on killing her, she'd be damned if she would make it easy for them. Taking a firmer grip on the iron pan, she instinctively leaned her weight forward. "Yellow Dog killed your sister."

The girl advanced. "I heard the warriors talking. He was paid." She pointed an accusing finger. "You are the seed of a murderer."

Emma's own temper, long smothered by duty and the molding hand of her aunt, burst through the fissures created by her immersion in this savage world. "My father killed no one. He is a good man." *Even if he's not a good father,* she silently added. And deep down, she had to believe he was a good soldier. Hadn't he moved through the ranks and earned numerous awards and recognition for his dedication? Dedication to negotiation and peaceful commerce with hostile natives. Too bad he hadn't given fatherhood the same devotion, she thought bitterly.

The Indian girl advanced, her face contorted with fury. But before the confrontation could continue, Striking Thunder entered.

"*Henakeca!* Enough! Leave us, Tanagila."

Emma didn't flinch from the glare the girl sent her before leaving in a swirl of shiny black hair. Instead, she shifted her feet and faced Striking Thunder. For long moments, he said nothing, just watched her, his features impassive. Nervous, she licked her lips and shifted her grip, her palms damp with sweat. But when his gaze latched on to her mouth, she took an involuntary step back.

"Come with me." He stepped out, glanced over his shoulder and waited.

Emma didn't move. "Why? Are you going to allow those women to stone me?" Her grip tightened on the handle of the skillet, her knuckles turning white.

He pointed to the iron pan. "You have no need of a weapon. You will not be harmed. Did I not give my word?"

Emma took a deep breath. She had no choice but to trust him. Dropping her weapon, she stepped outside, her heart pounding. Instinctively, she braced herself for the impact of stones. To her relief, nothing was thrown from the crowd of watching women. When Striking Thunder moved away, she followed, staying right behind him.

Groping fingers reached out to tug at her hair and dress. Fighting her panic, Emma bit back her cries of protest, unwilling to show these women her fear. With each breath coming in shallow gasps, she forced herself to walk like a lady, with her head held high, shoulders straight and her arms at her sides. She might be here against her will, but she refused to cower before these mean-looking women.

Striking Thunder led the white woman through the village, his thoughts dark as the sky above. He had but one pressing need: rid himself of his unwanted captive—and fast. Moving among his people, seeing the strong, healthy brown bodies of the children who ran alongside, strengthened his resolve. His people came first. Their

health, happiness and survival depended on his ability to
lead. And in order to be a good leader, he needed a clear
mind. Once he gave the woman over to Star, no unbidden
thoughts of her would distract him from his duties.

A gust of wind swirled around him. *Emma,* the spirits
seemed to whisper. He pressed on, refusing to think of
her by name. She was a white woman, his captive, nothing more, nothing less. But he made the mistake of glancing over his shoulder to see if she followed and found
himself staring into eyes a fascinating shade of green,
somewhere between spring grass and tree moss. Fear
made them nearly translucent. He scanned the rest of her
features. Her skin, where not burned by the sun, was pale
except beneath her eyes; there dark smudges signaled her
true state of fatigue. She looked fragile, vulnerable.

Yet her exhausted state did nothing to dim her beauty
or ease the sudden tightening of his loins. Had he been
too hard on her? Pushed her beyond her limit? Part of
him regretted her trauma, wished he could have released
her as he'd originally intended. But then she wouldn't be
here where he could gaze upon her beauty or further
explore the passion he'd sensed in her, had unleashed for
a short, brief sampling. Angry with the direction of his
thoughts, he glanced away and lengthened his stride. His
nostrils flared. He was a warrior, in control.

The spirits had led him to her, given her over into his
keeping and now, they sought to further test his worthi-
ness by tempting his flesh with her beauty. Pride squared
his shoulders as shouts of praise from his people followed him. Their faith in him strengthened his resolve.
Taking a deep breath, he accepted the challenge the Great
Spirit had put in his path. The white woman's hair, the
color of flames raging across the prairie, would fuel his
need for revenge, and her eyes, green as new growth
sprouting after the desolate winter, signified hope.
Renewal of life. A better life for his people. And her lips,
full, pink and tempting—

His blood pounded painfully in his lower region when

he recalled those lips' texture and taste. Grateful to reach his sister's tipi and put an end to his tormenting thoughts, he turned in relief.

Behind him, Emma stopped. For a split second, time stood still as they faced each other. He stared at her mouth, felt her lure, fought her magic. The words of his people broke the spell. Soon, he'd be free of her unsettling presence. Staring down at her, he ignored the fear and uncertainty in her eyes. "You belong to me. You are my captive, my slave. You will live here with my sister, Star Dreamer, and help her. Remember what I said or you will suffer. How you are treated will depend on your own actions. Our way of life is harsh. Work hard and the women will treat you with respect."

Emma's eyes snapped wide, the dark center shrinking, the outer circle of green brightening before they narrowed to furious slits. Defiant, she thrust out her jaw. "I'm to believe that, after what I've seen? Listen to me, Striking Thunder. I am no one's slave. I am a victim, innocent, and what you have done is wrong." The wind whipped the long tangled ends of her hair over her shoulder.

The golden-red strands reached out to slide across his throat, a soft, enticing caress. He stopped breathing and clenched his fists, fighting the urge to reach out and rub the soft silk between his fingers. His nostrils flared, caught her scent. That, too, he fought. He pulled the tipi flap wide and motioned for her to enter.

Emma passed him then spun around, her eyes snapping with fury. "I will find a way to warn my father of your evil plans. It is you and your people who will suffer, Striking Thunder, if you do not release me." Glaring at him, she waited.

When that gently rounded chin rose, Striking Thunder couldn't help admiring her spirit and loyalty. Though he resented feeling any compassion toward her, wanted nothing more than to leave her unsettling presence, he was glad to see that she wasn't beaten. Remembering her words, he vowed to keep a close watch on her—from a distance—as he knew she spoke the truth. Loyalty to her father would force her to resist captivity and try to escape. When she did, he'd show her who was master.

Unwilling to allow her the last word, he yanked her back against his chest, his blood flowing fast as some inner part of him warmed to the challenge. "Remember that we are not the only tribe out there. There are other warriors who'd treat you as Yellow Dog planned. So be very careful, white woman. Here, though you are a captive, you are safe." He glanced at Star. "Do not give this woman any trouble."

Without another word, Striking Thunder released her and left the tipi. Outside, the clouds burst open and in seconds, he was drenched. The people of his village had already disappeared, preferring to seek their dry tipis and warm fires. Striking Thunder returned to his. Somebody had lit a fire and set a bowl of stew near it to keep warm. Heat from the fire stole over him yet he felt chilled inside. He glanced around, but nothing had changed. Everything was in its place—left by him or Meadowlark—yet something was different.

He picked up his meal and lowered himself to his thick sleeping mat to eat. Emma's scent, one of sunshine, prairie and woman tantalized him, surrounded him. Frowning, he moved to another pile of furs. It did no good. The memory of Emma sitting on his bed danced before him and the image of her in his tipi, brief though it was, overshadowed the lingering presence of his deceased wife. He tried to call to mind Meadowlark brushing her long black hair in the evening. He closed his eyes, remembering how she would wait for him to come to her mat but instead of strong, brown limbs reaching out to embrace him, pale white arms beckoned.

The vision of Emma lying atop his mat, her mane of red curls spread out over the dark furs drove him back out into the stormy elements. Thunder crashed overhead, lightning flashed, but Striking Thunder embraced nature's display of fury. Wading into the stream, his breath caught as the frigid, churning water pelted against him. He ducked his head under, welcoming the shock, the clearing of his mind.

Soon, the first snows would fall. There was much to be done to ensure there would be enough food to last the winter. But even while he should have been planning another buffalo hunt, all he could think about was the woman named Emma.

Chapter Ten

Outside, the gusting storm darkened the late-afternoon sky, and rain pelted the outside of the tipi with soft patters. A fire crackled in the center of the tipi and the warmth felt inviting. Emma was tempted to kneel and warm herself. Uncertainty held her back. What now?

Though Striking Thunder frightened her and she didn't trust him completely, she had an inkling of what he might or might not do. But the woman sitting and watching her from across the fire was unknown. Their gazes locked. Emma's, wide and apprehensive; Star Dreamer's hauntingly sad. Looking closely, Emma's throat tightened in response to her ravished features: Eyes swollen from crying, her hair, black as a raven's wing was butchered short, leaving ragged ends to frame her fragile, delicate face.

Seeing the inner torment reflected in her golden-brown eyes touched something deep inside Emma. She'd expected to be confronted with more anger and hatred, not this quiet sad-faced woman. After several minutes of silence, broken only by the snap of the fire and the gentle shower of rain, Star Dreamer stood. She was petite. Her deerskin dress hung from her slim frame and fell to her calves. When she placed a thick fur on the ground a short distance from the fire, her shoulders stooped as if weighed down. Lifting her arm, she pointed, indicating Emma should sit.

Emma didn't move. She couldn't take her eyes off the

White Flame

Indian woman's hands, where long angry gashes scored their backs, cut across her fingers and disappeared beneath the full sleeves of her garment. Ragged trails of dried blood mingled with the still-seeping wounds of the deeper cuts. When she sat, crossing her legs, Emma saw the same wounds covering her calves.

Emma had read about cultures where grief-stricken women inflicted wounds on their bodies and brutally cut their hair. She'd never seen it firsthand. Studying her, taking measure of the new circumstances she found herself in, Emma realized this woman had suffered a great loss at the hands of Yellow Dog. Her heart went out to the woman even though she knew nothing of her. With her own loss of her beloved aunt still fresh in her heart, compassion stirred. But even as she felt the woman's sorrow and pain, she couldn't help but worry over what would happen to her. From what she'd seen of the women in the village, their emotions ran high and they were therefore very unpredictable.

"Taku eniciyapi he?"

The words were spoken softly in a warm, slightly hoarse voice, minus the hatred and resentment she'd encountered earlier. Relaxing marginally, Emma lowered herself to the fur, nearly moaning in relief at the warmth of the fire.

Star Dreamer repeated her question in English. "What is your name?"

All anger toward Striking Thunder and his people faded in the face of this woman's bereavement. Though Emma refused to believe her father had anything to do with what Yellow Dog had done, she couldn't bring herself to add to Star Dreamer's pain and grief. "Emma." Her voice came out hushed and subdued.

"I am Star Dreamer, sister to Striking Thunder."

Looking close, Emma saw the family resemblance. The knowledge that he'd placed her with his sister eased some of her apprehension. Her gaze fell to Star Dreamer's hands.

Star Dreamer held up her arms and turned them in the firelight. "You cannot understand, but here, it is the custom of our people to mourn in this fashion. In some tribes, a woman mourning the loss of a husband or son will cut off her fingers." The first spark of emotion brightened her eyes. She shrugged, humor threading through her voice. "My mother abhors that custom and forbids it of her children."

Emma shuddered at the thought of hacking off one's own digits. But she understood the pain of loss. Though it had been six months since her aunt had passed away, she still missed her, still mourned her deeply. "Who—I mean—?" Feeling like she was intruding where she had no business, she let her voice drift.

Star Dreamer closed her eyes. Tears streamed unashamedly down her cheeks. "My husband."

Emma laced her fingers together tightly, unsure of what to say or do. If this woman lost her husband and Striking Thunder his wife, how many more of those other women had lost a loved one? The true extent of her situation, of what her father was reputedly responsible for, hit her. "Do you blame *me?*" Though she feared the answer, she had to know where she stood if she were to survive until March—assuming Striking Thunder kept his word and released her.

Star Dreamer stared at her for a long time with eyes gone suddenly dark and blank as if she no longer saw Emma. Just when Emma feared she was going to faint or have a fit, she spoke, her voice whisper-soft.

"No. You had no part in this." She fell silent and with obvious effort, pulled herself back from where she'd gone.

Putting Star Dreamer's strange behavior down to grief, Emma vowed to learn all she could while she had someone willing to talk to her in English. Over the course of traveling with Striking Thunder, Emma had learned that most of his people spoke some English. Like her brother, Star spoke fluent English. Later, she would ask how they'd learned and from whom. Smoothing her skirt out in front of her, Emma she bravely asked, "If you do not hate me or hold my father responsible, why do the others?"

Star Dreamer stood, fetched a small tin coffeepot, dumped in what looked to be herbs, then added water. She set it at the edge of the fire, on top of a thin layer of glowing embers. Resting on her heels, she stared into the red and yellow embers. "They do not understand that you belong. In time, they will learn this. The spirits never lie."

A chill darted down Emma's back. What did she mean? She belonged in her home in St. Louis. "I think you misunderstand. Your brother promised to return me to my people after—" She couldn't say it. Just thinking it made her feel ill. "He's wrong. I know he is," she whispered, her chest tightening with fear.

Star Dreamer removed the pot from the fire. She poured some of the brown liquid into two cups, and held one out. "Then you must not lose faith in your father. Time will tell. But for now, you are tired. When *Wi* rises to show her face, I will instruct you in your new duties."

Taking the tin cup, Emma took a cautious sip. The brew was strong and sweet, and utterly unexpected. Her brow lifted in surprise. "Tea?"

A faint smile crossed Star Dreamer's lips. "My mother's favorite."

Emma closed her eyes and savored each sweet, wonderful swallow. When she was done, she cradled the warm tin cup in her hands. This small kindness wasn't what she'd expected. If she were to accept her status as a slave, which she did not, she'd have expected anger and blame.

Watching the fire die down, she felt mesmerized by the orange-red flames. It had been a long day, one filled with emotional upheaval. Setting the cup down, she fought a yawn and lost. With the warmth of the fire surrounding her, bathing her in its cocoon of warmth, all she cared about was laying her head down to sleep. Her vision blurred. When Star Dreamer touched her shoulder, Emma started.

Placing a wooden bowl of steaming water beside her, the other woman spoke, "You will feel better if you wash first. I will be back."

From the water, Emma took out a small beige cloth and rubbed it between her fingers. It wasn't woven material but it was incredibly soft. "Thank you," she murmured. As soon as Star Dreamer left, Emma roused herself. On her knees, she patted her sunburned face carefully, then applied the same care to her arms and the scabbing wounds around her wrists. Whether they healed with or without scars, she knew she'd never forget the days of brutality and the sheer terror of Yellow Dog's torturous game with his knife.

The shudders rose from deep inside her. Her fingers trembled and her throat tightened with remembered fear. She closed her eyes and fought the feeling. "He's dead. Gone." Speaking the words aloud gave her an enormous amount of comfort but the damage of those horrible days was irreversible. Breaking free from the despair sliding over her like a dark cloak, Emma removed her soiled and ruined stockings and scrubbed her legs clean from her thighs down to her toes harder than was needed.

Staring at her raggedly torn skirt and pieced-together bodice. She hesitated. If she took off her dress, there was a good chance she'd never get it back on and secure. As it was, she'd had to tear more strips off her hem to keep the bodice secure as the material continued to tear downward. With a sigh, she adjusted the tied strips and washed the best she could without removing the dress.

Not knowing when Star Dreamer would return or where she was to sleep, Emma turned her attention to her hair. With no brush, she used her fingers to comb through the hopelessly snarled strands. It didn't do much good. There was just too much dust and dirt in her hair. She needed to wash it.

The flap opened, letting in a stream of cool air. Emma

scrambled to her feet, but it was only Star Dreamer returning. The woman handed Emma a long dress made of softened deer hide. "This belongs to my sister. I will leave you to change. Tomorrow, you can bathe in the river and wash your hair."

Emma stroked the dress in her arms. Like the wash-cloth she'd used, the garment was butter-soft, pale brown and absolutely beautiful. She held it up, loving the way the fringe dangled from the hem, the yoke and from the sleeves. She fingered the various lengths of fringe then traced one finger along the scalloped yoke. She longed to shed her dirty and disreputable dress and slip into the incredible softness in her arms. Yet, she couldn't. To accept it, and wear it in favor of her own dress, meant accepting her role as a captive, a slave. That she would not do. Her dress might be in shreds but not her pride and dignity. No one could take that from her.

She handed the dress back then clasped her hands behind her back. "Thank you, but I cannot accept this." A long silence filled the tipi. Fearing she'd hurt the other woman's feelings after receiving nothing but considera-tion and kindness, Emma softened her rejection by adding, "It's very beautiful."

Star Dreamer stared at her for long moments. Emma stood her ground. Finally, Star turned aside and set the dress down. "As you wish." Quickly, she spread a pile of furs along one side of the tipi. "Lie down so I may tend your face and wrists. Then, you will sleep. We start our day early."

Emma stretched out on the soft cloud of fur beneath her. While Star Dreamer gently massaged a brownish ointment onto her wrists, she told Emma what to expect come the new day. Barely listening, only bits and pieces penetrated the thickening fog closing in on her. "Prepar-ing the buffalo hides, filling water pouches, gathering firewood, grinding cherries, caring for children—"

It all swam together and made no sense to Emma who could not focus on what Striking Thunder's sister was saying. By the time Star Dreamer finished her wrists and arms, Emma, unable to remain awake, fell into a deep sleep, hardly aware of Star's gentle fingers smoothing healing salve over her face.

When she'd done all she could to ease Emma's injuries, Star Dreamer pulled a thick buffalo-fur robe over the white girl whom she'd seen in her visions. Fetching another thick fur, she draped it around her own shivering shoulders as she stared down at Emma. One day, she'd be family; her *tanke,* sister-in-law. Thinking of Striking Thunder, she smiled. The attraction between them was there. But accepting his future, his fate, ah, that would not come easily or without pain. Moving back to her spot near the fire, she sat huddled beneath the fur's warmth. As the quiet of the night descended, her gaze darted around the shadows of the tipi, seeing past images of her husband. Fresh waves of grief oozed through her veins.

She closed her eyes but quickly opened them when the familiar and nightmarish visions of the past few weeks replayed themselves: the attack of the hunting party, her own husband's death, and finally, the white girl with red hair riding free across the prairie.

Moaning and rocking, she wished Two-Ree were there to comfort her. She hated the gift of sight, fought the onslaught of visions, but most of the time, it did no good. And as the event they warned of grew closer, the visions grew in intensity, came uninvited and without warning. And often, by the time she figured out the hidden meanings, saw what the spirits were trying to tell her with her heart and mind, it was too late.

Like Yellow Dog's attack. By the time she'd warned her brother, it'd been too late and as a result, she'd lost her husband. Guilt mingled with grief. She'd failed. Not only herself and her brother, but her people. If only . . .

Star dropped her head onto her updrawn knees as silent tears streamed down her face. How could she ever hope to make up for the loss of her children's father? Two-Ree had been a loving, kind and gentle father and husband. Turning her face to one side, she glanced at two small, empty pallets near the back of the tipi. Her children were with her mother and father. She wished they were here. She needed to hold them close. Thinking of Morning Moon and Running Elk, a new worry plagued her—raising them alone.

Perhaps she should accept her brother-in-law's offer to take her as his second wife. It was oftentimes the custom when a woman lost her husband. But as quickly as the thought entered, Star discarded it. She had no desire to marry ever again. She had her children, had already seen them as strong, healthy adults and knew she had nothing to fear for them. But her heart? She'd never risk losing her heart to another, not as long as she retained the gift of sight.

How she longed to be like everyone else. Other women had the advantage of being blissfully unaware of their husband's, son's or daughter's deaths. Not her. She'd seen her husband's mortal wounding, felt his pain and the loss of his spirit leaving his body. A cry tore at her throat. No. Never would she go through that again.

Her gaze fell on her sleeping guest. While her visions of this woman were sketchy, she'd known that Emma would be important to their people—and not just for revenge as her brother thought. For that reason, she hadn't said anything to her brother, choosing instead to confide in her husband. If Striking Thunder had known that Emma would one day become his wife, he would never have gone after her. The thought made her smile and forget her own problems for a few precious moments.

Her elder brother was much too serious. She knew him well, knew that he denied himself even the simplest of needs in his quest to put duty first. This woman would teach him much about himself. She also sensed that Emma wasn't what she appeared to be, that she, too, would change and find herself.

Emma moaned in her sleep. "*Renny*—" The name fell from her lips.

Responding to the desperation in Emma's voice, the edges of Star's sight blurred, grayed as a vision took hold. She whimpered, protested. Too many. Too fast. But tonight she was just too tired and spent emotionally to fight them. She closed her eyes and braced herself for more nightmarish revelations of the future.

But this one was different, new, fresh. In her mind's eye, she saw a young girl running across the prairie. She was fast, her legs a blur as she ran in wild abandon. She had red hair, darker, like the burning embers in a fire. As Star watched, the child cried out in glee.

Star smiled and relaxed and absorbed the images and the colors of emotion. The girl was playing with other children—Indian children—her laughter rang out as they all collapsed onto their backs to watch soft white clouds scroll across the blue sky. The appearance of her brother surprised her until she saw him take the child up onto horseback and ride off with her.

Then the vision cleared, bringing with it a sense of peace. Star moved around the fire and tucked the fur around Emma's shoulders, grateful to know that soon, the two sisters would be reunited. "Shhh," she whispered, "your sister is safe." As if she heard the words in her sleep, Emma calmed.

Outside, ignoring the storm, Tanagila paced furiously in the dark, her long black hair whipping side to side. No one, especially some white woman, would take Striking Thunder from her. At fifteen winters, she was now a woman and was determined to take her sister's place as Striking Thunder's second wife. Her brother, Waho, four winters older, had told her why the woman was here, as bait, but that didn't reassure Tanagila. She had only to look upon Striking Thunder's mother to know the dangers of a white woman's presence in their village. Striking Thunder could decide to follow in his father's path.

"What is wrong, Tanagila?"

The deep, husky voice startled her from her thoughts.

She spun around to see a warrior of medium height and build step from the shadows.

Tatankaota, whose name meant "many buffalos," approached, moving on silent feet. "Why do you wander alone in the dark? It is not safe to be out here."

Tanagila's heart sped up but she didn't make much of it. He'd just startled her, that was all. His gaze roamed over her and it pleased her to know he wanted her for his wife. He was one of the most handsome warriors in their village with his strong jaw, high cheekbones and long hawkish nose.

Tatankaota had already made several offers to her father for her, more than any other warrior, but even before her sister was murdered, Tanagila had held hopes of becoming Striking Thunder's second wife. Oftentimes, sisters of the first wife were secured to help the first wife with the many chores and give her companionship when the warriors were out hunting, or warring.

"You were not at your tipi when I came to speak to you." He lifted his arm to reveal his blanket.

Tanagila eyed the blanket and frowned. "I am not in the mood to talk this night. I have much to think about." In reality, she did not want to encourage him. At first, the attention she'd received from him since becoming a woman had pleased her. But his persistence was driving her other suitors away.

Tatankaota squared his shoulders. "I made another offer for you this night."

Frowning, Tanagila chewed her lower lip. Her father was urging her to marry, and Tatankaota, five winters her senior, seemed the most persistent. "I do not wish to marry. I've told my father this."

The warrior, far from being discouraged, grinned. "I've waited long for you, Tanagila. I will wait until you are ready." He looked pleased with himself. "Do you not want to know my offer?"

Curious but refusing to show it, she shrugged. "It matters not. I won't marry you or any other warrior."

He narrowed his eyes. "Even our chief?" His voice dipped, showing the first hint that he wasn't as calm or patient as he pretended.

Her gaze snapped to his. "That is not your concern, Tatankaota."

His confident grin reappeared. "Ah, but it is. You will marry me and only me. I've offered six horses and six buffalo hides as well as some of the white man's tobacco that your father loves. He stepped forward, shook out his blanket, and wrapped it around her damp shoulders. Drawing her close, he brushed her lips with his.

Tanagila's head fell back before she realized what she was doing. His lips touched the pulsing hollow at her throat then trailed up the taut skin to her jaw.

"I won't—" His mouth stopped her flow of words when he claimed her lips in a kiss that lasted no longer than a heartbeat.

"It is not thoughts of our chief that stir your blood, *kechuwa, Tanagila*, my darling hummingbird, who tries to flit from flower to flower." Lifting his head, he ran a finger down the gentle slope of her nose. "Think upon my offer. Don't keep me waiting long. We are wasting needless time. I want you."

Watching him disappear into the darkness, Tanagila felt torn and confused by his actions. Realizing he'd done this to her purposely, she narrowed her gaze, angry at his underhanded methods. She vowed not to have anything to do with Tatankaota, and she'd ask her father to reject his very generous offer.

Chapter Eleven

The sound of a hushed childish voice lured Emma from a
deep sleep. She smiled. Renny, habitually up before the
sun, always bounded into her sister's bedroom to wake
her. "Go 'way, Renny," she moaned, "it's much too
early." After going so long on so little sleep, she longed
to remain abed the rest of the day.

Renny! Emma bolted upright, eyes blurred and heart
pounding. "Renny?" she called, glancing around the cir-
cular enclosure. It took a few minutes to orient herself,
and remember. When her eyes focused, she spotted two
children, a young girl and boy, watching her solemnly
from the open flap of the tipi. Both had straight black
hair. Her back slumped. No Renny.

Emma closed her eyes against the sting of tears and
dropped her forehead onto her knees, willing herself to
be strong. A soft touch to her shoulder made her glance
up warily. A young girl, around Renny's age, stood in
front of her, staring down at her with compassion. The
expression reminded her of the way Star Dreamer had
looked at her the night before, so she assumed this girl
was her daughter and the boy her son. Looking into those
dark eyes that were watching her so intently, Emma had
the strangest feeling this child knew how she felt. Not
wanting to frighten the girl, Emma forced a smile. "What
is your name?"

There was no answer. The boy, around five, shouted
something then ran outside while the girl moved to a pal-

let next to Emma's and sat. Wondering what she should do, Emma stood, remembering first to check her torn bodice and adjust it. Her gaze fell upon the beautiful dress Star Dreamer had offered her last night. She regretted not accepting it; her own dress was soiled beyond repair and wouldn't last much longer.

Using her fingers, she attempted unsuccessfully to untangle her long tresses. Once again, the girl came to her and this time, she held out a comb. Nodding in thanks, Emma took it and ran it through her hair. Feeling only slightly better, she went to stand in the open flap. Her stomach fluttered with nervous anxiety. What was expected of her? She had no idea what to do next.

Once again, her silent watcher came to her rescue by pushing past her and taking her hand to lead her out into the bitterly cold morning. Emma shivered as the air seeped through the thin fabric of her dress, reminding her that winter was fast approaching. Their destination was the river. At the water's edge, Emma spotted a small clump of bushes. Grateful for the privacy, she ducked behind them and relieved herself, using her skirts as a shield. After, she knelt on the wet bank and splashed water over her face, then rolled up her sleeves and washed her hands and arms.

"You may bathe if you like."

Emma glanced over her shoulder at Star Dreamer, who stood next to her daughter. At a softly spoken word from her mother, the child left. Turning her attention back to the water, Emma longed to scrub her body clean of the grime that clung to her, but wasn't about to strip out in the open or enter that cold water. She'd catch her death for sure—if she didn't drown. The river wasn't large but it moved quickly and looked to be deep in the center. She shook her head. "Too cold. I'm fine." From the corner of her eye, she saw Striking Thunder approaching.

Overhearing her refusal to bathe, he frowned. "My people bathe each day. You will join them each morning." He stopped next to his sister.

Emma noted both he and his sister had straight shiny black hair and eyes the color of richly turned earth. She tilted her chin. "I won't bathe in water so cold. I'll catch my death for sure." Lifting a brow, she added, "And you surely wouldn't want that."

Striking Thunder lifted a brow in warning, then pointed to her dress as he addressed his sister in their guttural language. Whatever Star Dreamer replied, it made Striking Thunder's brows lower in displeasure. He folded his arms across his chest. "You were given clean garments last night, were you not?"

Emma's hands fluttered to her chest, self-conscious of the state of her dress but pride dictated that she remain firm to keep what little independence she had. "I prefer to wear my own clothes."

Black brows shot up. Striking Thunder strode forward until only a few feet separated them. "Were you not warned to do as you are told?"

Emma glanced away.

He forced her to look at him by tipping her chin up with one finger. "You will bathe, then change into the clothing given to you. And when *Wi* shows her face once again, you will rise with the others and bathe."

A long-buried rebellion within Emma rose to the surface. She was tired of taking orders, of being told what to do, first by a father who'd destroyed her carefree childhood, and now some savage intent on killing that father. Well, she wouldn't do it. Emma stood her ground.

"I won't bathe in the river."

Without taking his eyes off Emma, Striking Thunder said something to his sister. Star Dreamer hurried away.

Striking Thunder advanced until he stood toe to toe with Emma. With compressed lips, he reached out and turned her around so that she faced the water. Before Emma had a chance to wonder what he was going to do, she heard the rending of cloth seconds before she felt the icy brush of air on her back, from neck to the base of her spine. Screeching in shock, she held the dress to her breasts and rounded on him but he swept an arm around her waist and lifted her off her feet. To her horror, he waded toward the middle of the stream.

Emma panicked and grabbed on to Striking Thunder's shoulders, but he dumped her into the water. She gasped at the shock of the cold water, barely having time to close her mouth before the water closed over her head. She flailed her arms and kicked. Strong hands hauled her up. Coughing and choking, she clung to Striking Thunder. He thumped her on the back, then carried her toward the shallows. Releasing her, he stared down at her. "You will also learn to swim."

Too furious to consider her words, Emma smacked the surface of the water and shouted, "Go to He—"

"Careful, Emma. Do not push me."

A soft voice from the bank drew their attention. Star Dreamer, along with her daughter, stood behind Striking Thunder. He held out his hand. Star Dreamer tossed him a bar of soap. He handed it to Emma. "You will give me the dress."

Seeing no point in further refusal, especially as he'd destroyed the dress completely, and her teeth were starting to clatter, Emma ducked down until the water rose higher than her chest and slid out of her clothing. Hating the look of triumph on his face, she wadded the ruined cloth into a ball then threw it at him. Striking Thunder caught it and left without another word.

An hour later, Emma had to admit she felt better. Not only was she clean, with her hair in two neat plaits, but she was warmer. The dress Star Dreamer had given her had long sleeves and, beneath the long skirt, she wore a pair of fur-lined leggings. On her feet, she wore lined moccasins. When her new mistress called her, she obeyed, after all, it wasn't Star Dreamer's fault her brother was a hateful, arrogant bastard.

Thus began her first day among a tribe of savages.

From her place beside the smoldering cook-fire, White Wind stopped grinding pine nuts for their midday meal and watched the white girl follow her daughter across the camp to where several buffalo skins were pegged to the ground. She wasn't sure how she felt at the sight of a captive woman among them. Their *tiyospaye*, or clan, never took captives.

One pale braid fell across her shoulder. She stared at it. More white than yellow, it reminded her that though she'd lived as an Indian for more than twenty-eight years, she, too, was part white and had once been brought to her husband's tribe against her will as a young woman.

Fondly recalling her first meeting with the golden warrior she'd married, White Wind chuckled softly. The night she'd run away from her loathsome guardian, Golden Eagle had followed her and refused to allow her to continue on her own, alone in the wilderness. Instead, he'd promised protection against her stepfather, and to help locate her true father if she stayed with him. She had stayed, not knowing he was to wed at the end of that summer to a woman of his father's choosing.

Her eyes misted over as she recalled that summer long past. Life had been good, she mused. She had four wonderful children and a new daughter-in-law, her son Wolf's new bride. And soon, she'd have more grandbabies. But even those happy thoughts couldn't erase the worry when she caught her elder son, Striking Thunder, watching the white woman he'd brought to their village. She knew the details and didn't like the situation, not one bit.

Warm hands closed over her shoulders. "Do not interfere, my wife."

White Wind glanced at her husband. "What our son plans is wrong."

"Our son is chief. He will do what is right."

Tilting her chin in a manner that let him know she wasn't going to be put off, White Wind stood. "Yes, my husband. Striking Thunder will do what is right—or deal with his mother." With that, she stalked away.

Golden Eagle glanced skyward and implored the spirits to watch over his family. For the most part, his wife had adapted to the Indian ways, except with regard to family. She tolerated no distance between her and her sons, nor did she hold to the belief that a son fell to the jurisdiction of the father and other male role models. If he or either of their sons did something to displease or disappoint her, she made it very clear and as a rule, the males in his family quickly conceded to her wishes. It was a vast source of amusement to the rest of the tribe.

He was joined by their youngest daughter, White Dove, who sat beside him around the warm fire. In her hands, she held a half-dozen dried and straight shafts for making arrows. Arrows. He shook his head. His daughter's skill in making and shooting them was as good as any of the male warriors in his tribe. Pride filled him. How could she not be, with her aunts instructing her?

Again, his family had broken tradition. Both his sister Winona, and his wife's sister Wildflower, had been raised in an unorthodox manner—and both had encouraged Dove to master skills boys learned, whenever they visited. He sat a bit straighter. Of course, he too, took pride in Dove's natural ability. She'd learned from the best—him.

"Mother is angry."

Golden Eagle met his daughter's sparkling hazel eyes with a lift of his brow. "Angry is not what I'd use to describe your mother's feelings on this subject."

Dove grinned. "I'd hate to be my brother right now." She pointed at White Wind and Striking Thunder.

Golden Eagle spotted his wife and son arguing. He stood. "We need meat for the evening meal."

Standing as well, Dove lifted a brow in perfect imitation of her father. "Coward."

Glancing over his shoulder, Golden Eagle vowed to stay away for the rest of the day. He eyed Dove. "You coming or staying?"

Grinning, Dove followed him into their tipi and fetched her quiver of arrows and bow. "I'm no fool."

* * *

134

Striking Thunder watched Emma. Kneeling on the cold ground, she rubbed the cooked brains of the buffalo into a hide stretched between wooden pegs. He was somewhat surprised to see her dipping her hands into the mixture that would make the hide supple. He'd have expected her to refuse, finding it much too disgusting as most white women would have.

The white woman worked well and wasn't giving Star trouble; he had no reason to stand watching her. He had work to do—warrior's work—yet when he forced his feet into motion, they led him closer to the woman. Near her, Star and Morning Moon removed flesh and hair from another hide. Their last hunt had been successful. He drew in a deep breath, reminded that he'd also lost his wife and others had lost their loved ones during that outing. He put his grief aside to be dealt with later.

Emma stood and stretched, drawing his gaze to her figure. The buckskin dress, belted around her waist with a strip of leather, revealed a figure with nicely rounded hips, full breasts, long legs and nicely shaped calves. Most Indian women were shorter, but on Emma, the added inches enhanced her feminine form.

She turned, as if sensing his presence. Their gazes clashed. With a look of dislike, she stepped around to the other side of the hide, pointedly ignoring him. Unable to allow the challenge to go unheeded, he followed and stood close. She worked the white paste into the hide, ignoring him.

He should have been pleased, but the fact that thoughts of her kept him from his business irritated him. Her hands shook, belying her appearance of calm and when she clumsily spilled some of the precious mixture, he felt better. She wasn't unaware of him, either.

Finally, she turned to him. "Must you stand there? It's cold and I wish to finish so I can wash my hands of this . . . this icky stuff." She rubbed her fingers together.

Striking Thunder pointed to the spilled patch of white

soaking into the earth. "Each animal has only enough brains to tan itself. Be careful not waste it."

Emma's jaw dropped as she turned her hands over and stared at them. "What did you say?"

Striking Thunder indicated her grayish-white hands. "Brains. We use the animal's brains to soften its skin. They are precious and are not to be wasted."

Seeing the color fleeing her face, Striking Thunder raised an eyebrow, amused. "My sister did not tell you what it is you are using?"

"N-no. She didn't," she whispered. Lifting her gaze to his, her eyes suddenly rolled back in her head.

When her body crumpled, he reached out and caught her. All feelings of triumph fled at her reaction. Yes, he'd wanted to shock her, wipe that haughty look from her face, but not make her faint. Now what?

His mother shoved past him. Her furious bright-blue eyes glared at him. "Fetch water."

Striking Thunder did as he was bid. In minutes, Emma came to. Her hands had been washed clean of the brain-and-sage mixture. Sitting, she took several deep breaths then burst into tears. In over his head with a weeping female, he took a step back, but at the look White Wind sent him, he stopped. Star Dreamer rushed over, and when she learned what had happened, sent him a look that he knew well. She led Emma away, leaving mother and son alone.

White Wind stood. "I will speak to you, my son." She walked away from the gathered crowd.

Though he was a grown man and chief of their tribe, Striking Thunder felt like an errant boy about to be shamed. But nothing she said would change his mind. Though she wasn't happy about Emma and the circumstances in which he'd brought her to the village, she would just have to accept it.

"You should be ashamed of yourself for what you did—and for what you did to her earlier down at the river. You should never have brought her here. I ask you to release her; return her to her people and forgo this plan of revenge. It is not right."

Striking Thunder clasped his hands behind his back and unlike most Sioux men, he met her gaze squarely with his own. "I respect you, Mother. You are wise, but the white girl is none of your concern. I am chief. I will decide what is right."

Keeping his features impassive, he winced inwardly at the look of fury on her face. From the corner of his eye, he saw his father and sister ride away. He wished he dared to ride after them. He stifled a sigh. Chief or not, when his mother was determined to have her say, nothing stopped her.

"I am disappointed in you, my son. More violence and killing will not bring your wife back. The white woman had nothing to do with the killing of her or the others."

He sighed. "I know this and for that, I have promised no harm would come to her. She will be returned to her people unharmed."

"And that will put her mind and heart at ease when she knows you plan to use her to kill her father? What if her father is innocent of the crimes Yellow Dog accuses him of committing?"

"I know the truth."

"Do you? And if you are wrong? What then? What of her?"

Tired of having his judgment questioned by the women who surrounded him, he held up his hand. "Enough. I will not release her or be swayed by emotion. I am a warrior. I have responsibilities to our people. We are fair. I will give the white woman's father a chance to prove his innocence. If he cannot, he will die. The needs of The People will be met."

White Wind's gaze held a hint of troubled sorrow. "And what of your needs? When will you tend to those?"

As he'd done, she held her hand up when he opened his mouth to remind her that avenging his wife's death was one of his needs.

137

"Do not say it." Her gaze softened. "Think you that this mother does not know you married Meadowlark to appease the council who wished to see their young chief married and settled? Though you found some happiness with her, she did not lay claim to your heart. A mother knows this, so do not try to tell me otherwise."

Striking Thunder didn't bother to deny it. She was right. "That has nothing to do with the girl or what will be."

"True. I cannot force you to change your mind, but I will have your promise that you will keep her from harm. At least you had the good sense to give her to Star. I've heard Waho's grumbles. He and his sister are very angry about your decision."

Striking Thunder reached out to tug gently at one of his mother's long braids. Always, the color—or lack thereof—fascinated him. "My mother will not worry. This chief will deal with Waho and will keep the woman called Emma safe. He has already given his word."

White Wind's gaze sharpened. "Do not think I haven't seen you watching her with that same hunger as many other warriors in our village. I expect my son to keep her safe from all, including himself." They stared at each other in silence. Finally, without another word, White Wind walked away.

Striking Thunder turned his glare toward the white woman. Her hair, bright in the afternoon light lit a fire in his loins. He hated to admit, even to himself, that his mother was right. He wanted nothing more than to take Emma to his sleeping mat and make her his. He was grateful his mother had not extracted a promise from him. He wasn't sure he would have been able to give it.

Chapter Twelve

Sitting in the cool shade, Emma leaned against the side of a tipi, her stomach still queasy from the discovery that she'd had her hands up to her elbows in boiled brains. Drawing her knees to her chest, Emma hugged them tightly, feeling weak and washed-out after her hysterical bout of tears.

Frowning, she fought both embarrassment and humiliation. She'd never fainted and seldom cried. But since leaving the *Annabella*, everything had changed. How could she endure this? She wasn't cut out for this sort of life. Despair brought fresh tears to her eyes. How would she make it until March? She couldn't scrape flesh and hair from hides, skin animals or—she shuddered—rub brains into the skins. And God only knew what else they'd ask her to do.

Her resentment toward Striking Thunder grew. He'd known perfectly well she didn't have any idea what she'd been rubbing into that skin and had purposely set out to shock and humiliate her. Her gaze shifted to where he and a woman with white braids argued. Who was she? Like the other women, she dressed in a simple, unadorned dress made from softened hides but her hair held faint traces of pale yellow. She wasn't Indian. Was she a captive, too? Observing her and Striking Thunder, Emma could tell neither was happy with the other.

The woman spun away and Striking Thunder glanced over his shoulder and speared Emma with a look of displeasure. Whatever they argued about concerned her. Good. Emma hoped the woman made his life difficult. He deserved it for doing this to her. She sent him a pleased smirk and had the pleasure of watching him stalk off.

Her stomach settled, and her resolve returned. She'd survive—somehow. Turning her thoughts from the horrible experience, she took the opportunity to study her surroundings. The village was alive with activity. Several women sat and gossiped while grinding nuts and dried berries, others stooped over the funny-looking pouches that hung from tripods. Steam and aromatic scents rose from them. Earlier, she'd watched a woman bent-over with age add water and hot rocks to one of the pouches. This was apparently how they cooked their stews and heated water. Emma grimaced and decided she didn't want to know where the elastic pale pouches came from.

But what amazed her were the children. Even in the cooling weather, most ran around naked. From one group of women or men to another they would hurry. Some reached out to sample food being fixed or just plopped into an empty lap. No one minded. Three small naked boys ran in front of her. They stopped as one and stared at her, their eyes wide. Hesitantly, she smiled. Their round, brown faces split into huge grins. The bravest one came close. He reached out and touched her braid, then jumped back as if afraid he would burn himself.

Finding relief in such innocence, Emma laughed softly and held out her long braid. The other two bravely stretched out their arms to touch the red rope. All three broke into excited speech then ran off, shouting to a group of older boys. But when she spotted Morning Moon and three other girls playing with miniature tipis and dolls, she thought of Renny and her two favorite dolls, the ones that had once been Emma's and were locked in the trunk aboard the *Annabella*. Renny would love to have an Indian doll and tipi to play with.

"Where are you Renny?" she asked quietly. "Are you well?" Was her sister being taken care of? Fed? Treated well? From what Emma saw here, the Indian people cared a great deal for children—but what about a white child? Would they treat her as a slave and mistreat her?

Morning Moon glanced up. Emma stared into her wide, far-too-serious dark eyes. The girl stood and came to Emma. She removed a long beaded necklace from her neck and silently slipped it over Emma's head. With one last solemn look, she ran back to her friends.

Fingering the beaded gift, Emma studied the design. A round leather medallion with two stick figures beaded into the center hung from a narrow strip of leather. The figures, one tall, one shorter stood with their hands clasped. Emma felt her throat clog. It reminded her of a mother and daughter. Or two sisters, one older, one younger. She stroked the intricate patterns of color circling the two figures, and felt a strange sense of hope and peace steal over her. One day, she and Renny would be reunited.

Startled by the thought that seemed to come from nowhere, she glanced back at Morning Moon. How had the girl known? Staring at the gift, Emma shook her head. Of course she hadn't. It was just wishful thinking on her part, the need to believe that she'd find Renny. The two figures hanging between her breasts must represent Morning Moon and her mother. Emma decided later she'd make sure that the girl hadn't given away something she shouldn't have.

A shadow fell over her and destroyed her moment of peace. "The white girl is weak. Lazy. Cannot do woman's work." Tanagila stared down at her with contempt, then said something to her companion, a girl of the same age but several inches shorter and a lot rounder. The two laughed and walked away.

Emma glared after her. "I do plenty of woman's work," she muttered, thinking about the town house and all it took to run it with only two trusted servants: a housekeeper and cook who were more family than hired help. But even with them, Emma had done her share of housework, shopping and planning the meals. And she hadn't had a nanny. Care of her sister had fallen to her. Careful not to think about how she'd failed at that one, she focused on her fainting attack. "I just never had to do this kind of disgusting work."

Though Star Dreamer had told her not to worry, that someone else would finish the hide, Emma felt guilty watching the other women working hard in the sun. She tried to tell herself she wasn't one of them, that she didn't have to do this kind of work, but some spark of pride took hold. She'd never been accused of being lazy in her life.

Across the way, Tanagila stopped at the hide Emma had been working on. She threw another contemptuous look at Emma, tossed her head and picked up the wooden bowl holding the boiled-brain mixture. The message was clear: Tanagila was pointing out to the others that Emma couldn't do her job, couldn't pull her weight.

Emma stood. Darned if she'd allow that hateful girl to think she was superior just because she could stick her hands in a bowl of icky white stuff. She'd show them that she, Emma O'Brien, was no pampered white woman. She could do anything they could.

Overhead, a loud caw sounded. Glancing up, she spotted a raven perched on one of the poles sticking out from the top of the tipi. It flapped its wings and cocked its head, its beady eye fixed on her hair. She shook her finger at the bird. "Don't think it." For some reason, Striking Thunder's bird liked her hair and when it got the chance, it tried to yank strands from her head.

Reaching Tanagila, she snatched the bowl from her. "I finish what I start." Ignoring the girl and those around her, Emma drew in a deep breath, and willed herself not to think about what she was touching. *Pretend it's paste,* she ordered herself. White paint, flour and water, anything.

Holding her breath, she dipped her fingers in, knelt and resumed her task.

Early the next morning, Emma rose stiffly when called. She ached from her neck to her calves from the hard work. Yawning, wishing she could have snatched a few more hours of sleep, she followed Star Dreamer and her children out of the tipi. There, they were greeted by two women, one older, one younger. Emma was surprised to see the white woman who'd argued with Striking Thunder yesterday. Her eyes were a startling deep blue.

Star spoke. "This is my mother, White Wind."

"Your mother?" Emma's jaw dropped as she glanced from Star, who looked like the other Indian woman, back to her mother. "That means you're also Striking Thunder's moth—" Horrifed, she clamped her mouth shut.

White Wind laughed softly. "Yes. Striking Thunder is my son."

At her side, a younger woman with hair the color of rich maple syrup grinned, her eyes, a paler blue, sparkled with mischief. "I am White Dove, younger sister to Striking Thunder."

She leaned forward to whisper, "I know it is hard to believe to look upon us, but white blood runs in our veins, though, I think my brother Striking Thunder rejected his white heritage, even in the womb. From the time he entered this world, he has denied that part of him." At a frown from her mother, Dove stepped back with a shrug of her slim shoulders. "It's no secret how he feels," she said, not looking the least bit repentant.

"Dove, behave yourself," White Wind scolded, her voice firm.

The three women fell into their native tongue, which was fine with Emma. It gave her a chance to absorb the fact that Striking Thunder's mother was white. Maybe she'd be able to enlist the woman's help. If she and her son had been arguing about Emma yesterday, then she couldn't be too happy with him.

When they reached the edge of the water, the women removed their clothing. Dove ran out into the middle of the stream to greet her friends while Star Dreamer saw to the bathing of her children in the shallows. Emma hesitated, unable to imagine bathing so early in the cold water, let alone stripping down and bathing in a group. It seemed so strange and barbaric. And to bathe both mornings and evenings!

White Wind removed her fur-lined leggings. She smiled encouragingly at Emma. "It's not as bad as it seems. You'll get used to it."

Not sure if she could go through with it but wanting to keep White Wind near to talk to, to find out where she stood, Emma sat and slowly removed her moccasins, wincing as each movement stretched her sore, stiff muscles.

"You are in pain?"

"Just a bit achy, that's all." Emma rotated her stiff shoulders and stretched out her arms. "I'm not used to tanning hides." She eyed the flowing river. "A hot bath definitely sounds much better."

White Wind sighed. "Ah yes. I do enjoy them still."

At Emma's look, she confessed, "When I go to visit my other son who lives in the cabin I grew up in, I do indulge myself in hot baths. But here, we bathe in the river. You will learn that nothing is wasted, not food or water or time and energy. These women wouldn't think the time it takes to haul water and heat it and pour it into a tub worth the effort—even if they were willing to carry around a tub. Moving as we do from camp to camp makes it impossible."

Emma studied Striking Thunder's mother. "Are you here against your will?"

After a moment, White Wind sighed. "No, child. I'm here because I chose to be." She spread her hands. "Understand that while I don't agree with my son for bringing you here or even agree with his plans, I am Indian."

At Emma's disbelief, she smiled.

"My father is White Cloud of the Hunkpapa tribe of the Sioux. Many years ago, I, too, was brought here against my will. I know how you feel, but there is nothing I can do to help you."

Emma's shoulders sagged. "I understand."

White Wind bent down to touch her shoulder. "No, child, you do not." She waved a hand toward the women in the water. "These women are my family and friends. I may have been unwilling in the beginning, but I chose to stay and adopt the lifestyle of my father's people. I am one of them. By choice."

"I won't stay. Striking Thunder is wrong about my father." Emma said the words bravely, defiantly.

Removing her dress, White Wind's blue eyes darkened. "Like his father, my son is a good man."

Emma rejected the statement with a shake of her head. "I don't believe you. He only cares about what he wants. He doesn't care that my sister who is only nine years old is out there alone somewhere. If he cared, he'd help her, at least find her and bring her to me so that when I'm released, we will be free together." Her voice broke and to hide her futile tears, she turned her head to the side.

White Wind sighed. "I truly wish I could help, child. I will give you this, and hope it brings some measure of comfort. My people revere children—all children, no matter the skin color. The horses Yellow Dog traded her for are Cheyenne. They, like the Sioux, treasure children. Be assured that your sister will be treated as any other child." With that, White Wind waded out to join the women, leaving Emma alone with her thoughts.

"No one help you, white girl." Tanagila laughed and walked past. After dumping her clothing in a neat pile out of reach of the water, she entered the river without hesitation and smirked at Emma as she ran her hands down her slender waist before submerging herself beneath the gently flowing river.

Though she hadn't said a word, Emma felt the sting of her challenge. The other girl assumed Emma was ashamed of her white body. Well, she wasn't. She knew enough of

145

men to know they appreciated her curves and the size of her breasts. She'd show Tanagila and the rest. If they weren't ashamed of their bodies, then neither was she.

She lifted her skirt, hesitating one last time, battling her shyness. Gathering her courage, she pulled her dress over her head. Fingers of cold air brushed her skin and puckered her nipples. Feeling conspicuous with flesh so pale and breasts much fuller than most of the women present, Emma ran into the water and quickly submerged herself beneath the freezing-cold river.

To her relief, no one paid her any mind. Around her, female chatter and laughter filled the air. There was a great deal of splashing and joking. Some of the women even swam, ducking their heads beneath the surface. Emma admired their oneness with the water.

Keeping to the shallows, she washed, dunking her head to wet her hair, then washing it using the root of the yucca plant Star Dreamer had swam over to give her. By the time she was done, her teeth were chattering so hard her jaw hurt with the effort to still them. Working up the courage to stand and leave the water, Emma was startled when a sleek, dark head surfaced unexpectedly near her. Tanagila rose from water. Leaning forward, she hissed, "You not belong here." Hate filled the young maiden's eyes.

Tired of the girl's harassment, Emma narrowed her own eyes and stood, pleased she had several inches' advantage over the shorter Indian maiden. "You think I'm here of my own free will?"

"Leave."

Emma snorted her disgust. "I'm just going to walk out of the village and no one will stop me?"

"Tanagila help you. Meet here tonight. I bring you horse."

Not trusting the Indian girl, Emma left the water to dry herself off. Tanagila followed.

Sending Tanagila a look of disgust, she asked, "Do

you really expect me to trust you? Besides, Striking Thunder isn't going to let me go. He'll follow."

A sly look came into the other girl's eyes. "I will make sure he does not know you are gone. I will say that it is your woman's time, that you are in the woman's hut."

Emma wanted nothing more than to make good her escape but when she did, it'd be on her own without anyone—especially a troublemaker—knowing. "No. I shall stay and convince Striking Thunder that he is wrong about my father."

"You are a fool." Her expression changed to one of malicious delight. "After he kills your father, he'll sell you for many horses." Tossing her hair, sending drops of water flying into Emma's face, she stalked off.

Biting her lip, Emma watched her go. A small hand slipped into her own. Glancing down, she stared into Morning Moon's troubled gaze.

"She lies, seeks to trick you like *sungmanitu,* the wily coyote. You are wise, like *sunkmanitu tanka,* the wolf." A funny look crossed the girl's features and for just a moment, her eyes went blank.

Worried, Emma bent down. "Morning Moon?"

The little girl started and pulled her hand out of Emma's. "I will watch over you." With that, she walked off.

What a strange comment for a child to make, Emma thought. Morning Moon was so different from her own energetic sister. She fingered the talisman that the child had given her and wondered if she'd ever see Renny again.

Lying in bed, Derek cursed his carelessness. It had been eight days since his carefully laid plans had gone awry. So far, there had been no word from the search party. And when it came, he feared the news wouldn't be good. Emma would never survive captivity with Yellow Dog. Derek shoved the rough, itchy blanket off him and stood. He had plans to make.

147

Doctor Gilbert O'Sullivan, a seasoned physician who had been with the Army for more than thirty years, stopped him from walking out the door. "Captain Sanders. You have not been given permission to leave that bed."

Derek frowned. "I'm fine. I need to be out there, searching."

Gil's features softened. "Now, boy, you can't blame yourself. You did the best you could. You're in no shape to ride out."

"I can't stay in bed a minute longer."

Not one to overly pamper his patients, the doctor nodded. "Fine. But until your wounds have completely healed, I want to see you each morning."

Derek nodded then left. After dressing in a new uniform, he left the fort through the open gate. When he arrived at a small group of soiled and tattered tipis, he stopped. From inside several came the sound of rutting men and squealing women.

The women who occupied these tipis relied on soldiers to give them work—laundry or prostitution—both appreciated by the lonely soldiers far from civilization. Some soldiers even went so far as to marry their whores.

His mouth hardened. Not him. Not like his traitorous father who'd left him and his mother to go to California with his squaw in search of gold. When *he* married, it'd be to a lady who had money or connections. Or both. Like Emma. He put thoughts of Emma from him when he reached Wild Sage's tipi.

Grunts and moans came from within. Without bothering to announce himself, he strode in, surprising a soldier in the process of bedding the tipi's mistress. Derek fingered the bag of cheap baubles he'd picked up from traders traveling up the Missouri River then jerked his thumb over his shoulder. "Out!" He ordered the private.

A look of intense pain crossed the young soldier's features. "Aw, Cap'n, not now—" he groaned, his hips moving faster, frantic.

Derek reached out and yanked the panting man off the

woman bucking beneath him. "I said out. Now!" He tossed him out the door along with his trousers and boots and ignored the laughter that came from others who had witnessed the soldier's plight.

Unbuckling his own trousers, but not removing them, he knelt over the woman. Reaching out, he squeezed one plump breast. At her moan of pain, lust fired his blood. "Have you missed me, Wild Sage?"

Her brown eyes widened when he pinched a dark-tipped nipple, but she nodded and knowing what he expected, she took his hard shaft into her mouth. Derek groaned, it'd been so long, he couldn't stop the release that came almost immediately.

After he refastened his trousers, he reached into his shirt pocket for a pouch.

Emptying it onto the dirt floor, he watched Wild Sage's eyes grow round with greed. But when she scrambled to her knees to take the cheap jewelry, he grabbed her pudgy fingers.

"Not so fast." Scooping them up, he handed her a bracelet and pin. "Do as I say and I'll give you the rest."

Wild Sage nodded. "Wild Sage please Captain, Captain give Wild Sage many nice things."

Derek paced. "I seek information on a woman captured by Yellow Dog."

At the name, a look of fear entered her eyes. Though they weren't of the same tribe, everyone in this area knew of the warrior. "Yellow Dog mean. He kill Wild Sage if I help enemy."

He waved her fear aside and clasped his hands behind his back. "The woman is the colonel's daughter. I will protect you, but I need to know where she is, if she is still alive. You will find out for me."

When she still looked reluctant, Derek grabbed a handful of her hair. "Do it or I'll see you banished from the fort." His gaze hardened. "Without the protection of the soldiers, anything could happen to you." His voice dropped, low and cold. "Understand?"

"Wild Sage understands."

Laughing softly, Derek pulled her long stringy hair just hard enough to force her to look at him. "Good. Now understand this. You're mine and I don't share my squaw with anyone. You want to spread your legs, you spread them for me."

Again she nodded but it wasn't enough. He yanked, harder.

"Only you, Captain. Wild Sage please only you."

Freeing his swollen flesh once more, he smiled and shoved her down onto the hard ground. Dropping his trousers, he shoved her legs apart. "Very good, bitch. Now would be a good time to show me how much you missed me."

Chapter Thirteen

The land of rich, summer golds turned brittle and dull as fall prepared to give way to winter. Temperatures rose and fell wildly, as if Mother Nature couldn't make up her mind as to which season she preferred.

Wandering freely around the village, Emma tipped her head back, seeking the warming rays. She suspected the first snows weren't far off. The last couple of weeks had been rainy, cloudy and cold. Hugging herself, she stared up into the brilliant blue sky, finding in it a renewed sense of hope that one day, her life would return to normal.

She shivered as much from the temperature as from fear of what her future held. That morning when she'd gone down to the river to bathe, the dry grass had crackled under the thin layer of frost coating the prairie, and still they had bathed. To her surprise, no one, including her, had taken ill from the exposure.

And if she really were honest, she'd admit there was something invigorating about starting the day in this fashion. Unlike bathing in hot water, which tended to relax and leave her lethargic, cold water got her moving with a spurt of energy that seemed to carry her throughout the day.

In addition to her deerskin dress, she wore a pair of leggings lined with rabbit fur and her feet were kept warm in a pair of lined moccasins made by her own hands. The soft, pliable upper pieces came from the hides she'd prepared, as did her leggings, and the soles from an old smoked top of a tipi. Even the rabbit fur lining them came from her efforts. And if the fur was pieced together because she'd torn it during the skinning process, well, only she knew—and Star who'd had incredible patience in teaching her what she needed to know.

Passing a group of adolescent girls, Emma noticed they were studying a group of boys the same age. She smiled. Some things were the same no matter the language or lifestyle. This was her favorite time of day. Done with her chores until time to start the evening meal, she had the freedom to do as she chose—unless she wanted to ride.

She made a face. She wasn't allowed near the horses. She stopped in front of a colorful tipi. So far, her favorite pastime was to study the paintings on the bleached rawhide. Some consisted of crude drawings, childlike in their form, while others were quite good, their painter a skilled artist.

Sighing, she wished she knew what each symbol meant, what story it told, but sheer stubbornness kept her from asking and taking advantage of the opportunity to learn about a different culture by experience rather than from a book or newspaper account.

Showing interest might make it seem as though she had accepted her role of captive—and that she refused to do. She did what was expected of her, mostly because Star was kind to her and Emma didn't want to be a burden to the grieving woman. Many nights, Emma woke to the sound of soft tears. She also acknowledged that she could be treated far worse if she rebelled so she'd slid into the routine demanded of her, embracing the hard work so that each night, she fell into bed too exhausted to lie awake and worry over the future.

But most of the labor required of the Indian women was repetitive and mindless. It left her free to think— too much sometimes—while she worked. Stopping at the edge of the village, she stared across the prairie, praying her father would find her before the snows made searching impossible. That was her only hope. He had to find her before Striking Thunder had time to prepare his trap. Not once did she allow herself to question whether her father was out searching. For her own sanity, she had to believe he was.

The long afternoon loomed before her. If she were home, she'd have spent the afternoon curled up in her favorite chair in front of a fire in her mother's parlor, or if the day was particularly fine, she'd have spent a couple hours in the park with her paints. Even that option was out. She didn't have a pencil or even paper to sketch with and wasn't about to ask for the use of their Indian dyes.

Walking past a group of older men telling stories to children of all ages, she smiled. Some of the youngest ones had fallen asleep, pillowing their heads in the lap of an older child beside them. Too bad she didn't understand enough of the language to listen from a distance.

Emma glanced around the quiet village. Different groups of women and girls of all ages chatted as they sewed or made sinew. Others sat around just visiting. She supposed she could join Star and her group and learn to bead and quill but she shied away from becoming involved any more than what was required of her. To join them in this social time meant encouraging friendliness, which risked forming attachments. And first chance she got, she planned to leave. She thought of the stash of dried meat and berries hidden among her things. Unlike Striking Thunder's mother, she wasn't going to be here long enough to adopt this way of life.

Pulling the end of her belt up, Emma counted the tiny lines she'd scored on one side. One for each day since Striking Thunder had found her. She figured it had to be near the end of October, now. Mentally, she ticked off the months. Six more to go before Striking Thunder released her. Six before he planned to kill her father. Six before she could arrange a search party for her sister.

Rounding another tipi, she came to an abrupt halt. Her absentminded meanderings had led her to the back of Striking Thunder's tipi. And it was just her luck that he was there, painting a scene on the bleached hide. She grimaced. Though Star Dreamer wasn't demanding, Striking Thunder made sure she was always kept busy.

Though he seldom spoke to her and never openly criticized her, his watchful silence spoke more than words when she did wrong; like the time when she'd torn a hole in the hide she was scraping because she wasn't being careful, or whenever she burned a meal. And it wasn't just him either. Others made their feelings known just by their silence. But as she improved, she'd also felt their unspoken praise.

This method of not openly criticizing one another was a major difference between the Indian world and hers. Being shamed and feeling humiliated among one's peers was a far better tool than words raised in anger. It was much more subtle, and more compelling.

Leave, she commanded herself. The last thing she needed was another encounter with the arrogant warrior. But she didn't leave. Running Elk hurried up to his uncle and without any sign of impatience, Striking Thunder stopped what he was doing. The sight of him crouched down with his arms around his nephew held her enthralled. He was teaching the boy how to shoot his bow and arrows.

Emma grinned. Running Elk never put the bow down, he even slept with his prized possession. From the cadence of Striking Thunder's voice, she knew he was telling the child another story, a form of instruction, she'd come to realize. Sliding into the dark shadows between two tipis, she watched. Despite her resentment of Striking Thunder, she admired his patience with the young and his concern and respect of the elderly.

Running Elk shot off an arrow. It flew straight and true, landing a short ways away. The boy ran off to fetch it, shouting his happiness. Striking Thunder stood, smiling. The love and pride on his face touched a deep chord within her. With a start, she realized that because he thought himself alone, he'd lowered his guard.

Her own pulse quickened. The softening of his features made him one handsome man to look upon. Especially when he only wore his breechclout and left his hair unbraided as it was now. She loved his hair. Long, baby-fine, it fell in ripples halfway down his bare, golden back. Her fingers itched to go to him and feel its silky texture. Alarmed by the urge, she took a step back to beat a hasty retreat before he found her watching him. But without turning to face her, Striking Thunder spoke. "Do you not have work to do?"

Embarrassed to be caught staring at him, Emma's good mood shifted. Her first impulse was to turn tail and leave before he found more work for her. No. She was fed up with his constant hounding. She did her share of work and was entitled to her share of free time. So she sauntered over. "Nope. I'm free to spend the afternoon as *I* like. *Star* thinks I work hard."

Dipping one end of a slender bone into the paint, Striking Thunder returned to his work. "My sister is far too easy on you. As you have nothing to do but stand around, you may fill my water pouches and fetch more wood for the fire. That should keep you busy until time to prepare the evening meal."

Narrowing her eyes, Emma decided it was time to play the game. She kept her eyes trained on the figures and shapes decorating his tipi. "Star Dreamer is kind, thoughtful and fair. Something her brother is not. He would take away this woman's free time when she has earned it."

Startled at her show of defiance and her method of turning the tables on him, Striking Thunder glanced at her. She meet his gaze. Green eyes clashed with brown. He grunted and went back to his work. "Then you will do as I've asked later."

Pleased to have won that round even if it meant more work later, Emma walked around him to study another scene. She recognized his black raven and was impressed by the lifelike effect of the bird soaring over the taut hide with a herd of buffalo running below. She glanced up. The bird wasn't in sight. Good. The stupid raven was always swooping down to try and pluck her braid.

Moving on to another scene, she lifted her brows at a brown hawk, eyes closed, its wings pulled back as it arrowed down the canvas from a gray cloud as if about to strike an unseen target. Next to it, Striking Thunder had painted the same bird with its beak wide open. And from brilliant golden eyes, jagged bolts of lightning flashed into the dark sky painted around it. The bird looked fierce and angry. She slid her eyes sideways. Much like the artist who'd drawn it.

"You're good," she admitted grudgingly, moving on to the scene he was currently painting. It showed two warriors. One with his fist held high in victory, the other, crumpled at the victor's feet. Looking closer, seeing the yellow-painted face, she realized the slain warrior was Yellow Dog. She shuddered and stepped back as if the slain warrior could still reach out and do her harm. And in a way, he still could. Nightmares from those terror-filled days still haunted her. "Rather violent for my tastes, but good."

Striking Thunder ignored her comment. Pointing to a fort surrounded by wagons and people, she asked, "What's this one about?"

Expelling an exasperated breath, Striking Thunder glared at her. "Do you not have anything else to do?"

Emma glanced over her shoulder at him, pleased to have irritated him. Normally in her presence, he remained stoic and unemotional, barking out his orders. She held up one hand and ticked off her fingers. "Let's see. No books lying around to read. No carriages to take me shopping. No balls to attend. No letters to write. No mail service, even if there were and," her voice broke slightly, "and no little sister to chase after. So no, guess there's not much to do out in this barren, godforsaken land."

Using the sharp bone he used as a brush as a pointer, Striking Thunder indicated various groups of women sewing or painting quills. "There is much you could do instead of asking questions of this warrior."

Emma lifted her shoulder. "Why bother? By the time I master those skills, I'll be gone. When I return to St. Louis, I won't have need of deerskin dresses."

Striking Thunder narrowed his eyes, a sure sign that she was pushing his patience. Good. How many times since her arrival had he driven her to the point of anger, knowing full well she couldn't say anything?"

Setting the bone down, he regarded her with contempt. "No. You'll return to a life centered on proving how much better you are than your neighbor. You'll go about each day without realizing all you have to be thankful for in your quest for more. And you won't care about the cost to the land or the people, as long as you have what you want in your search for happiness."

His counterattack stung. "That's not true."

"No? How many dresses hang in your closet? How much material is wasted by clothing thrown out because the styles change each season? How many women wear a garment only once and discard it?

"Your people seek *things* to make them happy, to make them feel important yet most of it sits and gathers dust. Always, the white man has need for more. Bigger houses. More land. More wealth. Look around you. We only have what we need."

Slapping her hands on her hips, Emma glared at him. "It's not fair to compare us. We live differently. You can't judge us because we don't live as—"

"Savages?" He bit out the word. Placing his hands on her shoulders, he spun her around to face the rest of the village. "Look around you, Emma. We have so little, and yes, we live primitively by your standards, yet all we need

157

is here. We are rich in our *lives*, not in our bank accounts. It is people and families we value, not objects. You think you live a superior life, but you are no happier."

What he said was true. His people were not only happy but content. She shrugged free of his disturbing hold. "How do you know so much about it?"

Striking Thunder grinned and looked pleased with himself. "It is wise to learn all one can about your enemy. Do we not know how each animal lives? We study them, learn from them and use the knowledge they give us." His grin turned wolfish. "With the whites, it is no different."

Turning serious, he stared over her head, his eyes coming to rest on each of the people in his village. "My mother made sure her children were educated in both their Indian and white heritage. Each spring, my brother White Wolf, who lives among the whites, and I go to your towns to trade and buy supplies. There, I see your houses of wood and stores filled with goods and places where men drink your spirits and leave swaying on their feet. Are they happy with their minds clouded by alcohol?"

Emma paced. "Some may not be happy, but most are."

"And you, Emma. Were you happy in your house of wood?"

The question took her by surprise. It was the first time he'd asked her a personal question. And it struck a raw nerve. For only here had she begun to see that in truth, she'd been very unsatisfied with her life. Out here, there were no restrictive conventions. Here one could, and was encouraged to, speak one's mind. And for reasons she didn't understand, though she was a captive, she felt free for the first time in her life.

She did not admit any of this to Striking Thunder. She squared her shoulders and lifted her chin. "Of course I was happy. It was my life, one taken from me first by Yellow Dog then by you."

Striking Thunder's features gentled, his eyes softening. "Then why did you leave your home? What drove you to travel a long distance to a land unsafe for white women?

Do not lie and tell me you were happy, Emma. In your eyes, I see it isn't so."

Mesmerized by the unexpected tenderness in him, she whispered, "You wouldn't understand or care." Some part of her wanted him to care. This was a side of Striking Thunder she hadn't seen. Not only had he backed down on his orders—by action if not by words—but he allowed her to voice her views, allowing her to come to her own conclusions. But his insight into her own heart left her reeling and wishing that he truly did care.

Striking Thunder reached out to finger one golden-red braid. "That is where you are wrong, white woman. There is much about you this warrior understands." Tugging gently on her braid, he drew her close. Tucked out of sight from the others, they stared at each other, devoured each other with heated gazes. Emma held her breath. With his gaze alone, she felt kissed. But it wasn't enough. He'd touched her mind and heart, now she wanted him. His mouth hovered just over hers. Their breaths mingled, hot and sweet.

His hand slid from her braid to the back of her neck. She leaned into that warm hand and waited, her lips parting with breathless anticipation. Finally, his mouth whispered a kiss across her lips. Lifting up, Emma sought more. Striking Thunder obliged in a slow, tender and thoughtful kiss that sent shivers of pleasure down her spine.

The kiss lasted forever and stayed sweet until noisy shouts of children running toward them intruded. Striking Thunder broke the contact. Four boys ran past yet their gazes remained locked, each longing for more of what the other had to offer. Striking Thunder reached out to stroke her cheek. "You make this warrior want what he cannot have, white woman.

His kiss, his gentleness made her yearn for the forbidden as well. Gone was the ruthless warrior. The change confused her. "You say you understand, yet you would kill my father and deny my sister the father she so desperately longs for?"

Striking Thunder's hand fell to his side. He stepped away, his eyes hard. He drew his lips together in a line of displeasure. "A man who abandons his family and destroys others doesn't deserve the gift of life."

Emma paled, shaken by his quick mood change and his belief that he had the right to judge and take lives. "Who appointed you God?"

His head lifted and his hands bunched into fists at his side. "I am chief. It is my duty to see justice served when wrongs against my people are committed."

"And if you are wrong? Who will pay the price? You? Your people? No. It will be a young innocent girl—if I ever find her. Think of that when you contemplate killing him." Furious, Emma stalked away, her afternoon ruined by a stubborn, arrogant and frustrating warrior whose kiss transported her to a heavenly world where everything turned soft and wispy as the clouds floating across the blue sky.

Across the village, she stopped. Anger, frustration and confusion boiled inside her and screamed for release. Why *him?* Why did he have to stir her and make her long for things she couldn't have? She pulled at her fingers and searched around her. If she didn't find a distraction, she'd go mad. If she were home, she'd take her paints and canvases outside and lose herself in her drawing until her mind and emotions equalized but here, she had nothing.

She kicked a rock. It landed in a fire pit in front of her and sent a partly charred stick flying into the air. It hit her dress, leaving a line of charcoal down the front of her skirt. Emma started brushing it away then stopped to stare at it. Charcoal. She picked up the stick and drew another line on the underside of her garment. Excitement grew as she varied the thickness of the strokes. Surveying the lines, she grinned. Crude, but it might work. Filled with purpose, Emma went to Star Dreamer's tipi and slipped inside.

Striking Thunder felt guilty on two accounts. One for

upsetting Emma needlessly. Her praise and appreciation for his work pleased him—too much—as did her response to his kiss. And two, for withholding the knowledge of her sister's whereabouts. He frowned, torn by her pain and worry.

The horse Emma had taken from Yellow Dog had belonged to the Cheyenne who'd traded horses for the girl. With faint paint marks remaining on the animals haunches, Striking Thunder had traced the animal back to his owner—and Renny.

Knowing how much Emma worried, he was tempted to call her back and give her peace of mind on that account but instinctively, he knew it wouldn't be enough. If she knew Renny was in the region, she'd insist upon going to her or upon him bringing her here. And that was out of the question. In case his plan to lure the colonel into a trap failed, he needed the two sisters apart. Besides, once she had Renny with her, there wouldn't be any reason for her not to run.

No, it was better for her not to know where the child was or that he'd purchased her. It was bad enough that Renny knew he had Emma. He thought back to his first meeting with the sullen and unhappy child who kept trying to run off to find her sister. He grinned inwardly. How alike the two were. So spirited. So loyal. And when Renny turned those beseeching blue-gray eyes on him, he'd lost the ability to remain impassive. She'd reminded him of Emma so much, he'd finally given in and reassured her that Emma was safe.

The sullen and depressed girl had turned eager and demanding, insisting he take her to Emma, but Striking Thunder had managed to convince her that it wasn't yet possible. He'd found himself promising they would be together come spring. His story that her Indian owner demanded many horses and buffalo robes for her release and that it would take most of the winter to gather them had worked. And for good measure and to distract her, he'd given her one of the horses he brought with him as payment for her after she'd promised to stay where she was and give her owner no more trouble.

Unlike Emma, who was nothing but trouble.

Anger rolled through him over his conflicting emotions. The woman was his captive, the means to avenge his wife's death and the others', but he couldn't help feeling compassion toward her. From what she'd told Star, she'd been given the task of raising her sister at a young age. This he didn't understand. How could any father turn his back on his own children? In his eyes, Colonel Grady O'Brien had failed in his most important duty—family.

With only half a mind on his work, Striking Thunder watched Emma enter Star's tipi. When she came out a few minutes later she carried a piece of rolled-up rawhide and took it to Star. His sister handed her the knife she was using. Emma cut the hide into many small squares, then handed back the knife.

Curious, Striking Thunder picked up another piece of bone made from the porous edge of the buffalo shoulder. The honeycomb composition held paint and let it flow onto the sun-bleached hide smoothly. Again, his attention wandered to Emma who had settled beside a fire, off by herself. Her hair caught the rays of weak afternoon sunshine, adding a wild splash of color to a drab, colorless scene.

He couldn't understand his fascination with her hair. He'd seen many white women with hair of all colors. Even the harsh, dyed-red hair of the women who worked in the saloons. So why did Emma's draw him? What made her so different that he couldn't dismiss her? Abandoning his own artistic endeavors, he watched, curious to see what she was up to.

Taking several thin sticks, she set them into the glowing embers, allowing them to catch fire before removing them and blowing out the flames. To his amusement, she used the tips to scratch something onto the cut hide. Over and over, she repeated the process. He took a step toward her to see what she was up to then stopped. *No. Leave her. Banish her from your thoughts.* Taking his painting implements down to the river, he rinsed them and put them away then decided a ride in search of game would clear his mind. Taking his bow and quiver of arrows down from the pole on which they hung, he stepped outside.

Once more, his gaze sought Emma. Oblivious to those around her, the force of her concentration reached him from across the village. What was she doing? Every so often, she stopped to reburn the tips of her sticks. Over and over, she dipped her sticks into the fire and pulled them out then scratched the hide with them.

Slowly, a crowd gathered around her. Curiosity got the better of him. Shoving his way through the throng of hushed watchers, he peered over Emma's shoulder. He expected her to glare at him as she always did whenever he came near, but she seemed totally engrossed in what she was doing. "Drawing with burned sticks?" He made his voice derisive.

Glancing at what she was doing, he received a shock. Captured by her crude method of sketching were three women. Singing Sun cradled her infant to her breast, while her mother, Red Woman, stitched beads onto a pair of moccasins and looked on. The love between the three was clear. Two tipis formed a background behind the women. As alive as the subject themselves, Emma had captured the essence of motherly love, whether with an infant or grown daughter. He picked up another square of hide from the ground beside her.

His gut tightened. Star Dreamer stared out over the plains. Her hair, trimmed and evened out by Emma, now framed her face—but in her eyes, he saw that familiar faraway look. With a few strokes and some clever shading, Emma had captured both the grief and the haunted look in Star Dreamer's eyes that spoke of visions.

Ignoring him, Emma added a couple of finishing strokes to the portrait of the two mothers and the infant.

Only then did she glance over her shoulder at him. Their gazes met, their faces only a few inches away. Her eyes glowed, the color darker than normal, a dark, smoky green signaling the extent of peace within her. She waited.

He felt uncomfortable in the face of her talent but fairness demanded he tell her what he thought, honestly. "You are good," he said, giving her his first compliment.

Her lips curved slightly. "I know."

Staring at her softly parted lips, Striking Thunder felt the urge to lean closer and kiss her. It didn't matter that his people surrounded them, he wanted her. And that realization brought him up short. He stood and stalked away, the drawing of Star clenched in one hand.

Emma watched him go. His praise left her feeling warm and satisfied, which unsettled her. She didn't need anyone's praise of her work. She drew for her own satisfaction, not to please others. Angry with him, and with her circumstances, which had forced her to draw with such primitive instruments, she glanced down at her work and had to admit, it was one of the best drawings she'd done. The artist in her had seen with her heart, not her mind, and with that clarity of vision, she'd perceived her subjects without anger, resentment and prejudice.

Her breathing grew rapid as she really studied her own work. This wasn't the image of hideous savages. It was a symbol of motherhood, of the bonding of women. Somehow, she'd come to view these people as humans who shared a love of life and who supported one another. She glanced around, seeing the wonder in the faces as they compared her drawing to the subjects across from her. Some smiled at her, others nodded in approval.

Unsure of what this meant but afraid of the change she'd undergone without even realizing it, Emma shivered. For the first time since she'd been taken prisoner, she felt no resentment, no anger toward these women. Suddenly, she needed to get away from them. She had to think. Signing her name out of habit, she stood and walked over to the young mother. With her first genuine, friendly smile, Emma held out the square of rawhide.

Hesitantly, the young woman, around her own age, took it. When she looked at it and realized Emma had drawn her and her infant and her mother, her eyes widened with pride and pleasure. Grinning broadly, she showed the others, her guttural voice filled with excitement.

"Pilamayan," she said shyly.

Emma accepted her thanks, then fled to Star's tipi. Inside, she flung herself down onto her pallet and rested her chin on her fisted hands. Striking Thunder was right. His people were happy, content. Whether it was working or playing, there was a closeness among them that her upbringing lacked. In fact, she'd never seen such devotion and communal support, especially with regard to the elderly and young. Nor had she ever met such giving people.

Small things, like a simple gift made from braided grass or a colorful quilled pouch brought them more joy than some women ever experienced when receiving gold and diamonds from their husbands.

Flipping onto her back, she stared at the intense blue sky peeping in through the top of the tipi. Her throat clogged, and tears gathered in her eyes, and ran down the sides of her face. Today, she'd broken her vow to remain distant, to keep solitary and not allow herself to care about these people. It was easier—and safer—to view them as a lesser race, as savages, for she knew if—when—her father found her, the soldiers would more than likely destroy them.

Emma bit back a sob. She hadn't wanted to care. But God help her, she did. She did. The thought of that young mother and her baby dying brutally shattered the last of Emma's barriers. Turning back onto her stomach, she wept.

Chapter Fourteen

The yellow-gold of the summer sun setting over the prairie colored her vision. Star smiled dreamily as the gold glittered and sparkled. She closed her eyes, grateful that this vision lacked the violence and death of her more recent ones. She relaxed and gave herself up to the images floating across the backs of her closed eyes.

An eagle, with a brownish-red tint to his feathers, materialized. Lifting her hands, she joined the eagle and they glided across the golden haze. She and the eagle became one. The bird dipped, soared and scanned the land below, his cry loud. She sensed he searched not for prey, but for something lost. Puzzled, Star tried to see what it was he sought. Below them, the *maka* boasted a pale green carpet as the barren winter retreated under the promise of spring.

With a shriek of victory, the eagle folded its wings and dove toward a spot of bright color amid the green and gold landscape—a red flower. Suddenly, *Heca*, the buzzard who signaled the end of cold weather, appeared. Star cried out a warning but was too late. The ugly black bird swooped down, and with his sharp talons, plucked the flower. The eagle gave chase and the vision slowly faded.

Still caught in the throes of her vision, Star frowned and tried to make sense of what she'd seen but the glittering golds dulled, the sky darkened, until there was nothing left to see. Opening her eyes, she realized she was trembling, a sure sign that there was more to this vision than she understood. What did it mean? Though it made no sense—and most of her visions didn't in the beginning—she sensed it would play an important role in her life.

Around her, women laughed and talked as they worked. Several still exclaimed over the portrait Emma had drawn. But Star battled her own demons. Carefully, she stitched the moccasin she was quilling, but her mind wasn't on her work. It was on the unsettling vision. Who was the eagle and what of the flower?

Glancing around, she spotted Emma. Her hair glinted in the afternoon light. With sinking certainty, she knew Emma was the red flower that the buzzard had carried off. But it made no sense. The girl had no enemies. Who wished her harm? And the eagle? It couldn't be Striking Thunder. He was the black raven. Besides, when she'd flown as one with the eagle, she'd sensed a closeness between them, a special bonding of souls.

Star bit her lower lip. She didn't want to know her future or anyone else's. Two-Ree's death haunted her, as did guilt. And with the guilt came the soul-ripping question: Could she have saved her husband's life? If only she'd paid more attention to her visions instead of fighting them, perhaps she could have stopped him from going after Yellow Dog with her brother.

Most of the time, she realized the significance of her visions in time to do something about them. But twice in the last few months, she'd failed. Once with Meadowlark's death, and then her own husband's. That the visions were tied together, along with the arrival of Emma, wasn't lost on her. She now knew Emma's role and understood why the spirits had reclaimed Meadowlark. But why her husband?

Earlier that year, she'd seen the danger surrounding her brother, White Wolf, and his wife, Jessie, in time that her father, who'd still been chief, could arrange a rescue party. All had turned out well. Wolf and Jessie, now known to their people as Wild Rose, would return and run a school for the Indian children.

Star looked forward to the end of the following summer. Another smile, this one wide and dreamy spread across her features. They wouldn't return alone. But she kept to herself those sweet visions of the future.

She wished all her visions were of happy events. Why did she have to see danger and violence? If only she could stop her prophecies forever. Her people thought highly of her gift but no one understood how debilitating it was. If it were up to her, she'd gladly give up knowing the future and live her life as a normal person.

Tipping her head back, she tried rolling the tension from her shoulders. Maybe she should take her children and leave the village. If she weren't here, living so close to the land and the spirits that inhabited her world, maybe the visions would leave her. She frowned. But where would she go?

The eagle. In her vision, they'd become one as they'd flown across the blue sky. She longed to leave, to fly away and be free, but as quickly as the thought came to her, she banished it from her mind. Standing, she shook away the notion that she could ever leave. This was her life. There was no other for her. After putting her things away in her tipi, she wandered down to the river. Normally, the rushing of the water soothed her. Not today. She feared what tomorrow would bring.

"Ina?" Morning Moon called out to her mother.

Turning, Star held out her arms to her daughter.

"You had another vision. It troubles you." It was a statement, not a question.

Staring at her daughter's worried expression, Star's heart thumped. *Oh, please*, she begged the spirits. Do not do this to her. The one thing Star prayed for daily was that Morning Moon would never know the pain of having the gift of sight.

"Yes. How do you know?" Kneeling, she fingered one of Morning Moon's long braids. "Tell me you haven't had visions, daughter."

Morning Moon reached out and patted her mother's cheek. "I see in your eyes when you are worried."

Breathing a sigh of relief, Star led Morning Moon to a tree near the edge of the water and sat, drawing her onto her lap, grateful for her daughter's comforting presence. "That is good."

Mother and daughter sat in silence with the sound of water gurgling past them and the whisper of the wind caressing them. Star leaned her head back and willed the tension to leave her body. With her eyes closed, she didn't see Morning Moon's eyes glaze over or the frown that crossed her features.

Striking Thunder returned from his hunt empty-handed, hungry and in a foul mood. With his thoughts centered on the white woman, he'd been careless and had scared away an entire heard of elk. Unwilling to admit to defeat, he'd traveled far, searching for game but even the rabbits had eluded his swift-flying arrows.

But what really rankled was that he, a great hunter and warrior, had allowed his thoughts and concentration to slip. And the one he held responsible sat with his sister and her children, eating as if nothing had happened. His gaze fell to her mouth when her tongue snaked out to lick her bottom lip. Recalling the feel of that full bottom lip sent his blood singing through his veins. Fury followed hard on its heels.

Her father was a murderer, responsible for the death of Striking Thunder's young wife. So why did he have the irresistible urge to storm over there, take her in his arms and carry her to his tipi? She was a slave, not a revered visitor, yet as he watched, Singing Sun approached her and presented Emma with a bag made from the fur of the coyote.

"The white woman is a talented and skilled artist."

Glancing at his father who'd joined him, Striking Thunder shrugged. "Many people can draw."

"How many can capture a woman's grief with only burned sticks and rawhide?"

Striking Thunder folded his arms across his chest. Fairness dictated he give credit where it was due, even if he hated to utter the words. "The white woman is good, but she is still only a slave." He indicated where Emma sat. "Have my people forgotten that she is the daughter of a man who seeks to rid the land of The People?

Golden Eagle lifted a brow. "Is the daughter responsible for the actions of her father? Do we not judge others on their own goodness and worth? Our people know this and accord her the respect she has earned."

The reprimand made him wince. Emma *had* proven herself worthy of his people's respect, starting the day she'd returned to finish tanning the hide she'd been assigned. Grudgingly, he agreed. "My father is wise. Yet, she is here for only one purpose. When we have no need of her, I will return her."

Golden Eagle remained silent for a moment, his gaze on Emma. Then he slowly pulled his hands from behind his back, holding up a sheaf of parchment paper, a pencil and a steel pen with a half-full bottle of ink. "You will do what must be done when the time is right. But while we have such talent in our midst, your mother would like to have a drawing of each of her children." He handed the items to Striking Thunder.

Striking Thunder frowned at the items. "Why does she not ask the woman herself?"

"She is your captive. Your mother does not wish to interfere."

With a bark of disbelief, Striking Thunder fixed a skeptical gaze on Emma who now held Singing Sun's infant daughter on her lap. The picture touched him. Emma would make a wonderful mother. Long before the women had accepted her, the children had been drawn to her. With her experience raising her sister, she had a special affinity with the young. "We know that nothing would stop my mother from interfering if she deemed it necessary."

"That is true." Golden Eagle chuckled, and without giving his son the chance to reply or protest, he walked away whistling.

Striking Thunder stared at the paper, tempted to return the items to his mother. Let *her* ask the white woman. Yet, what was the use? She'd insist and in the end, he'd still have to do it. "Mothers. *Women,*" he muttered, giving in to the inevitable. When he arrived at the group of chattering females, they all fell silent. Emma shifted her gaze from the baby to him. He held out his mother's gift.

"These are from my mother. In return she'd like you to draw each of her children. And her husband," he added, knowing she'd want one of Golden Eagle and his father would not have passed that on.

Emma's eyes shone with pure pleasure. "Paper." Her voice shook with awe. She stood. Before he realized her intent, she'd thrust the baby into his arms so she could examine the pencil and pen.

In his arms, the infant squirmed and turned its head toward Striking Thunder, rooting for nourishment. With a soft chuckle, he touched the child's downy cheek. The baby latched on to his finger and suckled until it discovered there was no milk there. But before it could wail its displeasure, Singing Sun returned. He gladly gave over the infant and put it to her breast.

Unbidden came the image of Emma's breasts, creamy and full, the tips puckered. Perfect for suckling, for drawing those pouty nipples into his own mouth to taste and draw out to full beaded tips. Unsettled by the course of his thoughts, he stepped back, fighting his attraction to Emma. He was a warrior. When he took a wife to his tipi, it would be an Indian woman, one with whom he could have Indian children, one whom he could respect. Not one who made him forget his goals, forget who and what he was, a chief with a duty to protect his people. Yet, he

171

had no trouble envisioning him handing her a child—their child to put to her breast.

He took a step back. To keep the barriers raised between them, his voice turned harsh. "I forbid you to sketch me."

Emma shrugged. "All right."

Taken aback by her easy acquiescence, Striking Thunder stalked away. Her indifference stung, which made him all the angrier. She shouldn't matter to him. But somehow, she did. And no matter how much he tried to tell himself that only vengeance mattered, it wasn't true anymore.

The night was clear and bright when Emma slipped out of the tipi. Though every muscle in her arms and back ached, restlessness made sleeping a luxury that evaded her. She had no idea if the guards posted at night would try to stop her. Her steps were cautious as she made her way through the tipis.

To her relief, no harsh voice shot out of the dark to order her back to the tent, so she continued. Silence surrounded her. Even the dogs who barked during the day were quiet in their slumbers.

Above, jewel-bright stars twinkled against a brilliant blue-black backdrop, and to her left, a pale crescent moon hung low on the horizon. Turning in a slow circle, Emma drew comfort from the vastness of the heavens stretched out in all directions. When had she last stepped outside her town house in St. Louis to view the night sky? She couldn't recall ever taking the time to enjoy the beauty and peace the night sky offered. Her eyes roamed the heavens, tracking one glittering star to another.

She took a deep breath. Brisk, pure air permeated her lungs. No choking chimney smoke. No noxious odors of human waste and rotting garbage. But what really amazed her was the absolute quiet. No disruptive sounds of horse-drawn carriages rumbling down the streets at all hours of the night, or drunken neighbors shouting and

singing when they returned from parties to disrupt night-
time sleep.

Though the land was wild and primitive, Emma discovered it offered its own brand of sophistication, one she not
only appreciated but desperately needed in her constant
state of emotional turmoil. The fact that it was this very
same wilderness, the untamed savageness of the land, that
had put her in her current state of distress, didn't bear
thought.

She'd survive this experience, but in order to do so,
she needed to learn all she could so that when she left,
she'd be able survive her long trek back to the fort. She
frowned. How would she escape? Everywhere she went,
they watched, especially Striking Thunder. And like earlier that afternoon, if he found her idle, he would find
another chore for her to do. She wished she dared tell him
what he could do with his chores, but his warning kept
her quiet.

It rankled her status as slave. It was wrong for humans
to treat their fellow humans in this manner. Emma now
had an appreciation for those who fought for freedom.
She wandered down to the stream and stared out over the
dark water.

Freedom.

It meant many things she was discovering now that
she'd lost it. Not only did it mean to be physically free to
come and go as one pleased, there were deeper implica-
tions. Free to choose, free to live one's life as one
wished. The thought crept into Emma's mind that desire
for freedom had been the driving force behind her decision to board the *Annabella*. Freedom from unwanted
responsibilities.

With nowhere to run and hide, the glaring truth
slammed into her. She'd yearned to be free to follow her
heart, and free of the duty of raising her sister. Pain
slashed through her as she bared her soul to the moon and
stars and her own heart.

And what she saw made her cringe. She'd been selfish,

when she'd taken it upon herself to reunite her sister and father. Though she hadn't realized it at the time, she couldn't deny it now. She hadn't been taking Renny to see their father just for the girl's sake. Her true and hidden goal had been to make Grady O'Brien take back his duties as father so she could pursue her own happiness. Art school. Social pursuits. Travel. Anything. Everything.

A lump formed in her throat, and she hugged herself, chilled by her realizations. By her own actions, she was free from that one binding duty. Tears slipped down her cheeks. What she wouldn't give to have it back, to have Renny back beside her. She was no better than her father. She'd been ready to abandon the one person who needed her the most. Not only that, but Emma needed Renny, needed her sister. She would never forgive herself.

A cricket sprang from the damp earth, momentarily startling her. Around her, the distinct sounds of the night cocooned her in their sweet melody. Insects hummed and buzzed, owls sent their eerie *hoo-hoos* through the air and beside her the river flowed, blending the sounds into one masterpiece.

Rubbing her upper arms, Emma wished she had the courage to leave—now—this very night. But she consoled herself with the thought that she was smart enough to realize her circumstances could be much worse. Indeed, with Yellow Dog, they had been desperate. At least here she was safe—and she no longer doubted Striking Thunder's word. No one had tried to do harm to her.

But the question remained: Would he really release her in March? And if he did, what sort of life would she have? Would she be one of those poor, despised women society pitied, and what if Striking Thunder succeeded in killing her father? Then she'd truly be alone. An ache rose from her heart to her throat. Somehow she had to warn her father. Then together, they'd search for Renny. If it took the rest of her life, she'd gladly spend it searching. She wouldn't give up until Renny was back where she belonged—with her.

White Flame

With a sleepy yawn, Emma decided she'd better return to her bed before Star Dreamer woke and found her gone. The last thing she wanted was to have anyone think she'd run off. Only by having the freedom to move at will would she survive her captivity and succeed in escaping when she had her plan worked out.

She turned to retrace her steps. A dark menacing figure loomed over her. Before she could scream, a large hand covered her mouth.

Chapter Fifteen

Fear clouded Emma's mind when a strong arm jerked her roughly against a solid muscular chest. To her horror, she was carried away from the village. Her heart lurched. Kicking and thrashing, she fought for freedom. Terrified, she bit down hard at the hand covering her mouth. Her muffled screams broke the peace of the night.

"*Inila!*" A voice grunted in pain near her ear. "Silence! Do not scream."

At the sound of Striking Thunder's voice, Emma stilled. Without the fear of abduction distorting her senses, she became aware of him: his scent, one of wood smoke and pine, and the feel of those arms, firm, yet gentle on her, leaving no bruises. Though relieved, when he set her down and removed his hand from her mouth, she whirled out of his grip. Fury at what he'd done raced through her, chasing away the prickles of fright. They faced each other with twin stances of fury.

Striking Thunder shook his hand. "Must you use your teeth on my flesh?" He glared at her, reminding her of the time she'd bit his lip.

Emma tipped her chin. "Serves you right. If you don't want to be bitten, keep your flesh away from my teeth."

Lightning-fast, Striking Thunder snagged her by the arm and brought her close. "Do not bite me again, white woman."

Unafraid, Emma shoved him away. With hands on her hips, she glared at him. "What do you expect when you sneak up on me like that? How was I supposed to know it was you?"

"That is the point. You *had* no idea who I was until I spoke."

Breathing hard, she drew on her outrage to stand up to him. "And who here would dare touch me? You promised I'd be safe. If I'm not allowed to go for a walk by myself, then just tell me so. Of course, that wouldn't be as much fun as scaring a poor woman. Is that how you get you fun?"

Striking Thunder's eyes narrowed to two furious slits. "Do not push me, Emma. As long as you obey our rules, you are free to move as you please. But not at night. It is not safe."

Emma snorted and sent him a look of derision. "Don't try to frighten me with tales of bears and wolves. I'm not stupid. If there were any wild animals—besides you savages—around, the dogs would bark."

Striking Thunder advanced. Emma stood her ground until inches separated them.

"Savages are precisely who you need to fear when you wander alone in the dark."

Emma rolled her eyes, but he jerked her chin up and forced her to meet his angry glare. "Did you hear *me* behind you? If I'd been the enemy, you'd have been dead or long gone by now. Tribes raid other tribes for prizes and even pleasure. And you, Emma, with your flame hair and white skin, are a prize."

His gaze dipped to her heaving bosom. "A prize any warrior would risk war over." Releasing her chin, he trailed the backs of his fingers along her jaw, down her throat and down the center of one breast. His voice lost some of its angry edge. "No one will steal you from this warrior. You are mine." He lifted a hand to still her protest. "Like it or not, you are mine."

Emma closed her mouth. It was a waste of breath to state she belonged to no one, so she didn't bother. Instead, she poked him in the chest. "And was that why you were following me? Or were you afraid I might run away?"

His features eased and one corner of his lip quirked upward. "You wouldn't get far on foot, my spirited captive, so do not try anything so foolish. I'll follow and find you before *Wi* rises fully in the sky."

Frustrated at the truth of his words, she seethed. So much depended upon her and yet, she felt so helpless. "You won't get away with this. Your plan to kill my father will fail."

This time, Striking Thunder chuckled. "And who will stop me? You? I think not. You will serve me well by luring your father and the captain to me when the time is right."

His reminder that once again, she was only bait, a convenience to be used for his own needs, not a person with thoughts and feelings and needs of her own brought forth fresh waves of resentment. He didn't care about *her,* just her use for his own plans. He was no better than her father.

To Grady, she was caretaker of his house, business affairs and daughter, which allowed him to shake off his responsibilities and go off to do whatever he wanted with no worries and no encumbrances. Why was it men never gave any thought or consideration to her? Well, she'd had it: With her father. With Striking Thunder. Rebellion rose like a geyser bursting from the earth. Too many years of doing what was expected, of following convention and rules set by others, burst through the locked cavern of her heart.

Her father might not be here for her to tell him what she thought of him, but from now on, Striking Thunder would learn she was not some object or possession to be jerked around at will. If she wanted to walk, she'd walk. She stalked downstream, away from his smug arrogance and the sleeping village. He followed, running in front of her to block her path. "You have been out here long enough. Return to your bed."

She ignored the voice of reason that suggested she back down and return to Star Dreamer's tipi posthaste. "Go away, Striking Thunder. I'm not a child to be ordered to bed. When I'm tired, I'll return on my own. If it will make you leave me in peace, I'll stay close to the village."

"I will stay with you."

"I don't want your company. I don't even like you, so go away and leave me alone." She spun around to return. His voice stopped her.

"You liked me well enough this afternoon," he reminded.

Recalling that shared kiss sent her heart skipping erratically. She eyed him over her shoulder. "Well, I don't anymore."

Rather than grow angry, his lips quirked in amusement. He joined her, purposely standing close. "Challenging me?"

Folding her arms across her breasts, Emma firmed her jaw. "If you like."

Striking Thunder reached out and cupped her jaw with one hand, his thumb moving rhythmically just below her ear. "Should we put that to a test? If I decided to make you mine, you would not resist." He grinned his hateful arrogant grin. "In fact, my flame-haired beauty, you'd beg me to teach you the ways between a man and woman."

"I'd die first," Emma scoffed. The first misgivings were beginning to assail her. The warmth of his fingers cupping her chin were doing strange things to her. Avoiding his eyes, Emma lowered her gaze to his sleek chest. Her breath hitched in her throat. Before boarding the *Annabella*, she'd never even seen a bare male chest and since coming to Striking Thunder's village, she had come to appreciate what the sight of a nicely bronzed and well-developed chest did to a woman's heart.

And *his* naked chest had drawn her admiring glances more often than she was comfortable admitting. Urges she couldn't put a name to took hold. Earlier, when he'd kissed her behind his tipi, she'd longed to press her lips to his chest and explore that hard, sinewy flesh. The urge to run her fingers over that flesh and across his beaded male nipples left her weak-kneed.

Startled by the direction of her thoughts, Emma flushed. Staring deep into his glittering dark eyes, she noted the desire lurking deep in those fathomless orbs. *Run*, the voice of reason screamed. But she couldn't move. His gaze trapped her in a sensual fog. Nervous, she licked her lips, recalling how his mouth felt, tasted. Here, with only the stars above as witnesses, she wanted him to kiss her again.

His palm slid up one side of her face in a move so sweet and tender, Emma surrendered to the lure of the night and her own hidden need to be touched and loved. She leaned into him, her body softening with yearning.

Triumph filled Striking Thunder's voice. "You belong to me. If I chose to touch you, I will. And if I chose to kiss you, I will." His voice dropped to a whisper. "If I decide to take you to my mat, you won't resist."

Emma held her breath, torn by the promise in his words and his utter arrogance. But when his hair, a thick curtain of straight black silk fell forward and brushed her cheek, all thought of protest fled. Blood rushed to her lips, and her breasts swelled in anticipation. He angled his head. Her eyes drifted shut. She waited long agonizing seconds before his mouth slanted over hers, tender and coaxing, barely touching hers.

She moaned, tried to lift up onto her toes to make him kiss her as he had before, but Striking Thunder teased her until she thought she'd burst with the need for more. As if he could wait no longer, his mouth captured hers fully. She responded with a long, heart felt whimper. Leaning forward, she allowed his hard frame to support her. "Please."

"Yes." His thumb pulled gently on her chin. Her jaw dropped in response and Emma cried out in relief when his lips traversed hers with compelling mastery. Gone was the teasing, taunting, proud warrior. In his place stood a man whose touch freed her soul and bared her heart. When his tongue snaked past her teeth, her lips parted on a breathy moan, unconsciously inviting him to deepen the kiss.

Striking Thunder slid one hand to the back of her neck as he slipped his tongue slowly inside her mouth. Though he'd kissed her in this fashion briefly before, this time was different. He went slow, he teased and he coaxed. Emma tipped her head back further, giving him the access he sought. Her entire body from her head to her toes, felt both weak and alive. Sliding her hands up his chest, she reveled in his hard texture. Taking her time, she stopped to rub her fingers over his flat, brown nipples. His chest rose rapidly in response.

She wanted this. *Needed this.* It'd been so long since she'd felt strong arms around her, been able to let someone else take charge. In many ways, she'd been on her own since the day her father rode off. She'd had to be strong, but now, she readily gave herself over to this warrior who stole away her breath and all rational thought. Right now, she was simply a woman with needs of her own and he the man who could meet them.

He lifted his head and stared down at her. Emma reached up and traced his moist lips with her fingers. He bent his head, drew one finger into his mouth and suckled. She gasped and pulled her hand back. His eyes, nearly black with emotion, beckoned. Rising onto her tiptoes at the same time his head lowered, she met him in a kiss that exploded with frantic need.

Following his lead, Emma tentatively pushed past his seeking tongue and traced his lips with hers in the same manner he'd done. He groaned, his fingers dug into her hair as he held her close. "Yes," he whispered when she hesitated. He opened his mouth wider, inviting her to taste him as he'd tasted her.

Emma accepted his invitation shyly. His tongue

retreated, hers pursued, then in a game of tag, roles reversed until it became unclear who chased after whom. As one, their mouths fused, mated. Each took, each gave. Each learned the feel, texture and taste of the other. Striking Thunder trembled when she drew his lower lip into her mouth and gently bit down. And she went weak at the knees when he drew her tongue into his mouth and suckled.

With a ragged sigh, they drew back, gasping for air. He ran his hands along her jaw, then down the sides of her neck. His lips followed, blazing a trail along her jaw and down her throat, stopping at the pulsing hollow. With her head thrown back, eyes closed, Emma moaned and threaded her fingers through his long, cloud-soft hair when he found another weak-knee point. She twisted her fingers into his hair to keep from falling.

"Emma," he breathed, moving to explore her collarbone and the place where her shoulder and neck joined. Her head lolled to one side. Her hands slid down to his shoulders. "Oh, yes." She was vaguely aware of his large hands drawing her close, melding them together front to front as he explored her back but she startled when his fingers closed around her buttocks and drew her hard against the cradle of his hips.

After a month in the village, living closely with these people who didn't hide their natural reactions or smother the sounds of lovemaking at night or even worry about the firelight inside their tipis throwing their shadows on the white hides, she had a pretty good idea what the hardness pressed against her belly meant.

Striking Thunder was aroused and he wanted her. The realization sent a warm glow through her. Heat pooled at the junction of her thighs. He wanted her. *Her*. Oh, many people might need her, want her to take care of them but this was different. And for once, she needed to know there was someone there for her, someone she could lean on. And with startling clarity, after seeing him with his family, his nephew and niece and holding Singing Sun's infant daughter, she knew Striking Thunder had it in him to love with his heart and soul should he ever give it again. How she envied his wife.

Reality slammed into her. His wife was gone. Murdered. And he blamed her father and meant to kill him. What was she doing? How could she be doing this with a man bent on revenge, murder. This wasn't some suitor out to woo her. This was the enemy.

Her captor.

He pulled her back to him. "Shh, do not be afraid. Let me show you how it is between a man and woman."

Her body swayed. She wanted him badly, wanted what he could give her, but her mind rebelled. Shocked and terribly afraid of the wondrous sensations he'd aroused in her, she had to stop him. For her own sake. Taking a deep breath, she shoved him away. "No. This isn't right. You have no right to do this, to touch me in this way. Only my future husband has the right to do this."

As if he'd been dashed with cold water, Striking Thunder's head reared up. He cursed, low and harsh. But instead of putting more distance between them, her words appeared to trigger a white-hot fury in him. He crushed her to him in an iron-tight hold. Roughly, one hand yanked her chin up, forcing her to look at him.

"Do not throw up at me that bastard you mean to marry." His voice roughened. "He won't ever touch you or marry you because he'll be dead, like those innocent people he murdered."

Realizing he thought she'd been referring to Derek when she'd been vague, Emma cringed. She had no intention of marrying Derek, had only told Striking Thunder that in the beginning to make him think her important enough to leave alone. But she didn't tell him that. If thinking she still planned to marry the captain washed away the desire in his gaze, good.

Her own behavior from the minute she'd seen him that night appalled her. What had happened to the proper lady she'd once been? Aunt Ida would roll over in her grave if she could see Emma now. Where was this rebellion and temper coming from? She was a lady. Ladies didn't give in to fits of anger or try to start battles with the opposite sex. Or kiss and be kissed senseless under a wild canopy of stars.

But out here, far from proper society, it seemed as though she'd lost the ability to act like a lady. She licked her lips, confused by the churning emotions coursing through her. And when his lips lowered and stopped a mere breath from hers, she knew the need to be touched, held, and loved was stronger. She didn't protest when he wound his hands roughly in her hair and forced her to look at him.

"You belong to me. No one else." He held her face tenderly.

His mouth played with hers, coaxed and teased her. There was no one else. Just him. She moaned, moved her lips against his, met him kiss for kiss. His hands shifted to either side of her head, hers slid over the whipcord strength of his shoulders. On fire, Emma burned for more as he roused a deeper response from her.

Her hands roamed his body, and her hips, driven by a pulsing need deep within, moved restlessly, brushing against his hardened sex. His fingers trailed down her back and pressed her firmly back against him. Heat, intense and driving, filled her. His hips rotated against hers.

Harsh moans filled the air. His? Hers? She didn't know, didn't care. She ached with a need unlike anything she'd ever felt before. And when he pulled back, she protested.

Striking Thunder throbbed with the desire to bury himself deep inside her. Holding himself back, he trailed his lips downward, and lowered them to the damp barren ground. Taking the fur robe she'd worn over her shoulders to ward off the chill, he spread it beneath them then stretched out next to her with one leg slung over hers.

Tenderly, he feathered his fingers over her breasts and

down her flat belly. Watching her, he learned the shape of her as he followed the contours of her body over gentle curves and dipping down into flat valleys.

Leaning over her, his hard chest pillowed by the soft swells of her breasts, he caressed the side of her face with one hand. She turned her head into his embrace with a deep sigh of surrender. The soft breathy sound nearly broke his control. He longed to move over her and join himself to her. But he waited. Watching Emma as she experienced each new step of the mating act held him enthralled.

Holding her wide and wondering gaze with his, he used his knee to nudge her legs apart. Her eyes widened and she stiffened slightly. He lowered his head to reclaim her mouth. When he felt her relax, he pressed his thigh against her woman's mound. With a startled cry, her hips jerked off the ground but she didn't stop him. He slid his other hand beneath her dress, which had ridden high up one soft, slender thigh. "*Kopegla sni yo.*"

Emma shuddered when she felt his fingers caressing the inside of her thigh where her leggings were tied, high beneath her skirt.

In English, he said, "Don't be afraid." But she was. Something was happening to her when he touched her. It didn't hurt, exactly, yet she was filled with an odd ache. A pleasant one, though. Unable to stop it, and not wanting to, her arms tightened around his neck, slid down his shoulders and skimmed over his back. With each gasping breath, her breasts lifted and pressed into his chest, igniting every nerve with soul-searing heat. As soft as her dress was, the material abraded her sensitive nipples.

Incredible, never-before-felt sensations filled Emma as Striking Thunder stroked her in slow, tender circles, moving up her thigh to that place that ached worse even than her breasts, which felt heavy and swollen. She shifted. A tendril of cool air brushed against her legs when Striking Thunder pushed her dress higher.

Her body felt on fire and only he could offer her cooling relief. When his lips moved to her throat, she threw her head back. Overhead, stars twinkled down at them and the flow of the river added a sweet whisper of background music. The night darkened and lengthened. But for Emma, there was only now. Him. This. Her eyes closed on the wonder of it.

He murmured something against her throat. Though she didn't understand, her body responded to the tenderness of it, and when his fingers inched higher, parting her, exposing that hidden core, she shied away from his touch and the intense pleasure-pain he brought her. Fear burned the edges of the fog surrounding her. Her eyes flew open and her lips parted in a protest that died as a hoarse whimper.

He touched her there again. "Shh, relax. Let me give you release."

Emma had no idea what he meant, didn't need to. When his palm pressed hard against that moist area, he ignited an intense pulsing deep in her center. Her hands fluttered toward him, unsure if she meant to push him away or pull him closer.

He grabbed one hand and kissed her palm, her wrist. Her other hand fell uselessly back to her side. Her fingers dug deep furrows into the thick fur beneath her. Lifting her hips, she rolled her head from side to side. "Please. I—I'm not sure—" Each time she thrust upward, touched him, something snapped. It made thought, speech impossible. Oh, God, she wanted his touch, harder.

Gently, Striking Thunder kissed her while his fingers circled her swollen flesh, until she thought she'd surely die from the intense pleasure. Then he removed his hand but before she could protest, he slid one finger lower, parting her further. She gasped when he slipped inside. In, out, and using his thumb, he circled her throbbing heart, playing her until she thought she'd burst with the pleasure of it.

Her head rolled back, emphasizing the white column of her throat. His mouth took up her invitation, his teeth nipping the taut skin, his tongue trailing a heated path from jaw to collarbone. The sensations, so many, so incredible left Emma shaking and wanting. More, lots more. Her back arched and her legs shifted, stiffened, then trembled as she sought something, just out of reach. His finger delved deeper, pressing upward inside her at the same time his thumb pressed down. He increased the rotation across that overly sensitive, previously hidden and untouched flowering bud.

He swallowed her soft cries and just when she thought she couldn't take any more, she came apart in an explosion of incredible pleasure. Jewel-bright colors dazzled her and carried her upward to mingle with the glittering diamonds sitting in the night sky, just waiting to be plucked before she fell back to the earth.

Chapter Sixteen

Captivated by Emma's passionate surrender, Striking Thunder felt awed by the look of wonder on her face. He smiled, and though his own desire throbbed painfully, witnessing her release held a sweetness of its own. Holding her close, the rapt pleasure on her face fascinated him. Never had he seen a woman lose herself so completely. More than anything, he wanted to lose himself in her passionate embrace and follow her lead. Their coupling would be wild and uncontrolled.

Without conscious thought, his fingers combed through her mound of red curls in a soothing fashion then trailed upward beneath her dress to caress the soft, white skin of her flat belly. Her ragged gasps slowed and her soft sighs mingled with his harsher breaths as his body burned hotter with need.

Emma turned to him, lifted a hand to cup his jaw. "I never knew it could be so wonderful between a man and a woman."

Striking Thunder ached. Neither had he. Not like this with just him giving the pleasure. He and Meadowlark had never taken turns so that each could witness the other's passion. Their matings had been just that. She'd wanted to bear him children. He'd wanted children. It was all part of life's circle. Everything was a circle. A bird's nest. His tipi. The sun and the moon. Life was a circle.

To his dismay, the passion he'd shared with Emma

made it increasingly clear that he needed what she offered. She was part of his life circle. And until this moment of truth, Striking Thunder might in time have accepted another arranged marriage and been content with friendship and respect, as fulfillment of that nev-erending circle—but not now. That would never be enough. He frowned. Why was he thinking about love? There was more to life and marriage than love. Mutual respect and affection formed a satisfactory alliance.

Passion wasn't wise. Passion led to loss of control, which was something he demanded of himself. The knowledge that he wanted nothing more than to claim this woman as his own at whatever cost to himself made him roll away. To rebuild the barriers between them, and to deny himself the trembling in his limbs and the burning need in his heart for her touch, he stood, his voice harsh. "I warn you now, white woman. Do not challenge me again or you will bear the consequences."

With regret he watched Emma's gaze widen and the remnants of passion flee from her soft, green gaze. "Next time you want me to kiss you, just say so. No need to challenge me." His gaze dipped. "Subduing that stubborn streak of yours is a pleasant diversion, but I'd prefer not to have others witness our loving. Next time, come to my tipi. It's a much more private place."

He ignored the twinge of guilt at the brief flash of pain that swept across her features as she scrambled to her feet and straightened her dress. But again, she surprised him. No tears fell from those moist, wide eyes.

Instead, she thrust her stubborn chin at him. "You have an overinflated sense of self, Striking Thunder. There won't be a next time."

Striking Thunder reached out and pulled her to him, his lips covering hers in a hard, demanding show of mas-tery. When her lips softened on a moan, he released her with a self-satisfied grin. "You lie, white woman. This warrior can lay claim to your body anytime. It doesn't lie."

To himself, he admitted that if she were to take him at his word and come to him and demand he finish what he'd started, he wouldn't be able to refuse her or himself. To his immense relief, she only glared at him. He pointed toward the tipis behind them. "*Iyunka yo!* Go to bed. You've wasted enough of my time this night."

Emma's eyes snapped with fury. "That was unbelievably cruel, Striking Thunder, but what can one expect from someone who goes around kidnapping innocent women and plotting murder?" Defiantly, she stalked away, then turned, purposely eyeing the swollen ridge of flesh beneath his breechclout. "And you certainly didn't think I was wasting your time a few minutes ago."

Her words struck Striking Thunder right where it still hurt. Though he yearned to bring her back and finish what he'd started, he didn't. Instead, he followed and made sure she returned to his sister's tipi without mishap. Then he went to his own lodging. He didn't need her. He could find his own release.

But just inside the door, he froze, his eyes traveling around the interior. The fire still burned, the embers hot when they should have died down long ago. He sensed he wasn't alone. His hand dropped, ready to grab his knife until he spotted his late-night visitor in his bed. "What are you doing here, Tanagila?"

The young maiden sat up. Furs from his bed covered her shoulders, but didn't hide the fact that she wore nothing beneath them. "I am here to give myself to you. It is my duty to care for you, to see to your needs."

Striking Thunder entered. Though he was swollen and ready, the sight of her did nothing to him. The burning need cooled. "Return to your father's tipi. I have no needs to be attended to this night."

Tanagila stood, unashamed of her nakedness. Her eyes fell to his breechclout and the erection he could not hide. "I offer myself to you in place of my sister. I am healthy and will bear you many strong sons and daughters. It is only right that a great chief such as you have a wife and family. Is this not the way of our people?"

Holding the flap open, he motioned for his unwanted visitor to leave. Wearily, he shook his head to take the sting from his words. "I have no desire to take a wife at this time. Leave and do not come back uninvited."

The young maiden bowed her head, hiding her expression as she scooped up her clothes, slid her dress over her head, then walked out without a word. Dropping the hide door, Striking Thunder rubbed the back of his neck. *Women.* They caused too much trouble. Tanagila he could handle. She was young and thought she was in love with him, but Striking Thunder knew about Tatankaota and how the other warrior felt. Tatankaota would make a good husband for her if he had the patience to win her heart.

Emma was another matter. He couldn't deny his attraction to her, nor his desire to have her. He frowned. Not just desire. She captivated him. And not just her body. Everything about her drew him. Her insight into his people, her courage, her loyalty and yes, her beauty.

Just thinking about her soft body pressed against his made him tremble. Hearing in his mind her soft cries and gasps made him break out in a sweat. Recalling her face, and remembering her lying there, with the moonlight bathing her; watching her as she found her release; all haunted him. Emotions crowded into his mind and needs—his own—gripped his heart. He feared her passion—and his need for it—more than any warring tribe.

"No!" He would not give in. Striking Thunder left his tipi and took off running to rid himself of his restlessness. When he returned tired and wet from bathing in the river, he went and gathered some supplies, ready to leave at first light. He had to leave to put her and this madness in perspective, to see it for what it was—a weakness, a test he could and would overcome. Stretching out on his pallet, unable to sleep, he watched the night pass through the open top of his tipi and admitted that for the first time in his life, he was running away.

With the cold wind sweeping across the bleak prairie, Emma welcomed the bitter chill to drive the heat of desire from her veins. She drove herself relentlessly, doing her best to keep so busy that she couldn't think about Striking Thunder or what had passed between them the night before. Just remembering it left her embarrassed beyond words.

Taking two full waterskins to an elderly couple, she made sure they had enough wood for their fire and allowed them to feed her, knowing her company meant as much as her help, even though they spoke little to one another. After caring for her aunt for so long, it seemed perfectly natural for Emma to turn to those who needed assistance but would not ask.

By afternoon, tired from lack of sleep and from pushing herself just to keep occupied, she agreed to show Morning Moon and several other girls how to draw with her makeshift charcoal pencils. The Indians weren't the only ones who could improvise and make due with what nature provided. To her surprise, Morning Moon caught on quickly, grasping the concept of light and shadows and depth. Rather than tackle something simple such as a tipi like her young friends, the girl had insisted on drawing a portrait of a young girl.

Star joined them and, while Morning Moon and her friends drew, she and Emma started grinding dried strips of buffalo into a fine powder, which would later be mixed with ground cherries and fat. But even between the girls' requests for help and the wrist and backbreaking work of pounding the meat, Emma wasn't able to put Striking Thunder from her mind for long.

Pounding stone against stone, she sent chunks of meat flying. She didn't want to remember what had passed between them and she certainly did not want to dwell on the incredible pleasure he'd given her. Yet guilt wavered with the desire to experience his wondrous touch again. He'd been so tender and considerate, a side she'd seldom seen in him. She picked up the chunk of meat, brushed it off, then pounded it, ignoring Star Dreamer's questioning look.

What happened last night should never have happened. Not only weren't they married, but she was his captive, his prisoner. She needed to concentrate her energies on getting free so she could start her search for Renny. She blanked her mind, tried to focus on her goal and remember who and what she was. She was Emma O'Brien, a white woman. She didn't belong out in this wilderness. Her place was back in St. Louis with her sister. So why was she fantasizing about a handsome warrior when she had no business longing for such things? But no matter what she said to herself, her body refused to acknowledge the social and circumstantial differences between herself and Striking Thunder.

Her fingers stilled. What would her world be like once she returned? Staring down at the brownish-red crumbs in her stone bowl, she tried visualizing her former life. Somehow, after the daily freedoms from the censoring eyes of white society, Emma wasn't as eager as she'd once been to return to days filled with so many rules.

Star poured her powdered meat and cherries into a pouch. Emma added her own ground mixture to Star's and set her stone bowl down. She shook out her aching wrists then helped Star add melted lard to it. After mixing it, Star took the cooling pemmican to the tipi. Alone, Emma glanced around, searching for Striking Thunder among the incoming warriors.

"Emma, did I do this right? I want to draw your sister."

With a suppressed sigh, Emma turned her attention to Morning Moon and her sketch. Her breath caught in her throat. While the drawing was rough and quite crude, Morning Moon had drawn a pair of wide eyes in a hauntingly familiar-shaped face. While none of the other features were true to life, the eyes—

Oh, God. She pressed a hand to her throat and stared at Renny's eyes. The shape, the wide-eyed intelligence, and the mischievousness were all there and made Emma want to weep. But she didn't want to frighten Morning Moon.

She smiled weakly. "You did an excellent job." Taking the stick from Morning Moon, Emma added a couple of lines and rubbed the charcoal in, shading them to give the drawing depth. "There."

Morning Moon closed her eyes then nodded. "Yes. That's better." Then she frowned. "I can't seem to get the nose or mouth right. I can't see them so good."

Emma couldn't help but wonder what the child meant. Morning Moon couldn't know what Renny looked like—unless she'd used Emma as her model in the assumption that the sisters looked alike. That was the only scenario that made any kind of sense. Though Renny favored their mother and she their father, there was enough resemblance between them that the relationship was obvious.

Tweaking one of Morning Moon's black braids, Emma hugged the girl. "Do not be in such a hurry. It takes time and lots of practice to be able to draw people." The girl nodded then ran off to join her friends. Star rejoined her and together, they started in on the evening meal. After a few minutes, Emma glanced around again. Still no sign of Striking Thunder. And though she told herself it was good, that she didn't need or want to see him, she missed his arrogant presence.

"My brother has gone."

Startled, Emma eyed Star. She didn't bother pretending not to know to whom the other woman referred. "Gone? Where?"

Shrugging, Star used a forked stick to remove a hot stone from the fire pit. She dropped it into the pouch of water hanging from the cookfire tripod. Their method of heating water without the use of pots still amazed Emma. She eyed the stomach lining of a buffalo, which served as their container. It was clever, yet disgusting—especially as someone would eat the pouch after the meal was served from it. "I do not know. Our warriors often go off alone, sometimes for many days." Her gaze sharpened on Emma's. "You were out late last night."

Emma felt her skin flush. She glanced down at her trembling hands. "I couldn't sleep, so I went for a walk."

Worry lined Star's forehead. She leaned forward. "You must be careful. Do not go far."

"I know. Your brother informed me."

At that, Star lifted a brow. "And when did he tell you this? Last night?"

Remembering all that had happened between them, Emma flushed. "Yes. He followed and explained the dangers, making his point." Her mood darkened when she recalled his method of proving he spoke the truth. Glancing at Star, she frowned at the look the woman wore.

"I think he did more than talk to you last night."

Emma narrowed her eyes, glad the other women had gone off to tend to their families. "What makes you think that?"

Star reached out and ran the tip of a finger along each cheek and the flush staining her still-pale skin. "This."

Horribly embarrassed, Emma crushed the dried herbs and added them to the simmering water, keeping her back to Star. "Well, I'm glad he's gone and I hope he stays away."

"He's confused."

Emma snorted. "He's arrogant and insufferable."

After considering Emma's words, Star agreed and added some white roots to the stew. "Yes. He is. But you must understand why. He has great responsibility as our chief. My brother has always taken that responsibility seriously, putting duty above even his own needs. He has yet to find balance. You will help him."

"Me? Not a chance. I'm not going to have anything more to do with him." She tilted her chin defiantly.

Star only smiled, which worried Emma. She knew about the woman's supposed ability to see future events. While she wasn't sure she believed in such things, Star

Dreamer's calm acceptance of her from the beginning made her uneasy. "Don't even think it," Emma warned.

The Indian only grinned more widely, then ducked her head to hide her expression.

"I'm serious, Star. I don't plan on staying a moment longer than necessary." Realizing she might sound ungrateful for the woman's kindness to her, she added, "I do not mean any disrespect. You've been kind but this isn't my world."

She stared out toward the hills. "Besides, how could I stay with a man who intends to kill my father? No. There is nothing here for me. When the time comes, I will leave."

Star laid a hand on Emma's arm, her gaze serious once again. "Be careful, Emma. There are many changes to come. Do not act rashly." She stood and walked away, leaving Emma alone.

With a few minutes to herself, Emma picked up her pad and a pencil whittled to a point. Already it was a short stub. With a sigh, Emma knew it wouldn't last much longer. White Wind had given it to her. In return, as Striking Thunder had asked, she'd sketched Dove and Golden Eagle. She'd already done one portrait of Star, capturing her haunted pain. Striking Thunder had returned it so that Emma could present it to his mother.

Emma grinned. Dove, Star's younger sister, had been easy and fun to draw. She found the woman to be high-spirited yet deep; there was a steel core that drove her to be constantly challenging the warriors. There was a complexity and a need to prove herself in this fashion that the rest of the women lacked.

Emma regretted that she would never meet Striking Thunder's brother White Wolf, who was in Oregon. She'd have liked to meet the last sibling in this close-knit family. Willing her mind to empty, she sketched. And as the form took shape, she was disconcerted to recognize Striking Thunder's features staring back at her.

Having put off drawing him, she allowed her hand to

move across the page, stroking and shading. Perhaps if she drew him, she'd rid herself of his haunting image. Her mind wandered. She'd gotten little sleep the night before. All during the long hours of darkness, she'd replayed the scene beside the river, felt again his lips, hands and fingers moving over her body. Just thinking about Striking Thunder brought on the familiar throbbing. She shifted on the hard, cold ground.

"This is crazy," she muttered. What was wrong with her? Something in him called out to a part of her she'd never known existed. Here, with these people, she'd found the freedom to be herself, to explore and discover who she was.

She recalled that young girl standing on the doorstep, calling out to her father, crying until her aunt had brought her back inside and told her she must not cry anymore. Young ladies had to be brave. They didn't show the world their sorrow, they hid it beneath a cloak of dignity. And from that point, her life had changed, ruled by those who needed her to be strong. She'd been molded, trained to hide her feelings, ignore her emotions and follow the rules, even if they went against everything within her.

Until now. Here, away from the stifling confines of proper society, she was discovering just who she really was and what she wanted from life. And it wasn't to be molded into what some boor of a male thought a woman should be. Forget being serene, always acting proper and ladylike, and the rule that a young lady should never challenge or argue with a man. She grinned.

Though she was a captive, that didn't stop her from arguing with Striking Thunder. He challenged her as no other male ever had. When they entered a discussion, it was as equals—both with separate and defensible points of view. And like yesterday afternoon and last night, she'd stood up to him. It had felt good. Whether or not it had been wise to do so was another matter entirely. Which brought her full circle—back to last night and the knowledge that if he came to her now with the promise of more of what he'd shown her last night, she would go—willingly—and consequences be damned.

Like a butterfly emerging from its cocoon, Emma stretched her mental wings and with her transformation, came the discovery of a woman with dreams of her own family. She longed for her own child, yearned also for someone to love her and put her needs first. She needed someone to lean on and trust to be there for her, no matter what. Grimacing, she was truly afraid she'd found that person: Striking Thunder.

She, Emma O'Brien of St. Louis, was falling hopelessly in love with the maddeningly arrogant Indian chief who had freed her inner spirit and shown her there was much more to life than she'd ever imagined. Closing her eyes, Emma knew true fear. Somehow, she had to stop this from happening, for it was a dream beyond her reach.

Setting the pencil down, she opened her eyes and stared at the portrait she'd drawn without any real thought or effort. While she'd expected to see Striking Thunder's stoic features, what she saw made her heart thump.

The features of the man she'd drawn bore little resemblance to the Indian chief she knew well. Somehow she'd captured Striking Thunder as he had looked last night. His hair, wild and loose, framed his face; his eyes, slightly hooded, promised total fulfillment. And his mouth . . . Oh Lordy, just staring at those full lips stirred her blood anew and made her long to lose herself in his warm embrace.

He was right when he'd said all he had to do was touch her and she'd gladly give herself to him. Just thinking of what he'd done to her, what he'd made her feel and where those clever fingers had touched made her tremble. But it was more than that. It was *him*—Striking Thunder, a man loyal to a fault to those he loved—who called out to her heart. What would it be like to be put first by him, to be his top concern?

Heaven.

And she knew he had it in him. Lord help her, she wanted it. All of it. To love him and have him love her in return.

Standing, Emma ran to the tipi and hid the drawing. "This can't be," she whispered. Yet it was. She loved Striking Thunder.

The temperature dropped drastically. Grady braced himself against another bitterly cold gust of wind. Soon, the weather would force him to give the order to turn back. The search party wasn't outfitted for heavy snows.

The idea of giving up, returning without his girls, sat like a heavy weight on his shoulders. It had been a month since he'd learned of Emma's capture and left the fort under the temporary command of Captain Derek Sanders. He needed to get back to his duties, but how could he leave when his daughters were out here, somewhere? He had to find them. *I promise, Margaret Mary, I'll find them. I'll find our girls.* He closed his eyes against the tormenting guilt. He'd failed Margaret Mary with the greatest gifts she'd given him. And he'd failed Emma and the daughter he'd only seen once, the day he'd left to return to duty. No. He'd left to run and hide, using the army as a shield.

Only now did he admit that his sister had been right. He'd run from his grief, shut himself off from the two most important people in his life. He drew a deep, shuddering breath. Oh, he'd meant to return. One assignment. Six months. That was all he'd planned to take. But one assignment had led to another and six months had bled into years. It had become easier not to return and face his loss. For not a day went by that he didn't miss Margaret Mary and her sunny smile, twinkling eyes and contagious laughter. Not a night passed that he didn't mourn the loss of her warm body next to his, cradled in his arms with the sweet scent of her luring him to sleep.

And now, faced with the results of his selfishness, Grady knew true despair. Not only had he abandoned his children, he'd selfishly denied his sister a life of her own by dumping his children upon her. He prayed for forgiveness. With nearly every breath he took, he prayed.

Please, God. Forgive me. Let me find my girls.

Please, God. Give me another chance. I'll take care of them. I'll never leave them again.

Please, God. Keep my girls safe.

Over and over, he prayed, but so far his search had turned up nothing. Day after day, they searched Indian villages but found no trace of them. Today had been no different. He glanced around the gathered Arikara Indians, mostly women and children. Some wept. Others huddled together. The warriors stood stoically, surrounded by his soldiers whose rifles were poised and ready.

His gut tightened as he stared into the wide, frightened features of the women and children. He was a peacekeeper by nature. Now he'd become the aggressor. Rage filled him. These people had stolen more than his daughters. They'd ripped out his heart and soul. He gripped his reins. His horse snorted in response. Taking hold of himself, he relaxed his fingers and banked his fury.

He would not take out his anger on the innocent, especially women and children—though many under his command wouldn't hesitate to destroy the village, steal what they could and kill every "savage." But Grady was nothing if not fair. He'd mete out justice to only those responsible. Grady narrowed his gaze, his jaw tight. Yellow Dog would pay dearly for this crime. The return of one of his men drew his thoughts back to the ongoing search.

"They's not here, Kern'l. No sign of 'em neither." The speaker, a soldier with no front teeth, sent a stream of tobacco onto the ground. "Whaddya want us ta do now?" One by one, each soldier rejoined him. He motioned for Zeb. "Ask again."

Zeb stepped forward and spoke to an old man with long, flowing white hair. There was much hand gesturing. Finally Zeb turned back to him. "Says he knows nothing about any white woman or child with red hair."

"Damn. See if he knows where to find Yellow Dog. Make sure they understand that no one here will be hurt. I only want Yellow Dog. He will hang for slaying my soldiers and taking Emma and Renny."

Once again, Zeb turned to the Arikara chief, but before he spoke, a woman stepped forward and chattered at the old man. After several minutes, Zeb, his features drawn with worry, returned to the Colonel.

Grady's chest tightened with fear at the look on Zeb's face. "Well, what happened? Tell me!"

Zeb pointed to a woman. "She says Yellow Dog was killed by the Sioux. She, along with the rest of the women and children escaped. The next morning when they returned, it was to find all their men, including Yellow Dog, dead. This is the tribe of her husband's family. She has returned here to raise her children."

"Did she see my daughters?" Excitement warred with fear. Oh, God, how would he live with himself if anything had happened to his little Emma?

After Zeb repeated the question, the woman turned to him, her voice earnest, yet frightened. "Says Yellow Dog returned with a woman with hair the color of fire, but she never saw a child. And after the attack, the woman was gone."

A young boy stepped forward. He showed no sign of fear as he spoke to the chief. "Now what?" Grady demanded.

"This boy is the woman's son. He says he knows who killed his father and the rest of the Arikara warriors."

Grady turned to the boy. "Speak, boy. Who?"

At a nod from his chief, the boy said, "*Waagliheya Wakiyan*."

Zeb glanced at Grady. "Name means Striking Thunder."

Grady knew that name, knew of the young chief who was determined to protect his land from the white man. At the thought of the fierce Sioux holding his daughter, his heart plummeted. He turned his gaze toward the west, toward Sioux land. His hopes of finding Emma and Renny alive dipped. The Sioux were the fiercest and most feared tribe in the region. They would be the hardest to subdue if it came to a battle to free Emma, even supposing he found her.

The Sioux traveled and lived in small groups during most of the year, spreading themselves out across the plains and at the end of summer, they gathered in great numbers for celebrations and to conduct their sun-dance ceremonies. With winter approaching, they'd be even more spread out. Even the individual clans tended to separate along rivers in the winter, which made gathering them together for searches difficult.

Grady scanned the sky, noting the dark, ominous clouds. Another blast of cold air stung his cheeks. "We've got to find them."

Zeb frowned. "Beggin' yer pardon, Kern'l, but the snows are comin'. We don't have much time left and we's nearly out of rations."

He considered his options and realized Zeb was right. Grady motioned for the soldiers to mount and when they were a safe distance away, he called a halt. His contingent of forty soldiers were bone-tired and cold. Culling out ten of his best men, he sent the rest back to the fort.

He pointed his horse to the west and motioned the small group forward.

Chapter Seventeen

On foot, Striking Thunder wandered for a day then headed into the Black Hills, toward the towering great gray rock jutting from a thick nest of pines and spruces. There, he would seek answers. It was there he'd had his first vision and learned that his sign in times of battle would be a flaming arrow.

Another more recent vision had provided him with his raven as a special helper. Now he returned to seek new answers with regard to the white woman. Here, he'd lament and beg the spirits to tell him how to cleanse himself of her strong appeal. Reaching the base of the rock, he started his climb. Buffeted by frigid winds, he scrambled for a hold, his fingers so cold that he no longer felt them.

At the top, he tossed down his bundle of supplies: a warm robe, his bow, his quiver of arrows and his shield—the only items needed by a warrior on the move. Inside the robe, he'd carried rocks. Taking them out, he set one down then placed the other four at points far around it, forming a large circle. Around his waist, he had his sacred medicine bundle.

Wearing leggings and a buckskin shirt made by Meadowlark in preparation for the forthcoming winter, he lifted his hands to the heavens. Fringe dangled from his arms, playthings for the wind to toss and tangle. He turned in a circle, stopping at each direction to give a prayer, his voice loud and true as he lamented.

After an hour, he went to the edge of the cliff and surveyed the land that stretched out into eternity. As far as the eye could see, prairie, broken only by the occasional rolling hill or flat-topped mesa, met his gaze. Plumes of smoke from several campfires drifted toward the heavens.

Returning to the circle formed by the four rocks, he untied his medicine pouch. From inside, he pulled out some sweet sage, crushed and sprinkled it across the rock that was inside his rock-formed boundary. Then he donned the newly tanned robe he'd brought. He'd painted it with white streaks of clay to signify purity.

His hands held up he continued to lament, asking *Mahpiya,* the spirits of the heavens, to honor him with another vision. As he did so, he walked slowly from rock to rock, staying inside the bounds he'd outlined. His feet moved painfully slowly. One full circle took him nearly an hour. When darkness fell, he sat but still chanted.

For the next two days, he alternated between walking, sitting and standing. He took no food or water. His voice grew hoarse. Cold, exhausted and hungry, he refused to let up. He had to prove to the Great Spirit that he was worthy of a vision.

Emma fretted over Striking Thunder's absence. It had been several days. How long would he be gone? She seesawed between wanting to see him one last time and the need to escape before he came back.

"You are quiet these past few days, Emma."

Starting guiltily, Emma glanced over at Star. She truly liked the woman; she had become the older sister Emma had never had. If only circumstances were different. "I must be tired," she offered as an excuse. The last thing she needed was for Striking Thunder's sister to learn of the turmoil she fought.

Star gave her a penetrating look but didn't question. Instead, she packed her and her children's belongings, as Emma did the same with her own. Once again, the tribe was moving to a new location. Within minutes, the tipi was dismantled, their poles tied to the horses to form travois on which all their possessions were carried. Emma trudged alongside the horse.

At her side, Morning Moon slipped her hand into Emma's. Emma's heart tugged for the bittersweet relationship she'd formed with the girl who reminded her of Renny. She missed her sister—missed her terribly—and not a day went by when she didn't think of and pray for her. How could she ever have thought she could turn the girl over to their father? Only now did she realize just how important Renny was to her. And when she found her, she'd never let anything separate them. Fighting tears, she took a deep, shuddering breath.

"You are sad."

Emma glanced down into Morning Moon's intense brown eyes. Her first reaction was to lie and make excuses but she couldn't. Though the girl was just a year older than Renny, there was something mature about her. She was a quiet and reserved child, but at times, like now, those young eyes held a world of wisdom in their depths.

"Yes, I am sad."

"You miss your sister."

Again Emma nodded. "Yes, I miss Renny."

Morning Moon tipped her head to one side. "I'd like to know more about her. Tell me about her."

Star joined them. She spoke to her daughter. "You must not ask questions. You made her cry."

Emma brushed back the tears. "No. It's okay. I'd like to tell you about Renny." Star already knew how her father had left her and Emma's devotion to Renny. So she pulled from her heart anecdotes of her sister's escapades. They headed north. The Black Hills were on their left and the river to their right. At the split in the river, they changed course, heading west. Emma kept track of their position.

A halt was called near the base of the hills, the site for their new camp. But this time, instead of forming several circles within circles, each family set their tipi up along the banks of the river. That evening, they had visitors in the form of a group of warriors on horseback, who were greeted warmly and with much enthusiasm. Emma turned to Star Dreamer. "Who are they?"

Star was evasive. "They are Cheyenne."

"Are they friendly?"

"We are friendly with the Cheyenne."

Emma, her time with Yellow Dog still fresh in her mind, looked doubtful. One warrior glanced at her and when he came near, she refused to cower though she wondered what would happen should he decide to claim her and take her from the absent Striking Thunder.

When he reached out to finger one of her long braids, she stepped back. Forget being brave. She'd run like mad if she had to. No one was taking her anywhere. But to her surprise, he turned his attention to Star Dreamer and said something, using hand gestures as well. He pointed to her hair several times, then returned to the fire where his warriors were eating the meal being served to them.

"What was that all about?"

Star Dreamer didn't answer. Her manner turned evasive once again. "He just made a comment on your hair." Standing, she hurried to her parents' tipi to help her mother serve hot stew to their guests.

Emma, relieved to have the visiting warrior occupied, stood. Perhaps she'd spend the evening in the tipi. Striking Thunder's warning of tribes was ringing in her ears. But before she could slip inside, a resentment-filled voice stopped her.

"Star does not tell all."

Recognizing the spiteful tone of Tanagila, Emma was tempted to keep going and ignore the troublemaking girl. She was tired of being taunted every time they came face to face. Yet, something in the girl's voice made Emma glance over her shoulder. "If you have something to say, Tanagila, say it. I do not care to decipher your riddles tonight."

Something in the girl's features changed. Her gaze shifted, turned sly and calculating. "This maiden knows what you do not." Grabbing Emma by the arm, she pulled her away from the camp. "Come."

Emma tried to stop but was dragged along. Finally, Tanagila stopped next to a tree. The dark shadows concealed them. "Star Dreamer not tell you Night Hunter has captive with red hair."

Emma eyed Tanagila. "So? What does that have to do with me? I feel for the poor woman, but there is little I can do?"

"Ah, I never said it was a woman."

It didn't take but a split second for the words to sink in. Emma closed the distance between them. "It's a child?"

Tanagila smirked and walked past Emma. "Now you understand."

Emma grabbed her arm. "Wait. Tell me. Where is his village?"

"I do not know." With a shake of her head and a slyly cast glance, Tanagila smiled coyly. "I could find out."

At that, Emma snorted in disbelief. "Why would you help me? Do you expect me to trust you?" Thinking furiously, she knew this could be her chance. So far, there'd been no hope of escaping. The horses were too well guarded. But if she had help?

Intense, all coyness gone, Tanagila lowered her voice. "You have no choice but to trust me, white girl. I want you gone."

She was right. There was no choice for Emma. If Renny was safe, and in Night Hunter's village, she had to go after her. No matter the risk. "How am I to get my sister from Night Hunter's village?

Tanagila shrugged. "I will give you a horse. You will go. That is all I care about."

Emma knew the girl was threatened by her presence. It was no secret Tanagila turned down other warriors' bids for marriage because she wanted the chief. But to consider Emma a threat? She flushed, recalling what had happened between her and Striking Thunder and conceded that the girl had every right to be worried—not that Striking Thunder would marry a white captive.

That desire, that hope that she shared with this girl gave her the courage to accept her offer. "All right. You find out, but I will decide when and how I leave."

The girl nodded. Emma hurried back to the tipi. Inside, she paced. She had to leave immediately, before Striking Thunder returned. Even then, what she planned was risky. She knew only too well she risked capture again, but she had no choice. She had to find Renny.

Staring out into the night, she considered several plans. The village was spread out, which meant there wouldn't be as many watchful eyes. And though the weather had turned cold, she had warm clothing and a thick buffalo robe. She grew warm. It was the one they'd nearly made love on.

Pacing, ridding herself of that memory, Emma focused her attention on what she planned to do. Though the dangers were great, there was no choice. To die trying to rescue her sister was better than to live with the guilt of betrayal if she did nothing.

Hugging herself, she knew once she left, there would be no turning back. She'd have to find Renny and get them both back to the fort safely on her own. Her mind turned to Striking Thunder. He'd come after her, of that she had no doubt. Her only hope lay in getting a large lead on him. Though her mind was made up to leave before he returned, the thought of never seeing him again sent black despair seeping into her heart. But once again, family must come first.

For two days, Emma hoarded food, careful to take only her share and eat little. Tanagila had given her a general idea where to find Renny and she was anxious to leave. But she cautioned herself to do it carefully and methodically, so she watched, learned the routes of the guards and studied the layout of the land when she went to gather wood. The only thing that worried her was acquiring a horse. Stealing one was out. Not only were they well guarded but stealing was a severely punished crime. Of that, she'd been warned.

But, there was one horse, the one she'd stolen from Yellow Dog. Technically, it was *her* horse. Just because Striking Thunder had taken it from her didn't make it his. So be it. She'd find a way to get it. Passing the small lodge reserved for women during their monthly bleeding, she glanced inside.

It was empty. She'd spent one week there, in the company of several other women. Rather than feeling ostracized, the women used that time to gossip, rest and work on whatever they wanted. Other women brought food and water. Returning to the hut, she studied it. Smiling, she went to find Tanagila. They had plans to make.

That afternoon, she packed the belongings that she would take with her and moved into the woman's lodge. All the next day, she went through the motions of a woman having her flow. Star brought her food and she accepted it but declined any company, pretending to be in pain. She felt terrible for deceiving her, but it couldn't be helped.

That night, when no sound came from the sleeping village, Emma dressed warmly and pulled a dark buffalo robe around her shoulders and head. Taking a deep breath, she slipped out of the hut and into the dark. Around her waist, she'd tied bundles of food, and on her feet, she wore her lined moccasins. With silent step, she followed the river east. As arranged, Tanagila had left her horse with added supplies tied to her back. Mounting, she kept the horse at a walk, glancing constantly over her shoulder. In her mind, she replayed the directions she'd been given. *When the river splits, follow it to the south, keeping the Black Hills to your right*. Night Hunter's camp was located further south from where they'd last been camped. Though Emma worried about finding it and freeing her sister without being captured herself, she had to try. Even if she were caught, then she'd be with Renny. Together she'd find a way for them to escape.

When she deemed she was far enough from Striking Thunder's tribe, she urged the horse into a steady gallop. She had to put as much distance between them as possible. Her only chance lay in having Striking Thunder's people believe she'd ridden east, toward the fort. They wouldn't look for her in the west.

Striking Thunder sat in his circle atop Great Gray Rock, palms up, eyes closed, facing east, waiting for the appearance of *Wiyohiyanpa*. Today, the spirits would talk to him, guide him. After two full days with no food, water or sleep, his body was pure, cleansed. And spending those days walking within the confines of the rocks, praying and lamenting, never stepping out of the circle, his mind was now ready to receive a vision.

Standing on weak legs, he swayed in the wind. He continued to chant, his voice low and hoarse. The hours passed. The sun rose into the sky and still there came no vision. His vision blurred, his mind wandered, and his legs shook. By afternoon, the air had turned bitterly cold, promising snow, yet he persevered.

But by nightfall, he had no choice but to sit, cross-legged, the backs of his hands on his knees, palms up. His lips moved, yet no words sounded. He closed his eyes, focused his mind on that to which he sought answers: the white woman and her hold over him. Why did she affect him so? Why could he not put her from his mind? Even now, images of her danced behind his eyes: her head tilted back, exposing her long, slender neck, her mouth, slightly parted, her eyes closed, her red-dusted lashes dusting her cheeks. Her hair spilled down her back and swayed against her buttocks.

He sucked in a breath. The image of her became so startling clear then shifted, blurred and reappeared, but this time, he saw himself, in an identical pose. Moving slowly, the couple in his vision came together. Heads and bodies moved close until they touched from the chest down. Their arms lifted; their palms pressed together over their heads.

Then they turned so they were back to back. Their hands lowered to their sides, fingers entwined. Again, they tipped their heads back, faces to the moon rising above. Her head rested on his shoulder, his leaned against hers. They were one. Red hair mingled in the breeze with black. Warmth surrounded him, inside and out. Curls of wind wound around them, lifting them high above the ground.

Then, without warning, a jagged bolt of lightning shot from the sky, separating them. Emma faded into the darkness. Striking Thunder fell back to the earth. Standing, he found himself surrounded by enemies on one side and his people on the other. They crowded around. Shouting, gesturing, demanding. Louder and closer, until they blurred into one mass and he could no longer see, no longer feel.

Emma! Where was she? Cold. He felt so cold. The vision faded. Opening his eyes, he realized the cold came more from within but he was too exhausted to give it thought. Laying on his side, pulling his buffalo robe over him, Striking Thunder slept.

Chapter Eighteen

Pinkish streaks across the sky heralded the arrival of the new day. Sun lifted himself over the horizon and leaving his wife, Old Woman Moon, in their lodge, took his place in the sky. Peeping down, he sent fingers of light over the mountains, chasing away dreams brought on by his counterpart, *Hanwi*. Seeing the still form of an Indian warrior asleep on top of Tall Rock, he sent a beam of warmth sliding over the warrior, warming him, luring him from the darkness of the night.

Striking Thunder woke as soon as the ray of light struck his closed eyes. Before taking refreshment, he stood and greeted the four superior gods and their associate gods. First, *Inyan,* the Rock, ancestor of all gods and all things; then *Maka,* the Earth, mother of all living things. *Skan,* the sky, and source of all force and power sat in judgment of all gods and spirits. Last of the superior gods, but the highest ranking among them was *Wi,* all-powerful, defender of bravery, fortitude, generosity and fidelity.

After performing his morning rituals, Striking Thunder drank a little water from his pouch and chewed a piece of jerked buffalo meat as he stared out toward the distant plains. With his mind clear and his body refreshed, his vision returned to him with startling clarity. In the clear, cold light of day, he gave it careful thought and consideration. Though visions were usually interpreted by holy men, Striking Thunder knew he and Emma were to become lovers. That didn't surprise him. He'd been fighting the inevitable.

But the difference in his acceptance of it came with the knowledge that Emma would leave when the time was right. That had been the message of their abrupt separation. Rather than feeling pleased, the thought left him feeling bereft. Yet keeping her was out of the question. Letting her go was as it should be, and this laid his mind to rest with regards to Star's visions of Emma. He'd feared Emma's presence in his life would become permanent.

His life was mapped out. When the time was right, he'd take to his tipi another wife, one of his own, an Indian maiden who would give him strong sons and daughters, as his mother had given his father. He didn't think of his mother as white. Her Sioux blood flowed strong in her, and she'd passed it on to her four children. Even his brother who lived among the whites did so to help The People. His spirit was Sioux, even if his eyes and hair were not.

But Emma was wholly white. She had nothing to offer the Sioux. *But she has much to offer you,* his heart cried out. A lump formed in his throat when he recalled the feel of her, the taste of her, and the sound of her passionate cries in his ear. His heart jumped and his body sang with a life of its own. He craved her, craved what she and only she could offer him. Never had a woman touched his heart as this white woman had.

A shaft of sadness arrowed deep into his heart. He had to remain strong. There was no room for weakness. She was his only until he'd avenged the death of his wife. After that, she'd no longer be needed. In the meantime, he'd take her to his tipi and rid himself of his obsession. Then, come spring, he'd send Emma back to her people.

Satisfied, he gathered his supplies then remembered how cold and alone he'd felt toward the end of the vision, just before he'd slept. Frowning, he glanced around, wondering if that had been part of the vision, or if it had been his body's reaction to the weather and lack of food and sleep.

As much as he longed to put it down to the latter, he couldn't. In a vision, everything was important. Even colors and patterns. And the more he thought of his vision, the more confused he felt. Though he was eager to see her again, now that he had the spirits' blessings to take her to his mat, a niggling worry ate at him.

He buried it. What would be would be. The will of *Wakan Tanka*, the chief god, would be revealed in time.

Leaving the top of the tall granite rock, he drank more clear, cold water from the stream and ate a bit more. After a quick wash, he headed east, taking the direction in which he knew he'd find his tribe. Each tribe moved in a fairly set pattern. A warrior could always find his people, no matter how long he'd been gone.

Forging his way through the thickly wooded forests, Striking Thunder quickened his pace when the first fat snowflakes fell. By early afternoon, the storm broke, coating the land with a blanket of white. Finally, he came within sight of his village. He slowed, took stock of the scattered tipis. Some lined the bank, others were set up a short distance away.

After stowing his weapons in the tipi his mother or sister had set up for him, he started a small fire to warm the enclosure, then went to find Emma. During the day, she would continue to help Star Dreamer, but her nights now belonged to him. At Star's tipi, he hailed, "*Hau,* my sister."

Star Dreamer opened the flap. "*Hau,* my brother. It is good to have you back." Her gaze roamed his features and like him, she gave none of her thoughts away.

Striking Thunder entered and addressed his reason for the visit. "Where is Emma?"

"In the woman's lodge."

Striking Thunder couldn't help the stab of disappointment at the news. All during the day he'd envisioned the night to come and only now, faced with the prospect of postponing his plans to take her to his mat, did he realize how much he'd been looking forward to the night.

Morning Moon glanced up from a oval-shaped piece of hide and called him over to see her work. He stared down at her crude portrait of a laughing young girl. Brushing the girl's braid over her shoulder, he hunched down at her level. "You are very good." It was obvious that Emma had been instructing her, which reminded him of the day she'd done the same with him.

Staring closely, something about that picture drew his attention. It seemed familiar. Only the eyes stood out with clarity. The rest was slightly blurred, though the mouth, that hint of a grin reminded him of a mischievous imp. Something in that simple sketch of lines and smudged charcoal drew him. The eyes, he realized, and that mouth. They belonged to Emma's young sister.

He lifted a brow. How could Morning Moon know what Emma's sister looked like? He tipped her chin and stared into her eyes. Morning Moon stared back but revealed nothing, avoiding the question in his gaze. When her glance slid to her mother, he knew it would have to be later, when they were alone. For a long time, he'd suspected she had the gift. Seeing this drawing confirmed it.

Turning to give his nephew equal time, he ran his fingers over the new larger bow the boy had helped his grandfather make and promised to take him out hunting soon. Preparing to leave, he noticed Star's haggard appearance. Concern rose. He went to her. "You have had more visions?" He kept his voice low, knowing she didn't like to discuss them in front of the children.

She shrugged but wouldn't meet his gaze either. "Nothing I can make sense of." Her voice was bitter.

Pulling her to him, Striking Thunder held her close. Most men didn't demonstrate their affection to their female family members but his mother had known none of that. Her children had grown up showing their love for one another and consequently, they were close. "The spirits will reveal all in time."

Star stiffened in his hold. "But will it be in time for the

knowledge to be of use?" She tore free, wrapped her arms tightly around herself. "I couldn't save even my own husband. His death is my fault," she whispered, so softly that he barely heard.

He frowned. "What nonsense do you speak? It was not any fault of yours."

Star Dreamer lowered her head. Tears coursed down her cheeks. "You're wrong, my brother. If I hadn't fought the messages of the spirits, I could have warned him. He could have stayed behind and been alive today."

Her inner torture made Striking Thunder angry. He loved her so much and wished she could come to terms with her gift. If only he had the words of wisdom to help her accept what was. But he could dispel this one foolish belief she clung to. "No," he said, his voice hard. "You are wrong." Forcing her to meet his gaze, he willed her to open her mind to the truth of his words. "Had you seen his death, had you warned him of your vision, do you think your husband would have remained behind?" He waited a heartbeat. His fingers pressed firmly into her shoulders. "Your husband's place was at my side."

He gentled his tone, his fingers moving soothingly down her arms. "Knowing does not always change the outcome. Many times our people have benefited from both your visions and those of our grandmother but we can't change the plans of the Great Spirit. He is our creator and he chose to call his brave warrior home.

"I know your words to be true, my brother, but still the guilt remains." She drew in a deep breath. "I cannot help but fear the next time. Will I fail to warn of danger? Is what happens a result of 'what is to be' or is it a result of my failing to understand? This is what I cannot live with—the knowledge that I might have been able to prevent the death of both your wife and my husband." She glanced over at her children. Running Elk sat with his bow and tiny quiver of arrows in his lap, and Morning Moon played with her doll and tipi.

"I give thanks that I have not passed this gift on to my

daughter. Though you disagree with me, it is a curse, one I would never wish to impart onto another."

Striking Thunder frowned, his gaze resting on his niece. She seemed oblivious to their conversation, yet he had the feeling she knew exactly what they discussed. He decided now was not the time to voice aloud his own suspicions that Morning Moon had inherited the gift of sight from her mother and grandmother. Time would tell. Star Dreamer interrupted his thoughts as she told him of Night Hunter's visit.

With much to think about, he bade his sister and her children good night. Leaving the tipi, he stood undecided. Emma still did not know Renny lived with Night Hunter and his wives. Worried that the Cheyenne warrior had come to tell him that the young girl needed him, he decided this was another good time to go visit Emma's sister. He'd promised the girl to come whenever she needed him.

Staring at the lodge, he wished he dared go inside to see Emma, to tell her of his plans to leave and that when he returned, she'd share his mat. But men were not allowed in that lodge. Perhaps he could speak with her through the door. Keeping his voice low, he called out, "Emma?"

There was no answer. He called her again, louder. Still no response. Worried that she might be ill, he eased the hide flap aside a mere inch in order to scan the inside. A voice behind him startled him.

"My son. What are you doing?"

Striking Thunder felt relieved to see his mother. Letting his hands fall to his sides, he explained, "I came to check on Emma but she does not respond to my call."

White Wind tilted her head to one side. "You wish to speak with her?"

Hesitantly, he nodded. White Wind tried to hide her smile but failed. Striking Thunder scowled at his mother's back as she bent down to enter the lodge. Seconds later, White Wind rushed out, her features drawn with worry. In her hands, she held several sheets of paper.

"She is not here. I only found these." She held out several sheets of papers that had come from the supply she'd given Emma.

Stunned, Striking Thunder took the fluttering papers but didn't look at them. A new worry took hold. If Emma was not here, or in the tipi with Star, or in his tipi, where was she? Closing his eyes, he knew. She'd run away. And with what Star had told him of Night Hunter's reaction to her hair, he suspected she'd somehow learned where her sister was and had set out to find her.

Guilt swept through him. This was exactly the reason he hadn't said anything to Emma about her sister's whereabouts. He knew she'd risk her own life to go after her. Now, with a storm brewing, her life was in danger. Running to his tipi, he gathered fresh supplies. With the snow storm outside worsening with each passing hour, there was no time to lose. Grabbing his snowshoes and extra furs and his supplies, he draped a thick robe over his back and set off on foot. A horse would only slow him.

Emma struggled through the worsening storm. Her destination was the thick stand of trees off to her right. There, she prayed, she'd find shelter. The wind gusted. Her mare shook its head and stumbled in a deep drift. "I'm sorry, girl," Emma murmured, rubbing the animal between its ears. "But we can't stop now."

An hour later, Emma reached the edge of the white-frosted hill and the sheltering pines. She dismounted and tied the horse to a tree. Another burst of cold air sang through the trees. Shivering, she pulled the robe around her tighter. Her feet were numb with chill, and she no longer felt her fingers. To conserve warmth and protect her face, she tucked her chin and mouth down beneath the thick fur and exhaled, trying to warm herself with her own breath. A fire. She needed a fire.

Gathering some small sticks, she tried to remember

Star's instructions. But with the wind, it was hopeless. She sat back on her heels and choked back the tears. She was cold and so tired. And wet. She stomped around, trying to warm herself. When that didn't work, she found the thickest tree trunk to shield her, sat and ate a piece of hard, dry bread and a strip of jerked buffalo meat. Then, utterly miserably, she waited for the storm to abate.

The afternoon wore on and the snow grew more blinding; the storm was turning into a full-fledged blizzard. She fretted over the delay the weather caused. By now, Star would know of her escape and would have alerted the warriors. Emma longed to forge ahead, but it would be foolhardy to do so with a blizzard raging around her.

Moving as quickly as her freezing limbs would allow, she gathered fallen branches and brush, piling them several feet away from the tree trunk to form a sheltering barrier of sorts. She pulled long, thin branches from several smaller pines then laid them over the top of the three-foot-high shelter, crisscrossing them to keep them from being swept away by the strong hand of the storm. Next, she piled snow around the base. After clearing the snow from the inside, she had a small enclosure with just enough room to squeeze into and huddle back against the tree trunk.

Outside, the loud snap of a snow-laden branch breaking startled her. Her horse snorted and thrashed, trying to free itself. Fearing she'd lose the animal, her only form of transportation out of this harsh land, Emma crawled from her shelter and untied it. She needed better shelter for the horse. But where? The sudden loud wail of wind slamming through the treetops sent the mare into a blind panic. Already skittish from the storm, it danced and snorted in a circle around Emma, finally pulling free from Emma's icy fingers. Emma dove after her but fell. The horse ran off. "Oh, no," she cried. "Come back!"

Scrambling to her feet, Emma quickly realized she had no hope of catching the animal. She needed to get back to her own shelter before the storm obliterated her footprints. Retracing her steps back, she crawled back into her shelter, distraught and sick with fear. Alone, scared and cold, Emma hugged herself tightly and listened to the wind howl outside.

Time lost all meaning. Cold seeped into her bones and her eyes grew heavy. Blinking rapidly, she rubbed her eyes and fought the urge to sleep. But after a while, she put her head down onto her knees and pulled herself into as tight a ball as she could in a futile attempt to keep warm.

Her eyes drifted shut. For a minute, she promised herself. She'd just rest her eyes for a minute.

Grady led his group of exhausted soldiers onward, toward the hills. Despite the turn of the weather, he pressed forward, driven to find his daughters. At every Indian camp, they stopped and searched then rode on to the next. But the results were the same. There was no sign of Emma or Renny, and no one who could or would tell him where to find Striking Thunder's camp.

Frustrated, he stared out at the hills. Time was running out with the arrival of snow. They weren't equipped to spend the winter on the plains. If only he could get someone to tell him where to find Striking Thunder, but the Indians were tight-lipped and protective of their own.

Two days later, the first snows fell, slowing their progress further. The Black Hills were still a fair distance away. Zeb rode up beside him. "The men are tired, cold and hungry. You've got to turn back, Kern'l. The storm is worsening. I know you want to find your daughters, but we risk starving. Our food is nearly gone and game is scarce."

Grady rubbed his gloved hands over his beard, dislodging flakes of clinging snow. He knew the scout was right, but *damn!* Everything in him rebelled against giving up. His girls were out here, he knew it. He *felt it*.

Lifting his pistol, he fired off five shots in a pattern. Nothing. No sound. No shouts. If Emma was nearby, would she recognize the old code they'd once shared? Memories flooded his mind. Whenever Emma got into trouble, his wife had punished her by confining her to her room. Dinner had been brought to her but without her favorite course—dessert. Grady, unable to deny his daughter anything, had always sneaked into the nursery late at night, using his secret knock. Together, he and his daughter had shared dessert and a glass of milk.

He knew Margaret Mary had known of his giving Emma dessert on the sly. She'd even seemed amused by his sneaking it to her, but she'd never said anything to him and he suspected that was why she'd punished Emma so. It was enough to get across to Emma that she'd done wrong, yet, it allowed him to reassure her that both he and her mother loved her no matter what she did. Bittersweet memories continued to wash over him.

No matter what it took, he'd find his daughters. Taking his field glasses, he searched the area. Nothing but white. *Wait.* Near the hills, he spotted movement. Disappointment rose when he realized it was only a horse. Reloading, he fired off five shots and waited. Using his binoculars, he scanned the area. No sign of movement. Even the horse was gone, scared off by the gunfire.

With tears in his eyes, he pulled his treasured lock of hair from his pocket. How could he leave, give up? How could he have left her in the first place? Defeated, he closed his fist around that lock of hair, and gave the command to turn back.

Emma dreamed. Once again, she was a young child. A soft knock sounded on her bedroom door. One, two. Pause. Then the third, fourth, and fifth knock in rapid succession. She giggled. It was her father, using their secret code. He entered, slipping inside with a finger pressed to his lips. In his hands, he carried a bowl of Mama's apple pie, two spoons and a glass of milk.

"Papa!" she squealed, jumping up to hug him.

He set down his offerings, swung her up in his arms

and crushed her to him in a bear hug. We must be quiet or your mother will hear."

Emma nodded. She'd gotten in trouble and her mother had taken away her dessert. But Papa always sneaked her some. Nestled against his solid warmth, they giggled and ate their dessert, and when he tucked her beneath her thick coverlet, it was with the certain knowledge that he loved her. The dream faded as cold seeped into her bones but over and over, she heard the loud knocking pattern. Only, now it sounded like gunfire.

One shot, two, followed by silence then a third, fourth and fifth in rapid succession. Then silence. It was repeated. Startled, confused, she sat. "Papa?" She listened. It came again. "Papa!" she shouted, her voice thick with sleep. She fought her way from the stick-and-brush enclosure, now covered with a thick layer of snow, and fell into the deep snowdrift.

Struggling to her feet, silence and blinding white greeted her. She stumbled forward. "Papa," she screamed again and again but the wind absorbed the sound. "Please," she gasped. "Papa, I'm here. I'm here." Sobbing, she fell to her knees and prayed for the signal to sound again so she'd know which way to go. But there was nothing more. Only cold bleakness.

Snow swirled around her, coating her, clinging to her hair, making sight impossible. Had it only been a dream? Wishful thinking on her part? Shivering uncontrollably, Emma struggled to find her shelter. To her dismay, in her haste to leave it, she'd destroyed it. Suddenly, she was tired, too tired to care. Falling onto the pile of fallen branches and pine boughs, she curled up into a tight ball.

Chapter Nineteen

Night fell, bringing chilling temperature drops. Calculating the path Emma would hopefully take to reach Night Hunter's village, Striking Thunder had a fair idea how far she'd gotten. By not stopping, he hoped to overtake her. By his estimations, she had nearly a day's headstart on horseback but in this weather, a horse wasn't much of an advantage. Snowshoes strapped to his feet allowed him to keep up a steady pace.

Every so often, he stopped to listen for any sound of her or her horse but the only sound he heard was the wind slinging snow across the plains. Dressed in his warmest clothing with a thick furry buffalo hide wrapped around his shoulders and covering his head, the biting wind still managed to seep through and sting his face.

What about Emma? Just thinking of her out here, alone, shattered his control and sent ripples of apprehension through him. She wasn't accustomed to traveling in near-blizzard conditions. Would she take shelter or keep going? Did she have enough robes to keep from freezing?

At mid-morning, he rounded a small curve in the river near the base of the hills. His eyes hurt from the blinding snow and the cold wind. Head down to get some relief, he almost missed seeing the dark brown horse near the trees. The animal lifted its head and shook its mane at him. With a surge of excitement and hope, Striking Thunder recognized the animal as the mare Emma had stolen from Yellow Dog to make her escape.

When the horse trotted over, he grabbed the lead rope, and swept the blanket of snow from its back. He checked for signs of injury. Relieved to find none, he scanned the area. Where was Emma? She wouldn't have left the horse to roam loose. Which meant it had either broken free from being tethered or the mare had thrown its rider. A slight lessening of wind and snow allowed him to scan the area but visibility was still poor.

Worry churned in his gut. Everywhere he looked, he saw white, no bright patch of golden-red. Realizing Emma could be nearby, or several miles away, hope of finding her dimmed. She could be unconscious, lying beneath a layer of snow within several feet of him and he'd never know. Guilt raged inside his heart. This was his fault. If he'd brought Renny to her, she'd never have run off in the middle of a winter storm to find the child.

Tipping his head back, he let out a long, loud cry to catch the attention of the spirits. Then he begged for their help. "You spoke to me. Gave me the white woman known as Emma. Lead me to her so I might fulfill my vision quest."

To his relief, *Mahpiya*, heard his invocation and took pity on him. Though the clouds above him remained swollen, the snow slowed to sparse flurries. Striking Thunder gave thanks then resumed his search. He didn't have much time before the heavens once again dumped a load of snow on the land. Painstakingly, he checked along the riverbanks and then moved up to the base of the hills, looking for any sign of Emma. Nothing.

"Emma. Emma." Over and over he called her name. Where was she? Was she injured? Dead? His gut tightened at the thought. He couldn't lose her. The sudden and unexpected sight of Black Cloud flying overhead drew his attention. The bird normally stayed sheltered within the protection of trees during the storms. But it circled, its caw loud in warning.

The sharp report of gunfire followed, startling both him and the bird. The raven flew into the thick cover of forest. Striking Thunder stood, poised. When the shots came again, the same pattern as before, he listened to the echoes. Whoever it was, they were close. Half a mile at the most. Scanning the snow-covered prairie, he couldn't see anyone. Who was out there? Friend or foe?

Leaving Emma's mare beneath a tree, he slid into the forest and climbed rapidly. From his vantage point, he was now able to spot a small dark blur marring the blanket of white. A tribe on the move? Not likely in this weather. With sudden insight, Striking Thunder knew they were soldiers. Emma's father hadn't given up the search. He hunkered down to watch. If they continued toward him, he would have to abandon his search for Emma and go warn his people.

After another volley, silence fell. Then, to his relief, the distant dark speck faded as they turned back. After another few minutes, they were gone entirely. Striking Thunder headed back down the snow-covered hill. There was no time to lose. He had to find Emma.

The wind chose that moment to wail through the trees, bringing with it a sudden onslaught of snow flurries as the heavy clouds released their burdens once again. He froze in his tracks to listen to the wailing wind. Was that a cry he heard? A woman's voice? Again, it came. *Emma!* It had to be her. She was here, somewhere.

"Emma!" The blast of cold air tore the words from his throat. He slid and slipped down the hill and plunged among the trees, unable to pinpoint where her voice had come from. He turned in a slow circle. The raven left the shelter of the trees and perched on top of a pile of snow, plucking at some pine boughs.

Striking Thunder ran past, keeping to the edge of the forest, sure she would have taken refuge among the trees. But there were so many trees. With a flap of wings, Black Cloud landed on his shoulder. Striking Thunder pressed the edge of his hand against the bird's feet to remove it. He didn't have time for the bird right now. He had to find Emma.

But when the raven stepped onto his fingers, a glint of red tangled around one of the bird's claws caught his attention. Striking Thunder stopped and pulled the single strand of hair free. Emma! The bird was forever trying to pluck at her bright hair. He held the bird at eye level. "Oh, wise bird, my helpmate, you know where the woman is. You came to me in my vision. Now show me." He tossed the bird into the air.

The bird flapped its wings and returned to the pine boughs where he'd perched moments ago. Again, he plucked. Striking Thunder lurched forward, and he saw it. Shoving through the knee-deep snow, he caught a glimpse of Emma's golden-red hair.

A frantic voice broke through the white fog shrouding Emma in a cloak of silence. Her lips moved. "Papa." She tried to move, but couldn't feel any part of her. Her eyes refused to open. *Trapped.* She was trapped in a world of blinding white. The voice came again, urging her to break free of the numbing bliss stealing over her. She tried but didn't have the energy.

Emma had no idea of the passage of time or how long she lay in a numbing world but with a suddenness that caused pain, the cottony cocoon vanished beneath an onslaught of needle like pain traveling through her fingers and feet. A voice demanded that she wake. She cried out, but her voice was only a hoarse croak.

"*Kikta yo.* Wake up! Open your eyes!" Striking Thunder commanded, rubbing her fingers.

"Hurts," she gasped, opening her eyes. Her vision cleared. Striking Thunder leaned over her, his features tight, his lips compressed.

He speared her with his piercing eyes. "You are lucky to be alive. You nearly died out in that storm." He stood.

Too confused to understand his anger, Emma cried out, "Don't leave me." Her teeth chattered uncontrollably.

He bent back down, lifted her head and held the water pouch to her lips. She drank then he laid her down, tucking the fur tightly around her. "Shh. Relax. We're safe from the storm in a cave. I'm not going anywhere."

She watched him walk over to a fire and toss bits of bark onto the glowing fire. Emma turned her head. Firelight danced on the gray walls. Grotesque shadows danced and loomed and made Emma nervous. When he returned to her side, she breathed easier. Striking Thunder continued to massage her hands and feet. Slowly, the warmth from the fire stole over her but it wasn't enough. She shivered, her body wracked with cold and incredible sharp stabs of pain as her blood began flowing again.

She opened her mouth to ask him how he'd found her but Striking Thunder stood and, with quick movements, shucked off his clothing, all but his loincloth. He moved beneath the furs and took her in his arms, pulling her back tight against his front, curling his legs around her.

Emma, to her dismay, realized she was naked beneath the fur, but the warmth from his body stealing into hers stilled her protests. Slowly, her body calmed. One of his hands rested just beneath her breasts. She grabbed hold of him. "Don't leave me," she repeated, afraid.

"Mni kte sni yelo. I won't go. Now sleep. *Istima yo."*

Emma allowed the soft caress of his deep murmurs to lure her back into a dreamless sleep. Just before darkness closed over her, she whispered, "Papa was here."

She never heard Striking Thunder's, "I know," or saw the tenderness in his gaze as he watched her sleep. And she didn't feel the press of his lips just below her ear as he shifted and drew her even closer to his body's warmth.

Striking Thunder woke to the soft warmth of Emma's body wrapped around his. He smiled and pulled the furs tighter against them. Outside the cave to which he'd brought Emma yesterday, the ravaging storm continued. Pain lanced his heart when he realized how close he'd come to losing her. And the realization that it mattered shook him deeply. He shouldn't care. But he did, and not just for his plans of revenge. He stared at the rocky ceiling.

227

Emma, with her brave spirit, her loyalty to her sister and father, her gentleness with the children of his tribe, and her incredible talent for seeing what most whites didn't, had broken through the protective layer he'd built around his heart. No longer could he keep his emotions at bay. His heart and mind warred with the knowledge.

Shifting his gaze to the woman asleep, her head pillowed on his shoulder, Striking Thunder found Emma staring at him with sleep-clouded eyes the color of a misty lake. Lifting his hand, he brushed a bright red strand from her face and trailed his finger down the side of her cheek. "Foolish woman." His voice was tender.

Tears pooled in Emma's eyes. "I tried to find Renny. Night Hunter has her." Her voice came out a mere whisper. "But I failed again." Ashamed, she turned away.

Gently, Striking Thunder tipped her head back, forcing her to look at him. "Explain how you failed again?"

Emma stared at him, her eyes wide and troubled. "I didn't protect my sister. I should never have left home and exposed her to this danger."

Striking Thunder absently rubbed her hair between his thumb and forefinger. Though the wilderness was no place for a white woman and child, he'd never have met her if she hadn't gone in search of her father. "It was meant to be . . . "

Tears slipped down the sides of her face. Her lips trembled. "How can you say that?" she cried. "Those soldiers were murdered because of me. If I'd stayed onboard the steamboat instead of being in such a hurry, none of this would have happened. Yellow Dog would never have seen me, or attacked those soldiers to get me." She closed her eyes and pressed her fingers to her lips.

Striking Thunder recalled the grisly scene of ambush and could only imagine the terror she'd gone through. "It does no good to torment yourself with blame. I cannot explain, except to say that my sister foresaw your coming. You were meant to be with us for this short time. The spirits have spoken."

Emma's eyes flashed with denial and anger. "Don't expect me to believe that I'm here just so you can try and have your stupid revenge."

Rolling over, he covered her body with his and cupped her face between his hands. He didn't want to talk about her father or even think of him. "Then believe you are here for me. For this."

Gently, he covered her mouth with his own. Her lips parted with a sigh and he slid his tongue inside, basking in her sweet moistness. With his touch alone he sought to convince her that this—they—were meant to be. He knew the rightness of it. He only feared that after experiencing all this woman had to offer, he'd never be able to let her go. But that was months off. After all, if the spirits had given her to him, he had to believe they would give him the strength to do right by his people.

Emma broke off the kiss with a moan. She shifted beneath him. Her gaze grew wide as if she just realized she was naked beneath the furs. Her fingers spread across his bare chest. "We can't do this."

Bringing her hand to his mouth, he kissed her palm then each finger. "Yes, we can. We will." Striking Thunder lowered his head back to her mouth, kissing away her protests. Against his chest, he felt the soft swells of her breasts. Needing to see her, feel her, all of her, he lifted his head and tossed the fur off him.

Glancing down between them, he reacquainted himself with her full, pale breasts. "Beautiful," he said, his voice hoarse with need. He scooped one full mound into the palm of his hand then lowered his head. Reverently, he kissed the pink bud, first with his mouth then by sweeping his tongue over the firm, beaded tip.

Her chest rose beneath him and her soft whimper wrapped him in silken threads, binding him to her. His need for her grew and he moved to her other breast, then did what he'd longed to do that first night when he'd seen her bare flesh. He buried his head between the generous swells and inhaled deeply, filling his nostrils with her scent and warmth.

Lost in a sea of incredible sensations, Emma threaded her fingers through Striking Thunder's cloud of dark hair, holding him to her breasts, lifting herself to encourage him to continue his fondling. Whether it was his fingers kneading her, or his warm mouth drawing her aching nipples inside to suckle with urgent need, or his tongue snaking out to tease her sensitive flesh, Emma was on fire. Gone was the cold of the night before.

Her heart pounded furiously, her skin flushed with heat and need as Striking Thunder ignited her passion. His palm slid down her belly, and he lifted his head. With eyes glazed with need, his fingers found that hidden part of her that swelled beneath his touch. Her hips lifted and she pulled him to her, claiming his lips in a kiss that demanded as well as gave.

Secluded in the cave with the sound of the storm outside, Emma felt a tide of passion cresting within her. She pulled her lips from his, but kept her hands wrapped in his long hair as need swept her into another world.

Striking Thunder bent his head and nuzzled her neck. "Feel my fingers." He increased the pressure of his rotations and stroked faster. "Feel what I give you."

"Yes," Emma cried. "Oh, yes." Thought fled as need took over. There was nothing else. Only him. This. And like the night under the stars, her body shook with pleasure, seeking an end yet wanting it to go on forever. This time, when her hips jerked, once, then twice, she was prepared for the loss of control as she found her release in a sunburst of color.

Slightly embarrassed by her reaction, she kept her eyes closed and concentrated on calming her ragged breathing, but Striking Thunder had other plans. Encouraging her to part her thighs wider, he slid one finger, then two, deep inside her. Sensitive to his touch, she arched her back. He withdrew his fingers. She moaned in protest.

He moved over her, settled his thighs between hers. His moan joined hers. "I need you. All of you." He spoke the words against her mouth and slid his manhood across her where moments ago, his fingers had stroked.

Emma felt his male member against her, throbbing in time to her own racing heartbeat. She moved against him, oblivious to all but the aching need to touch and be touched by him. The friction of him sliding along the outside of her slick heat sent shivers of delight through her.

Striking Thunder supported his weight on his hands and threw his head back as if the contact were too much. Glancing up at him, seeing the look of pain mingling with need, Emma realized she affected him the same way. Heady with the knowledge, she reached between them and slid her fingers down his chest, over his flat belly to where his dark curls blended with her reddish ones. As he stroked between her moist lips, she caressed the tip of his velvety softness.

The pressure built. *More.* She needed more. "This is— it feels—"

"*Woitonpe!* Wonderful. Right. As it should be." He took a ragged breath, then claimed her lips once more, his tongue thrusting in time to their hips.

Emma grabbed hold of him as her body began the incredible ascent for the second time, but before she found release, Striking Thunder lifted himself from her and settled himself more firmly between her thighs. She felt the tip of him probe at the junction between her legs. She moaned, feeling as though she stood at the brink of something incredible. Tightening her hold on his shoulders, she pulled him to her. Her hands roamed from his sweat-slick back down to his smooth buttocks.

A look of pure anguish etched his features. "Let me have you, flame of my body. Let me come into you, now."

"Yes," she whispered and braced herself for the pain she knew would follow. Beneath her fingers, his buttocks tightened and with one quick, smooth thrust, he slid past her barrier and deep into her, making them one.

At the piercing pain, her nails dug into him and she bit her lip to keep from crying out. Murmuring soft words of comfort, he bent his head to her breasts and held himself still. Slowly, the pain ebbed and she became aware of only a sweet, pulsing fullness within her. He threw his head back. "Can't wait. Move with me." He pulled out then inched his way back inside.

Afraid to move for fear of more tearing pain, Emma braced herself. But there was no pain, only a growing ache that built with each slow stroke. As passion built, his thrusts grew harder, deeper until her own needs equaled his. The throbbing centered where they were joined and grew, intensified with each stroke, driving her further toward the pinnacle of pleasure she knew awaited.

"Now, *kechuwa,* join me."

Striking Thunder's features contorted. With one final, deep thrust, white flames of passion rippled through them, sent them soaring high on a tide of blissful surrender.

Chapter Twenty

Striking Thunder collapsed beside Emma, pulling her against him, keeping them joined, unwilling to let her go. Nothing mattered. Only him and her, and he refused to consider the future or how he could let her go. He stroked her hair and listened to her ragged breathing. The only other sound was the occasional pop of embers. He didn't get up to rebuild the fire. "You are mine now."

Emma's fingers trailed along his jaw. "I have to find Renny."

He tipped her chin. Striking Thunder knew she was serious. She'd die trying to find her sister and while he admired her spirit and show of loyalty, he also knew just how close she'd come to succumbing to the blizzard. If he hadn't found her . . . He banished the nightmare of those hours after he'd found her and his fear that he'd been too late. "You promised not to run away."

A spark of resentment flashed in her eyes. The color deepened. Sitting, she pulled the buffalo fur around her and moved away from him. "I also said I'd find my sister. I meant it. I will do whatever I have to."

Sitting on the fur he'd worn during his search for her, he studied her. "Even die trying?" Her reply wasn't needed, nor was it given. "How will dying help her?"

Emma shifted her gaze from his. "I cannot sit and do nothing."

Striking Thunder sighed. Standing, he moved to the fire and added more fuel. The time had come to bring the child to his village, both for Emma's own safety and his own plans. The soldiers coming this close worried him. He had no idea if they would return or if they'd left the area for good. He couldn't risk Emma leaving again.

The wind whistled past the entrance to the cave, sending a cold draft to disturb the dancing flames. Lost in thought, Striking Thunder struggled with what he knew he had to do. Though it meant putting his own people at risk to have them both together, he would fetch Renny. But what if Emma decided to run away and take the girl with her? He was fond of the child and didn't want to see her life risked. He went back to Emma and slid beneath the fur. Reaching across the space separating them, he pulled her back to him. Stiff and protesting, Emma resisted.

"What would you do to get your sister back?"

She stilled and lifted haunted green eyes to his. "Anything," she whispered.

"I will take you to your sister if you will agree to move into my tipi and stay with me until the time comes to release you. You must also promise not to take her from my protection and run away. I ask for your promise not to endanger her life."

"I would never put her life in danger."

Emma reacted automatically with indignation, as he'd known she would. He hated the pain his demand would cause but he needed her word. He lifted a brow.

Emma paled and buried her face in her hands. "Oh, God, I've done nothing but put her at risk since leaving home."

Pulling her to him, he felt as low as a snake for making her feel worse than she already did. But he had to prevent her from ever doing anything so foolish again. If he hadn't found her, she'd have perished in the storm. He pushed the terrifying thought from him. "Promise me this."

Emma drew a deep, shuddering breath. "I promise. I'll stay with you if you take me to Renny."

Pulling her hands from her face, Striking Thunder lowered them to the mat of furs beneath them. "We cannot leave until the storm stops. The child is safe and protected. In the meantime, I think I know how we can pass the time." Lifting up onto his elbows, he used his tongue to stroke her from the tip of her breasts down to her flat belly. Her breathy moan told him she agreed.

Two days later, Emma and Striking Thunder left the cave to enter a world of white silence. Trees rose from the ground, their heavily laden boughs weighed down with snow. Above them, a crystal-clear blue sky greeted them and rising high, the sun provided a comforting sight.

Emma lifted her face to its weak warmth and breathed deeply of the fresh crisp air, grateful to find there wasn't so much as a breeze. With no lasting effects from her experience in the blizzard, Emma followed Striking Thunder down the hillside, allowing him to help her when the ground turned slick with snow already melting. When they reached flat land, he pulled her to him. "Remember your promise."

She tipped her head. "Remember yours."

He leaned forward and kissed her hard on the mouth, as if he couldn't help himself. Then he lifted her onto her horse. The animal had been sheltered near the cave in a thick stand of trees and seemed eager to move on. Emma was glad the mare had survived the storm. "I can't believe I'll see Renny soon," she whispered, closing her eyes, finally able to rid herself of her last image of Renny screaming as she'd been torn from Emma's arms.

"You will see her tomorrow."

True to his word, Striking Thunder led them in the direction she'd been headed when the storm hit. As he didn't seem to be inclined to talk, Emma thought back over the last two days spent in the cave. The time seemed dreamlike. Nothing more had been said between them about her father or even the fact that soldiers had been close. They'd spent their time huddled beneath the furs sleeping or making love.

Emma smiled in remembrance. She'd had no idea there were so many different ways to bring one to the brink of pleasure, especially with one's mouth! She tingled between her legs just thinking about Striking Thunder's insistence that kissing her there was acceptable. Oh, it *was*. It was more than acceptable.

Watching him as he led the way, her heart swelled. During their time in the cave, he'd been so gentle, so patient with her inexperience. Without a doubt, in these last two days, she'd fallen completely and irreversibly in love with her warrior.

And that admittance brought up questions like what to do about it. She didn't know, but for now, she'd take what she could. They stopped to rest and eat. When it was time to go, Striking Thunder approached and helped her to her feet. But instead of releasing her, he pulled her close, a familiar glint in his eyes.

She glanced around. There was no shelter. "Not now? There's no shelter." Her voice ended on a squeak.

His lips curved into an amused grin. "Here. Now." He slid her dress up over her hips, pulled his swollen manhood free, then lifted her onto him. "Wrap your legs around my waist."

Emma did and held on as he stroked them both to a fast and furious release. Afterward, she rested her head on his shoulder. "I can't believe how much I want you."

Gently, Striking Thunder lowered her. *"Minseya, kechuwa. Minseya."* He kissed her, long and slow.

Emma sighed. She didn't know what he'd said but she loved the tender sound of it. After a moment, Striking Thunder stepped away, then fixed his clothing while she did the same. They continued their journey to Night Hunter's village.

The closer they got, the more worried Emma became. She voiced her fears. "What if they won't give her to you?"

Striking Thunder stared straight ahead. "They will give her to me."

She wished she felt as confident. Her sister had been right when she'd accused her of being a bore. But what choice did she have? Raising a child essentially on her own was a huge responsibility. Recalling Star Dreamer and Striking Thunder's reaction to her father's abandonment, some of her guilt eased. Responsibility for Renny had been one unfairly thrust on her. But instead of the familiar resentment, Emma longed for a second chance. She'd gladly embrace being boring if it meant having Renny back at her side.

Thinking about her life, and having to go back to a strict, confining lifestyle, something deep inside Emma rebelled. Staring around her, she realized she didn't want to return to that life and the same predictable routine day in and day out. There was no spark, no grand adventure to liven it—except Renny's escapades. She shifted on the back of the mare, startled by her train of thought. What nonsense was this? She belonged in St. Louis. It was home.

Wasn't it? Rubbing her fingers, she glanced down, forgetting she no longer wore gloves to pick at when she was uncertain or nervous. Of course it was, she chided herself. And if not there, certainly in some other town. *Or out here?* a small voice whispered.

Emma shook off the ridiculous notion. What was wrong with her? As if she could live in the wilderness, roaming from spot to spot endlessly! It was an absurd notion. When the time came, she'd return home to the secure world she knew so well.

But instead of representing happiness and security, the thought of once again taking up her old life made her feel caged. Yes, she'd have security, but freedom would once again be lost to her.

With nothing to do but think and ponder, Emma searched her heart and soul, confused by her conflicting emotions. She studied the scenery, looking for answers.

It was so peaceful out here, a painting waiting to be captured on canvas. The rising tower of rock and trees awed her and when she lifted her face to that incredible sky, she wanted to spread her arms out and embrace it all. She wanted to be as free as the birds soaring overhead.

But she didn't hold her arms out or jump off the horse and run just because the thought of doing so made her happy. Instead, she restrained herself. Her upbringing did not allow her the freedom to act in such a manner. Emma frowned. There it was again. That word. *Freedom.* Why did it keep popping into her head? In St. Louis she was free. A respected citizen. Here, she was a captive. No rights. No freedom.

No, that was not true. Since Striking Thunder had brought her to his village, she'd felt more free than she'd ever felt before. The differences came to her. Here, she was no longer hemmed in by what others said and believed. From her own personal experiences, she'd been able to draw her own conclusions and in fact, survival had forced her to do so. With Yellow Dog, her perceptions of the Indian race had mirrored those of society as a whole. He'd been a savage bent on harming others. But that perception couldn't be more wrong with Striking Thunder or his people.

No one in the Sioux village told her how to think or act, and despite her status as a captive, her captors hadn't forced her to do more work than any other woman. They were not like those of her own race who owned slaves and worked them long, cruel hours and considered them less than human. Striking Thunder's people had treated her with respect and acceptance.

That was the key. Acceptance. They had accepted her for who and what she was, judging her only on her own merits. That was where her sense of freedom lay. Even her art reflected her freedom of choice—her subjects. She'd always yearned to draw and paint what she wanted, not what others told her was "ladylike."

She wanted to run across the land with her arms outstretched, and she needed to give in to her temper occasionally and express herself. And most importantly, no matter where she went in the future, she wanted to take a stand and be herself.

Rubbing the mare between its ears, Emma smiled at the ever-changing landscape, the canvas on which she longed to paint herself and her dreams. In her mind, she painted a tipi—Striking Thunder's—and inside, embraced by the warm glow of the fire, she sat with her family. In her arms, she held an infant to her breast and across from her, two black-haired children sat beside Striking Thunder, her husband. That was the image she longed to paint on the canvas of her future.

Acting on impulse, she slid down from the horse and sank into the melting snow. With a shout of pure happiness, she held her arms out and ran, twirling around and around, with her face to the sky above.

Striking Thunder watched Emma with a smile. He felt her wild abandon and understood. No one knew better than he the weight of responsibility and duty. Though he did not resent his position or the behaviors and expectations imposed on him, he occasionally longed to shed them and just be himself.

And right now, watching Emma, he wanted to join her. Her contagious laughter drew him, reminded him of his mother. He fondly recalled from his childhood how she had always laughed, and always his father had responded. How many men in his village so openly declared their love and affection for their wives? Not many would come home after a long day of hunting and take their wife to their mat, uncaring who knew.

His people still regarded his parents as a pair of young lovers.

He stopped. And why not? For the first time in his life, Striking Thunder understood his father and his need to come home and make love to his wife. Giving in to that same need to openly express what he felt, Striking Thunder set his bow and quiver of arrows on the ground and took off after Emma with a shout of his own.

He chased after her, she tossed snow at him and he retaliated by tackling her and sending them both rolling through the slush. Like children, they played, laughed and ran, unhampered by responsibility. By the time they resumed their trek, shoulder to shoulder, Striking Thunder felt lighter in heart and soul than he could ever remember feeling.

Early the next day, Emma and Striking Thunder were greeted by Night Hunter and two other warriors. Anxious, Emma followed the men into the village; it was much like Striking Thunder's. Women stopped what they were doing to stare at her but this time, there was no hostility. They were curious, nothing more.

Emma glanced around for her sister, but didn't find her among the familiar sights of women going about their chores and children running around. Where was she? Was Renny still here? Impatiently, she waited. After several minutes of talk and hand motions, Night Hunter left. "What's happening?" she asked Striking Thunder.

Striking Thunder glanced down at her. "Your sister will be brought to us. We will wait here."

Now that the moment was upon her, Emma felt afraid. She plucked at her fingers until Striking Thunder put his hand over hers. She read the question in his eyes and voiced the fear that had her stomach churning. "What if she hates me?"

He frowned. "Why would your sister hate you?"

Emma rubbed her arms. "For not protecting her."

Striking Thunder sighed. "She does not hate you."

"How can you be so sure?" Emma's stomach tightened.

"Do not make yourself sick worrying over what is not." He tipped her chin and forced her to look at him. "Let it go."

Emma knew he was right. What had happened couldn't be changed. If Renny resented her, she'd just have to deal with it as best as she could. But what about him and his determination to lure her father into a trap?

"And you, Striking Thunder, can you let it go?"

His eyes darkened. "It is not the same. You did not kill anyone."

Emma drew a deep, shuddering breath, recalling the soldiers. "That's a matter of perspective. And if Renny had died out here, her death would have been my fault."

Striking Thunder was saved from having to respond by a child's shout.

"Emma!"

With a joyful cry, Emma whirled around. "Renny!"

She held out her arms and caught her sister in a bear hug. Laughing and crying, she stood, holding Renny close. "Oh God, I've missed you. I didn't think I'd ever see you again," Emma sobbed, overcome by relief and love. "I'm so sorry this happened to you. I promise to make it up to you."

Renny leaned back, her dark blue eyes alight with mischief. "I missed you, too, Em. Guess what, I have two horses of my very own! Can I take them back with me?"

Laughing out of sheer relief, Emma would have promised her the moon. "Absolutely." Setting Renny down, Emma knelt and ran her fingers down her sister's untidy braids. "Some things haven't changed."

Renny frowned, then looked worried. "I ruined my dress, Em. That's why I'm wearing this one. You're not angry are you?"

Emma grinned. "Guess what. I ruined mine, too."

Giggling, Renny glanced up at Striking Thunder. "He is very nice, Em. And he has lots of horses."

"Yes, he is. He saved me from Yellow Dog. You'll get to know him when we go back to his village."

Dancing on her toes, Renny looked puzzled. "But I already know him. He paid Night Hunter three horses for me, then gave Red Rock, that's Night Hunter's wife, a horse of her very own to take good care of me until he came to take me to you. Imagine, Em, *four horses!*"

"Are you sure?" Emma frowned. What Renny said made no sense. If her sister had seen him three times, then he— She lifted her eyes to Striking Thunder. He meet her questioning gaze briefly, then his gaze skittered away. The truth slammed into her.

He'd known. For two months, she'd nearly worried herself sick, wondering and worrying about Renny and he'd known all along where her sister was. Keeping her features schooled, she spoke to Renny. "Are you ready to go?"

Unaware of the mounting tension, Renny nodded. "Almost. I'll go get my things." She started to run off, then turned back. "You won't leave, will you?"

Emma reached out and pulled her back into her arms for another reassuring hug. "Never. I'll never leave you. Now hurry."

As soon as Renny ran off, Emma stood with her hands on her hips and faced Striking Thunder. "You low-down slimy snake. You knew! You knew all along where my sister was and you never said a word."

Striking Thunder had expected Emma's anger. He didn't deny her accusation. "I had my reasons." He didn't elaborate. A warrior had no need to explain himself.

"Reasons! You let me worry myself sick. Even in the cave, when you knew how I felt, you didn't say a word."

Keeping his features impassive, he stared straight ahead. "I do not have to explain myself to you."

Tears of fury beaded in Emma's eyes. "You tricked me. You tricked me into agreeing to share your tipi."

Striking Thunder glared at her. "No. I made a bargain. I said I'd bring you here and I did. You will keep your part of that bargain and move into my tipi when we return."

Emma drew herself up. "Yes. I will keep it. But listen well, Striking Thunder. I agreed to share you tipi. Not your mat. I won't come to you willingly. You will have to force me." Renny returned leading two horses. Emma stalked off to help her.

Night Hunter, who'd returned, stared after Emma with an appreciative smile. "Your woman is very angry. She challenges you."

Striking Thunder smiled. The fire in Emma's eyes fascinated and drew him. His blood sang and every nerve in his body felt alive. "It is good for a warrior to have challenges."

Chapter Twenty-one

Riding across the barren prairie in search of game a month later, his words continued to mock him. True to her word, Emma had moved into his tipi upon their return. Renny had not. The girl stayed with Star Dreamer. Emma hadn't felt it proper for the girl to witness what went on between a man and woman—not that anything had happened between them, a fact that sat sorely with him.

Except for sharing his mat, Emma did everything a woman did for her warrior. When he hunted, she cooked, preserving or sharing what they didn't consume. With the harshness of the cold and wet weather, she repaired his clothing and even made him a new shirt and moccasins. But there was no joy in what she did. It was done in an unemotional, methodical, controlled manner. The laughter and spirited arguments between them were gone.

The warmth and passion she'd ignited in his heart had been cruelly snuffed, all because he'd kept her sister's whereabouts from her. Pulling back on the reins, he stopped. Fisting his right hand, he lay it over his heart. His heat beat, gave him life, yet inside, there was a cold, dark void that left him aching with sorrow.

He'd tried to make amends, tried to talk to her but she refused to listen. When he brought up the sensitive subject of her sister and his duty to his tribe, she walked away from him. No one else dared to treat him so. He was chief. A courageous, smart, cunning warrior. He'd counted numerous coups, led successful raids and won the admiration and respect of his people. He didn't need hers, yet he pursued, tried to win her back. All because he *wanted* her approval, needed to see her smile and gaze at him with love in her eyes.

He spent his days hunting far and wide to bring back all manner of game, sat around the fire at night fashioning tools to ease her workload and went to neighboring tribes, traded for small treasures, including a nice short-handled knife, but still, she withheld her forgiveness. His fist tightened against his aching chest. Not even a gift of three bags of powdered paint, a whole range of painting implements he'd made, and hard-to-come-by squares of hide and smooth bark had softened her. He'd thought those supplies would bring a smile to her eyes but, no, she refused to touch them.

He scowled. He'd been so sure that, given time, she'd come to her senses. She felt betrayed, hurt and angry, and he understood that. But his people came first. He didn't have to explain himself—yet he'd tried to explain that things had been different before they'd become lovers. Before she'd run off, he hadn't realized that to Emma, her need to find Renny was as vital to her as breathing. If he'd believed she'd have risked her life to go to her sister, he'd have brought them together sooner. By not telling Emma, he'd put her life in danger and had nearly lost her.

An ache rose deep inside him. He wanted Emma, longed for what they'd shared in the cave, needed those carefree moments where they could act like children and run wild across the prairie, but most of all, he wanted her in his arms each night. But he stubbornly refused to force the issue. He wanted her to come to him. He wanted forgiveness and understanding.

Many hours later, he returned to his village, his horse loaded with enough meat to feed three families but his heart still empty. Sitting on his horse at the edge of a ring of tipis, his hungry gaze searched for Emma. Frustrated, nearing the end of his patience, he felt tempted to go to her and say, *enough!* The white woman should be grateful he'd found Renny and purchased her from Night Hunter. Was the girl not happy and healthy and robust as any other child in his village?

Though the air remained brisk and cold, most of his people preferred to be outdoors. His gut clenched when he still saw no sign of Emma. Where was she? He urged his horse forward, scanning quickly. Had she run off again? Whenever his duties as chief took him away from his tribe for days at a time, he feared he would return and find her gone.

This time, he'd led a raiding party to take back some horses stolen from them by some Cheyenne. He smiled, his dark thoughts momentarily lifted. Raiding in the winter had become a way to pass the time, enhance skills and prove greatness. Seldom was there bloodshed. The object was to move in and out without the other tribe knowing until it was too late.

Across the way, Renny and Morning Moon rounded a tipi and ran over to him. "You're back!" Renny shouted. "I'll take care of *Zuya Yanka.*" She reached for the reins of his war horse. It amused him to see how much she loved horses. His brother White Wolf, who raised and trained horses, would have appreciated the girl's shared obsession with the beasts.

Seeing the child reassured him somewhat. Emma had not run off. She would never leave her sister behind. Striking Thunder spent a few minutes answering Renny's questions and talking to Morning Moon.

He dismounted, unloaded his weapons and game, then allowed Renny and his niece to lead the animal away. Staring after Morning Moon, he knew he had to talk to her about her visions. If she had the gift as he suspected, then their people had once again been honored by the spirits and there would be much celebrating. Frowning, he worried about Star's reaction to it. Soon, he would have to broach the subject but not yet, not while she still grieved.

Juggling his shield, lance and bow in one hand, he lifted the carcasses of two rabbits and a scrawny prairie chicken in the other and strode into his tipi. A blast of warmth greeted him from the banked fire. Everywhere he looked, he saw evidence of Emma's hand. He turned in a slow circle. Something was missing.

Emma. The knowledge that each evening she was here made him eager to return home each night. And on those occasions when duties took him away days at a time, a strange restlessness took hold. She was a special addition to his life and he missed her. His shoulders sagged.

Frowning, Striking Thunder tried to distract himself by putting away his supplies, but he couldn't stop thinking about the white woman. At first, he'd referred to her as such to distance his emotions. Now, it was with affection. She was his woman. His white woman. His Emma, the flame of his heart.

In a few short months, she'd become his lifeline and without her comforting presence, he felt lost and lonely. The realization did not sit well with him. Reaching out, he stroked his feathered headdress. Each feather cascading down the pole from which it was hung, he had earned. "I am a warrior. I am strong, brave and fearless." The words he spoke were true, with no conceit. They were plain fact, not that it helped. When it came to the white woman, he was weak in mind and heart.

"What need have you for one white woman who causes you to lose concentration and forget your destiny?" Yet the thought of setting Emma free left him strangely depressed. Could he keep her? Refuse to let her go? No. He'd given her his word to release her once he had no more need of her.

You have *need of her,* his heart cried. It jumped. Had his father and brother not taken a white woman for their mates? Yes, but it was different. In his father's case, White

Wind's father was Sioux. And his brother lived among the whites. By marrying Jessie, he had fulfilled the vision their grandmother had foreseen. With Striking Thunder, it was not possible. Pain cleaved his heart in two.

"You have duty to your people," he told himself, but where those words had once instilled pride, now they left him feeling bereft. Stalking back outside, Striking Thunder headed for the river. A cold dousing would ease not only his heated loins but perhaps numb his heart and soul to this pain.

To his dismay, he found the person responsible for his inner torment sitting near the bank, knees drawn to her chest, her chin resting on her fisted hands as she stared out across the fast-moving stream. Coming to a halt well behind her, he hesitated, loath to disturb her. No. That was not true. He was afraid of another rebuff.

The sun dipped low on the horizon and its light fell on her head, lighting the candle of his heart. The sight warmed him from the inside out and just being near her brought him peace and contentment. Closing his eyes, Striking Thunder finally admitted the truth.

He'd fallen hopelessly in love with the white woman. After weeks of denying it, he could no longer ignore the fact that he loved Emma O'Brien.

Why her? Why did she carry him to the highest level of passion both of the flesh and of the mind? What was it about her that forced him to give up the tight band of control he kept on his emotions? Being around her, talking to her, added something to his life that he'd been missing. He saw his own world with a new understanding through her eyes and when they made love, when he gave her pleasure, it took him to heights never before reached.

"She reminds me of your mother."

Striking Thunder glanced over at his father who'd joined him. Still reeling from his shocking discovery, he felt vulnerable—something else he'd never experienced. He frowned. He wasn't sure he liked all these new unfamiliar emotions. A great warrior had to be in control.

"She has no Indian blood." He said the words to convince himself more than his father that what he felt and yearned for was wrong.

Golden Eagle lifted one brow. "Is blood and the color of the skin more important than what is in the heart? Are you less Sioux because of your mother's white blood? Though your woman's skin is white, her spirit is Sioux."

Recalling her drawings, Striking Thunder knew his father spoke truthfully. "She is only here for another few months."

Nodding, his father folded his hands across his chest. Silence gathered in the dimming light. "I still remember bringing your mother to my village. I had promised her safety but couldn't keep her for myself as I was committed to marry her younger sister." He chuckled. "We did not know Wildflower was her sister then." He sighed contentedly. "But I fell in love with a spirited white woman named Sarah. I would have done anything to keep her at my side."

"Even start a war?" Striking Thunder asked.

Golden Eagle spoke, his voice low and husky with emotion. "No. I would have done my duty. I would have married Wildflower to prevent war."

Striking Thunder nodded. "As I must do mine." Luckily for his father, Sarah's father had been none other than White Cloud and as his eldest daughter, she and Golden Eagle were allowed to marry and fulfill the pact between the two tribes. If only it were so simple for him and Emma.

His father spoke. "Time will reveal what is to be." Then he launched into a story of how he had not revealed the truth of his promise to marry Wildflower to Sarah and how she'd run away, refusing to allow him to explain about the marriage agreement. "I finally took her away where we could be alone and made her listen to what was in my heart." Golden Eagle turned and left.

Striking Thunder considered his father's words. In keeping with their ways, his father had not told him what to do but had told him a story that made him think. Staring at Emma, he smiled. If his father could swallow his pride and take the woman he loved away to make her see reason, then so could he.

Sitting on the bank of the river, misery and heartache overwhelmed Emma. Why did love have to hurt? Striking Thunder had betrayed her in the worst way. Though she knew she couldn't stay here with Striking Thunder forever, she'd thought that she'd found something special, wonderful, to carry with her always. But no. He'd allowed her to worry and suffer needlessly. For that, she couldn't forgive him.

When she thought of all the tears she'd shed, the worry that had made her sick to her stomach and the guilt that had wracked her with each passing day, her anger renewed. How could he have done that to her, to any person? He'd proven he was heartless and didn't care about anyone or anything except getting what he wanted.

She needed to believe he cared for her, at least a little. But did he? Had it all been an act? She rubbed her eyes and moaned. Oh, what was the point in this torture. She had Renny back. Her sister was safe and happier than she'd ever been. Wasn't this enough? This was more than a case of simple hurt feelings. She loved Striking Thunder. No matter what. "Fool." The word came out as a mere breath of air. Emma rose, unable to stand the inactivity any longer. Feeling sorry for herself wouldn't help. She needed to keep busy.

Turning, she stopped, her breath hitching in her throat. There he stood, the object of her troubling thoughts. They stared at each other for long moments, then he came toward her and held out a thick robe.

"Put this on."

Emma put her hands behind her back and eyed him. He also wore a warm fur slung over his shoulders. "Why?"

"We are leaving."

Glancing over his shoulder toward the camp, Emma frowned. "What do you mean, leaving? Where are we going?"

Striking Thunder draped the fur around her shoulders and tied it so it wouldn't fall off. "We are going where we will be alone. We will talk."

Pulling back, Emma shook her head. "No. I'm staying here. I have nothing to say to you." She feared being alone with him. If he touched or kissed her, her heart and body would override her mind. He didn't love her, not the way she needed to be loved. Only by keeping her distance, both physically and emotionally could she guard what was left of her heart.

She walked past him but he swept her up into his arms and strode away from the village.

"Put me down," she ordered, pushing at the hard wall of his chest.

"No."

She glanced around wildly, searching for any excuse to stop him. "I can't leave Renny. She'll worry."

"No. I told her we would be gone."

Tears pricked her eyes. How could she stand firm if they were alone? "You are nothing but a big bully, Striking Thunder. Why can't you leave me alone? Haven't you done enough?"

Stopping, but not releasing her, Striking Thunder stared down at her with surprisingly gentle eyes. Her breath caught in her throat. "No. Don't—" But her words were lost when his lips descended. Though he did little more than brush his lips across hers, it weakened her resolve.

He tightened his hold. "This warrior wishes to tell you what is in his heart." His gaze grew intense with emotion. "I was wrong to keep news of your sister from you. It was not my intention to cause you pain."

The fight drained from Emma. Her head fell to his shoulder. "You hurt me. You knew how much I worried, yet you let me suffer."

Striking Thunder sighed. "I told you she was safe, that the Sioux and Cheyenne treated children well, no matter the color of the skin or hair. You did not listen."

Emma lifted a hand to his jaw and forced him to stop and look down at her. "You spoke in general terms. I had no way of knowing you spoke of her. Still, you knew I worried, as much as any mother fears for her child. You did not say the words I needed to hear. Words I needed to know." Her voice broke. "I've done so much harm in leaving home to bring her out here. I'll never forgive myself for putting her through all this."

Striking Thunder set her down but still didn't release her. "Does your sister look as though she harbors ill effects? She has not been mistreated, not by the Sioux or Cheyenne. Even Yellow Dog did not harm her."

At her questioning look, he confessed, "I asked her during one of my visits," he said simply. "She made it quite clear that she was angry with him for his mistreatment of you and of the horses he stole from the soldiers." Striking Thunder chuckled softly. "In fact, from my observations of her, I believe your sister is happy. Was that not your goal when you brought her out here?"

He cupped her face between his warm hands, and his eyes held hers. "Where is that unhappy child? I have not seen her."

Emma searched his gaze then tipped her head back to stare up into the sky. As she thought of what he'd said, she noted the orange streaks spreading across the horizon. Soon it would be dark but she felt safe out here with Striking Thunder. He waited patiently for her answer.

Finally, she nodded. "You are right. Renny hasn't been this happy in a long time." She pinched his chin playfully. "Of course, you bribed her with horses of her own."

"It made her happy."

His words caused tears to spill from her eyes. "Happier than being with me?"

Striking Thunder groaned. With his thumbs, he wiped the moisture away. "Never. Always, she asked about you. And Night Hunter knew he was to bring her to me should she grow unhappy. Please. Do not cry, Emma. *Kiyapi kahaha kin,"* he whispered and undid her braids. Bringing a fistful of her red hair to his face, his eyes reflected the brightness of the moon and a sheen that bespoke his own tears.

"Flame of my heart." His lips brushed hers briefly. Instantly, need and passion ignited. The kiss turned frantic as long-suppressed emotions rose to the surface. Lowering her to the ground, Striking Thunder cradled her in his lap, tightening his hold on her.

By the time they broke apart, darkness had fallen completely. Above, a silvery moon rose slowly to shine among the stars. Emma reached up and untied the leather thong binding Striking Thunder's hair into two braids. Using her fingers, she separated the strands. "Where is it you planned to take me, my fierce warrior?" She glanced around. Total darkness surrounded them as well as silence. In the far distance, she saw the fires from their camp but here, they were alone.

He grinned down at her. "Here will do." He spread his fur robe beneath them.

Emma kneeled before him as he pulled his shirt over his head. His cloud of black hair framed his face and flowed partway down his chest. Without taking her eyes off him, she slowly pulled off her dress, then winced when the cold air slithered across her nakedness.

Striking Thunder drew her close. His hands roamed down her back, leaving a trail of burning heat that matched the flame of desire in his eyes. Cupping her buttocks, he pulled her into the cradle of his hips. His mouth lowered to hers. "I will keep you warm."

Shivering, but not from cold, Emma had no reason to doubt him.

Two young girls surveyed the moonlit land. "Where did they go?" Renny whispered with a frown. She glared at her friend. "I told you we were too far back."

Morning Moon peered into the darkness, then put her hands on her hips. "If we had been any closer, my uncle would have known we were following."

Renny rolled her eyes. Morning Moon was so cautious! "But now we don't know where they are. Now what?"

"We go back before we are missed."

Glancing around the shadows, unwilling to admit she didn't like being out in the dark, Renny nodded. "Okay." The girls retraced their steps. "Will Emma and Striking Thunder fall in love with each other?"

Morning Moon frowned. "I can't tell."

Renny skipped a couple of steps, forcing her new friend to do the same. "Well, I hope so. I like living here."

This time Morning Moon rolled her eyes. "It is the horses you love."

Giggling, Renny nodded. "I'm going to stay here and raise horses just like your other uncle, the one who's gone. And maybe I'll even marry an Indian. That way, we can be together forever." Stooping to grab a rock, she tossed it into the river. "Who are you going to marry? I like Brave Rabbit. He's handsome and runs fast. I think he will make a fine warrior someday."

Morning Moon wrinkled her nose, then stopped. Her eyes glazed over.

Renny stopped as well and watched. It was unnerving when this happened but her friend didn't seem to mind, so she waited with as much patience as she could. Luckily, it never lasted long. After a few seconds, Morning Moon resumed walking.

Hands on hips, Renny stared after her then ran to catch up. "Hey, what'cha see this time?"

Morning Moon shook her head, her eyes wise beyond her years. "I can't always tell. But I know we will be together, as sisters. And I saw you grown with a man—"

"A warrior like Striking Thunder?"

"Don't know what he looked like but he's tall. Real tall." Then she lowered her voice to a whisper. "And I've already seen the face of the man I will one day marry."

"Honest?" Renny thought this gift to be one of the most amazing things she'd ever encountered. "Who is he? I won't tell."

Morning Moon shrugged. "I don't know. I only know he comes from far away."

"That's it?" Renny watched her friend's brows pucker as they did when she thought really hard.

"He dresses in strange clothes."

Renny sighed, then remembered what else Morning Moon had said. She reached over and grabbed her friend's hand. "I'm glad we will be sisters."

"Me, too," Morning Moon said.

Hand in hand, the girls skipped back toward their village. Rounding a bend in the river, both girls stopped when they saw Golden Eagle and White Wind taking a stroll in the moonlight.

The adults frowned in unison. "It is late, too late to be wandering," White Wind admonished in her quiet voice.

Renny gazed up at her with adoring eyes. "We were following my sister and Striking Thunder. We wanted to see if they were going to ki—"

Morning Moon stepped on her foot.

"Hey—" Catching her friend's glare, she closed her mouth.

Golden Eagle speared them both with his sharp gaze. "Return to your tipi."

Hearing the authority in his voice, Renny didn't hesitate. She grabbed Morning Moon's hand and pulled her into a run. While she adored White Wind, she wasn't so sure about the woman's husband. He looked much too serious all the time.

Behind them, Golden Eagle chuckled. "That one is full of spirit and will cause much mischief."

White Wind sighed. "She and Morning Moon remind

255

me of Winona and Little Bird. Your little sister was forever getting into trouble and Little Bird just seemed to be there. Much like Morning Moon."

Golden Eagle smiled at his wife's wistful tone and understood. "Come spring, I will take you to visit my sister and her family." He pulled her into his arms. "Let us walk." He indicated a different direction than the one his son had taken. "I feel in the mood to share the moon and stars with my wife."

White Wind smiled coyly. "Only the moon and stars, my husband?"

With a low, throaty growl, Golden Eagle swept her into his arms, his strides long and hurried.

Beneath those very same stars, Emma lay satisfied and happy. Maybe she'd been too hard on Striking Thunder. After all, he had made sure Renny was safe. Not just safe, she conceded, but happy and content. From her talks with her sister, Emma knew Renny had not wanted for anything, nor had she ever been mistreated. And though she didn't agree with Striking Thunder's reasons for keeping her in the dark, he had provided for her sister. Finally, with a sigh of relief, Emma let her anger go. It was just too taxing on the spirit and soul.

Emma snuggled closer to Striking Thunder. He nuzzled her neck.

"You will share my mat now."

Tipping her chin up, Striking Thunder kissed her long and slow. Breathless, she traced the fullness of his lower lip with the tip of one finger. "Are you asking or telling me?"

Striking Thunder frowned. "Does it matter?"

Though it didn't, as she'd already planned to forgive him, Emma wanted to see what he'd say. "Choices are important."

Striking Thunder sat and pulled her up with him. "Then I will ask. Will you share my mat and let me love you? Will you greet this warrior with a smile when he returns home each night?"

Though there was much still unresolved between them, Emma felt her heart swell with love. "Yes, I'll share your mat and more. I'll share your life." Risking the words, she added, "I love you, Striking Thunder."

Silence. Emma feared she'd ruined the peace between them, but his features softened in the moonlight.

"You are the flame of my heart." He pulled her on top of him. "Love me. Make me yours forever, my love, my *wasicun winyan.*"

Emma pushed him down and slid her body over his. Her lips rested on his. "Yes, my *tekihila*. My love. This white woman is yours."

Chapter Twenty-two

Spring crept across the land. Tiny green blades of grass pushed through the wet earth, prairie dogs scampered, played and groomed themselves beneath the golden sun spreading its warmth across a land eager for the change of seasons.

The promise of renewal lifted the spirits of the people who lived off the land as well. Laughter and excitement replaced dreary frowns, and those who'd fallen ill over the winter and survived felt a lightening in their spirits.

One such woman, Weyanna, whose name meant Little Woman, greeted Emma with a smile that split her aged face in two.

Emma reached out and greeted the old woman, thankful to see that her eyes were considerably brighter beneath their drooping lids. *"Hau, Uncl. Toniktuka he?"* In halting Lakota, Emma asked her how she was feeling.

Little Woman lifted a thin, wrinkled hand in greeting. *"Mabliheca yelo."*

Kneeling, Emma helped her to sit. "I am glad you are feeling better," she whispered. Over the winter, she'd grown fond of the widowed woman who'd fallen ill. Balancing a bowl of rich broth, greens and fresh meat, Emma spooned the nourishing meal to the old woman who ate with more appetite than before.

Emma would never forget coming to check on her and finding her on the floor, her frail body wracked with fever. For a month, she'd helped Dove, whose knowledge of herbs made her the tribe's healer, nurse her, staying with her long into the night.

With a strong will, Little Woman had made a painfully slow recovery. And as a result, they'd formed a bond. Emma thought of her as her *uncl,* her grandmother, and Little Woman now called her *cunksi,* daughter.

Setting the nearly empty bowl down, Emma went to a pile of furs and picked up a large, soft robe—one she'd fashioned for Weyanna over the long bleak winter days. She settled it around the woman's frail shoulders, then helped her outside where she made her comfortable on another pile of furs waiting in the warm sunlight. Seeing that she was settled and her friends were already approaching for a spot of gossip, Emma left.

A group of girls ran past. Renny, among them, stopped and held out a miniature tipi and said something in Lakota. Emma only recognized a couple of words and shook her head. Her sister had definitely picked up the language faster than she had.

"Would you care to try English first, then repeat what you said, slowly?"

Renny giggled. "I'm sorry, Em. I didn't even think. But look at what White Wind gave me. My very own tipi. I get to paint it myself, too! And when I play with the other girls, I'll have my own toys."

In her arms, she carried a doll Star Dreamer had shown Emma how to make. She and Renny had celebrated Christmas on their own, as close to the day as Emma could figure. Her sister had given Emma a leather bracelet, which she never took off.

"Gotta go, Em. Bye." In a rush, Renny ran to catch up with the others.

A low, throaty chuckle sounded close to Emma's ear. Striking Thunder's strong hands pulled her against his hard chest. "*Weshawee* is happy?"

"Yes, Renny is happy."

Together they watched the girl run after Black Cloud; the bird had snatched her doll from the ground beside the miniature tipi. Emma laughed. "I should have used black hair."

Striking Thunder chuckled and fingered her red braids.

"And you, Emma? Are you happy?"

Taking a minute to consider his question, Emma glanced around. Five months ago, she'd have laughed at the very thought that she could be happy out here with these people, but surprisingly, she was.

No. Not just happy. Content. Little Woman had become a part of her adopted family, and Star, an older sister. And Striking Thunder? He'd become her mate. He was all the things she'd ever yearned for. Kind and caring, even if a bit arrogant, he was a good provider, and most of all, he was her companion. Someone she could talk to and share her thoughts with.

Emma's lips curved and her hands slid down her dress to rest on her belly. If she was right in her suspicions, he'd given her a child of her own.

Striking Thunder gripped her a little harder as if anxious for her reply. "You take so long to answer. This warrior fears you are not happy."

Resting the back of her head against his shoulder, she smiled. "I am happy. Very happy."

Striking Thunder wrapped his arms around her and nuzzled her cheek with his. "Perhaps you would care to return to our tipi. This warrior might know how to make his woman even happier."

Emma turned in his arms. "I think it is my turn to make you happy." She leaned forward and whispered in his ear what she wanted to do to him when they reached their tipi.

His eyes sparkled in anticipation. "Only if I get to do the same to you, *kiyapi kahaha kin*."

With a sigh, Emma leaned forward. She loved it when he called her "Flame of My Heart" and prayed it was so.

One person in all of Striking Thunder's tribe resented the obvious love between their chief and the white woman.

Tanagila couldn't understand why Striking Thunder preferred the white woman over her. Reaching the river, she knelt to refill the water pouches.

With her father and brother bringing pressure for her to accept Tatankaota's marriage proposal, her time was running out. To stall her father, brother, and the persistent warrior, she'd agreed to think on his latest offer but in reality, she needed the time to figure out a way to get rid of the white girl. She'd almost succeeded last time but Striking Thunder had recovered the woman. No one knew of her role in Emma's flight.

Standing on the bank, she watched the swollen river rush past. Overhead, the night stars winked down at her and night sounds surrounded her. The peace calmed her somewhat, as did the clear notes of a flute in the distance. Some warrior was courting a maiden.

She closed her eyes, giving herself over to the magic of the night, pretending it was Striking Thunder who played a love melody to woo her. The music grew louder, the notes more sensual. Tipping her head back, she swayed in response.

When the last note died away, she sighed. So entranced was she, she never heard Tatankaota approach. "When we are man and wife, I will play for you every night."

Jarred back to reality, dismayed to have found herself responding to the magic of *his* flute, Tanagila moved away. "I have made no decision."

The warrior put the flute to his lips and sent another string of notes floating across the land. When he stood close, he dropped the hand holding the wooden instrument so he could lean forward and draw her to him with his other arm. He smiled gently then lowered his head and kissed her.

His touch, the warmth of his mouth against hers weakened her resolve not to have anything to do with him.

Finally, he lifted his head. "You will agree. Already you are mine. Your heart knows this and soon, your mind will also learn.

Breathing hard, she backed away. "Do not be so sure. There is much for me to consider."

"If you are waiting for our chief, you will wait long. His heart belongs to the white girl. All others see this."

Tanagila narrowed her eyes. She hated hearing the truth from him. "It won't last. Soon, he will return her to her people."

"So naive you are, my darling hummingbird. He will not release her. And I do not think the woman wishes to leave. Now that her sister is among us, she is happy." He grinned, looking very pleased.

She tossed her head. "And how happy will she be when she learns our chief is nearly ready to take her father's life, avenging my sister's murder?"

The warrior frowned. "This is her life now. She will understand."

Staring at the warrior who now made her heart thump wildly, Tanagila laughed. Did he really believe that? And more importantly, did Striking Thunder think he could kill the woman's father and nothing would change? She sobered as a thought came to her.

What if the white woman didn't know? What if she, in her stupidity, actually thought Striking Thunder would give up his quest for revenge because of her? Her grin turned to a smirk. Yes, she would believe that. It was time for someone to inform the white girl of the facts.

"What thoughts take you from me?" Tatankaota's gaze searched hers.

Schooling her features to hide her glee, she bent down and picked up the water pouches. "It is not proper for us to be out here alone. I must return to the tipi of my parents." She walked past him. His hand snaked out and stopped her.

"Do not think to cause mischief. The spirits have already chosen the next bride for our chief."

Standing on tiptoe, Tanagila brazenly pressed her lips to his to distract him. "This maiden has decided that you may walk her back." With that, she swung around and headed toward the camp at a slow walk.

Tatankaota, mesmerized by the teasing sway of her hips, the brush of her long hair against the gentle swell of her buttocks, forgot all else but her. Grinning from ear to ear, he put the flute to his lips. All who heard his music knew where his heart lay.

Grady returned to the fort from his daily ride just before the gray clouds released their springtime burdens. He'd decided the time had come to renew his search for his daughters. March had arrived and soon, the extra men he'd requested would arrive, allowing Grady to form larger search parties. Though the fort was closing, he'd been given permission to remain a bit longer to search for his daughters.

But before he headed back out into Sioux territory, he had some issues to settle. In his office, he sent Perkins to fetch Captain Sanders. While waiting, he pulled the lock of Emma's hair from his pocket and stared at it. The captain was Emma's only chance at a normal life after he found her—and he had no doubt that he would find her.

It never occurred to him that Derek would refuse. He had several new assignments to tempt the captain. Nice, safe desk jobs in booming cities that offered all the amenities one might wish for. A knock sounded. "Enter," he called out, tucking the precious lock of hair back into his pocket.

Sanders entered and saluted smartly. Grady returned the salute and took his seat behind his desk. Instead of taking the chair opposite, the captain remained at attention, looking sharp as ever in a clean, neatly pressed uniform. His dedication to personal cleanliness was just one aspect of the man Grady admired. The other was the man's determination to progress through the ranks.

Though it was no secret that Derek wanted command of the fort, and didn't know that soon the fort would close, Grady hoped to make it up to him with a nice promotion and a large dowry. Pointing to the chair, Grady ordered, "Sit, Captain. This is an informal meeting."

Derek lowered himself into the chair but did not relax his body. "What did you want to see me about, Colonel?"

"You're a good soldier, Captain. I don't know that I could have managed to keep things running here without your help."

"Only normal, sir, considering what has happened. You know I want to help. We will find your daughters."

But in what shape? Grady worried, his gut twisting with renewed fear. With his knowledge of Indians, he didn't fear for his youngest. She was a child and most of the Sioux tribes would not harm an innocent child. No. It was his elder daughter's fate that gave him nightmares. Just thinking about what he might find made him break out in a cold sweat.

"I won't beat around the bush, Captain. You know as well as I what Emma faces when we find her." He speared Derek with his worried gaze. "If word gets out that she spent the winter as a captive, her life will be in ruins."

Derek didn't hesitate. "You know how I feel, Colonel. We will marry as planned. There won't be any reason for anyone to know."

Grady sat back in his seat, feeling a small measure of relief. "No one would blame you if you changed your mind."

Derek frowned. "Have *you* changed your mind?"

Shocked, Grady leaned forward. "Good heavens, no. I just wanted to be sure of your feelings on this matter."

Derek looked him straight in the eyes. "My feelings have not changed."

"That is good," Grady said. "Any word from the scouts yet as to where this Striking Thunder's village might be found?"

Derek shook his head. "No. I will continue to ride out

and ask questions. No one around here knows or if they do, they won't tell."

Grady stood. "Be careful, Captain."

"Yes, sir." Derek stood and spun around sharply to leave. Then as if he'd thought of something, he hesitated at the door. "Colonel, it might be best for all concerned if Emma did not return to society for a while. After we're married, we could stay here."

Grady frowned, then understood. "We will see how she is when we find her. If she is overly distraught or not thinking right, I will bring in the best doctors." He made a mental note to pull strings and leave enough soldiers here to guard his daughter if needed until she could return to St. Louis.

"Yes, sir."

Derek saluted smartly, then left, ecstatic. Command of the fort was as good as his and soon, riches beyond his wildest dreams would follow. His lips twisted briefly into a grimace. If only there was a way to secure his position without having to take Emma as his wife for even a brief period.

He'd hoped that the colonel would never learn where she was but that hope had died when the search party had returned two months ago. Chances were, once the search resumed, they'd find her alive. All they had to do was locate Striking Thunder's village.

But Derek was ready for Emma's return. Yes, he'd marry her, and shortly after her father left for his new post, Emma would fall victim to an unfortunate accident or perhaps he would make it look as though she'd taken her own life. After all, it was common knowledge that captive woman sometimes went mad.

Even though he had it all planned out, it bothered Derek that others would know he'd married soiled goods. Everyone knew he didn't share his women. He didn't relish being the center of the men's ribald jokes and comments.

Maybe he should convince the colonel to split the search, then Derek would have a chance of reaching her first and making sure she didn't come back alive. If he found the colonel's younger daughter, he would still remain in the man's good graces. He knew of only one person who could take him to Striking Thunder's village.

Leaving the building, Derek hesitated when a group of soldiers rode up. They dismounted and one man, wearing the rank of sergeant stopped in front of him and saluted.

"Where can I find Colonel Grady O'Brien, Captain?"

Derek indicated the door at his back. "In there. What is this regarding?"

"I have a letter to deliver from headquarters." The sergeant stepped close. "Y'all will be glad to know, the army is closing down this godforsaken fort. Wasted money spent on it. Not even a decent river landing."

Stunned, Derek's mouth moved. "No. *This cannot be.*" He plucked at his mustache. "You must be mistaken, soldier."

Roberts shook his head. "No, sir. It's all here in this letter. Everyone's being reassigned, effective immediately. The colonel, he already knows, but this letter makes it official. Guess I'd better get this to him then head out. Got my orders to continue upriver to Fort Randall and report to the general there. That's where most of y'all will go."

Derek thought fast. They couldn't close Fort Pierre. He couldn't leave. Too much was at stake. Then the real truth hit. The colonel knew he wouldn't ever have command of the fort and when they found Emma, he'd still be expected to marry her, only it'd all be for nothing.

Roberts left but Derek was lost in a sea of fury.

Gone. Destroyed. All his dreams of the future lay in ruins. Without the might of the U.S. Army behind him, he had no chance of finding that river where nuggets of gold flowed in abandance. He pulled his last remaining nugget from his pocket. Alone, it would fetch him a fair amount of money, but not enough.

He wasn't going to live in some falling-apart shack or in some rundown farmhouse when he left the service. He needed money and lots of it. Lifting his head, he thought of Wild Sage. He was willing to bet she knew where to find the gold. He straightened. He'd force her to take him to the source. With her, he'd be able to move through Indian territory, especially if he were dressed as a trapper.

Gathering his gear, he froze. The army. His enlisted status wasn't up for a year. If he refused to marry Emma, there was a good chance his next post would be in some other godforsaken place, like some fort along the Oregon Trail to protect immigrants. He was stuck having to marry Emma.

Unless she wasn't found alive. Filled with purpose, he left his room. Soldiers gathered outside stepped back quickly, giving him a wide berth as he slammed the door behind him then strode out into the rain.

A short while later, he stormed into Wild Sage's tipi. She and another woman jumped when he entered. Wild Sage paled. "Do you know of a Sioux chieftain named Striking Thunder?"

She and the other woman exchanged glances. "He is great chief. All know him." Wild Sage stood.

Derek stroked his chin, considering his options. "Can you find his tribe?"

Wild Sage hesitated and clutched her hands tightly in front of her. "Each tribe moves. Very hard to find."

Derek studied her. Instead of fear in her eyes, he saw evasiveness. Two long strides brought him to her. "You lie, bitch." He yanked on her hair.

She cried out. "Why you want know?"

"I need to find the colonel's daughter before he does. You will take me there, help me get her. If you don't, I will kill you and leave you to the buzzards."

Her eyes went wide with fright.

"And after I take care of Emma, you will take me into those hills and show me where to find more of this." He held out the gold nugget.

"Hills sacred—" She broke off when he yanked her hair. "Wild Sage take you."

"Wise, bitch." Glancing around, Derek's gaze fell on the other woman. He'd forgotten she was still there. When she stood and headed for the door, he stopped her.

The fear in her eyes confirmed she'd understood enough of what he'd said. "Now, where do you think you are going, old woman?"

She struggled. Her long nails raked down his face. Taking his revolver from his belt, he slammed the butt into her head. She slumped to the floor. Wild Sage cried out and ran to her.

He grabbed the squaw and threw her to the ground. "Shut up." With the roiling emotions and rage running through him, he needed release. Removing his belt, he snapped the leather loud. Wild Sage cowered and whimpered, bracing herself for the first blow.

Chapter Twenty-three

Grady, informed that an Indian woman had been found near death from a blow to her head, strode into the infirmary, his steps hurried, his boots loud on the wooden floorboards. "Where is she? What happened?" His bellow woke any patients who were sleeping. Doc Gil left a bed and hurried down the aisle toward him.

"Beggin' pardon, Colonel, keep it down."

Glancing around, seeing several familiar faces, he nodded. "Sorry. What's going on? Who is this woman?"

"Some old Sioux woman. Got knocked on the head and lost a lot of blood before she was brought here. Zeb's with her now along with some other squaw who insisted on staying with her." Gil stopped. "She ain't gonna make it."

Reaching the narrow cot, Grady stared down at the old woman. Around her head, white strips of cloth had been wound to staunch the flow of blood. Kneeling, he took the woman's frail hand into his. "Who did this to her?"

Zeb spoke to the woman standing to one side of the bed in halting Dakota. She spoke, her voice faint and trembling.

Zeb lifted his puzzled gaze. "She says 'the Captain.'"

Searching the woman's features, Grady saw stark fear in her eyes. He glanced down at the dying woman then back at Zeb. "Sanders? Is she sure?"

Zeb nodded. "She and some others saw him go into Wild Sage's tipi, heard him beating her. When he left, taking Wild Sage with him, the women went inside and found this woman in a pool of blood."

Grady glanced back down at the old woman. Her breathing had grown shallow. "Why would he do this?" He looked to Zeb.

The scout scratched his head. "I don't know, Kern'l."

A voice across the room called out, "Beggin' yer pardon, Colonel, but that squaw there speaks the truth when she says the captain is mean."

Grady went to the cot where a young soldier lay sweating with fever. "Ben, isn't it?" The boy nodded. "Explain yourself?"

"Yes sir. It's just that the captain, well, he has a mean streak, especially toward the women. Hates the Sioux." The boy looked uncomfortable then continued. "Well, it's just that he's pretty rough with them, you know, when he goes to their tipis. . . . He leaves them pretty beat up."

Grady knew the men used the women as prostitutes, but this? How could he not have known about this?

Thinking back over the meeting he'd just had with Derek, Grady replayed it and had a hard time believing what he was being told. "Colonel?" Ben lowered his voice so no one else could hear.

"Heard Gus braggin' one night how he and the captain—along with those other men that got themselves kilt—was goin' around harassing them Indians and raping their women. I didn't believe Gus, just thought he was just tryin' to impress us."

Feeling sick at heart that his judgment had been so far off, Grady patted the boy's shoulder. "Thank you, soldier. You rest and get well."

Turning on his heel, he left the sickroom. Forgetting to keep his voice low, he shouted, "Zeb, take me to where that old woman was found."

A short while later, he arrived at the tipi belonging to Wild Sage. He went inside to search, but aside from the spot where the woman had been found, there was nothing there to give him any clue as to what was going on.

Outside, he strode over to where several women huddled. Motioning to Zeb, he asked questions. Learning of the captain's darker nature chilled Grady's blood. He now had a pretty good idea of the cause of anger and unrest in the area. Another soldier rode up and confirmed that Derek's horse was missing from the corral. He also mentioned the captain's fury in the officers' quarters.

Confused and concerned, Grady tried to make sense of all this. What had happened from the time Sanders had left his office to his escapade with Wild Sage to put him into a rage? He'd seemed eager to please and in good spirits, especially when they'd talked about promotions and Emma. A chill went through him. Did Derek not want to marry Emma? Had he said he would just to please him, to get into his good graces?

Grady recognized Sanders's driving desire for promotion. It had been one of the traits he'd admired in the man. If the man had changed his mind about Emma, felt he couldn't marry her because of her captive status, would he have come right out and said so?

The answer was no. Grady knew Derek would not have risked angering a colonel by refusing to marry his daughter. He'd wanted the promotion, the command of the fort.

That thought stopped him. Now things were coming together. With the arrival of Roberts and the official transfer papers, the captain must have learned that Fort Pierre was to be abandoned—and with it went the promotion he wanted.

Motioning for his men to follow, Grady headed for the corralled horses. To what lengths would Sanders go to keep from marrying Emma? With the death already of one woman, Grady feared he knew.

Sitting outside, Emma glanced across the fire at Dove.

271

Instead of sewing or preparing sinew, beading, or any other normal task on which most women spent their time on, the girl stripped feathers for the prepared arrow shafts in her lap.

The soon-to-be arrows had already been nocked and scored down the side to keep the arrow straight and so that it would have good spirit. Now, she stripped feathers for the next step. The feathers were of all shapes and sizes and had been sorted into lefts and rights.

Between them, a huge hunk of meat cut from a prime antelope roasted over the fire. Returning warriors strode past, eyes straight ahead, heads up and shoulders back. None looked at Dove or the meat, which amused Dove to no end. She wore a pleased grin. Her skills with a bow continued to be a source of friction between her and those warriors who had once sought to court her. How could a warrior impress her with gifts of fur when she could easily procure her own?

Curious, Emma set down the shirt she was painstakingly beading. "Why do you do it?"

The other girl glanced up and grinned, her pale blue eyes sparkling with deviltry. "When I marry, it will be to a great warrior, one who is brave, cunning and handsome."

She bit gently on the end of a quill to hold it steady and proceeded to strip the feathers from it in one smooth pull. The two vanes were also put into different piles. Vanes from the same feather were never used on the same arrow.

Emma glanced around, her gaze falling on one unmarried warrior after another. They all seemed to meet Dove's requirements. "Aren't there already so many to choose from?"

Dove snorted and shook her head. "The warriors of my tribe are all the same." Pride laced her voice. "All are brave, smart and fearless. But none are special. The one I will give my heart to must be different. He must prove himself to be above all others."

"So you challenge them so they will prove themselves?"

Dove giggled. "No. I challenge them because it's fun to watch them squirm."

Staring at the other girl in disbelief, she burst into laughter. "Dove, you are incorrigible."

Star joined them. "You will meet your match one day, sister of mine."

Dove scoffed, then narrowed her eyes. "Have you had a vision? Have you seen this warrior who will be greater than all?"

Star chuckled. "I have seen the one who will one day win your heart. You will learn that love is the greatest gift a man brings a woman. I will say nothing more on the matter."

Emma chuckled and watched, vastly amused as Dove tried to ferret the information from Star. But Star remained tight-lipped. Finally, Dove jumped to her feet and stormed off.

"That was quite mean of you to tease her so, Star." Emma was glad to see a spark of mischief in her friend's eyes.

"Yes, but no worse than what Dove does when she torments so many braves."

Emma tilted her head. "Have you really seen her future?"

A secret grin flashed before Star bent her head to her task.

"You are a wretched tease today." Emma kept the conversation light. Talk turned to the many tasks that fell to the women during the spring. It was a busy time, one Emma embraced as it kept her troubled thoughts at bay.

She loved Striking Thunder and wanted to stay with him, but they did not discuss the future; neither was willing to ruin what they had. But as time went on and nothing more was said about her father, Emma began to hope that love had changed his mind. Now, with a babe on the way, Emma had to choose: stay or return to St. Louis.

She frowned and paused in her work. What if Striking Thunder didn't want to marry her? Could she be content to share only his tipi and mat? She didn't know.

Stretching her cramped fingers, she glanced at the sun's position then put her beads back into her small, palm-sized pouch. Pride filled her as she ran her fingers over the designs worked onto the pouch she'd made. Getting to her knees, she glanced at Star. "Time to start the evening meal—"

Emma sat back on her heels. Star's eyes had gone distant, her face pale and white. "Star?"

"Murderer." The whispered word held fear. Her eyes had turned nearly black and were wild. "Do not trust him." She shuddered.

A cold sliver ran through Emma. Concerned, she reached over to hold Star's hand. "Who, Star? Who is it? Can you describe him?" Was it her father Star was warning of? No. Please, God, don't let her father be the monster these people thought him to be.

Weeping softly, Star trembled. Worried that her friend was having a breakdown, she motioned White Wind over. Star, still held in the grip of the vision, rocked back and forth.

"Soldiers. One not dressed as the others. Hatred lives within." She stopped, gasped, then continued. "There is good among them. Not all bad. Confusing. Two beings. The eagle and the buzzard. But I can't see. I don't know." Her voice turned gritty. "I can't help."

White Wind murmured to her daughter. Emma could only wait and watch helplessly. Finally, Star's eyes cleared but her features remained pinched. Together, she and Striking Thunder's mother led Star to her tipi. Emma heated water for tea, all the while thinking of Star's words but not knowing what she'd meant. After a while, Star fell into a troubled sleep.

"I will take the children with me."

Emma nodded. "Renny can stay with me. I don't wish to burden you with so many children in your tipi."

White Wind smiled. "It will be good to have them with us. Our tipi is empty now. Besides, Morning Moon and your sister are inseparable."

The reminder worried Emma. What would happen to Renny if they had to leave? She was so happy here.

Nodding, but unable to put aside the fear that the idyllic bliss she'd been enjoying would soon come to an end, Emma returned to her own tipi to start the evening meal.

A shadow fell over her but when she saw whom her visitor was, Emma went about her business, ignoring the hateful girl. Tanagila, not one to be put off so easily, toed some dirt into Emma's fire.

"Do you not have your own chores to see to?" Emma glared at her.

"I came to talk to you."

"We do not have anything to talk about."

Tanagila smirked at her. "Foolish white woman. You think to make your life among the Sioux."

Emma shoved past Tanagila, forcing her to step away from the smoking fire. Bending down, she laid more kindling over the flames. "It is none of your concern, *Tanagila*."

She deliberately used the girl's name, knowing it showed disrespect. She found it odd yet rather charming that Indians didn't overuse given names, believing they were sacred and should only be used to show respect. To use a person's name all the time meant one didn't respect that name or the person.

Eyeing her with narrowed eyes, Tanagila smirked at Emma. "Wrong, white woman. Soon, you will be gone." She preened and strutted around the fire, sending more sprays of dirt onto the flames. "Then our chief will marry as is his duty."

Exasperated and wanting nothing more than to be rid of the irritating girl, Emma stopped her food preparations. "I have work to do, and who says I'm going anywhere?"

Exploring the contents of a pouch holding dried berries and fruits, the girl helped herself to a handful.

"My brother, Waho, says you are to be returned to the fort soon, after our warriors kill your father."

Emma's heart thudded. Though she'd thought about the future earlier, hearing someone else speak of it jarred her back to reality. "That was months ago."

"Wrong again, white woman. They go out into the prairie to meet and plan so no one will tell you. Soon, they will send someone to the fort with proof that you live and lure your father here."

"No. Striking Thunder won't do it." Yet, Emma realized he'd been gone a lot lately. Many times, he'd come back without any game. What was he doing out there all day if not hunting?

Tanagila laughed. "Why not? Just because you share his mat? He must do his duty. He must avenge the death of my sister."

Duty. The word left Emma trembling, for she knew only too well Striking Thunder's obsession with his duty to his people. But that was before they had become lovers. Before he brought Renny here. Surely he wouldn't make an orphan of her little sister?

Emma spun around. This was a vicious lie. It had to be. "No. I won't believe you. You only seek to cause trouble because it is me he wants, and not you."

Her words hit their mark. Tanagila flushed. "Ask him," the girl hissed through clenched teeth. "You will see that I am right. You are nothing. When he marries, it will be to another Sioux maiden. He has only used you to warm his mat at night as no pure maiden would do so." With those spiteful words, Tanagila sashayed away, leaving Emma in a state of turmoil.

Emma moved through the rest of the late afternoon troubled. As much as she hated to believe anything that hateful girl said, the seed of doubt had been planted. Could Striking Thunder, after all they'd shared, still carry out his plan to murder her father in cold blood? Her heart screamed no, but her mind knew he put his people and their needs above all others, including his own. But if he loved her—

The truth slammed into her. Putting her hand to her mouth to still the trembling of her lips, Emma stumbled inside the tipi and fell to her knees on the pallet she shared with Striking Thunder. While she'd told him she loved him, he'd never repeated the words to her. Endearments, especially during their lovemaking, yes. But actual words and declarations of love, no. Not once.

Stop this. All you have to do is ask him when he returns. But no matter what she said to herself, she couldn't stop worrying.

By dusk, she'd worked herself into a nervous state. When he returned, tired, hungry and only wanting to eat and go to bed, Emma couldn't bring it up. She couldn't risk destroying what they had. And when he held his arms out to her, she went. Held securely in his arms, surrounded by his warmth, Emma shivered.

"What is wrong, white woman? Are you cold?" His voice revealed his exhaustion.

Tears threatened her at the tenderness in his voice when he spoke those words. Once, they'd been uttered with derision but now, he used them as an endearment. She opened her mouth to ask if he loved her but the words refused to be spoken.

Closing her eyes, Emma struggled between loyalty to a father she hadn't seen in nine years and the man who held her so lovingly, whose voice sent warmth darting through her veins. She buried her face against his neck and held tightly to him, afraid he'd fade away. She pressed her naked body to his.

Though the chill came from within, she whispered, "Yes. I'm cold. Hold me, Striking Thunder. Just hold me."

Emma woke to warm breath brushing over her neck. She smiled. Striking Thunder always woke with his need for her in evidence. She'd long ago decided it was silly to sleep with her dress on.

"You are awake."

She kept her eyes closed. "No. I'm dreaming."

"Ah, can you feel this in your dreams?" His hand slid over her bare breast, his fingers plucking the beaded nipple.

Arching into his touch, Emma tried to keep a straight face. "Um, I believe so."

"How about this?" His warm, wet mouth closed over the nipple, drawing it into his mouth to suckle. Then he flicked his tongue across the sensitive tip, made much more so by her expectant state.

She couldn't answer and when he slid his mouth down her belly, she lifted her hips eager for the kiss he'd plant there. He didn't disappoint her and when he deepened the kiss, thrust into her with his tongue, she moaned. "Don't stop."

He lifted his head for a moment. "But you are asleep. This is only a dream."

Heat pooled in her loins, she throbbed with need and with every stroke of his tongue across the swollen heart of her, Emma gasped. "But what a dream." Tangling her fingers in his hair, she held him to her, needing the release only he could give her. And he didn't disappoint. In a burst of heat and flame, she soared to a shuddering ecstasy.

Striking Thunder moved over her. "Look at me."

She focused on his handsome face and smiled.

"Feel me. Feel all of me. Together we fly as one." He slid into her slowly, his features contorted with his own need for release.

Reaching down, she took his male flesh in her hands and caressed him. He groaned and lowered his lips to hers. With quick sure strokes, he set the pace. Emma slid her hands to his buttocks and urged him faster. "Now," she cried as each stroke pushed her closer to the wondrous peak.

"Yes." With one last stroke, his cry rose to mingle with hers.

Striking Thunder knew he had to get up and start his day, yet he felt reluctant to do so. Holding Emma, listening to her breathing even out, left him content to stay right where he was. She stirred.

"I love you, Striking Thunder. I could lie here with you forever."

Her declaration of love warmed him as it always did and left him feeling a bit in awe. "You are my heart. You make this warrior happy. But now I must bathe and make ready for my day or the women will pity you for having a man who is lazy."

Emma sat up when he did. Her gaze searched his and he had the feeling that she expected something from him. He kept his tone light so as not to ruin their morning of sweet loving.

"All know I have the bravest, smartest and most handsome warrior in this village."

Though her words were light, there was something in her voice that gave him pause. He playfully mocked a frown. "Only in this village?" Standing, he donned his breechclout then strapped his knife to his calf. Another one dangled from the thong around his waist.

Her eyes held a hint of sadness and worry, as did her voice. "In all the land."

No longer able to deny something was wrong, he returned to her. Squatting, he tipped her chin up and stared into her eyes. The paler-than-normal color signaled her fears. "What troubles you?"

She tried to pull away. "Nothing. I'm just tired."

"Liar," he said. "Tell me."

Her gaze searched his. "Do you love me?"

The question took him aback. He thought it obvious that he did. "Do my actions not prove my feelings?"

"You have never said the words."

He frowned. "Are words more important than actions? Did I not just show my love to you?" When she remained silent, he realized she truly needed to hear the words. Cupping her face, he leaned forward and kissed her.

"Yes, *kiyapi kahaha kin*, flame of my heart. This warrior loves you."

Relief spread across Emma features and brightened her eyes. "Do you want me to stay with you?"

"Always."

With a cry, she threw her arms around his neck. "I'm so glad. I was afraid you didn't love me and that you would send me back. Now we can be together forever. We can send word to my father not to search for me or Renny. I'll tell him I'm happy and want to stay here."

Striking Thunder went still. He pulled back. Emma stared at him, her gaze wide and questioning. He stood. His stomach felt like a great stone had just dropped in it.

Emma got to her knees. "Striking Thunder, I love you. Things have changed." She licked her lips. "My father. You won't—I mean, you no longer need—"

"Revenge?" he asked softly, fighting to control the rising fear inside him.

She nodded. "You have me. We have our love."

Striking Thunder slung his quiver of arrows over his shoulder. "Our love has nothing to do with what must be done."

Emma shook her head. "No. If you love me, you can't kill my father. You wouldn't be able to cause me this pain."

His heart turned to stone. "I have my duty."

"What about me? What about Renny? He is our father. Do you truly expect us to be happy here, for me to stay with you if you murder my father?"

Striking Thunder turned slowly. "Are you saying if I kill your father, you will leave?"

Tears fell from her eyes, yet her jaw was set firmly. "If you love me, you won't do this." Emma glanced down at her fingers then lifted tear-filled eyes to his. "I can't stay with a man who puts duty to others before his family, as my father did. He rejected us to go fight his causes." She eyed him squarely. "And fighting for the rights of Indians is one of them."

He snorted derisively. "So *you* say. I have seen differently."

"No. You haven't seen. You believe the words of a liar. I have my father's letters, which prove his dedication and while I will admit that it is an honorable cause, Renny and I have suffered because of it. He chose to dedicate himself to others not to his family. I won't live like that ever again. If you cannot put me and my needs above that of your people's, then we have nothing."

Angry that she didn't understand and frantic at the thought of losing her, Striking Thunder asked, "What about the pain your father caused the people in this village? Would you deny them the satisfaction of knowing their loved ones' murders have been avenged?"

Emma held out her hands, palms up. "There are other ways. What you plan is also murder."

"In the eyes of my people, our laws, it is the only way."

"You would risk every woman and child in this village over the deaths of a few? The soldiers will destroy everyone here." Emma lifted her chin. "If you kill my father, you will be responsible for what happens. Can you live with the massacre of your people?"

Striking Thunder didn't reply but neither did he soften.

Emma's shoulders sagged. "*My* duty is to my sister. Her need to meet her father brought us here. Even though our father has chosen to lead a life away from us, he is still our father. I cannot condone what you are planning to do. I carry his blood in my veins. If you feel the need to kill him to avenge your wife's death, then you shall have to kill me as well, for I will try to stop you."

She stood, donned her dress, then began packing. "Do what you must. I will have nothing more to do with you. I am moving back in with Star."

Furious, Striking Thunder glared at her back. But she didn't turn around. He stormed out of the tipi, hurt and angry. How could she ask this of him? Already he'd put her and his own need for her above his duty. But to expect him to allow her father to go free was impossible.

He could not abandon his need for vengeance and remain honorable. For him to do so was wrong.

He had a duty to his people. To their dead.

Stopping at the edge of the river, he closed his eyes. But what about him, his needs? What about the love between him and Emma? He loved her, wanted her for his wife—but that was out of the question. Needing to be alone with his turbulent thoughts, he ran along the banks until he reached a secluded area. Stripping, he threw himself into the cold, fast-moving current.

The water matched his blood. He felt frozen, his heart shriveled into a tight hard ball. How had this happened? He'd allowed himself to believe he could keep his white woman always. Shame filled him when he recalled his vision. In it, Emma had left him. In his fascination and happiness with her, he'd forgotten this. Anger filled him. He'd failed the spirits' test, and failed his people who looked to him to guide them and keep them safe from the encroaching white settlers.

They expected their chief to be strong. Wading out of the water, he dressed then fetched his horse and joined his waiting warriors. Together, they rode out across the plains. He was chief. He was beyond normal temptations and weaknesses of the flesh. For just a moment, he'd been tempted to do as she'd asked—to let her father live. More than anything, he wanted Emma at his side, forever, but he could not do as she asked.

His heart ached, urging him to return to her and put the sparkle of love back in those soul-searing green eyes of hers. But he couldn't. To do so would be to betray everything that he was.

Chapter Twenty-four

Emma sat, numb with shock, long after Striking Thunder left camp. All her hopes and dreams lay shattered like broken crystal. In seconds, she'd gone through elation that he'd said he'd loved her to stunned disbelief that he would still seek vengeance against her father.

Finally, she roused herself. Sitting there, wallowing in self-pity wouldn't change anything. There were plans to be made. She couldn't allow Striking Thunder to carry out his plan. She had to leave and warn her father and, she prayed, save the village from the wrath of the soldiers.

At the door to the tipi, she glanced out. She'd miss this life but there was no choice. Spotting Renny across the way, shoulder to shoulder with Morning Moon, a new worry set in. What to do with her sister? Emma wouldn't risk Renny's life again by taking her from the protection of the tribe. There were just too many things that could go wrong: capture by hostile Indians, attacks of wild animals or getting lost and starvation. She would risk her own life, but not her sister's.

She slid her hand down her belly where a tiny new life grew. Striking Thunder's baby. By leaving, she risked her baby. That thought alone nearly made her abandon her plan, but then she looked around the tipi at all the familiar faces she'd sketched.

So many that she'd come to know and love. Little Woman, Star and her family, the children with their round faces and sparkling brown eyes. . . . Her stomach clenched. Oh, God, the children. If Striking Thunder killed her father, it was a sure bet that the soldiers would come and wipe out the entire village.

And she couldn't allow that to happen. "No more bloodshed," she whispered, haunted still by the massacre of the soldiers. Thinking of what she had to do, Emma wasn't sure what she'd tell her father. If he knew Renny was here, alive, he'd insist on coming to get her. That was out of the question. She had to keep her father and Striking Thunder far apart.

Well, she'd think of something when the time came. Maybe she'd just tell her father that Renny had been traded. It was the truth, though not all the truth. Then, she'd hire scouts to bring her back out here to fetch her sister. With her mind made up, Emma gathered what she'd need.

That night, when the moon had risen to its highest position, Emma walked quickly downstream where she'd hidden a bundle of supplies and her mare. She and her sister, along with several others, had gone riding earlier to search for fresh herbs. Using the excuse that she wished to bathe the horse when they had returned, Emma had left the animal hidden.

Mounting, Emma stared at the peaceful village for one last time then rode off into the darkness.

Tanagila watched from the shadows. All during the day, she'd observed Emma and knew she planned to run. Stupid woman. She'd really thought by sleeping with their chief, he'd do whatever she wanted. This time, there was no snowstorm to hamper her. And judging from the fury on Striking Thunder's features when he'd left, he wouldn't care enough to go after her.

She rubbed her hands together. Striking Thunder was hers. Slipping inside his tipi, knowing he and some of the warriors were gone overnight to meet with another chief, she twirled around. Soon, this would be her domain. She added more wood to the smoldering embers to keep the fire alive in order to ward off the night's chill.

The bits of bark and twigs caught fire. Light danced on the walls, chasing away the deep shadows. Glancing around, Tanagila noted the white girl's sketches of her people. She would burn them, she decided. But then she looked closer. Not only did she not have trouble recognizing the individual subjects, but hidden inside each sketch, some essence of that person came through. Mesmerized, she lost herself in the study of them. Some she took down and held out to the fire so she could see them better.

She loved the ones of the children. Happy, innocent and carefree, they brought a smile to her face. Then she found one of her father, sitting stoic and stern. It brought a lump to her throat, for beyond the outward calm and control he always maintained, there was a hint of sorrow in his eyes that lingered from the death of her mother three winters past.

Tanagila replaced her father's portrait and turned to go, suddenly unnerved to be here, where she did not belong, surrounded by her people. In the shadows, they seemed to look upon her with sad disappointment. Turning, she froze. There, hanging from a pole framing the door, she spotted a sketch of Tatankaota and some Indian maiden. She took it down with shaking fingers.

This one was different from the others. It wasn't just a bunch of charcoal lines. The white woman had used dyes to paint the couple. Seeing him staring at the woman with his heart in his eyes made her angry, until, with a start of recognition, she realized the woman Emma had painted beside Tatankaota was *her*. That couldn't be her. There was a softness about the portrayed woman as she stared up into the features of the warrior beside her.

Love. The truth stared her in the face. Her heart belonged not to Striking Thunder, but to this warrior who offered all he had, including his heart. Shocked, Tanagila realized she'd been blind to her true feelings toward the tall, brave and handsome warrior. She'd only chased Striking Thunder for the sake of her pride.

The white woman had seen her true heart. With her spirit lighter and her heart filled with the knowledge that she loved this warrior, Tanagila held the painted buckskin reverently. Would the white woman give it to her if she asked? She frowned. She'd been so mean to her and now felt bad. Jealousy had driven her to treat the redhead so terribly.

Then she remembered. Emma was gone, again at her hand. Glancing once more at the silent and disapproving faces around her, Tanagila backed up. Let the woman go. Let her return to her people where she belonged. Nothing had changed. In a few days, the plan to lure her father into their trap would be set in motion.

In the end, Striking Thunder would still kill her father and Emma would still leave. She left the tipi, taking the buckskin picture with her. Halfway to her own tipi, she stopped and glanced around. The white woman traveled alone. It wasn't safe.

Beneath the moonlight, Tanagila battled her conscience. Again, she stared at the sketch of herself and Tatankaota. The woman had given them a gift. She'd revealed their true natures, captured the very spirit of The People. Not only that, Tanagila realized with a sinking heart, she'd captured the heart of their chief.

There was no doubt that Striking Thunder loved Emma. Emma had become one of them. Little Woman had publically adopted her as her daughter.

And Tanagila, in her mean-spiritedness had put Emma's life in danger—again.

"No." Spinning around, she realized that she had to go after her. Taking one of her brother's horses hobbled behind their tipi, she led the animal away. When she reached the edge of the village, she took off after Emma. If she caught up with her in time, they could both return to their tipis before anyone knew they'd left.

It didn't take long to catch up with Emma, which surprised her. She'd have thought the white woman would be a lot farther ahead. Then she paused. That wasn't Emma up riding just out of sight. Someone else was following her. Slowing, not wanting to give her presence away, she palmed the knife she, like all women, wore strapped to their thigh.

Voices, childish and excited, reached her long before she made out the shapes of two riders on the one horse. She relaxed and put the knife away. Urging her horse forward, she caught up with two young girls who had some serious explaining to do.

The first light of dawn broke with a woman's scream. Warriors raced from their tipis, followed by the women. All paused in frightened confusion. When another scream rent the air, Golden Eagle pointed.

"The screams come from my daughter's tipi." He ran, followed by his wife and Dove. Entering, they found Star rocking back and forth, sobbing hysterically. White Wind ran to Star and wrapped her arms around her, trying to comfort her.

"They are gone," Star sobbed. "All of them. I could not prevent it. Again, I could not prevent it."

"Who, daughter? Who is gone?" Golden Eagle glanced around. Running Elk sat by himself, looking confused and frightened by his mother's wailing. Renny and Morning Moon weren't in the tipi.

"They went after her. They ride into the storm. It grows. It murders." Star's voice drifted, her eyes clouded.

Golden Eagle knew whatever visions had awoken her in this state once again held her in their grip. His heart clenched. At no time could he recall his own mother being so tormented by her gift of sight. Going to his daughter, he gripped her fingers tightly.

"Do not fight it. Look. Listen. Learn. You must tell me what you see." He roughened his voice to break through her fear.

"Speak!"

"Emma. She's gone. Rides toward the soldiers. A soldier rides toward her. His hair. Red. Great turmoil inside. Love and goodness surround him. No darkness. She's almost there but not alone. Others are with her."

Star's voice had calmed in her telling but the edge of fear returned. A storm, evil, cuts between them. Separates them. Emma rides into the storm, trusting."

Star broke off and fought the hold her father had on her. "No! No, don't trust him. Murderer. He will kill them all." Unable to continue, Star slumped into her mother's arms.

A short, tension-filled while later, she opened her eyes and fixed their haunted depths on her father. "Must go after them. Emma, my daughter and Renny and Tanagila. They follow the river, toward the soldiers, toward death."

Golden Eagle left the tipi at a run without asking anymore questions. If Star said they had to go, there was no time to lose. Back out in the open air, Golden Eagle sent two braves to find his son and the others, then hand-chose several other warriors to go with him. Quickly, everyone gathered weapons and made ready.

As expected, White Wind and his daughters joined him. Mounted, each wore a different expression. White Wind looked worried, Star fearful, and Dove determined as she swung her quiver of arrows over her shoulder. Mother and younger daughter flanked Star. Once again, they were a unit, inseparable in times of trouble.

With Golden Eagle leading the way, the group rode out.

Out on the open prairie, Derek had stopped for a few hours' sleep. The sun was just rising when something woke him. A light sleeper, he felt Wild Sage ease out of his arms. With a growl, he grabbed her and hauled her back. "Going somewhere, my little whore?"

Wild Sage cried out and cowered, covering her face with her hands.

Sitting up, Derek stared at her naked body, pleased by the bruises and bite marks marring her breasts. Served her right—her and her kind, luring white men from their wives and families.

His breathing grew shallow. Just like the squaw who'd taken his father from him and turned his mother into a hard, bitter woman. He scowled and fought for control. He'd never been good enough for Josie Sanders.

Always, she'd compared him to his father.

Always, she'd found fault.

Always, she'd harped.

Closing his eyes against the tide of pain, he comforted himself with the knowledge that Josie Sanders would never hurt him again. He'd taken care of her, shown her that he was a man. Man enough to kill. Remembering her fear and the way she'd begged him not to kill her calmed him.

Just thinking of the heady sense of power that came from being in charge brought an evil, feral grin to his face. Wild Sage cried out.

Finding her watching him, eyes wide with fear, he backhanded her. "Shut up," he snarled. "Make another sound and I'll kill you right here."

Wild Sage whimpered. Derek stared down at her. Lust pooled between his legs. Standing to remove his pants, he scanned the area out of habit. His hand stilled when he spotted a small group traveling toward him. Grabbing his binoculars, he studied them, then grinned.

"Ah, I couldn't have planned this better myself." Bending down, he yanked Wild Sage to her feet. "Get dressed and hurry." When she was done, he shoved her toward the horses. "Let's go. And don't try anything."

Galloping along the river, Emma kept her eyes focused ahead. At her side, Tanagila kept pace. "I won't return with you, Tanagila. Please, take the girls and go back."

Emma frowned at the two girls riding up ahead in twin

dresses of fringed bleached-white buckskin. Renny and Morning Moon chatted away as if this were a grand adventure.

Rubbing her forehead, Emma felt like crying. Renny wasn't supposed to be here. She was supposed to be back in the village, safe. According to Tanagila, who'd caught up with her last night, the two girls had been following Emma. Worry churned in her gut. She'd vowed not to endanger her sister again but here they were, unprotected in the wilderness along with Morning Moon and Tanagila.

"You must listen to me, Emma. I was wrong to cause trouble. My heart was jealous. Please turn back. No one will think bad of you."

Emma glanced at the girl, still surprised by her turn of heart. After confessing to finding the portrait of her and Tatankaota, she'd spent the remainder of the night trying to talk Emma into returning to the village. "Go to your warrior, Tanagila. Take the girls. I promise to return for Renny."

"Our chief loves you."

Emma shook her head sadly. They'd been over and over this. "If he loved me, he could not kill my father." Heartache brought tears to her eyes. She was right in what she was doing. Striking Thunder had his duty. She had hers. There was nothing to say so she remained silent, keeping her horse pointed eastward.

Tossing her braided hair, Tanagila reached out and stopped Emma's horse. "You don't understand. He must. It's our way."

Emma glanced over at the Indian maiden. "You don't understand that I also must do what I have to do." Reaching out, she put her hand on the other girl's shoulder.

"Do you not see what will happen if I allow Striking Thunder and the rest of your warriors to do this? If they kill my father, a colonel in the army, the soldiers will retaliate. They will wipe out your entire village as punishment. Is this for the good of your people? Do you want to see your innocent children and babies killed? And for what, revenge?"

Fighting weariness of both body and soul, Emma's voice broke. "It's wrong to kill, Tanagila. There is nothing anyone can do to bring your sister or any of the others back. Go back and warn your people to move where they will be safe. Take the children away."

Tanagila looked troubled, but stubbornly didn't turn back. Ahead, Morning Moon, seated behind Renny on the back of the horse, turned to look at Emma. Her eyes were dark and serious. Her heart went out to the girl. From what Renny had said, Morning Moon had known Emma was leaving and the two girls had followed.

Emma's heart grew heavy. She was torn. If Tanagila didn't turn back soon, Emma would have no choice but to return with them. She couldn't put Renny and Morning Moon at risk.

But what would she be returning to? A warrior who couldn't put her needs first? A chief who would someday marry one of his own? Suddenly, her future loomed, empty of love and laughter.

"Emma, look."

Drawn from her depressing thoughts, Emma glanced out across the prairie. Two riders were coming toward them. There was nowhere to go or hide. Silently, the group stopped and waited. As the pair of riders drew near, there was something about one of them that she recognized. Dressed as a trapper, there was no mistaking that moustache or gleaming blond hair.

"Derek!" Emma spurred her horse forward. He could take her and Renny to their father, leaving Tanagila and Morning Moon free to return. Then she would take her sister back to St. Louis and try to forget the handsome young chief who had stolen her heart.

With her attention focused on reaching Derek, Emma didn't hear Morning Moon call her back.

Chapter Twenty-five

Striking Thunder caught up with his father by noon. Stopping briefly so that Golden Eagle could fill him in, Striking Thunder learned about Star's visions and the missing women and children.

Golden Eagle pointed. "They follow the river to the Big Muddy River." He glanced at his son. "There is another set of tracks. All seem to be traveling together but I do not know who the other is."

Striking Thunder rode toward the back where Star rode between his mother and sister. The three women stopped when he rode up. He looked into Star's eyes and saw her fear.

"Can you tell me anything more?"

Star shuddered. "Soldiers. A forked path. One leads to peace and happiness, the other is soaked in blood. Hatred destroys those who walk that path." Glancing at him, tears streamed down her face. "Choose wisely, my brother."

Striking Thunder frowned. When he rejoined his father, he suggested they head across the prairie to cut Emma and the others off. Agreeing, they crossed the river. The hooves of the horses thundered across the prairie. Staring straight ahead, fear for Emma's safety churned in him. This was his fault. He should have known she'd run again. With sudden insight, he realized he'd misread his own vision. Emma's leaving, their separation, had been a warning, not a prediction.

And because he hadn't shared it with their *wicasa,* their holy man, this mistake might very well cost him dearly—his heart.

Riding faster, he thought of Emma and the choice she'd made. Her father over him. While it hurt, could he blame her? Her sense of duty, like his own, was strong. His mind conjured up a child much like Renny, watching her father leave, not realizing he wouldn't be back. The image of that little girl, charged with raising an infant sister, haunted him.

But his need to avenge Meadowlark was different. Would his father not have done his duty and married Wildflower rather than risk starting another war? Yet his father had suggested that there was duty to oneself. What was his duty to himself? Everything he'd ever done had been for his people. Except Emma. Taking her to his tipi, keeping her, that had been for himself. Because he loved her.

The thought of losing Emma, the flame of his heart, left him feeling hollow and empty inside. Dead. And if he felt this way, it would affect his ability to lead his people.

And what about Emma? What was his duty to her? Marriage? Protection? Provider? All of these were a warrior's responsibility. But what about trust? Loyalty? Did he not owe her these? With a sigh, he put his troubling thoughts from him. There was much for him to consider. Right now, he had to find Emma and bring her back safely. Returning to the river, they followed it in silence.

The sun warmed the land. New grass formed a soft mat and tiny wildflowers added color and beauty. Striking Thunder appreciated none of it. By mid-afternoon, he was beginning to fear they'd lost Emma and the others. Ready to turn half of his warriors back, he glanced up into the sky and saw Black Cloud circling above them.

Suddenly, the bird shot across the sky. Following the bird's direction, he saw a large group riding hard toward them in the distance. Calling a halt, he watched.

When he saw the flags and uniforms of soldiers, he gave the signal to form a line. Bows were readied but he gave the command that none were to shoot unless he gave the orders. White Wind and Star stayed well behind the strung-out line of warriors. Dove took her place in front of her mother and sister, her bow and arrow at the ready.

Striking Thunder waited, his heart pounding, adrenaline pulsing through his veins. Emma's father had come. Emotions churned. Images of Emma over the last few months flashed before him. What he did now would affect everyone's future. He glanced back at Star. She seemed calm, which suggested the danger surrounding Emma was not ahead.

Glancing at his warriors, he also knew what he decided here would affect how they viewed him and his leadership abilities. How could he put love before them? How could he not? Around and around he went. Time became his enemy as the enemy advanced slower now. Soon, he must make his decision. Emma and love, or duty and revenge. It was a forked path before him.

When the soldiers stopped, the glint of light flashed on the metal barrels of their rifles. Silence fell as the two groups of fighters faced off. Striking Thunder had no trouble picking out Emma's father by his long red hair, blowing in the breeze beneath his hat. He kept his eyes trained on that man.

Finally, the colonel dismounted. He was tall, trim and wore a neat uniform. Another man, dressed as a trapper also joined him. The colonel gave the universal sign for peace with his hands and spoke the words. "I am Colonel Grady O'Brien. We come in peace."

Concealing all thought and emotion, Striking Thunder nudged his mount forward. His father moved with him, keeping back a bit so all knew who was in charge. Normally the Indians, even if they spoke the white man's language, didn't reveal that fact. But Striking Thunder didn't have time to play games. Emma was in danger, although, if her father was here, he wasn't sure from what or whom. Still, Star had seen something. He would be careful.

"You are on Sioux land."

If the colonel was surprised by his English, he didn't show it. Without turning, he signaled his men to lower their rifles. Standing straight and proud, his hands at his side and well away from his pistol, he stepped forward. "I am in search of my daughters."

"Look among us. Do you see your daughters?"

Grady's gaze scanned over Striking Thunder's warriors. "I seek a young chief by name of Striking Thunder. It is he who has my Emma."

"You said daughters." Striking Thunder knew with one slight motion of his hand that he could give the orders to cut down this man and most of the soldiers standing nervously behind him. Still, he hesitated.

Grady's voice caught. "I do not know where my youngest daughter is. The information I have concerns only my elder."

"And what information is this." Striking Thunder listened as Emma's father explained what he knew of Emma whereabouts. And he watched and judged. He saw no false concern and no hatred. The more the man talked, the less of a soldier he seemed. He became a father. A worried one.

The image was not what he was prepared for. Considering the man before him, and his sister's vision of two paths, he knew the choice rested with him. Not to kill this man and keep peace between the two groups of armed men, or to kill him, avenge the deaths of his people and cause bloodshed. Tension grew.

Two paths. One with Emma. One without. One filled with love and laughter, the other cold silence. But what about duty, his people. Suddenly, everything became clear. His first duty was to his own heart. Though her skin marked her white, her heart and soul belonged to the Sioux and his belonged to her. They were tied. One and the same. His duty lay with her and together, with her love, he'd be able to serve his people.

The need for revenge drained away. Yellow Dog, the one who had committed the murders had died. And if the colonel lost his own daughters, by their own choice to stay, wouldn't that be punishment enough? All he had to do was tell this man he didn't know of Emma and leave. The colonel would never need to know of his daughters' whereabouts. It was enough that they were safe.

As quickly as he gave thought to that idea, he discarded it.

Emma would not want her father to worry. But did this man who'd put duty ahead of his family truly care about his daughters? Did he deserve to know the truth? Striking Thunder decided to test him. While meeting with the other chiefs, he had taken the colonel's belt buckle. He pulled it out of the pouch tied to his waist and held it up. The sun sparkled off the silver and flashed. With a word, he tossed it to Emma's father.

Tension mounted as the colonel cradled the belt buckle in his hands. Lifting his eyes, Striking Thunder thought he caught a gleam of tears in his eyes. "This is mine, stolen from me months ago."

"Stolen or given to Yellow Dog as payment to kill the Sioux?"

Grady's head shot up. "Stolen. What purpose it served, I do not know."

"You did not give it to Captain Sanders with orders to use it as payment to Yellow Dog?"

The colonel drew himself up. Barely restrained fury flashed in blue eyes with a hint of storm in their depths. "Ah, now I begin to understand. Let me tell you, that in addition to searching for my daughters, I'm also after Sanders. I have reason to believe he means to harm my elder daughter."

"Why would this man want to harm your daughter?"

"I do not know for sure but he is dangerous. He has killed one woman and kidnapped another."

Before Striking Thunder could ask more questions, Star moved up next to him. She stared at Emma's father for a long time. "The Eagle," she whispered, then turned to her brother. "The white man speaks the truth. No darkness surrounds him."

The Indians withdrew a few feet and conferred. Grady sensed something deeper going on. Who was this warrior and what did he know? Tracing the initials on the belt buckle his daughters had given him, he also wondered how this warrior had come to be in possession of it.

Then with certainty, he knew. This had to be Striking Thunder, the young chief who'd killed Yellow Dog. He glanced around one more time. Where was Emma?

He longed to step forward and demand answers but he didn't dare, not with arrows pointed at him and his men. Though he didn't fear for his own safety, one wrong move could set off a bloody chain of events.

The two sides were well-matched. Even though his soldiers had rifles, those arrows would find their mark just as quickly as bullets. To still his impatience, he let his attention wander over the Sioux. To his surprise, there were three women. The one talking to Striking Thunder held his gaze.

She was a vision of loveliness with her short black hair and fragile features. And when she turned her gaze on him, her haunting beauty struck a chord deep inside him. She returned her attention to the other two women while Striking Thunder and the warrior with him dismounted and came forward.

Striking Thunder spoke. "I believe the father of Emma did not have anything to do with the killing of my wife or the others in my tribe. We, too, search for your daughters who left this morning."

"Renny? You have her as well?" Grady felt like weeping with the relief that both his girls were alive. "Thank God," he whispered softly, grateful his prayers had been heard and answered.

Striking Thunder sent him a pointed stare. "If you had not left them, they would not have come here."

Grady didn't refute the accusation, for it was true. No one knew better than he what his lack of responsibility had caused. He vowed to make it up to his children. But first, he had to find them. He eyed the young warrior with narrowed eyes, not sure he liked the possessive attitude this warrior—no, chieftain—showed, but now wasn't the time to challenge him.

"We shall speak later of how you came to have my daughters. Right now, I need to find Sanders before he harms them."

"We shall join forces. I shall tell you of my sister's visions."

Grady, still feeling incredibly relieved and lighthearted at learning his children were alive, nodded. "Zeb here has been tracking Sanders along the Cheyenne River. We've not seen any women or children traveling alone."

Striking Thunder glanced up river. "And we cut across the land to reach this spot as Emma and the others would not have gotten any farther than this since leaving last night, especially with the two young girls."

Grady and Striking Thunder turned as one to stare at the stretch of river snaking toward the hills. "Then Emma and Derek travel toward each other." Both men ran for their horses. Striking Thunder waited for Emma's father to join him. Then, with his father at his side, and Zeb at Grady's, the four men led the charge.

Chapter Twenty-six

"Derek, I'm glad to see you," Emma cried. She pulled her horse to a halt beside him. To her surprise, there was an Indian woman with him. She sat on her horse, bent over, her stringy black hair covering her face. Emma didn't pay her much attention.

"Emma! You're safe. You've had us all very worried." Derek dismounted.

Emma did the same. Suddenly, the Indian woman came to life. Her eyes, black and swollen from being beaten, went wild with fear.

"Run! He kill you!"

Startled, Emma glanced at Derek. Rage contorted his features. Emma backed away, suddenly recalling his treatment and derogatory comments about Indians while they'd traveled to the fort—and his dealings with Yellow Dog. Had Yellow Dog been telling the truth? Had Derek paid him to kill Striking Thunder's wife and stir up trouble.

No longer able to trust the captain, she spun around to remount and flee but the sound of a gunshot stopped her. With a cry of fright, she whirled around. To her horror, the Indian woman lay motionless on the ground, eyes staring blankly at the sky.

Lifting her gaze, Emma found Derek regarding her with a sneer. In his hand, he held a revolver, leveled at her own chest.

"Don't be in such a hurry to leave, Emma."

Shocked and scared, Emma strove to keep calm, but

having the pistol pointed at her chest made her hands sweat and her heart pound. "Derek, what is going on?"

Derek snickered. "Just some unfinished business, Emma, my dear. Now, be a good girl and move away from the horse."

He pointed the pistol at the group behind her. "Now, or one of them gets it next." His voice turned hard.

With a fearful look at Tanagila and the girls, Emma did as she was told. "I don't understand."

"Ah, you will, my dear. You will." Derek uncoiled a thin length of rope tied to his belt. He turned his attention to Tanagila. "You. All of you, get over here."

Tanagila and the two girls dismounted and joined Emma. Renny ran to Emma and pressed tightly into her. Derek grinned at the group, his gaze lingering on Tanagila. He tossed the rope to Emma and ordered, "Tie her hands behind her back."

For a brief moment, Emma considered refusing, but the cocking of the pistol spurred her to do as he ordered. She stepped behind Tanagila to bind her hands. To buy time, she asked him, "Why are you doing this?"

"Because your father expects me to marry you—but we both know you're spoiled goods by now, don't we, my dear?"

Without Derek knowing, Emma slid the small knife from her thigh and beckoned her sister toward her. Pretending to still be tying the rope, she cut a small slit in the doll the girl clutched and hid the knife there. Renny gave nothing away. Done, Emma stepped to the side. Renny moved close to Morning Moon.

"So, refuse to marry me."

"And spend the rest of my life in some remote, godforsaken land, living a life of poverty? I think not, especially as your father knows where you are and plans to come after you. Too bad, you know. You were my ticket to being rich."

He pulled out his gold nugget. "See this? There's more. Lots more in those hills." He eyed the dead body of

Wild Sage, then moved toward Tanagila. "And this pretty little squaw will take me to find the gold. Won't you."

Tanagila ignored him. Derek cut the dangling length of extra rope after making sure Emma had tied it good and tight. Then he stared down into Tanagila's impassive features. "Yes, I think I will keep you around for a while." He trailed the gun down her cheek. "It will be fun teaching you the meaning of fear." Derek glanced around and motioned to the two girls. "Now, them," he ordered Emma. "Tie *them* up." He cut the remaining rope in two.

Emma wrapped the rope around Renny's wrist in front of her, careful to keep the doll in the girl's palm, the concealed knife facing the child.

"Put her hands behind her back and get rid of that lice-infested doll."

Turning, Emma scoffed, "She's a child. Let her have it. Surely she's no threat to you."

Derek glared at her then motioned to Morning Moon. "Tie the brat now."

Before Emma could tie the girl's hands, her sister charged forward, her hands fisted in fury.

"I won't let you hurt my sister or my friend. You're mean."

Derek laughed and stuck out his booted foot, catching her in the stomach and shoving her back.

Renny stumbled back and fell, winded. Dropping the rope, Emma ran to her. "Leave her be."

Reaching down, Derek grabbed Emma's hair and hauled her to him. "If you're nice to me, I'll kill them brats clean. They won't suffer. But if you're not—" he fired off another shot, this one just over Morning Moon's head. "If you give me trouble, they will die slow, with buzzards and wolves circling them before they are dead.

Terror paralyzed Emma. She fought it, knowing she had to keep a clear head. *Please, Striking Thunder,* she prayed, *come, before it's too late. Please be following me.* "Please, Derek, listen to me. I ran away last night.

Tanagila, Renny and Morning Moon followed to stop me. Striking Thunder and his warriors won't be far behind. "Let them go and I'll go with you and help you get away."

Derek ran the cold muzzle down the side of her neck, then followed the path with his lips. "I don't think so." He lifted his head and tightened his hold on her arm. "What is this Striking Thunder to you? Your lover?"

Emma winced but didn't dare move with the gun moving up and down her throat.

Without warning, rage shook Derek. The gun rammed into the tender flesh beneath her jaw. "You're no better than the rest of those squaws, are you? *Are you?*" he shouted.

He shoved her to the ground and straddled her. The gun in his hand shook. "You're nothing but a whore. Like all squaws. You'll spread your legs and trap any man."

Intent on Emma, Derek didn't pay attention when Renny crawled to Morning Moon who'd already moved behind Tanagila. Morning Moon's eyes clouded over so Renny took the knife out of the doll and started sawing through the ropes binding Tanagila.

Striking Thunder rode hard, images of Emma and what they'd shared haunting him. On his left, Emma's father kept pace. The rest of their rescue party followed.

Though he knew he'd done the right thing by letting Emma's father know the truth, he feared that Emma, after seeing her father, would choose to return to her house of wood. Could he convince her to stay? Should he? The life they led was harsh. What if she couldn't survive? Yet how could he let her go? He loved her. She was the flame of his heart. She set his blood on fire, sent white heat through his veins. With her, he felt alive.

Before, he'd believed that keeping his feelings under tight control made him a better leader. But by denying his own passions and emotions, he'd limited himself, strangled his own growth. Now he saw the world through the colors of love, sorrow and grief. All had their place and made his world complete.

As in all things, they were part of the circle of life. And Emma, his white woman, his love, made his life's circle complete. She brought him love, had taught him to feel. Somehow, he had to find the words to convince her to stay with him. Pushing his mare, he sped across the short green grass. Clumps of moist dirt flew through the air.

Above him, Black Cloud flew. Touching the medallion around his neck, he prayed to his animal friend for help once again.

Find her. Find my love.

The wise bird soared through the sky. When the raven circled ahead, Striking Thunder knew they were close. Stopping, he waited for the others then pointed.

"They are ahead." He motioned for his warriors to split up and move to surround them. He had no idea if it was just Emma and the others, or if Sanders was with them.

The warriors dismounted and moved along the river's bank on foot, while others ran away from the stream in both directions to spread out and set a trap in case Derek tried to flee. Grady also gave commands to his soldiers. Half would stay back in case Derek fled toward them. The rest would stay with him and Striking Thunder.

Waiting to give his warriors time to get nearer was the hardest thing Striking Thunder had ever done. He wanted nothing more than to charge ahead. But when he heard the loud report of a gunshot, his heart stopped. "Emma!" With a cry of rage and fear, he jumped onto his horse and urged her forward. Nothing mattered. Only her. The sound of a second shot sent terror slamming into his chest. *Don't let me be too late.*

Closing in, he heard screams. Slowing to take stock of the situation, his father and Grady caught up with him. They swept forward together.

Emma felt the ground trembling beneath her. So did Derek. He glanced over his shoulder, then swore. Pulling her in front of him to use as a shield, he hooked his elbow around her throat and pressed the muzzle of his gun to her head.

With fear in her heart, Emma saw Striking Thunder arrive with warriors and soldiers, their guns and arrows pointed at Derek. Next to Striking Thunder, she recognized her father.

Her heart lifted and she cried out with joy. Striking Thunder hadn't killed him. For that, she was grateful. If she died today, her father would be able to take Renny home. Full of fear and thankfulness, Emma kept her gaze on Striking Thunder, trying to tell him with her eyes that she loved him.

"Put the gun down, Sanders," her father's familiar commanding voice boomed.

"Move any closer, she dies." Derek pulled her back.

"You can't escape."

"Wrong. If you try and stop me, she dies."

Emma tried pulling Derek's arm from her throat but he tightened his hold as he dragged her toward the horse. "Please, let me go, Derek. They won't kill you if you let me go."

"Shut up," Derek screamed, tightening his hold so that Emma could barely breathe. The horse, made uneasy by the tension, scooted away. Derek cursed.

Striking Thunder kept his gaze on Emma. A movement behind her caught his eye. Tanagila was free and creeping toward Derek on her hands and knees, the knife between her teeth. And Renny was standing, her doll held high overhead, staring into the sky while Morning Moon watched Emma. Fearing they'd do something to cause the gun to go off, he kept his eye on them. Emma's father, who'd also seen them, kept Derek distracted.

Renny moved forward and waved the doll in the air. The sun glinted off its bright red hair.

What was she up to? When the raven flew across the sky with a loud caw, Striking Thunder understood. He smiled reassuringly at Emma. "As the raven flies straight, his sharp eyes always searching for bright treasures, know that I love you, Flame of my Heart."

Derek sneered at him. "How sweet. Declarations of love."

Emma ignore Derek and spoke to Striking Thunder. "As I love you, my warrior whose aim is true."

Striking Thunder drew his arrow and watched Emma's eyes as she tracked the bird. When her gaze suddenly dove to the ground, he hissed beneath his breath low enough for only Grady and his father to hear. "Be ready."

As expected, the bird flew down toward Renny's doll with a loud, raucous cry. Startled by the appearance of the bird, Derek whirled around. That one moment of distraction, when the gun was shifted from Emma, was all Striking Thunder needed—but before he could fire off an arrow, Tanagila rose up and threw herself at Emma, knocking her out of Derek's grasp and onto the ground.

A shot rang out, then another. Derek fell to the ground. Both Striking Thunder and Grady ran forward. Reaching the two women, Grady gently pulled Tanagila off Emma while Striking Thunder gathered her into his arms.

She wrapped her arms around his neck and sobbed. "Tell me you are unhurt," he whispered, his heart pounding furiously when he saw blood welling from a small cut on her forehead.

"I'm not hurt. Tanagila? Is she—?"

Glancing over, Striking Thunder saw Tatankaota holding Tanagila. One shoulder was bare and bleeding from a gunshot wound. Grady and an army doctor, along with his mother and Dove, tended her. Listening to the doctor arguing with Dove lifted his spirits.

"She will be fine." Bending his head, he kissed her, uncaring who saw. "You frightened this warrior. I thought I'd lost you," he whispered against her temple, needing to tell her what was in his heart and to beg forgiveness.

"I was so scared that you wouldn't come." Tears swam in her eyes and her voice broke. She turned her gaze away from Derek's lifeless form. Mindful of the women present, someone had covered him with a coat.

"You did good, white woman, flame of my heart. This warrior is proud of you. You were brave and full of courage."

Emma reached up to cup his jaw. "No. I was foolish. I endangered the others by leaving." She stopped at the approach of a soldier. Her mouth moved yet no sound came.

"Papa?" Her voice came out a croak of wonder and fear.

Striking Thunder stood and drew her to her feet, then he stood back. She stumbled forward into her father's outstretched arms. Feeling let-down and strangely jealous, he turned away, willing to prove his love by letting her go if that was what she wanted.

Emma threw herself into her father's arms, weeping. "Papa. You're here. You came. I'm so sorry. I failed. I didn't keep her safe, Papa. I'm sorry."

Tears ran down Grady's face. "No, Princess. The fault lies with me," he said, drawing her onto his lap as if she were once again eight. "I should never have left you. I've been running, afraid to face my loss, afraid to face life without your mother at my side. I failed not only you and your sister but her as well. Your mother entrusted me with the two most precious gifts in the world and I never realized what I've missed. I'm a selfish old fool who would like to have a second chance to make things right."

Emma's heart felt like it would break. "Oh, Papa. I was so afraid."

Grady stroked her head. "I know, Princess. I know. Everything will be all right. We'll go home. Papa will make it right."

Before Emma could tell him she loved Striking Thunder, Renny shouted at him.

"No! No! I won't go back with you. You don't love us." Defiant, Renny crossed her arms across her chest and glared at her father. "He doesn't want us. I'm staying here."

Emma pushed out of her father's arms. "Renny, don't—"

Grady turned to face his younger daughter, whom he hadn't seen since the day he'd named her. "No. Let her have her say. She has every right—" His words died in his throat. "My God. You are the spitting image of your mother."

Renny stood in front of Emma. Her lower lip trembled. "That's why you hate me. I killed her."

Startled, Grady shook his head. "What nonsense is this?" His daughter's anger and pain drove the knife of guilt deep into his heart.

"It's not nonsense. That's why you didn't come back. You blamed me."

Shocked by Renny's pronouncement, Grady went to her on bended knee. "That's not true. That's not true," he whispered.

He searched her face, then lifted his gaze to Emma's. Tears fell from her eyes but she remained silent. Behind her, Striking Thunder massaged her shoulders. The realization that the three of them were united, a family without him, tore his soul in two. "Your mother died of the fever. It just happened. It was no one's fault. And I don't hate you. I've never hated you." He reached out and fingered her hair.

"So beautiful. The same shade as Margaret Mary's was." He smiled into her eyes—reflections of his own. The expression there reminded him of both Emma and her mother.

Renny stuck out her lower lip. "You didn't come back. Not never."

Drawing a deep breath, Grady nodded. "I was wrong to stay away. I failed you and your sister. But I promise never to leave you again. I love you and your sister very much, even if I haven't been around to show it."

Renny's eyes grew suspiciously bright. "I don't want

your love and I'm not going anywhere with you. I'm staying here. I'm not going back to that boring old house. I have horses here."

Grady's heart broke in the face of her resentment, but he accepted that he'd have to earn her trust and love. And he wasn't above a bit of bribery to do it. He couldn't lose her. Not now. Not ever again. "I'll buy you a whole stableful of horses if that is what you want, sweetheart."

Still looking uncertain, Renny shook her head then turned and ran to Morning Moon, who sat with her.

Emma placed her hand on his shoulder. "It will take her a while. She can be stubborn."

Grady stood and blinked back his tears. "Stubbornness is an O'Brien trait. I've got time." He took in the way Emma and Striking Thunder stood close to each other. He didn't want to think of what that meant for his elder. "I'm going to resign, immediately. We'll go home and maybe we'll move. I've always dreamed of buying land and settling down. Horses, cattle, it doesn't matter.

"What about you, Emma? Can you forgive me?"

Staring up at Striking Thunder, Emma smiled. "Yes. I can forgive you."

Grady frowned. The love was unmistakable. "You love him?"

Without hesitation, Emma nodded. "With all my heart."

"And he loves you. That much is obvious." Sighing, Grady put his hands on her shoulders, drew her to him for a long hug, then gave her hand to Striking Thunder. "True love, once found, should be treasured above all else."

"Thank you, Papa."

Grady left Emma and Striking Thunder. After only a moment's restraint, they reached for each other and held on as if afraid to let go. She drew back and searched his eyes. "You didn't kill him."

Striking Thunder slid his hands up the sides of her neck. "I couldn't—even before I knew that he was innocent, that it had been Sanders who paid Yellow Dog."

"But your duty—"

"Is to you, now. You and any children we have. You are my heart, my soul. You are my white woman. My white flame. Will you stay with this foolish warrior? Be my soul mate. Love me forever."

"Yes. Yes. Yes," Emma cried, throwing herself into his arms.

Striking Thunder picked her up, uncaring of who saw. "We shall marry as soon as we get back." His voice turned stern. "And you must never run off again."

An impish grin curled Emma's lips. "Are you telling or asking?"

Striking Thunder smiled down at her. "I'm begging."

"Then I promise never to leave you again. But there is something you must promise in return."

"Anything."

"I will wish to travel to see my father wherever he settles with Renny. He deserves a chance to get to know his grandchild—and Renny will make a wonderful aunt, don't you think?"

It took a moment for the words to sink in. "A baby. We are going to have a baby." He turned to the others and shouted. "I will be a father soon!" He spun her around in his arms.

Laughing, Emma made him put her down when the others crowded close. Golden Eagle hugged her then turned to Star. "What is it to be?"

Emma noted that the strain of the vicious visions had left Star. Her eyes clouded over but her features remained serene. Then she smiled. "The child will be strong and healthy." She turned and walked away, her father following, trying to find out if he had another grandson or granddaughter on the way.

Striking Thunder and Emma both chuckled. Alone again, Striking Thunder kissed her, long, slow and thoroughly until the flutter of wings and the appearance of Black Cloud settling on Emma's shoulder disrupted him. The bird plucked at her braid.

Striking Thunder shooed the bird away then picked up Emma and carried her to his horse.

Realizing his intent, Emma waved to the group of warriors, soldiers and treasured family members. Off to one side, several soldiers were digging two graves.

Striking Thunder mounted and pulled her up in front of him. His warmth and scent surrounded her. She leaned her head into the cradle of his shoulder and when he wrapped one arm securely around her waist, she held him to her. Neither spoke as they rode away.

Hours later, as the sun began its descent, Emma sighed and nuzzled her cheek against his chest. "It's over."

Striking Thunder stopped and tipped her chin. "No, it's just beginning. I love you, White Flame."

Emma wrapped her arms around his neck. "As I love you, warrior of my heart." Reaching up, Emma drew his mouth to hers and kissed him, long and thoroughly, showing him exactly what she wanted. He lifted his head, his eyes heated with the spark of passion she'd ignited. She trailed her fingers down his jaw and slid them around his neck. "I want you, Striking Thunder."

He stared at her mouth. "We will go away, far away, where it will only be the two of us and this warrior will show you what's in his heart."

Emma glanced around. They were alone in the middle of nowhere. Not another soul in sight and no black raven circling her head. She smiled, finding new appreciation for the wide open plains that had once frightened her. With carefree abandon, she slid off the horse and twirled in a slow circle with her arms outstretched. Striking Thunder dismounted and with a laugh of pure joy, joined her, giving chase.

As one, they fell onto the carpet of spring grass. Emma reached between them and unknotted the thong around his waist, remembering a moonlit night when he'd taken her out into the prairie. "Here will do," she whispered, wickedly, "here will do just fine."

Dear Reader,

The U.S. Army purchased Fort Pierre in 1855 and kept it only a year. For the purpose of this story, I left a small contingent of soldiers at the fort through the spring of 1857.

I hope you enjoyed Striking Thunder and Emma's story. The *White* series continues with *White Nights*. This is the story of James Jones and Eirica Macauley, secondary characters from the book, *White Wolf*. Join them on the second half of the Oregon Trail as they risk everything for true love. Look for their story in April 2000.

For updated information, check out my website at http://members.aol.com/susanedw2u or write to me at:

Susan Edwards
P.O. Box 766
Los Altos, CA 94023-0766
(SASE greatly appreciated)

WHITE WOLF

SUSAN EDWARDS

Jessica Jones knows that the trip to Oregon will be hard, but she will not let her brothers leave her behind. Dressed as a boy to carry on a ruse that fools no one, Jessie cannot disguise her attraction to the handsome half-breed wagon master. For when she looks into Wolf's eyes and entwines her fingers in his hair, Jessie glimpses the very depths of passion.

___4471-4 $5.50 US/$6.50 CAN

Dorchester Publishing Co., Inc.
P.O. Box 6640
Wayne, PA 19087-8640

ICE &
Rapture

CONNIE MASON

Cool as a cucumber, and totally dedicated to her career as a newspaperwoman, Maggie Agton is just the kind of challenge Chase McGarrett enjoys—especially when he discovers that she hides skimpy silk underthings and a simmering sensuality beneath her businesslike exterior. Virile and all too sure of himself, Chase is just the kind of man Maggie detests—especially when she learns that he has no intention of taking her across the Yukon to report on the Klondike gold rush. Cold and hot, reserved and brash—Maggie and Chase are a study in opposites. But when they join forces in the frozen wilderness, the fiery sparks of their searing desire burn brighter than the northern lights.

___4570-2 $5.99 US/$6.99 CAN

Marriage By Design

Jill Metcalf

Her sign proclaims it as one of a number of services procurable through Miss Coady Blake, but there is nothing illicit in what it offers. All a prospective husband has to do is obtain a bride—Coady will take care of the wedding details. But it is difficult to purchase luxuries in the Yukon Territory, 1898, and Coady charges accordingly. After hearing several suspicions about Coady's business ethics, Northwest Mounted Police officer Stone MacGregor takes it upon himself to search out the crafty huckster. Instead, the inspector finds a willful beauty who thinks she knows the worth of every item—and he finds himself thinking that the proprietress herself is far beyond price.

___4553-2 $4.99 US/$5.99 CAN

San Antonio Rose

CONSTANCE O'BANYON

Sam Houston knows he needs all the help he can get to defeat Santa Anna's seasoned fighting men. But who is the mysterious San Antonio Rose, who emerges from the mist like a ghostly figure to offer her aid? Fluent in Spanish, Ian McCain is the one man who can ferret out the truth about the flamboyant dancer. Working under Santa Anna's very nose, he observes how the dark-haired beauty inflames her audience, how she captivates El Presidente himself. But as she disappears with a single yellow rose, he knows that despite the tangled web of loyalties that ensnare them, he will taste those tempting lips, know every secret of that alluring body. And before she proves just how effective she can be, he will pluck for himself the San Antonio Rose.

___4563-X $5.99 US/$6.99 CAN

Dorchester Publishing Co., Inc.
P.O. Box 6640
Wayne, PA 19087-8640

Please add $1.75 for shipping and handling for the first book and $.50 for each book thereafter. NY, NYC, and PA residents, please add appropriate sales tax. No cash, stamps, or C.O.D.s. All orders shipped within 6 weeks via postal service book rate. Canadian orders require $2.00 extra postage and must be paid in U.S. dollars through a U.S. banking facility.

Name_____
Address_____
City_____State_____Zip_____
I have enclosed $_____ in payment for the checked book(s).
Payment <u>must</u> accompany all orders. ❑ Please send a free catalog.
CHECK OUT OUR WEBSITE! www.dorchesterpub.com

FREE FALLING
STOBIE PIEL

How did anyone talk her into jumping out of a plane strapped to a man? And why didn't anyone tell her that man was going to be her wildly handsome ex-boyfriend Adrian de Vargas? Cora Talmadge never thought she'd see him again, especially not at ten thousand feet—but their "chance" encounter turns out to be the least of her worries. When she and Adrian are sidetracked by a mysterious whirlwind and tossed into nineteenth-century Arizona, extraordinary measures are called for. Unfortunately, she isn't quite sure that she is the woman to perform them. Lost in a world without phones, cars, or even Scottsdale, Cora wonders if their renewed romance can truly weather the storm, or if their love is destined to vanish with the wind.

___52329-9 $5.50 US/$6.50 CAN

BUSHWHACKED BRIDE

EUGENIA RILEY

"JUMPING JEHOSHAPHAT! YOU'VE SHANGHAIED THE NEW SCHOOLMARM!"

Ma Reklaw bellows at her sons and wields her broom with a fierceness that has all five outlaw brothers running for cover; it doesn't take a Ph.D. to realize that in the Reklaw household, Ma is the law. Professor Jessica Garret watches dumbstruck as the members of the feared Reklaw Gang turn tail—one up a tree, another under the hay wagon, and one in a barrel. Having been unceremoniously kidnapped by the rowdy brothers, the green-eyed beauty takes great pleasure in their discomfort until Ma Reklaw finds a new way to sweep clean her sons' disreputable behavior—by offering Jessica's hand in marriage to the best behaved. Jessie has heard of shotgun weddings, but a broomstick betrothal is ridiculous! As the dashing but dangerous desperadoes start the wooing there is no telling what will happen with one bride for five brothers.

___52320-5 $5.99 US/$6.99 CAN

Savage Revenge

A fiery Indian beauty, Haina will accept no man as her master, not even the virile warrior who has made her his captive. For years their families have been fierce enemies, and now Chance finds a way to exact revenge. He will hold the lovely Haina for ransom, humble her proud spirit, and take his fill of her supple young body. But Haina refuses to submit to his branding kisses and burning caresses. Only exquisite tenderness and everlasting love will bring her to the point of surrender.

___4255-X $5.99 US/$6.99 CAN

Dorchester Publishing Co., Inc.
P.O. Box 6640
Wayne, PA 19087-8640